CRASH

TAMARA LUSH

CRASH

The **PRETENDERS** Series

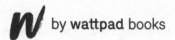 by **wattpad** books

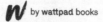 by wattpad books

An imprint of Wattpad WEBTOON Book Group

Copyright© 2023 Tamara Lush
All rights reserved.

Published in Canada by Wattpad WEBTOON Book Group,
a division of Wattpad Corp.

36 Wellington Street E., Suite 200, Toronto, ON M5E 1C7 Canada

www.wattpad.com

First W by Wattpad Books edition: January 2023

ISBN 978-1-99025-944-9 (Trade Paper original)
ISBN 978-1-99025-946-3 (eBook edition)

Library and Archives Canada Cataloguing in Publication information is
available upon request.

Printed and bound in Canada

1 3 5 7 9 10 8 6 4 2

Cover design by Leah Jacobs-Gordon

To Dino, the one I will love forever

CHAPTER ONE

EVIE

According to one of my business school professors, internships are supposedly like planting strawberries. You nestle the seeds in the ground, diligently water the sprouts, welcome the sunshine, then eventually, enjoy the delicious, ripe fruit that bursts with flavor.

"It's like love," she'd say. "Cultivate, nurture, then reap the benefits."

Now, I know nothing about love, and I'm only starting to be a halfway decent gardener. But this is my third internship, so I'm pretty knowledgeable in that department.

In reality, internships are like potatoes. After cultivating the plant, you dig into the earth, get messy, and eventually find a dirty, lumpy vegetable. Then you have to put in more time, and more work, before it turns into something edible. And even then, you might burn the spud to an inedible crisp while frying it in boiling oil.

My thoughts drift to french fries and my stomach growls, a Pavlovian response to my hunger. I shove aside a company brochure, check my phone, sigh. It's close to seven, and I should be home. Instead, I'm glued to my uncomfortable gray office chair on the third floor of the Jenkins Corporation office in downtown Atlanta, staring at a stack of files on my desk.

For a second, I rest my head on my forearms in the hushed office, trying to will away the hunger and, yeah, the boredom. The sooner I finish proofreading these memos, the sooner I can get home.

Thanks, Josephine, I mutter. Way to pile on in the last week of my internship. Normally I proofread marketing copy, the kinds of blurbs and snippets that showcase the company's charitable side. Charity is in short supply on the intern level, though. Even though I'm only making twelve an hour, the company treats me more like a junior public relations executive. All work and very little pay, for the opportunity to be considered for one of the few PR jobs that come open each year.

But my manager has already said there are no new junior PR positions this quarter, which means I'm out of luck. She'd assured me if there were available jobs, I'd be a shoo-in. But that and a dollar will get me a Beefy Potato-Rito on the value menu at Taco Bell.

Groaning, I lift my head and thumb through the files, my eyes feeling dry and scratchy from the harsh overhead fluorescent light. I'll never get home in time to make dinner. And I'll totally be too tired to work on that newsletter for the community garden in my neighborhood. Why did I volunteer to do that, anyway?

I pick up my cell and wearily tap out a text to my sister, Sabrina. *You're on your own for dinner tonight.*

She calls me five seconds later. Unlike the rest of her generation, my little sister loves to chat on the phone, probably because she enjoys hearing herself talk.

"I have to, like, cook?" Her tone is dubious.

"Sabrina, I'm going to be late. You're on your own for food. There's one of those microwave pizzas in the freezer, I think." I cradle my cell between my ear and shoulder, opening the cover of one of the files.

"Let me check." I hear her open the freezer door. "Oh, look at that. There are two pizzas. Want me to heat one up for you, Evie?"

My sister's melodic southern accent soothes my mood. It sometimes baffles me that we're related. I have an accent as flat and dry as Florida, the state where I was born. My sister is pure Georgia, where our family moved after Dad got a sales job here in Atlanta at the world's most famous soda company.

"No, I'll deal with it when I get home. Eat yours. Microwave only on medium. Four minutes. You good? And hey? No friends over tonight. You need to study for finals."

"But whyyyyy?" Sabrina's high-pitched whine fills my ear.

I don't have time for this tonight and I snap at her. "Stop it. No guests."

"The exam's hella simple. I was going to invite over Kris and Aiden and—"

"I don't care if the biology exam's easy. Keep studying. Alone. Love you." I tap the Off button on my phone, cutting her off midsqueal.

Studying is her priority, while working to keep us fed and sheltered is mine. It's hard to raise a whip-smart, risk-taking teenager, I've discovered.

Boys worship her (which is a little adorable). Adult men love her (which is gross). Hell, she's even confided in me that she's experimented with girls. (That's fine with me, whatever makes her happy.) She does a pretty decent job of keeping on task, but I'd never tell her that. I try to act like Mom and Dad would have, or how I think they would've acted, had they lived. Sometimes I try to channel their reactions, something that Sabrina hates. But I'm now Mom, Dad, and big sister. Or, according to Sabrina, a jail warden.

Our fights have gotten more frequent during her senior year, with all the parties, all the risky weekend outings, like tubing through river rapids, and all the overnight trips to theme parks in Florida.

It's my goal to get her to graduation next week and to an elite science camp in Boston for the summer. She's been accepted, even gotten a scholarship for 75 percent of the cost, and I'm determined to scrape up the rest. Maybe I'll take on additional shifts at the restaurant . . .

I don't even want to think about her college in the fall. That's what loans are for. God knows I have enough of them. I might have to defer them for the rest of my life, but at least I have a business degree. I'd hoped to go for my MBA, but Mom and Dad's fatal car crash killed that dream. Maybe someday.

Back to work, Evie.

Scanning the first page of the file and then a glossy brochure paperclipped to the folder, I spot the Post-it note left by Josephine, my boss. It's stuck to the brochure.

Proofread this marketing plan for spelling errors and then bring this entire file to Alex's office. Right away. He needs to sign off in person, and wants to see the attached brochure as it's printed.

The second underline is a bit of overkill, in my opinion.

I frown and flip the note over, hoping for more instructions. Alex's office? The managing director? I'm an *intern*. Interns *do not* casually drop off reports for upper management like that.

"Josephine?" She isn't just in my contacts; she's always at the top of my list of recent calls. Next to Sabrina, I think I talk to Josephine more than any other human.

"Hey. It's Evie. Sorry to bother you. Can you hear me?"

There's clicking and a fuzzy response. Dammit, she must be on the train, headed home to her house in the suburbs. The line goes dead so I text her instead.

You want me to bring everything to Alex's office? Do you mean Alex Jenkins? Or is there another Alex I don't know about?

Already I have so many questions. What if I find an error? How should I correct it? Do I go over the corrections with the managing director? That can't be right. Josephine's usual micromanagement style seems half-assed tonight. Something is amiss, and all the poop has rolled downhill and landed squarely in my lap.

I riffle quickly through the file, waiting for a text, not spotting any errors. It's such an unusual request from Josephine because she always deals with Alex directly. Why can't I email this? Does the managing director not know how to use PDF files?

The last thing I want is to bust into Alex Jenkins's office after hours. The thought makes me shiver.

Dale Alexander Jenkins isn't around much. Usually he's traveling the globe, running one part of the company or another.

Jenkins Corporation owns the world's largest tire manufacturer. The company was started by Alex's grandfather, according to a plaque in the lobby commemorating Dale Alexander Jenkins Senior.

But the conglomerate also recently acquired a line of chemical and industrial rubber products, a chain of sporting goods stores, and, inexplicably, a company that makes roofing supplies.

Rumor has it that Alex is angling to be the entire company's CEO—a job that's occupied by his father. His octogenarian grandmother, who is the chairperson of the company, is opposing the move, I've heard. It's not clear why she doesn't want him to ascend the corporate ladder, especially since he seems quite competent. I try not to pay attention to the rumors, though. They're none of my business, and likely aren't true.

I'm in the corporate communications department, which means I write feel-good stories for the company newsletter and copy edit press releases about Jenkins's "corporate citizenship."

Safety! Environment! Community!

Those are the company's three buzzwords, and they've been imprinted into my thoughts during my five and a half months here. They're on the company letterhead, at the bottom of my emails, in every news release. They're in my stupid dreams, ones where I push papers and type until my fingers ache. I wonder if Alex Jenkins knows his corporate communications intern has to work as a hostess at a fast-casual restaurant chain to make ends meet.

If those buzzwords float in my brain, Alex Jenkins is branded there, too. Because good lord, is he gorgeous.

Although I stare at him every day in our company literature— he's always smiling and self-possessed in those photos—I've only seen him twice in person. Once during a company-wide forum where he'd given a presentation, and once in the lobby of our building on a Saturday a couple of months ago. Both times I was shocked at how young he seemed—not a day over thirty—and how he had the most extraordinary way of looking both earnest and wicked.

I glance down at my phone, shaking off memories of Alex, the hot managing director.

Josephine, please text me back.

Staring out the window as the sun sets in downtown Atlanta, I have to force myself to shift my attention back to the stack of files. I'll never get home if I keep daydreaming. I open the glossy brochure and scrutinize the words on the front. It's a trifold, full-color, glossy-paper thing, the kind that's given to recruits at job fairs and corporate conferences.

When Josephine found out I was such a good editor, she'd unleashed me on all sorts of projects. If there's one thing I'm good at, it's details. I see the trees, not the forest.

My cell startles me enough to cause a yelp to burst from my mouth. Glancing at the screen, I notice two details: it's two hours after I usually leave the office, and it's Josephine.

"Hey! Thank God you called. About this brochure. You want me to bring it to Alex Jenkins's office? Do I have the right Alex? Or is it someone else? I wanted to double-check. Can't we email it?"

"Evie! Holy shit! No, we can't email it. Alex is going to a meeting in New York later this week and he wants everything to be perfect because of some huge deal. You haven't looked over the brochure yet? It's going to print tomorrow morning. I put that first in the stack, so you'd do it right away. Didn't you see the note?

Alex said he wanted to see the proof by eight thirty. Get your skinny butt up to his office NOW."

Shaking, I hang up. Yep. There it is. A second Post-it on the inside of the file folder says: *do this immediately!!!*

The three exclamation marks are the punctuation version of a punch in the gut.

Glancing through the slick, colorful brochure again, a pit grows in my stomach, because I haven't put enough time into proofreading the thing. It should only take me ten minutes to give it a first read, but normally on something like this I'd spend an hour.

As usual, I get caught up in the details. I find one small error where there should be a comma, and wonder if anyone but me will notice. I look at the time and gasp. It's eight fifteen. Maybe I'll explain to Alex that there's a minor typo and let him decide if he wants the brochure redone. Why he's even interested in this level of minutiae, I'm not sure.

The brochure's glossy paper practically slips through my fingers as I stuff it into the file and run for the elevator. Once inside, I punch the button for the top floor. I hate elevators. Loathe them. Normally I take the stairs when coming and going from the office. But I don't have time to dash up several flights right now, so I suck it up. Right now, I'm more afraid of my boss and not getting this project to Alex Jenkins than the elevator.

I'm sweating with anxiety by the time I'm halfway to the top floor. This is Atlanta's tallest office tower, and I must think about anything but this small, confined box hurtling up fifty-two stories. Dinner? My stomach growls and lurches. Whether Sabrina's doing her homework? Gah.

Or . . . Dale Alexander Jenkins, the younger. That's something curious to ponder. As I'm whisked into the upper reaches of the building, I idly wonder why everyone calls him Alex and not Dale. Maybe because his father and grandfather were named Dale? Maybe because Dale's an old-fashioned name? He definitely doesn't look like a Dale. I imagine him introducing his sexy self as Dale and almost giggle.

A soft sheen of sweat blooms on my upper lip as the elevator takes me up twenty more stories. It dings softly, and when the doors slide open, I shoot out into a vast private office.

It's low-lit, illuminated only by a green glass shaded desk lamp and the twinkling lights of Atlanta's business district below. Thankfully, there's no one behind the desk—although the room has the charged energy of a place that was recently occupied.

I haul in a lungful of air. My sense of smell is strong, and I detect notes of spice and musk. A man's aftershave. My gaze sweeps around the room. I spot a closed door in the corner where there's a coatrack with a suit jacket. Otherwise, the few pieces of sleek, dark wood and black leather furniture are the only things in the room.

Hesitantly, I take a few steps toward the desk, figuring I'll drop the file and run.

When I reach the desk, I open the file once again. That's my downfall, because I feel a compulsion to read the first paragraph of the brochure once again, to make sure everything's correct. I can't stand errors and feel terrible that I haven't proofread this file with my usual level of care.

Jenkins Corporation is North America's largest—

"Thank God you're here."

I gasp and drop the file at the sound of the growly, masculine voice. The brochure and the papers spill everywhere at my feet, like leaves in autumn.

CHAPTER TWO

EVIE

When I whirl in the direction of the voice, I see Alex, the company's managing director. All six-foot-something, dark hair, and blazing eyes glare at me from the door that had been closed a few seconds before.

"I-I . . ."

"Is that the Corp Comm file on the tire-recycling program?" he growls, and I nod enthusiastically. "Fucking marketing. They take so long with everything."

Hey! We do not! I want to shout, but he's obviously angry so I stand, frozen to the plush gray carpet.

"Gather those papers and get the coffee on. She'll be here soon."

She? Who? What?

"Uh, sir, I—"

Alex steps closer and his smell washes over me. *Whoa, yum.* I breathe deep a few times, trying to drag more of his scent into my nose. My heart pings around my rib cage.

"I told the agency that I didn't want the girls to call me 'sir.'" He gives me a once-over, and I detect a suspicious, or possibly skeptical, look on his face.

"Sorry, sir." I look up, then down at my feet. "Sorry, Mr. Jenkins, but I think there's been a mix-up."

"Yes. There has been a mix-up. Corp Comm has screwed up, and on top of that, the agency obviously sent me a temporary personal assistant who's subpar. Go get the coffee. My grandmother will go ballistic if I don't have something hot and alcoholic waiting for her."

I press my hand to my chest. His poor granny.

"The coffee's in there." With an arrogant gaze, he points at the door where he'd emerged, then walks around the front of the desk and sinks into the black leather seat. "And make it strong. Three fingers of Kahlúa—the bottle's on the table."

Shaking, I collect the papers and set the file on his desk. I guess there's no harm in making the guy and his grandmother coffee, right?

Sabrina would call me obedient for doing something like this, but I think it's old-fashioned manners. Even if Alex Jenkins is a prick. I'm an intern, and I'm here to make life easier for the employees. If I do, I'll be noticed and get a full-time gig. Maybe this is a test from the universe, and a full-time job at this company will magically open for me by tomorrow morning.

That's the kind of thing my business school advisor would say, although she never mentioned anything about what to do about arrogant managers. A sigh escapes my lips as I look around.

The room's something of a studio apartment, with a fancy stainless-steel coffeemaker on a sleek table near a small fridge, a clothing rack with identical dark suit jackets and white shirts, and a cozy-looking gray sofa that's aimed at a flat-screen TV.

He must work so hard that he stays here sometimes. I fiddle with the coffeemaker buttons. As the machine churns out the fresh-smelling brew, a disconcerting realization comes over me.

He thinks I'm his personal assistant.

It's kind of funny, really, a man so powerful not knowing his own assistant. But he'd said something about a temp, and with the mercurial temper he exhibited, I suspect that he goes through staff quite quickly.

Thank God I'm in a whole different department, away from such wrath. Even though he is impossibly good-looking, I'd hate to be around such arrogance for forty hours a week. And he's probably the kind of boss to make his secretary work overtime.

Wait. I'm working overtime. I calculate the time and a half in my brain and figure I'll get an extra . . . eighteen bucks in my paycheck if I work three hours of OT. I stifle a sigh.

First, I pour the coffee into a mug, along with a splash of Kahlúa, then wonder if I should use one of the carafes. Figuring that I'll bring some to him first to get his approval—he seems like the kind of man who wants to approve everything in his orbit—I straighten my spine and strut into the office with the coffee, trying to project an aura of inner confidence, as if I do this all the time.

I'm good with change. I can pivot. This isn't the worst thing that's ever happened to me.

He's sitting in the chair, his back to me, when I slightly bend to hand him the coffee. When he whirls around, his knees brush my bare legs and I become flustered. His arm flies up and knocks the mug out of my grasp. The liquid splatters all over his white shirt and my pink cardigan. He curses, loud and vulgar, and I yelp.

"I'm so sorry, Mr. Jenkins! Sorry, sorry, sorry!"

I spring back and run across the office into the adjacent room to grab a towel. This is a disaster, and all because I wasn't more assertive about who I really am. Towel . . . towel . . . towel . . . I snatch a fluffy white towel from a basket and run back in. Is the towel even clean?

This still isn't the worst thing that's ever happened to me, but it is pretty mortifying. By the time I fly back into the office, he has his shirt off. *Eep.*

I didn't know real-life men are this muscular. I've seen guys like that on TV, but figured that pecs and abs and whatever those muscles on a guy's side are called were all computer-generated trickery.

Alex Jenkins is like a damned Rodin statue. Hard, sculpted, and smooth. His skin is tan and . . . mercy, his shoulders have muscles on top of muscles, ones that I didn't even know existed on the human body. He must spend entire weeks in the gym. When does he have time to even work?

I shield my eyes with one hand.

"I'm so sorry, sir. You startled me, that's all. Here's a towel. I think it's clean. Maybe. I got it out of the basket." I hand it to him without looking. I feel my own shoulder with the opposite hand. Nope. I don't even have those muscles.

He utters a few more swear words. "Miss . . . Miss . . . what is your name, anyway?"

"Evie Cooper." I address the floor.

"Evie Cooper, look at me."

I raise my eyes, trying not to pay attention to his muscular arms, the planes and valleys of his six-pack stomach, the hardness of his pecs. I ignore the bronze of his skin and the sprinkling of hair on his chest. His beauty makes me feel naïve and inexperienced and completely, one hundred percent inept. I stare into his eyes, an act equally as dangerous as looking at his body.

He flings the soiled shirt into a wastebasket. "Get me a shirt and bring it here. And another tie. The red one. They're on the hook on the back of the door. And take off your sweater. Now."

I stand, frozen. He's telling me to take off my clothes. The very idea is exciting. And scary. "My . . . sweater?"

"There's coffee all over the front." He points at my chest.

A flush of embarrassment spreads across my face as I peel off my sweater. He wasn't asking me to strip for him. *Lord.* The coffee hasn't reached my black sheath dress. Thank goodness because it's my nicest work outfit, and I don't have money for dry cleaning this week. Or this month.

Looking about wildly, I wonder what to do with my sweater.

"Give it to me." He extends his hand.

Keeping my gaze on the floor, I hand it to him. Our fingers brush against each other, and a flare of electricity travels from my hand, to my arm, right into my chest.

I scamper away.

When I return, his back is to me, and he's staring out the window. The sound of me clearing my throat makes him whirl around.

"Sir. Mr. Jenkins. Here," I say, extending the open shirt in his direction.

He steps forward and my heart pounds as he comes closer.

I'm not used to being around masculine, powerful men. Okay, so I'm *rarely* around any men. I've kissed a few, but it's never gone further than that. Unsurprisingly, losing my parents and raising a teenage sister hasn't exactly done wonders for my love life.

Attempting to be professional—there's that obedient side of me again—I help slide the shirt over those powerful arms.

He stares at me while buttoning the shirt. "Not a great first day, Evie."

No kidding, dude, I wanted to say. Wait. *First day?* What's he talking about?

Wordlessly, I hand him the tie. I'm not going to argue because I assume that this will be my last day at this company, because he'll fire me soon enough, either when he discovers I'm not his temporary assistant or when he finds out I'm an intern in the incompetent corporate communications department.

He slides the tie through his collar and glares at me, an expression that is completely uncalled for, given the circumstances. "Can you help me, please, instead of standing there and gawking at my body?"

My obedient side is approaching a cliff and I narrow my eyes at Jerky McJerkface. There's only so much attitude I can handle. I stand in front of him, my breasts inches from his chest. God, why is today the day I wore my thinnest bra? I can see my nipples poking through my cheap dress. What a disaster.

Concentrate on the tie. Concentrate. My hands tremble out of fear and a touch of rage. I haven't tied a man's tie since my father was alive. If I think too hard about the last time I did that—the night he and my mother died two years ago in a car crash, when I was twenty—I'll want to cry.

This is not the time to cry. I am a damned mess right now.

Taking a deep breath, I put my hands on either end of the red tie and look into his face. It's then that I notice he's staring at me with something other than anger. An unfamiliar warmth spreads through my body, concentrating somewhere between my legs. His eyes are half-lidded, almost sensual. He smiles at me, but it's not a kind expression. It's dangerous.

"You do know how to tie a man's tie, don't you, Evie?"

"Of course I do; Which knot do you like?" My dad had taught me the Windsor knot, the half Windsor, and the four-in-hand.

"I like knots of all kinds," he murmurs. "Usually I'm the one tying them, though."

I pretend that he didn't make a stupid double entendre. I'm suddenly less enamored with his looks. Hopefully he'll fire me in the next couple of minutes. At least then I can go home and eat a frozen pizza. As if on cue, my stomach grumbles.

"Can't you tie your own tie, Mr. Jenkins?" I ask, my tone frosty.

CHAPTER THREE

ALEX

This temp's going to be a problem, and it's the last thing I need tonight.

For one thing, she doesn't seem like she's capable of performing the job. Not due to the way she spilled coffee on me, because hell, that was my fault. And it's not the tone of her voice, nor that snark she displayed when she asked whether I could tie my own tie.

No, there's something about her that doesn't seem qualified as an assistant. Like she hasn't been trained in dealing with the flow of an executive office. I can tell by the way she's pussyfooting around the place. It's puzzling. Usually the agency sends over confident women who have loads of experience.

Why the hell did my regular PA decide to go on vacation this week?

I take the tie from her and loop it around my neck. "Of course I can do it myself. See?"

She scrutinizes me with an adorable little frown as I loop the silk fabric around itself. This woman is distractingly pretty. But I can handle that. I'm not a Neanderthal. At least not outwardly. I'm rather complicated when it comes to women. I'm both Atlanta's most eligible bachelor (according to *Peachtree Magazine*) and "something of an overgrown fuckboy" (according to a woman I'd met in a bar recently).

The latter detail is one thousand percent false, but as I've come to realize, a rakish reputation—even a false one—is difficult to live down.

Despite all this, or maybe because of it, I have rules.

Not screwing an employee is one of those rules. It doesn't matter that Evie's eyes are as blue as the Caribbean, or how her pink lips pout as she watches me; I'm not getting involved with a subordinate—even one who is here temporarily. And I need to stop flirting and joking with her, for Christ's sake. I approved the company's new sexual harassment policy last week.

"Wait, no. That's crooked." She waves my hands away and undoes the tie while shaking her head. She reties it and straightens the knot at my throat. "There. You look way better than before."

What the hell does she mean by that? Save the snappy comeback, Jenkins . . .

"Thank you," I say briskly, trying to steer this situation back into something resembling an orderly office environment. "Now. Let's go over what I need for the next hour while Gram, ah, Eleanor, is here." I step behind the desk and point to one of the two chairs on the opposite side of the desk from me. "You're going to sit there. Eleanor will be there." I stack some papers hastily.

"Mr. Jenkins, I need to tell you, I'm not your assistant." She remains standing, behind the leather chair.

I raise my hands in a WTF gesture. "Then who are you? A woman off the street who enjoys spilling scalding coffee on men and showing off her Windsor knot talent?"

"Technically, you spilled the coffee on me. On my work sweater."

I pause to grind my molars together while I let everything sink in. Maybe I didn't hear her correctly, so I'll start fresh with an olive branch of kindness. "And I apologize for that. The coffee spill was my fault, I'll be sure to dry-clean your sweater. I'm sorry."

"Apology accepted." Good lord, this woman's attractive. Normally I don't like women with shorter hair, but the way hers brushes against her graceful neck? Hell, I could stare at that for hours.

"Did you say . . . work sweater?" I narrow my eyes.

"It's freezing on my floor. Subzero. You should really fix that. I keep a sweater here so I don't get frostbite." Her eyelashes are long and alluring. "And it would probably save the company money if you bumped the thermostat up a degree."

I pace around the desk. "What floor do you work on?"

"Third. I'm an intern in corporate communications. I came here to give you that file." She points to my desk.

I'm not usually caught off guard, but I am tonight, so I stalk back around the desk and sink into my chair. "You're an intern?"

"Yes. This is my postgrad internship. I graduated from Emory in December. Next week is my last here at the company. I've had a rewarding time here at Jenkins, so thank you for that."

"Good school, and it's great to hear you've gotten a lot out of your internship," I mutter as I impatiently shuffle files around my desk. I glance up and see more than a hint of pride in her eyes and feel bad for being so cynical. The woman's what, twenty-one? Twenty-two? I groan inwardly at the entire situation. Lusting after a girl nearly ten years younger *and* being harsh to a young employee who's trying to climb the corporate ladder? *Just great, Jenkins.*

"Do you happen to know where my temporary assistant went, Miss Cooper? And please. Sit. You're making me nervous standing there."

She shrugs her thin shoulders and perches on the edge of the chair. "How should I know? I walked in right before the coffee incident. I was delivering marketing reports and you startled me."

My gaze travels from her face down to her neck and I briefly catch a glimpse of her chest. Her curves are barely hidden by her dress. I scowl. "There was no one outside when you walked in? At the desk?"

She shakes her head.

"Dammit. The agency must not have sent a temp. Or the girl left. I don't know. This day's been busier than a mosquito at a nudist colony." I wait for her to giggle, but she doesn't. Tough crowd. "When my usual PA is on vacation, I go through assistants like you wouldn't believe. Swear to God, during the weeks Nadine's gone, I change assistants more than I change my sheets."

"I can't imagine why. You're so kind," Evie deadpans.

Everyone's a comedian these days. "I'm going to ignore that because I'm in a bind and need someone to take notes during this meeting. Can you please act as my assistant for the next hour? It won't be difficult. Sixty minutes, tops."

Her eyes lift to the ceiling as if she's thinking hard, which gives me an excuse to stare at her face. She crosses her arms over her chest.

"Please?" I push out a breath. "Listen, I'm sorry I called you subpar a few minutes ago. That was wrong of me. I'm under a lot of stress these days. Are you willing to stay and help?"

"I'm afraid it will cost you." She slants her mouth, as if to say, *What stress are you under, buddy?*

I stare at her incredulously. "You're an intern. You're supposed to do whatever anyone asks of you."

"You're keeping me here late. I'm only paid for thirty hours a week. I've already worked two hours of overtime, and whenever I work OT, I don't get paid. That's a labor violation." She straightens her spine. "I'm giving up important things by being here late."

Important things? At her age? Probably partying or screwing her boyfriend or drinking at some club with her friends. The nerve of this woman. But she obviously knows she has me over a barrel. "Okay, fine. I'll pay you double. Here." I take a blank legal pad and a pen out of a drawer and hand it to her.

She taps her foot. "Triple overtime."

I squint at her. She has a thin, delicate frame, and there's a defiant edge to her. An alluring, defiant edge. I've always loved a challenge. "Extortion. That's what you're doing. If you were a man, I'd tell you to go to hell."

"My professor says women should demand to be paid what they're worth. And what's it to you? It comes out to thirty-six dollars." She snorts. "I'm sure you have it in your budget. Or probably in change, behind the cushions of your couch."

We pay the interns only twelve an hour? *Christ.* I'll have to ask HR about this tomorrow before I go to New York. One more thing to deal with. I inhale deep. "Fine," I bite out. "Triple over-time. Now would you please get ready to take notes?"

"Why do you need notes if it's your grandmother? That's a little strange."

"Because my grandmother is the sharpest person on the planet, and I need a record of what she says to study it later. She's stopping by to drop off a list of ideas before she goes to the opera."

"Hmm." I can't tell if that's a judgmental *hmm*, or a *hmm* of agreement.

We stare warily at each other, and I swear, I imagine myself looking into those ocean-blue eyes right before I kiss her. Her eyes are the color of the water off the coast of St. Barts, which is where I went on my last vacation.

"But why?"

My brow forms a scowl. "Why what?"

"Why do you need to study what your grandmother says? Please explain the situation to me so I can perform my work duties proficiently." She taps the pen on the pad.

Massaging the back of my head, I try not to snap. None of this is Evie's fault. She can't help that she's not an assistant. She can't help that Gram is stubborn, or that Dad's pressuring me. Or that Beau, my slimy cousin who runs the sporting goods arm of my family's company, is once again trying to weasel in on what's mine. Perhaps I should send Evie away . . . but no. I need notes.

"Okay, here goes. I'm the managing director of this company." She nods, a look of annoyance on her face as I continue. "And my father is the CEO of the Jenkins conglomerate, which owns a tire manufacturer, a line of chemical and industrial rubber products—"

She interrupts. "A chain of sporting goods stores, and a new roofing supply company based in St. Louis. I proofread the latest annual report."

Does she expect a thanks? I plow on. "My grandmother is the chairperson of the board of the whole thing. The company was started by her husband. Dad and I want her to step down so he can be chair, and I can move into the CEO position."

"Okay, so what's the issue? You're all on the same team. You seemingly do a good job here. Or is this some sort of hostile takeover?"

I snort out a breath. "Yeah, right. *Hostile* is a good word. My cousin Beau—who's a managing director of another of my family's companies, the sporting goods stores based in Cobb County— wants the CEO role."

Evie tilts her head. "Ah, so this is some sort of *Succession* power play."

"What?"

"That TV show. Never mind. Why make your grandmother step down? Why can't you all continue the way you are? Or do you want more money or something? Is Beau older? More experienced than you? Or does your dad want more power?"

"Money's not the issue. Beau's only a year older, and we have about equal experience." Revenge against Beau is my driving motivation, but I won't tell dearest little Evie about my ulterior motive. "And Gram's old and she should enjoy what time she has left. Also, I am often at odds with my cousin over various, ah, things, and I don't want him to get this job. So, there's that."

At odds is a polite way of saying that I hate his fucking guts.

"Why not let your grandmother choose what she wants from her life? And why not try to run the company with your cousin, instead of trying to beat him at some invisible game? Wouldn't that be best for your entire family?"

I inhale a thin breath through my nose and stare at Evie. She has no idea that the Jenkins clan puts the fun in dysfunction, and if she knew what was good for her, she wouldn't ask any more questions. "Did you sign a nondisclosure agreement when you started your internship?"

She pauses to think for a moment. "I did. But what does that have to do with your cousin and you taking over the company?"

"Because my grandmother and I could discuss sensitive topics and I don't want you blabbing about them at the water cooler in marketing, and I definitely don't want my cousin to find out."

Her eyes narrow. "But wouldn't your grandmother tell your cousin that you discussed these sensitive topics? And I thought he works in a different division, in another county?"

"No chance of that. Gram's good at keeping secrets." Such as who's going to take over the company. Too good at secrets, in fact. "And Beau keeps an office here. He stops by sometimes so he can keep his foot firmly in the company door."

Evie pantomimes a zipper motion against her luscious lips. Then opens those lips. "The water cooler on the third floor hasn't worked for two weeks. But that still doesn't answer my questions."

Hell. I jot the words *water cooler–third floor* on a notepad. "Let's put it this way. My rivalry with Beau Jenkins—my cousin— is akin to that of the Atlanta Falcons and New Orleans Saints, and I want to come out on top. Ever since we were kids, we've competed against one another. Grades, colleges, sports; you name it, we've tried to one-up each other at it for years."

She blinks a few times, probably thinking my entire family is a bit unhinged. Well, we are.

I don't mention the other thing. The big event. The defining moment of my life. Don't need to get into *that* particular scandal with this sweet summer child.

My eyes flicker to Evie's hair, which is dark and straight and cut in a bob that falls to her shoulders—I know this because my sister, Savannah, once tried to tame her curls into this shape. Evie's soft-looking locks are perfect for the style. It's not sleek or severe. It falls to her collarbone, and something about seeing her dark hair touching her tan, freckled skin makes me want to brush it back and gather it in my hands. And kiss her collarbone.

Dammit, *stop*. She's an *intern*. More off-limits than an assistant. An inappropriate fantasy sends a burn of discomfort into my chest. I smile awkwardly at Evie, and she returns the expression. Dear God, she has the sweetest dimples. Didn't she say her internship was over next week?

"My dear, who is this?"

Christ. Cockblocked by my grandmother.

"Gram." I stand up, stride over, and give her a kiss on both cheeks. The room is clouded with Poison, her signature perfume. She hands me a thick, monogrammed envelope. I'm certain that Gram's ideas are on linen stationery inside, in her formal cursive handwriting in black ink.

Evie stands and faces my grandmother.

"This is . . . my assistant for the evening. Evie." I sweep a hand in her direction. "Evie, meet Eleanor Dorothy Jenkins, my grandmother and matriarch of not only my family, but this company."

With manners obviously learned at some finishing school for girls, Evie's eyes sparkle and she offers Gram a gentle handshake, the kind women do with their fingers.

"A pleasure to meet you," Evie says.

"Your assistant or your companion? I thought you'd sworn off the beautiful secretaries," Gram retorts, winking at Evie as she settles into her chair. Evie looks alarmed, and I cough. Gram is a pistol, and tonight could go off in a hundred different ways.

"Gram, you know I never get involved with the staff. Let me get you one of your special coffees. I'll be right back."

She lets out a hoot and looks to Evie. "Ooh, you've trained him perfectly, dear. Alex never gets my coffee. Well done."

Evie coughs in response.

There's no way I'm letting Evie around hot liquid again. And I need a minute to gain my composure. Tonight, I'm going to explain my latest proposal to save the company money—and once again, to not-so-subtly suggest that my grandmother give up her role as chairperson of the board and name me as CEO. I'm perfect for this new role, and desperate to prove to Gram and the rest of my family that I'm worthy of the job. My cousin simply cannot run this company. Beau can't have it all.

I hear my grandmother snort.

"Secretary, my ass. He's never dated his secretaries, but he's damned sure dated every other woman in Atlanta. I guess he's expanding his horizons. How'd he meet you, anyway? You seem a little classier than his usual."

I stab at the button of the espresso maker. As the machine whirrs to life, I pull out the bottle of Kahlúa and splash some into a mug, then down the whole thing in one gulp. Between a gorgeous, scrappy intern and a grandmother who doesn't have a filter between her brain and her mouth, this is going to be an interesting night.

I'm about finished with the espresso when I hear heavy footsteps in the office.

"Gram? Thanks for telling me you were stopping by the

building! Lucky for you I happened to be here taking care of a few things. Where's Alex? And who is this lovely lady?" My cousin Beau's syrupy, braying tone makes me stare conspiratorially at the coffeemaker, as if it's my only confidant in the world. Gram obviously called Beau and asked him to join us. *Hell.*

My cousin's arrival means that an interesting night has turned into a rotten one.

CHAPTER FOUR

EVIE

The sound of a second male voice makes me turn in my seat. "It's good to see you, Gram."

The man with the deep southern drawl walks over to Mrs. Jenkins and leans over to give her a peck on the cheek. In theory, he looks like Alex with dark hair and dark eyes, but on him, the features look a bit smarmy. I think it's the angle of his mouth, like he's perpetually smirking.

"Dear, this is my other grandson, Beau. Since I was stopping by here at headquarters, I thought I'd invite Beau to attend so I could speak with both of my favorite grandsons."

So, this was Alex's rival. "Oh, hi. I'm Evie Cooper."

He extends his hand and I almost think he's going to kiss my fingers, but instead, he shakes them like I'm a child. "A pleasure."

"What are you doing here?" Mrs. Jenkins asks him.

"Dad told me you were here, so I thought I'd pop in. Where's the big guy?"

"He's making us cocktails." She gestures toward the door leading to the small room, where Alex is. I'm acutely aware that the office smells like coffee, the stuff I spilled.

"Let me go say hey." Beau strides across the room and disappears behind the door.

I glance at Mrs. Jenkins, who chortles. "My grandsons are two years apart."

"How nice," I say blandly.

"Beau's the older of the two, and he's married. His wife is pregnant."

"Very nice." This all seems so odd, this family gathering on a random Thursday evening at the office.

She lets out a sigh. "I wish Alex would settle down like Beau."

"Mmm." I test the pen on the pad of paper. It barely works, and I scrawl a second, then a third, circle. All I want is for this night to be over, and to burrow into my bed with a book

I smile patiently at Mrs. Jenkins, who chortles as she says something about Alex's prior girlfriends. *Good lord, how many women has he dated?*

"You're far prettier." She looks me up and down, as if she's appraising a piece of furniture. "Even prettier than Rose."

Who's Rose? My curiosity is instantly piqued. "Thanks?" I say, then focus on the legal pad, where I write the date in careful block letters.

I keep an eye on Mrs. Jenkins, though, because I get the feeling she's unpredictable, like a wild horse. She's wearing some sort of gold lamé dress and tall black boots, which seems odd for a business meeting. Or the opera. Her lips are pink, her hair is black, and everything about her sparkles. Not in a bad way, but in a rich-lady-bling kind of way.

This evening grows stranger by the second. I swallow a lump of discomfort at how I'd challenged Alex for extra overtime. Probably a bad move, but something about him made me want to act a little more bold than usual. As if he wanted me to stand up to him. *Weird.*

And the way we stared at each other before his grandmother walked in made my body feel like it was on fire from the inside out. My heart still hasn't recovered. I scratch my wrist and press my fingers to the underside, where the vein is. As I thought: my blood is racing.

Asking for overtime pay was out of character. But I have the distinct feeling that he thought I should stay and pretend to be his secretary for free, and that irks me. He has all the money in the world and wanted to take advantage of my time. Lately I've been thinking about how some people have so much, while the rest of us spend our precious time catering to the people with everything.

Time I don't have. I could be hanging out with my sister before she goes away to camp, then to college. If losing Mom and Dad taught me anything, it's that life is short and that we should spend as many moments as possible with the people we love. The fact that Sabrina's leaving soon makes me proud of her, and a little despondent that I won't have her hilarious—and sometimes annoying—self in my daily life.

Chewing on a thumbnail, I worry about whether Sabrina is burning our apartment down while making pizza or having friends over and cracking open a case of beer. Panic begins to set in, and I lower my hand, knowing that gnawing on my digit is rude and gross.

"Humid night for June, isn't it?" I ask Mrs. Jenkins. Might as well make small talk.

"A real bitch out there." She says this so cheerfully and casually that I laugh. I like this woman already.

She leans toward me. "I know you're not his secretary. He always hires ugly ones. You don't have to pretend or sneak around. I know all about my grandson and why you're here."

"Why am I here?" I feel a little unsteady, like I'd fallen down some existential rabbit hole.

"Probably to shag him."

I press a hand to my chest. "I am not!"

She snickers. "I wasn't born yesterday, missy. And that's why I'm not going to give him what he wants. At least not yet."

I rub my lips together, both curious and mortified. "Okay . . . why won't you give it to him?"

"Hasn't he told you? No, he probably hasn't. Alex doesn't share details of the family with anyone. He's so private, like his father." She waves her hand dismissively in the air. "His father wants my position as chair, and wants to move Alex into the CEO job. I don't want to give in to them until Alex has demonstrated that he's grown up a bit and that his father is going to make the right choices for this company. They can't get everything they want because they're men and snap their fingers. That goes for my grandson Beau, as well. But he has his faults, too, though. Quite a decision between the two."

She shakes her head and purses her lips, and I'm left wondering about the Jenkins family tree.

Maybe this is how rich people do things. I hadn't grown up with money; my parents were solidly middle class in a small town an hour outside of Atlanta. We were the perfect American family—at least until they died. Then Sabrina and I were plunged into poverty. The struggles of Alex and his family's succession plans are about as foreign to me as flying a spaceship to Mars, and about as appealing.

Mrs. Jenkins pats my knee with her bright-pink nails that are the same color as her mouth. She's got to be at least eighty. This is a woman who has no fucks left to give.

"Now, you seem like a nice girl. A huge improvement on those other tramps he's been with. They want him for his money. You seem a lot nicer." She winks. "If he was serious about a girl like you, about settling down and not going to clubs every night, I might change my mind about him taking everything over."

"Is that supposed to be a compliment?"

Mrs. Jenkins cackles like a Disney villain. It makes me giggle, and we lock eyes, as if we're conspiring against Alex. Wait. Why would I do that? Still, it's hilarious, and part of me is sad that my internship is ending soon because this place has suddenly gotten about a thousand times more interesting.

Alex stalks into the room, holding a mug sporting the company logo on the front.

Beau saunters behind him, a tumbler of amber-colored liquid in his hand. I notice that next to Alex, he's a little taller and thinner, and his clothes are a bit baggy. Unlike Alex, he's not wearing a tie.

"Mind if I stay and listen, DJ?" he says to Alex.

"DJ?" I blurt before I can stop myself.

"Beau's childhood nickname for Alex," Mrs. Jenkins says in a helpful tone.

Alex sets the mug in front of his grandmother then slides behind the desk and clicks a pen. A deep scowl crosses his dark brow, and he looks anything but happy.

"That's fine, Beau. You'll probably be a bit bored, though, with all the business talk."

Beau sits on the leather sofa off to the side and spreads his legs. Stretches his free arm across the back of the sofa. "No worries. I'm only here to catch up. And if it's boring, maybe I'll grace the conversation with some of my brilliance."

I can't help but twitch my mouth into a wince. Beau is somehow fuller of himself than Alex.

Mrs. Jenkins snorts softly. "Come on now, boys."

Beau smirks and Alex's scowl deepens. There's a lot of competitive energy in the room, and it's making me uncomfortable. I clear my throat, wondering what Thanksgiving must be like in the Jenkins family.

Alex and his grandmother begin an instant verbal volley about the company's new initiative for recycling tires. She has some strong views that probably won't win her any awards with the Sierra Club. I'm relieved when I hear Alex arguing that recycling and being a more environmentally friendly company is extremely important to him. At least he's got that going for him.

Beau doesn't interject with words, but he chuckles, sighs, and rattles the ice in his glass whenever Alex speaks. Both Alex and Mrs. Jenkins ignore him, so I try to, as well. At one point he gets up and wanders into the other room, returning with a fresh drink in hand. Our eyes meet and he winks before he sits down.

I inhale sharply and glance at Alex, who caught all of that.

"Beau, if you're going to distract my assistant, I'm going to have to ask you to leave," Alex says in the lowest, most menacing voice I've ever heard.

"Boys," Mrs. Jenkins warns again.

A deeply awkward silence fills the room.

"Back to the recycling program," she says in a brittle tone. "How much is it going to cost us?"

I lower my head and focus on scribbling notes.

For the next hour, I try to follow along, all while observing the two of them interact. It's as if I'm watching one of those wildlife documentaries that Sabrina and I loved as kids, and I have to remind myself to keep pen to paper and not gawk. Eventually, I give up and interrupt to ask if I can record the conversation in order to take notes later.

"Great idea," Mrs. Jenkins says, reaching over to tap me on the knee. "This one's sharp."

"Absolutely not," Alex counters. "I don't want our conversation on someone else's phone."

Okay, then.

"If you're paranoid, it doesn't mean they're not after you," Beau quips. *Yikes.* No one laughs. But him.

I return to the pen and paper. Alex and his grandmother are quite animated, talking about business one minute and his parents the next. She thinks Alex's father wants to travel and "lounge around," and isn't really interested in running the company. She also muses aloud whether Alex or Beau would be better as CEO. It's like watching a tennis match, the two of them.

"I'm not sure now's the right time to discuss this. Dad would want to be part of that conversation." Alex's tone is flat.

"I, for one, would like to discuss this," Beau chimes in from the sofa. Alex sneers in his direction.

Mrs. Jenkins then pivots to the topic of Alex's sister, who apparently had a baby recently.

"Gabriella is the most precious little thing. I can't help but spoil her. I wish Savannah and Dante didn't live in Italy half the year. I'll spoil your children, too, Alex. You need to give me grandbabies before I die. You're already thirty-two."

Beau beams. "Do y'all want to see photos of the ultrasound?"

"No," Alex says brusquely.

Does he hate babies, or what?

"Later," Mrs. Jenkins says, waving her hand dismissively.

"And Gram, I'm thirty," he says, his jaw clenching. "Can we please concentrate on the new initiative? I know you've got some-where to be, and I have to fly to New York tomorrow."

Must be nice to travel like he does. I'll bet he flies first-class and stays at those hotels like I've seen on TV, the kind with the whirlpool tub and the stocked minibar and the fluffy robes. The nicest hotel I've stayed at was when I went on a class trip to Orlando in my senior year of high school. It smelled like mold, and we saw two cockroaches in the bathroom.

"Gram, I think at your age, it would be best if you enjoyed the rest of your years in retirement. Why do you want to work? Dad and I have this place under control." Mrs. Jenkins purses her pink lips, and I look over, eager to hear her response. Alex continues. "We've been profitable for ten consecutive quarters. Even during a reces-sion. I don't see why you don't trust Dad with the entire company."

Beau clears his throat.

"You want me to wander off into a pasture—in this case, Palm Beach—and die like an old animal. I'm still vital!" she insists.

"Of course you are, Gram. I don't want you to die in a pasture."

They argue more about family and business and, at one point, politics. Just when I suspect Beau has the good sense to be quiet, I sneak a glance at him only to see that he appears to be watching a video on his phone. What a piece of work, this guy.

I struggle to take notes. Am I supposed to write *all* this down? My head spins. Alex's sister runs an auto-racing team sponsored by Jenkins Tire, and is having a problem with one of the top drivers. Her husband has a thick Italian accent and he can be a little "dramatic," according to Alex. Mrs. Jenkins hates the governor. Alex's mom grew up poor in Alabama and was an exotic dancer when she went to the University of Georgia.

Wait, what? I look up in alarm. Beau laughs, but I'm not sure if he's laughing at the detail about Alex's mom or the video.

"She was not a stripper, Gram," Alex sighs. "She taught dancing lessons to put herself through college."

I look over to see Mrs. Jenkins sniff haughtily. "That's what she claims. Dreadful nonsense. I've never been convinced."

Yikes on bikes.

They turn back to business, and recycling tires, and I scribble faster. The company has fished two hundred thousand tires out of rivers and streams across America. Now they're discussing his sister's difficult childbirth and how she was in labor for a day and a half. Mrs. Jenkins shares something extremely private about the sister's anatomy. I scowl at the notepad. Some of this is entirely too personal, and I'm embarrassed to be here. The business stuff is easy, and I wish they'd keep it to that.

"You're not mature enough," Mrs. Jenkins declares triumphantly in a non sequitur after a five-minute conversation about wildlife habitat at their Savannah vacation home. "If I saw you settled down with a nice girl like this one here, I'd think otherwise. Be more like your cousin Beau."

Beau simpers at Alex, then me.

I almost choke on my own spit, but Alex glares at me and I stifle it with a cough. *Settle down with this guy? Is she high?*

"You're getting old, Alex. You've sowed your wild oats." She gestures a manicured, veiny hand in my direction. "Look at how well Beau's done with the sporting goods stores. Since settling down, he's been able to focus on his work."

The cords in his neck tense and he stiffens in his chair. "Please. I'm plenty mature. And yeah, Beau's done great. He's like the manager of a Foot Locker in the mall. He has no idea how to run a company as big as this."

"Hey," Beau protests. "Shut up."

Mrs. Jenkins straightens her spine. "Oh, no? He doesn't? The stores' year-over-year profit is up thirty percent. Can you say the same for this company? And he's doing it while starting a family, while you're faffing about." She turns to me. "All he does is faff. Good God. I'm late to the opera. I'd like to at least catch the second act. We've got a balcony box so I can slip in after it starts. I'm going down to the car. Are you coming with me?"

Mrs. Jenkins stands, and so do Beau and Alex. Alex walks around the desk, and she brushes off some invisible pieces of lint from his shirt. "You're finally learning to tie a proper tie. Thank God for that. You're so handsome. Your aunt wanted to stay in the car to watch that game show she loves. What's the name of it?"

Alex heaves a sigh. "*Family Feud*."

"That's it. Are you coming with us? Beau, are you joining me?"

"No, I've got to get home to the wifey. In fact, I'm headed out." He walks over and kisses Mrs. Jenkins on the cheek.

She warmly bids him goodbye. Beau smirks at Alex, whose face is like a granite mask, stony and emotionless. There's a weird dynamic between them, but I guess that's what happens when two competitive rich guys are both angling for a position that will make them even richer.

Beau saunters out and Alex exhales while rubbing his forehead. The energy molecules in the room seem to have expanded and relaxed the minute Beau left.

"Alex, how about you? Opera? Bring your girl, I mean, your secretary, along."

Me, at the opera? I try to shoot Alex a panicked glance, but he ignores me.

Alex shakes his head. "I have work to finish. Contrary to what you might think, I don't spend every night in clubs with models."

Oh, thank goodness, because I want to get out of here. The whole vibe is weird, weird, weird.

Mrs. Jenkins chuckles. "Sure, sure. You're a good boy. Perhaps someday you'll make a woman very happy. You'll be a pain in the ass to her, but you'll make her happy." She busses his face, then turns to me, wagging her index finger. "It's always the playboys who fall the hardest, you know. He came so close to falling several years ago, but then called the wedding off right at the last minute; couldn't give up his precious bachelorhood."

With that, she winks at me and flutters her fingers a wave. "Evie, a pleasure."

Alex's jaw is clamped together so tight that the muscles in his cheek are bunched into an angry knot.

I stand up quickly, flustered. The notepad tumbles to the floor and I try to pretend it doesn't exist. "Same. Nice to meet you." My cheeks feel hot. Now I want to know about Alex's near marriage. I hadn't heard *that* through the office grapevine.

He shoots me a glare over his grandmother's head then

propels her out of the office. I scramble to scoop up the notepad. I'm certain I screwed up the note-taking. Sinking into the chair, I review the notes. So many spelling errors. Sloppy handwriting. I'd have done so much better had I been able to use a laptop or record everything on my phone.

Alex strides back in, and it's as if he's taking up all the air in the room. It's also as if he ceased to notice me. He's back behind his desk, stacking papers. The look in his eyes is positively murderous.

"Here are the notes. Unless you want me to type them up." I gently slide the pad onto his desk, not wanting to drop, spill, or ruin anything.

He scans the pad. "Your handwriting's pretty good. I'll email you if I can't decipher anything."

"Thanks. I'll see myself out. I'll make sure to look for that extra cash in my paycheck."

He looks up with those intense eyes and I nearly gasp. I'm not sure if I should be scared or turned on, and I guess I'm a bit of both. Why does the most annoying man on the planet also have to be so handsome?

"How much do you know about me, Evie?"

I raise my eyebrows. Oh lord, this night isn't over. Panic rises in my chest when I realize my cell is downstairs and I haven't been reachable for over an hour. What if Sabrina had an emergency?

"What you discussed with your grandmother is the extent of my knowledge," I reply lamely.

"No office gossip?"

I shrug slowly. "I think it's common knowledge you are a-a man about town."

He screws up his face, as if he doesn't understand.

"An eligible bachelor," I offer.

He presses his lips together in a thin line and nods. "How would you like to know more about the company from an insider's perspective? Learn the ropes?"

I lick my dry lips, but I'm wary of what he's about to propose. "That would be wonderful, but I really don't think I'm cut out to be an assistant. I'm really much better at marketing and proofreading—"

"I was thinking about something different. Very lucrative, and very educational." A feral grin spreads across his face and my jaw drops. *A real job?*

"Wh-what do you have in mind?"

He chuckles a little. "I need to think about it first. Perhaps run it by my lawyer."

With that, he tilts his head down and begins writing something in a black notebook. He looks up, expectant. He's obviously finished with me, which is okay because being near him makes me feel squirmy inside. "Thank you for your last-minute help tonight. I really appreciate it. I'll make sure your sweater is cleaned and returned to you by tomorrow afternoon."

"Am I free to go?"

He nods and I turn my heel. When my hand is on the doorknob, his voice rumbles through my body and stops me in my tracks. "Wait. I'll call security so you don't have to walk to the parking lot in the dark."

"It's no problem, I take the train." I gesture to where I think the rail system is in relation to his office.

"The train?" He stares at me as if he's unaware that Atlanta has a commuter rail.

"Yes, you know, MARTA? I live pretty close to a stop."

"You don't have a car?"

I shake my head and take a step toward the door.

"Let me call a car to take you home. Please don't be stubborn. You shouldn't be on the train this late by yourself."

This late? What is he, a grandpa? It's only nine thirty at night. "I don't want to be a bother. I take the train all the time."

He shuts his eyes for a few seconds, as if he's trying not to get pissed. Then he stands, grabs the notepad I'd written on, and shoves it into a black leather briefcase. It's not an old-fashioned businessman briefcase; it's more like something you'd see in a men's fashion magazine. A bag that's minimalist and sleek. It's practically a work of art.

Like him.

I pull open the door, hoping to slink out. Being around him is too distracting, too nerve-racking. He's too handsome, and I feel awkward, like a voyeur, now that I've sat in on his private conversation with his grandmother. It's like I got an intimate peek at his life, and that makes me uncomfortable for some reason.

Slowly, I turn my body and take a step through the elevator door. Then I feel someone close behind.

"Evie, wait, I'll drive you home."

CHAPTER FIVE

ALEX

It was a total disaster having Evie Cooper take notes during that shit show of a conversation. I kept sneaking glances at her, ostensibly to make sure she was doing her job. But when she shifted in her chair and uncrossed, then recrossed, those long tan legs, I couldn't help but stare. And Gram saw everything.

Evie, thank God, didn't notice at all. She'd been absorbed in writing on the legal pad, pausing only to look up in utter confusion when my grandmother dropped an eff bomb or three. Or stopping to stare at my dense cousin and his ill-timed wisecracks. *Welcome to the Jenkins family, Miss Cooper.*

Still, she rolled with Gram's attitude and didn't seem impressed with Beau's brand of humor. A definite plus. Watching her interact with my family gave me an idea for a special assignment for sweet Evie. The seed of the plan came while chatting with Gram tonight. It's a little wild, but it could work.

There was a TV movie that I'd watched recently when I couldn't sleep. It was a romance, where the heroine needed to save her flower shop and inexplicably needed a fake fiancé. I'd tuned in at two in the morning, when I was stressed as fuck, hoping it would bore me to sleep. It hadn't. It reminded me of my sister, Savannah, and what happened between her and Dante.

And now I can't stop thinking about the movie's plot.

Or Evie.

Or how I want to crush my smarmy jerk cousin once and for all.

Evie's a perfect candidate for this plan since she's ending her employment as an intern soon. Still, this is an idea I need to ponder before I ask her to be involved. I do need to run this by my lawyer, and I want to get a read on her first. That's the other reason I want to drive her home.

Can we carry on a conversation together? Or will our moments be spent in awkward silence? I hate those moments of quiet when I'm with a woman. Makes me nervous, like I'm not doing enough to impress her.

Can I impress Evie?

Will she annoy me, like that one temp assistant a few months back who made the weird phlegm noise with her sinuses? Is she going to shift into being too flirtatious, too seductive, too tempting?

Hell, she's already too tempting. She's barely acknowledging my existence, which is a bit of a shock—usually women try to flirt with me. Now I'm standing next to her in the elevator, trying not to breathe in too deep. I don't want to inhale more of her intoxicating, sweet scent. I've been smelling it since we left my office then stopped on her floor to get her bag.

She's staring down at the floor, her beautiful face flushed. It almost looks like she's breathing fast, but I can't tell because she keeps doing this sexy thing with her mouth where she presses her lips together then plumps them into a pout.

The elevator opens to the parking garage and I hold the door. The flickering glance as she walks out—what's that about? I'm trying to do something nice here, and she seems annoyed. I want to drive her home since I was such an ass to her earlier.

"This way." I point to the space closest to the elevator. It's my reserved parking spot, where my true love and its electric charger awaits. "You're going to like my new car. It's literally the fastest in the world."

Like I do every day after work, I gaze upon my new toy with all the affection a man normally reserves for his lover. My candy-apple red Tesla Roadster. Zero to sixty in one-point-nine seconds, top speed of two hundred and fifty miles an hour. All electric. Limited edition. Elon Musk himself met me at the dealership and handed me the keys.

A dream machine for a gearhead like me.

I go to the passenger door so I can hold it open for Evie. She'll be so impressed by this.

Wait. Where's Evie?

I look up and she's ten feet away, closer to the elevator. She's not headed in my direction.

"Thanks, I'll take the train." She whirls and takes a few steps toward the elevator. I jog to her as she's pressing the button.

"Wait, wait, wait. No. I don't want you taking the train this late. It's unsafe."

She folds her arms across her stomach. "I take the train all the time at all hours. It's fine."

"It's not fine. There was an assault last weekend. I saw it on the news."

Evie rolls her eyes. "Whatever. I saw that story, too. They were drug dealers. I wasn't planning on buying cocaine tonight."

"Still. I don't want you taking the train with drug dealers." I pause. "Why are we even having this conversation? Get in the car and I'll drive you home. It's really no bother."

Evie nervously eyes the Tesla. "It looks like a race car."

"It is a race car." I chuckle, until I see her glare. "What? You don't like fast cars?"

"Not at all," she snaps.

"Okay. I promise to drive like Gram in a Cadillac in Palm Beach. C'mon." I hold my hand out, declining to tell Evie that Gram behind the wheel is a terror.

"Okay," she mutters, and walks past me, toward the car.

I follow, and open the door for her, which gives me a chance to inhale her perfume again. Slowly, while clutching her messenger bag to her chest, she eases into the black-and-red leather seat. I shut the door gently, as if not wanting to spook a wild animal.

Once I'm sitting next to her in the car, I fire it up with the keyless ignition. I love the full-throated sound of the engine, and I glance at Evie. She's staring straight ahead at the dashboard.

She's not impressed, even a little.

"What's your address?" My finger hovers over the in-dash GPS screen.

Evie tells me, and it's not an area I'm familiar with. I plug it into the computer. It's sixteen miles away, on the city's south side, in a suburb.

I pull out of the parking garage and onto the street, going slower than I thought possible with this car. She eases up on the death grip on her bag, and we ride in silence for several minutes.

Evie's sitting up straight in the seat, still staring ahead out the windshield at the road. When her eyes flicker to me a few times, I take this as an opportunity to ask about her. It's far preferable to thinking of my own issues, like Beau's naked ambition.

"Do you still live with your parents?"

"No, me and my sister."

"Is she older, younger?"

"Younger. She's graduating from high school in a couple of weeks."

I sense there's a backstory here. Why would a recent college grad be living with her teenage sister? Despite my own family's lack of decorum, I should know better than to pry into Evie's life.

"You and your sister? Where are your parents?"

"Dead." Her tone is flat, and I instantly feel like an ass for asking. "Don't say you're sorry. It's not your fault."

Aw, hell. This makes me feel like a total shit. But I'm even more curious about her background now. Not enough to ask more questions and come off like an even bigger jerk than I already am. "I'm sorry for sticking my nose in your business. I shouldn't have asked."

"It's okay." She focuses out the windshield. "Most people don't understand what Sabrina and I are going through."

"Try me. My friends say I'm an excellent listener."

She slides a glance to me while shaking her head. "Thanks, but I'll pass. You have enough going on, and don't need to hear about my woes."

What are her woes? A couple of minutes go by in silence. It's driving me crazy.

"What was your major at Emory?" I finally ask.

She huffs out a curt laugh. "What's up with all the questions?"

I lift a shoulder. "I want to get to know you better."

"Marketing, with a minor in business."

"I was a business major." I glance at her. She's a little more relaxed now, I can tell by the way her lovely eyes have softened.

"Where did you go to school?" she asks.

"University of Georgia. I almost didn't go at all, though."

She shifts in her seat to look at me. "Really? Why?"

"You don't know?"

"No."

"I used to race motorcycles. Semiprofessionally. Well, professionally. When I was a teenager and into my early twenties." A look of horror crosses her face, and I can't help but grin. "Probably your worst nightmare, I guess, if you don't like going fast. But I loved it. I loved speed. Still do, I guess."

"Why did you stop racing?" Evie's right hand is white-knuckling the door handle, but the curiosity in her voice is evident.

The GPS announces that I need to exit the interstate, and I slow the car. When I break at the end of the off-ramp, her body tenses.

I clear my throat. "I figured I'd eventually run my family's company, and it would be more responsible to get a business degree than travel the world racing a bike around a track at two hundred miles an hour."

"That sounds awful. The motorcycle part. Not the business part." She shudders. I'm not sure I've ever met someone who is so offended by speed.

"Do you miss it?"

"What? Motorcycle racing? Or going fast?"

"Both."

"Hell yes. But I still get a taste. You should see me when I go on the track at the Atlanta Motor Speedway. I have a supercharged BMW bike and a tricked-out Porsche. I know the owner of the track, and he lets me play a few times a year in the off-season."

This should really impress her. It's one of the biggest tracks in the country, and other than pro racers, few get to rip around the asphalt there.

She lets out a disapproving little grunt that somehow also sounds adorable. "Sounds dangerous."

Evie Cooper is not easily impressed, or maybe she's the most safety-conscious woman in the world. The GPS directs me onto her street. It's in a neighborhood that a few years ago would've been considered a little rough and one that you wouldn't walk in at night. Now the tired old bungalows with their stately yet scruffy trees are flanked by new boxy modern condos with minimalist landscaping. It gives the area a mismatched, chaotic feel.

"Danger's not a bad thing," I murmur.

Her house is a little yellow place with a bright light illuminating the dollhouse-like porch, like a small beacon in the dark. It's so small that I wonder if it's one of those sheds they sell at the hardware store. Okay, it's not quite that tiny, but it definitely fits the southern definition of shotgun shack.

"Thank you for the ride. I know it was probably out of your way. You probably live in some mansion somewhere in Buckhead." Her hair sways against her shoulders and the urge to touch her skin is back.

"I don't do mansions. I live in a condo a few blocks from the office." A penthouse, to be exact, but mentioning that here, in front of her tiny house, seems like bad form.

A frown crosses her face. "And you still drive to work?"

I shrug. "What can I say? I love my car. Hey, let me walk you to your door."

"No, no need." She unclips the seat belt and her hand flies to the door latch.

"It doesn't seem safe around here. Let me open your door."

"No, Alex. I'm okay. I know everyone on this street. And, anyway, danger's a not bad thing, right?"

For the first time since we got in the car, the corners of her lips turn upward, a genuine expression of mirth. It's like goddamned sunshine at midnight. If I was attracted to her before, I'm captivated now. She slips out of the car while I'm still grinning like a fool. I open the driver's door and stand between my open door and the Tesla, watching her glide over the broken concrete of her walkway. Her head's held high and there's a subtle yet seductive sway in her hips.

I lean on the roof of the car, enjoying her strut more than I enjoyed undressing my last one-night stand.

"Maybe I'll take you to the track someday and let you drive the Porsche," I call out, then immediately cringe. What am I? Lovesick? A teen rom-com screenwriter? The star in a boy band video?

She turns around and tilts her head. "You'd trust me with your precious car? Somehow you seem like too much of a control freak for that."

This makes me chuckle. She might not be impressed by my Tesla, or my connections, or my past.

But I'm impressed with her.

Taking a couple of steps back, she grins at me, then whirls and strides to the door, her hair floating behind her. Oh yeah. The feisty and stunning Evie Cooper might be the woman I need to help secure my place as the CEO of my family's company.

CHAPTER SIX

EVIE

When I walk into my house, Sabrina's on the love seat, the one near the window. She's obviously waiting for me, and it looks like she's slipped her head under the curtain. She flings the fabric around and I laugh out loud because she looks so silly.

"Who was that, Evie?" She has the narrow-eyed scrutiny of a grizzled police detective.

"Some guy from work." I let my laptop bag slide off my shoulder and down my arm. It lands with a soft *thunk* on a bench near the door. "Were you spying on me?"

"You work with a guy that has a red Tesla Roadster?"

The car was red? Hadn't noticed that detail. Probably because I was too busy gripping the door handle for dear life.

I have a pathological dislike for physical risk. It probably has something to do with my parents' fatal car crash, and I'm sure I should talk it out with a therapist. I'll be certain to do that right after I get a real job, health insurance, and pay off my student loans.

So, basically, never.

As I toe-heel my shoes off, I sigh while sizing up my little sister. "How does a seventeen-year-old know what a Tesla Roadster is?"

She undoes her scrunchie and shakes out her glorious mane of curly amber-colored hair as if she's a model in a shampoo commercial. "I read *Vanity Fair.*"

Rolling my eyes, I pad barefoot into the kitchen and pull open the fridge door. Staring at the juice, water, milk, and soda, my mind drifts to Alex.

There was something odd in the way he looked at me . . .

"Evie? Evieeee."

My sister's whiny voice snaps me out of my thoughts. I grab a soda and shut the fridge. "What?"

"Who was that? Seriously. You don't work with guys who drive cars like that. I've been to your office. The guys on your floor are lucky to drive Hondas."

I take a long guzzle. My mouth has been dry ever since I got into Alex's car. "He's the owner of the company." Pausing, I think of Mrs. Jenkins and her knee-high boots, and his cousin Beau with the permanent smirk. "Well, sort of. His family owns the company. He's the managing director."

Sabrina sits at our kitchen table and lightly smacks it with her hands. "Oh, is he old and gross? Do tell."

The last thing I feel like doing is explaining. But this is better than fighting with her over whether she can go to a party. "There's nothing to tell. I stayed late to check some reports, and I had to deliver the paperwork to his office. He drove me home."

No need to explain her about the coffee incident, the way he smelled, or how he stared at me like a lion about to eat his prey. Or about how incredible he looked when shirtless. Or about his foulmouthed granny. I crack a smile thinking about Mrs. Jenkins sucking down her boozy coffee, but my expression fades when I recall Beau's wisecracks. That guy struck me as a bit of a bully, and I'd almost felt bad for Alex having to deal with him.

My sister narrows her blue eyes and extends her hand. I offer her my soda and she guzzles. "You don't think that's a little weird, him driving you home? He's probably way older. Perv."

I lean against the counter. "Yeah, it is a little odd, I suppose. He's very . . ." I wave my hand back and forth in the air.

"Very what?" Sabrina belches, loud. For such an adorable little thing, she can be pretty disgusting.

"You are such a pig. God."

"He's what?"

"He's arrogant. Maddening. Controlling. Maybe even a bit of a jerk. Don't like him."

"Then why are you grinning?"

"Shut up. What about your biology final?" I try to channel our mom.

"I already know all the material and I studied tonight. A little."

My eyes sweep around the kitchen. Why is there always so much crap on the counter? I swear I picked up before I left, so how is there an open box of cereal, two glasses and an empty bag of chips lying around?

The better question is: why can't Sabrina pick up after herself? I toss the empty bag in the garbage and put the glasses in a cabinet stuffed with plastic superhero cups we've gotten from various promotions at the nearby convenience store. I keep meaning to go through this cabinet and throw stuff away, but there never seems to be time.

"A letter came from the science camp." Sabrina flicks through a stack of papers on the table and pulls out an envelope.

Frowning, I stare at the letter as if it were personally offending me. Mail was never good news. "Did you read it?"

"Nah. I figured that was your job."

Of course. Everything's my job. Is it normal for a twenty-two-year-old to feel middle-aged? I sink into the seat opposite Sabrina and rip open the envelope.

"'Dear Ms. Cooper.'" I huff out a breath. At least they've stopped addressing the letters to Mom and Dad. "'We regret to inform you that there was a water leak in the Suffolk Science Camp's main hall. The space was a large classroom used by MIT faculty and students, and the school needs to perform extensive repairs this summer prior to the fall semester. Because of this, we're moving the main camp sessions to a building adjacent to the MIT campus. The camp doesn't own this space, and we've been forced to sign a short-term lease with the owner for the summer. Because of this, we will have to levy an additional five-hundred-dollar charge to all campers this year. The accommodations for the camp haven't changed. We regret this inconvenience. Please don't hesitate to contact us with questions. The deadline for payment of this new charge is Tuesday . . .' Wait, this coming Tuesday? Sabrina, when did we get this letter?"

She reaches for the envelope and glances at one side, then flips it over. "Maybe last week?"

Panic pools in my chest. We even don't have enough for the

camp yet. "Why didn't you tell me when it came in the mail?"

She shrugs. "You go through the mail. Remember the last time you had me do it? I threw away half the bills we had to pay and the electricity almost got turned off."

"How the hell are we going to pay for this? I'll definitely have to pick up extra shifts at the restaurant." Maybe also beg the camp financial director for a payment plan.

"We'll scrape up the cash," she says confidently.

She always seems to have faith when I don't. "We're going to try. I'll deal with this in the morning." Maybe if I can work at the restaurant every night. And if I sell another piece of Mom's jewelry. There's still her engagement ring. The diamond must be worth something. It's a step I haven't wanted to take, and a spike of shame hits my gut. If only I could get a full-time job in my field . . .

"I can't deal with this now. I'll tackle it in the morning when I'm fresh."

On my way out of the kitchen, I pick up a dish towel that's inexplicably balled up on the floor. A scalding hot bath is what I want right now, the one thing that might calm the feeling that everything's about to fall apart. Sabrina better not have used all the hot water. This rental house has a hot water tank the size of a bucket, I swear.

"What does he look like?" Sabrina's girlish voice bounces off the kitchen cabinets.

"Who?" I know exactly who, of course. She's probably trying to take my mind off the letter. Or she's being . . . what's that word she uses? Thirsty? Yes, that's it.

"Your boss. Is he super fine?"

He's tall, dark and dangerous in both the most sublime and cliché ways. His eyes are midnight blue, so dark they seem black. His chest looks like it was the prototype for numerous statues of Roman gladiators.

"I dunno. Like a regular guy. Dark hair. Tall. I didn't really notice." I take a couple of steps into the living room, toward my bedroom. Our house is so small that you can get to any room in ten paces or less.

"You didn't notice. Yeah, *right*. What's his name?"

Heaving a sigh, I call out: "Dale Alexander Jenkins."

"Dale's not a sexy name."

"He goes by Alex." I push the door to my room open, all while thinking of him. It's far more fun to fantasize about his spectacular muscles than how I'm going to pay for my sister's camp.

When we were in his office, his gaze was superficial and flirtatious. Mocking and arrogant, even. But then something small and subtle changed in his demeanor. It wasn't when I tied his tie. Or when we bantered about my hourly pay. No, it was when we were sitting in the car.

I plug in my cell since it's nearly out of battery, then strip off my cheap dress and throw on my robe. There's no use thinking about Alex. He's older, he's rich, and he's my boss. As I walk into the hall and take the three steps to the bathroom, I crack a smile at how he'd said I could drive his Porsche.

As if. But the thought of us hanging out for the day makes me giggle a little.

He's the *boss*. At least for a few more days. Even if he is interested—and I'm one hundred percent positive he's not—he'd never make a move. It would be wildly inappropriate. So why can't I stop thinking about him?

I guess it was the way he studied my face when I spoke. The

way his eyes drifted to my mouth, and how his eyes lit up when I laughed. The way he asked me questions while we were in the car and made me feel like I was more important than anything else in the universe.

I stare at myself in the bathroom mirror, wondering why he seemed so interested. Could he tell that I'm tired? Stressed? Afraid? Other women my age go out to bars and clubs. They get their nails done and plan weekends on the beach in Florida with their friends.

My college friends all took jobs far from Atlanta, which means my closest female friend is Ida, the eighty-year-old woman who runs the community garden down the block.

Maybe I'll skip those normal life stages of career, marriage, and having children, and head right into the life of a retiree. One with a low-paying service job. I do kind of like bingo, or I did when I took Ida that one time.

That reminds me, I still need to do the community garden newsletter . . .

Probably I should take a quick shower and get to that newsletter, but I need to unwind. I almost never soak in a bath. Everyone deserves some self-care, right? I work damn hard.

Our tub is one of those old claw-foot types, nice and deep. It has a shower attached to a precarious oval shower curtain rod. We have to be extra careful when we slide the curtain, or the whole thing will come crashing down. Which has happened, more than once.

I crank the 1950s-era faucet and stick my hand under. The water grows hot almost instantly. I almost groan with relief and reach for the bubble bath I bought last week at a dollar store.

While the tub fills with suds, I brush my teeth and wash my

face with my drugstore cleanser. I'll bet Alex has all the best stuff. His bathroom must be incredible, and never run out of hot water. He probably buys his girlfriends those beauty products whose names I can't pronounce, the ones used by the TikTok models Sabrina likes.

It probably takes more than three steps to get from his bedroom to his bathroom, and he probably can't hear his sister snore in the next room because he doesn't live with anyone else.

The tub now filled, I undo the tie to my robe. When did the edges get so frayed? I guess I've had this a while. I dip a toe into the water.

Sucking in my breath, I ease in, inch by inch. I pull the shower curtain around the tub. It's a pretty, palm-tree-patterned curtain, one I'd gotten on sale last year. It makes me feel like I'm in a tropical oasis while I'm in the tub. Not like I've ever been to a tropical oasis.

I settle back into the water and allow my lids to flutter shut and my muscles to relax. God, this feels so good.

The water's hot enough to make me forget everything. The thousand dollars I already owe the camp on the payment plan, and the five-hundred-dollars on top of that. How we have exactly $128.42 in our bank account until payday next Friday.

Alex.

Alex and his midnight blue eyes. I inhale a nose full of jasmine-scented bubbles, wondering what happened to Alex's fiancé, and why he broke off the wedding. I'll bet the cause was dramatic and interesting, and I'm dying to know more.

Couldn't give up his single life, his grandmother had said.

What would it be like to be his girlfriend, even for a little while? I'm sure he'd be generous and buy gifts. There would be no problems covering an unexpected five-hundred-dollar bill. It's easy to allow myself to slip into a fantasy, like when I imagine winning the lottery. But instead of fantasizing about using the Powerball millions to open an animal shelter, I'm thinking of what Alex would do if he saw the unexpected summer camp bill.

Don't worry about this. I'll take care of it, Evie, he'd say in that commanding voice. It's the aural mixture of honey and smoke, I've decided.

He'd organize trips around the world and we'd stay in boutique hotels. We'd eat in places with real napkins, and when we lived together, the glasses in our cabinet wouldn't be plastic. But his money isn't what attracts me to him. I could give a fig about all the material stuff.

No, what's alluring about Alex is how he *noticed* me. His laserlike focus. On me, Evie Cooper, intern. Probably he's like that with everyone. But for tonight, I'm going to pretend he saw something special in me and—

"Oh my God, look at this!" my sister hollers. I hear the rattle of the bathroom doorknob and the creak of the hinges. There's no lock on the door, so of course she can barge in.

So much for quiet, private self-care. "What? I'm taking a bath. Can't I have one minute to myself?" I yell, even though I can tell she's already a foot away, separated by the shower curtain.

She lets out an ear-piercing squeal and I wince. A hand, holding a smartphone, comes through the gap in the curtain like a Broadway actress making a dramatic stage entrance. On the phone's screen is Alex Jenkins, grinning and dressed in a tuxedo.

Sabrina chortles. "Holy shit, look at this! Evie, Alex Jenkins is super hot!"

CHAPTER SEVEN

EVIE

"Welcome to Chili's. Would you like a booth or a table?" My smile is so practiced my cheeks don't even hurt anymore. With the couple standing before me, the guy is tall, well-built, and has near-black hair. Although he looks nothing like Alex, I'm somehow reminded of him anyway, which sends heat searing into my cheeks.

Oh, lord. When am I going to stop thinking about Alex? When he drove me home three nights ago, he firmly planted himself into the recesses of my brain. At first I only thought about him at night, before bed, replaying those moments we were together.

Then he emerged from the recesses and is now front and center in my mind. It's like a delicious secret that I'm keeping, but also ridiculous. Stupidly I'm allowing myself to think *what if*.

What if he was interested in me?

What if he took me out on a date?

What if he looked at me with those intense eyes all the time, and not in the office?

The couple, who are beaming, practically glowing they look so happy, inform me that they prefer a booth. For what feels like the millionth time tonight, I grab the menus and lead them to a booth four along the far wall of the restaurant. I make small talk about the weather, which is unseasonably hot. Management likes us to be "uber friendly." Those are their words, not mine. Uber. Friendly.

"I guess we'd better settle in for a long, hot summer," I chirp.

The humidity's been a killer lately. I'm not looking forward to walking home in this soupy, hot mess tonight. Or any other night.

"Can you bring us two margaritas right away?" the woman asks as we approach the table, her black Coach bag hanging in the crook of her arm. "On the rocks, no salt."

"Of course. And I'll get your server."

Besides home and the office, this is where I spend most of my time. At a Chili's on a main road in my suburb, located exactly 1,852 steps—a little less than a mile—from my house. I know the distance because that's what I do when my night shift is over. I count the steps on the way home, hoping I won't get run over when I cross Peachtree Avenue, abducted near the vacant lot, or murdered along the way.

I've worked at Chili's for six months. When I was hired, I was told that a server job, which earns more in tips, would open up soon. That hasn't happened, and I've stayed as a hostess because, well, Sabrina and I need that ten fifty an hour. And the waitstaff does share a portion of the tips. Well, most of them do. Tonight might be one of those lucky nights since it's Saturday, but then again, maybe not. Gabe—the stingiest server—is working tonight, and I suspect he's not going to divide a single penny of his tips.

Once the couple at table four is settled—in Gabe's section, no less, because he'd sniped at me earlier in the evening, claiming I wasn't giving him the good customers—I make my way back to the hostess station at the front. We're about an hour past the dinner rush, which means it's nine o'clock. Two hours until we close, thankfully, then another half hour on top of that for cleaning and closing up. By the time I walk home it will be well after midnight.

I flag Gabe down and clue him in on the margarita order.

"Did you already tell the bar?" he asks, bored. Gabe isn't bad-looking, but he'd be far more attractive if he wasn't so surly. It's as if a kind word can't cross his lips. All the hostesses hate him.

For some reason, my feet are aching something fierce tonight. Probably because I cleaned the house this morning, then ran over to my neighbor Ida's home a few blocks away. She made a casserole for Sabrina and me, which was incredibly kind. Sabrina wouldn't eat it because it had diced chicken. Apparently my sister's a vegetarian now. That's a new development.

"Fine, more for me," I'd told my sister as I wolfed a plateful down for lunch.

Sometimes I skip entire meals because we don't have a lot of money, so whenever free food comes my way, I take advantage of it. I almost feel a little ashamed that I had the casserole and a loaded baked potato here at work, while Sabrina had another frozen pizza, but oh well. She could've shut up and eaten the casserole.

I survey the laminated, erasable layout map of the restaurant's tables and swipe a little sponge to clean it off. As I'm arranging the menus, a deep voice startles me.

"Excuse me."

I look up and nearly gasp. It's the man who I seated, but once again, I'm reminded of Alex. This is ridiculous because this guy's nose is way bigger than Alex's. Why did my brain think it was him?

"Yes, how can I help?" I paste on my most accommodating smile.

The man leans in and down, as if he wants to share something private. I catch a whiff of his scent and it crowds out the pervasive smell of fried onion and beer that hangs in the air.

The guy's cologne is spicy and warm, similar enough to Alex's aftershave that it makes my stomach flutter.

"It's our anniversary tonight. We've been together a year. Can we do something special for my girlfriend, like . . ." He gestures with his hand, and the expression on his face is almost bashful. How cute.

"Aww, congratulations. What can we do that would be special? Do you want us to surprise her? Maybe bring a dessert with a candle?"

"Yeah, that sounds good. She loves chocolate. She's wild about chocolate cake. She's special like that."

Dude, who doesn't love chocolate cake? Still, it's incredibly sweet that he thinks his girlfriend's love for a common dessert is special. Isn't that what everyone wants? To find that one person who is enamored with how unique, how special, you are?

"I'll chat with your server and the guys in the kitchen. We'll come up with something fun. I promise."

"Do you all sing songs at the table? Like happy birthday, but for anniversaries?"

I bite my lip and shake my head. Birthday songs are the bane of my existence. I feel so silly when I have to clap and sing and parade through the restaurant. When I first started, I tried to hide whenever there was a birthday table, but my manager had taken me aside and told me that I needed to participate with enthusiasm. Uber. Friendly.

"No, we don't have a special song for anniversaries, I'm so sorry," I say.

"Okay, well, a cake would be great. Thanks."

The guy stuffs his hands in his pockets and ambles back to his table. When he's out of earshot, I let out a little sigh. Partially because I now have to engage in conversation with Gabe, and partially out of longing.

What would Alex do on our one-year anniversary? Surely he'd take me to some place nicer than Chili's. Probably one of those downtown restaurants, the kind that Josephine's always talking about at the office. Alex would definitely make reservations.

Holy crap. Am I losing my freaking mind? Standing here, mooning about the millionaire managing director. I console myself with the thought that Alex probably orders for his date, given how bossy he is. I'd surely grow annoyed with that in about three seconds.

What a waste of brain space. I should be focused on the email I got today from my alumni job network, one that contained an opening at my dream workplace: the Georgia Aquarium. Applying and getting hired there might solve all my problems. Or at least some of them, including the need for Chili's shifts.

Gabe passes by my station on his way to the bar, interrupting my thoughts, and I call out his name.

"I'm busy," he says, but he stops.

"Listen, the couple at table four. It's their anniversary. The guy would like to surprise his girlfriend with a chocolate cake. And a candle. Or you could do one of those sparklers like we do with birthdays. I can handle that part, if you're busy."

"I'll take care of it. Your job is to stay up here." Gabe rolls his hazel eyes as if I'd made the stupidest request in the history of Chili's, then walks away. That's how he's acted toward me for a couple of months; ever since I declined to sit at the bar with him after closing and drink beer.

I squint at his back. "You're welcome," I mutter, then in a whisper, I follow up with, "jerk."

More customers come in, people who got out of the seven-o'clock movie at the theater across the street. They're all raving about some new blockbuster superhero movie, one that Sabrina and I would love to see. But we don't have the twenty-eight bucks to spare for two tickets, and even if we did, I was short on time.

The more customers I seat the more it becomes apparent that I won't get out of here by eleven thirty. For some irrational reason, I don't like walking after midnight—as if the serial killers only come out at 12:01 p.m.—which means I'll either take an Uber home or ask someone here to drive me. And I hate asking people for favors.

My perma-smile thins as I seat six at a table, and my mood is going the way of my expression. Down, down, down. What is Alex doing tonight? Probably something fabulous. Isn't he in New York? I think that's what Josephine said.

I imagine him at some club, drinking a bottle of something expensive. Probably surrounded by women. Everyone would be in designer clothes, and no one would order a giant fried onion.

The thought of him lounging and drinking somewhere swanky

seems so supremely unfair, all of a sudden. Especially since every pore of my body, and my hair, smells like fried chicken and charred hamburgers.

This wasn't what I planned, working two jobs to eke out a living. Raising my kid sister. Spending Saturday night at a hostess station at a chain restaurant. Smelling like I dove into a deep fryer. When I come home from shifts here, I have to scrub and scrub to get the foul odor off my skin.

The couple celebrating the anniversary walks out without a thank-you, a smile, or even a nod of the head. Ugh. Why are people so rude?

Rarely do I throw myself a pity party, but tonight I feel one coming on. The image of a grinning Alex in his fancy car comes to mind, and instead of longing, I feel a tired, dull anger, laced with a thread of shame. Surely he knows how poor I am, and probably that's why he treated me with such kindness.

It was pity, not interest, in his eyes.

How is it that some people like him have all the luck? And how is it that I've had none?

CHAPTER EIGHT

EVIE

By the time I dash out of the train at my stop, weave my way around the stationary people on the escalator and hit the exit, I'm out of breath. Dammit. I grip my messenger bag tight. This exit is closed for construction.

"Crap!" Did I yell that aloud? No one seems to care, because the other downtown commuters are also swearing and groaning, annoyed that their nine-to-five has become even more annoying than usual.

I whirl around and power walk toward the southwest entrance, the one near the library. This will tack on an extra couple of blocks to my walk to the office. Let's hope I can make it before those angry gray rain clouds let loose. Thunder rolls in the distance and I catch a flash of lightning on the horizon. The storm's headed this way, according to what I saw on the weather app this morning.

It's Sabrina's fault that I'm late. Somehow she'd lost both sets of house keys this morning. Had I not been forced to sift through the dirty laundry pile this morning, I would've left on time. I dial her as I huff my way down Peachtree Street.

"Hey, sis." Her voice is sleepy. "I'm sorry about leaving the keys in my jeans pocket and stuffed in the laundry. I've been so tired from that party . . ."

I'd allowed her to go to one graduation party. How wild could a Thursday night party be? Epic, apparently. She'd rolled in this morning at four. The lack of sleep and the hours of worry were probably contributing to my foul mood. I'd let her go to the party because she only had a half day of school that started at noon today.

Today should be an exciting one—the final day of my internship. But like other recent milestones, this is one more grind to get through. The highlights of my day will be to make extra copies of my resumé using the company printer and apply for that open communications job at the Georgia Aquarium.

"Don't worry about it. Sorry I yelled at you. Make sure you eat lunch today, and can you call your doctor about your physical? You need a doctor's slip for camp. Don't forget, we haven't got a lot of time left."

"Are we going to have enough money for camp?"

"Yeah. Don't sweat it. The financial aid office and I are going to talk again this afternoon. Love you."

I hang up and shove the phone into my bag. The camp hasn't been happy about our inability to pay. But since Sabrina's one of the top-ranked science students in all of Georgia—and because she's one of the only girls enrolled—they "might be willing to make an exception."

Might. Assholes.

Camp costs, college applications, financial aid forms . . . the crush of paperwork is enough to make me cry. Since I've graduated, it's only fair that my sister deserves a good education, too. She shouldn't get screwed out of going to college because our folks died and hadn't saved a lot of money while they were alive. Still, student loans will only go so far, and I don't want my sister to join me in the ranks of the people who will be retired and still paying off student loans.

I have middle-aged problems, all right—but not middle-aged paychecks.

Finally, I arrive at work, and fling open the door to the building. I'm a half hour late on my final Friday during the last day of my paid internship. Maybe no one will notice. Or maybe everyone will, and I'd forever be known as the Intern Who Screwed Up.

I imagine my boss making a tsk-tsk noise to her superiors. *We were going to give Genevieve a job after her internship, but her performance was so dismal*, Josephine would write. *She couldn't even arrive on time.*

That's the other reason for my foul mood. What am I going to do now that my internship is ending? It hasn't paid well, but it's paid *something*. I've spent the past four nights applying for jobs on several career sites, followed by a text to my manager at Chili's saying that I'd be willing to work any and all available shifts starting Saturday.

Earlier in the week I had a little twinge of hope that Alex would get in touch with me about that special assignment he'd mentioned. But as the days dragged on, I realized that had been all talk on his part.

It's a good thing that I haven't run into him at the office since that night, because I'd probably say something snarky about getting my hopes up for a job. If I never see him again, it will be too soon.

Even though I'm in high heels and the gray sheath dress I wear every Friday, I half run, half walk down a hall and into the lobby of One Jenkins Plaza. My heels clack purposefully on the black marble tile floor as I head for the stairs to the ninth floor, where HR is located. I'm supposed to pick up an exit interview packet that includes an embossed certificate of completion, like a diploma. But even more useless.

I'm not going to chance taking the elevator. No way will I get in that death trap. For months, I'd told everyone taking the stairs was how I got my daily exercise. I don't mind escalators, because I can run up—or down.

It wasn't always this way. There was a time when I could mindlessly walk into an elevator and not give it a second thought. But after Mom and Dad's accident, one of the many anxieties that crept into my brain was the fear of being trapped like they'd been, in their burning SUV.

In an elevator, there's nowhere to go.

Today, the lobby must have been recently waxed, because my right foot slips on the shiny floor. I catch myself and swear under my breath. When I take another step, I slip again. The *hell*. I look down. There's a visible crack where my four-inch black stiletto meets the heel. These are my nicest work shoes. Mom had bought them for me as a gift two years ago, saying I'd eventually need a proper pair of heels for work. She'd bought them weeks before the car crash, and I'd worn them to her funeral.

I bend my knee and look down. Crap, the heel's loose. I want to run up the stairs, but don't want to risk busting the shoe even more. I groan silently. There's so much to do today. Maybe I'll have time to sneak down the block to the discount shoe store for a replacement pair.

Whether I have the cash for that is a different story. Glue seems like a cheaper plan B, if I can raid the supply closet.

And how am I going to make it to my office? I can take the shoes off and go barefoot, but the stairwell is gross. I glance at the mechanical lift from hell and gnaw on my bottom lip. Tamping down my fear, I see the doors about to slide shut.

"Hold that elevator," I call out. Trying to run on the balls of my feet so as not to put pressure on the broken heel doesn't quite work, and when I fling myself between the doors, my entire shoe gives way, pitching me forward—and smack into the hard chest of Alex Jenkins.

"Oof," he grunts.

It sounds like I've punched the wind right out of him. Probably because my laptop bag hits him square in the solar plexus, or maybe it's my shoulder that made contact with his chest. Or both. I flail a little, at least until he catches me by the shoulders with firm hands.

"Evie?"

I glance up, into eyes so deep blue, so glittering, they are the color of the night sky in the South. Goodness, he's even more attractive today than when I last saw him, what, two weeks ago? Dark stubble is sprinkled across his jaw, and the look is arrestingly gorgeous.

By the probing way he stares at me, it was as if he knows I'd been thinking about him nonstop. He grins and I catch a quick glance of his tongue touching his canine tooth. Like a wolf about to eat a girl.

"Alex. Hi." The tops of my cheeks flash hot. I wrench myself out of his grip and look down. Mortifyingly, my heel has twisted horizontally. I flatten my back against one side of the elevator and wish I could disappear.

"Good morning. You okay?"

I nod, my heart pounding. I'm not sure if it's because I hate being in such a tiny, enclosed space or that his sardonic expression is annoyingly alluring. He reaches past me, a strong, tapered finger hovering over the elevator buttons. I detect hints of nutmeg and wood and midnight kisses under magnolia trees in his aftershave, and it's wickedly sexy.

"I guess we're even now." His eyes sparkle like sapphires.

"Huh?" I arrange my bag on the floor, trying to hide my broken heel.

"I spilled coffee on you Friday night, and you smacked me in the gut while tripping into the elevator."

I squeak out a laugh and eye the doors with apprehension. We're the only ones in here. I can't decide if that makes me more or less nervous.

"Third floor, marketing?"

"No, I'm going to HR on the ninth."

He punches the Nine button, then the Fifty-five. Both light up, sending a spike of adrenaline into me. I hold my breath as the doors slide shut, balancing my right foot on the tiptoe of my broken shoe.

The elevator rises, and I shut my eyes. *Please let this be over quickly. Please. He's my boss and he's so freaking handsome. And he's a jerk.*

I hate that I'm battling both a fear of closed spaces, which is a trauma response from my parents' accident, and nerves from being so close to Alex. Sweat blossoms on the backs of my knees.

"I was going to visit you this morning to talk about a proposition—"

At the word *proposition*, my eyes snap open. A beat later, the elevator lurches up, then down. The gears or cables or whatever make a sickening, grinding *thunk*. I wobble and grasp for whatever's near.

That would be Alex's forearm.

Then the car plunges into darkness. I scream. Loudly.

"We're okay!" Alex shouts, taking my arm.

"The hell we are!"

"Don't panic. Really. We're not going to die."

When someone tells me not to panic, I'm inclined to do the opposite. In this situation, the only reasonable next step is to melt down. A wan red emergency light flashes, then flickers, casting a menacing hue in the small space and leaving me even more worried.

I slide out of his grasp, down the sleek wood-paneled side until my butt touches the floor. On instinct, I curl into a ball, tucking my head into my arms and bent knees.

"Hey, this happens sometimes. We'll be fine." Alex's voice is soft. The red light flickers off and I whimper. The warmth of his body is close to mine, and his spicy smell surrounds me. "You're trembling, poor thing. I'm going to call building maintenance. No, my cell doesn't have a signal."

I raise my head. Alex is kneeling in front of me, his phone illuminating the sharpness of his jaw. The air is already stuffy and humid, punctuated with his smell. My chest constricts and I make a sound that resembles a wounded animal.

This is my worst fear come to life.

I put my head back between my knees and start to rock.

"Don't panic," he says softly.

The sensation of his big hand on my shoulder comforts me a little. He activates his phone's flashlight, then leans up and opens a little box under the elevator buttons. It's an old-fashioned phone receiver, and Alex speaks into it.

"Hello? This is Alex Jenkins. I'm trapped in elevator number two. Yeah. Somewhere between the lobby and the ninth floor." There's a pause, and I whimper at the spooky silence. "A blackout? Throughout the city? A thunderstorm. I see. Don't we have a generator? Let's get this fixed ASAP. I'm with an employee who's having a panic attack. Thank you."

He gently sets the phone into the cradle. Awesome. Now I'm the intern with the panic disorder. A blackout. We might be in here for *hours*. I swallow a sob.

"The building has an emergency generator. This'll be fixed soon. Hey, don't cry." He shines the light of the cell on me.

My breath is coming in hiccups. "I'm sorry, I have a terrible fear of small, enclosed spaces. It's why I always take the stairs."

The light of his cell extinguishes and a second later, so does the red light. The darkness makes me hyperventilate.

"Do you want the flashlight on, or off? Which is more soothing?"

"On, I guess."

Does it really matter? Do I want to stare into his eyes when this thing plummets into the basement? He flicks the phone on again and I'm a little comforted by his nearness.

"I hate to feel you shaking like this. Do you want to hold my hand? Or can I put my arm around your shoulders? Is it okay if I touch you? To comfort you? I don't want to be inappropriate."

"This isn't some perverted way to get close to me, is it?"

He clears his throat. "I'd give you a snappy comeback but under the circumstances, I'll play it straight. The answer is no. And I won't touch you if you don't want me to. All I want is to calm you down; if you think it will help."

Comfort is something I haven't experienced in a long time. "Yeah, it's okay." I sniffle.

The light of the cell slices through the darkness.

"Here. Give me your hand."

Our eyes meet and time slows. He looks less devilish in the wan cellphone light, which is something I didn't expect. His eyes are soft—kind, even.

I hold out my hand, and he takes it. His skin is blissfully cool, and I know my palm is sweaty. He settles next to me, his back to the elevator wall.

Oh, he seems so in control. So strong. So *comforting*. But we're in the near darkness. In an elevator. I whimper.

"Shh." He scoots a little closer, and I can sense the warmth of his body.

"Breathe. We're going to be fine."

His voice has a gentleness to it, and I relax a little. I don't think I grasped how solid he was until this moment. I'd spent a good chunk of the past week looking him up online and reading stories about how he'd been a championship motorcycle racer in his late teens. Photos of him back then showed a lean, sinewy guy, but that was more than a decade ago. Since taking the helm of his family's company, he'd certainly become quite muscular.

At least from what I can sense in the dark. I breathe in his spicy aftershave, which is kind of soothing. I'm about to explain more about my claustrophobia when I get an idea.

"Distract me," I mumble. The elevator walls seem like they're closing in on us. "Tell me something interesting or funny to take my mind off this."

"Mmm. Distract you."

How can a thoughtful, gravelly sound be so tempting and dirty under these circumstances? That *mmm* hum resonates deep inside my core. *Oh, dear.*

"What if I explain the business proposition I mentioned when we last saw each other. Do you remember?"

I figured he was bullshitting me. My heart speeds up again. "I do."

"After our auspicious meeting in my office that night, and after seeing how my grandmother was so delighted by your charm and wit, I checked your employment records and know that you've done an excellent job for Jenkins."

"Thanks," I mumble. A vision of the elevator car tumbling, untethered, flashes through my mind.

"Your internship is ending this week."

"That's right." My tone is hesitant. Maybe he's going to offer me a job, and I won't have to worry about paying for my sister's books and back-to-school supplies. If I can get out of this alive, that is.

"It so happens that I need help over the next few months. It involves some travel, to Savannah, and to some spots around Atlanta. Maybe to New York." He shifts around, and I think I can feel the elevator bouncing. Or maybe that's my panic rising.

"I've never been to the Georgia coast. Always wanted to go, I've heard it's beautiful. I'm from Florida, originally."

"You are? What part?"

"I was born in Tampa."

He squeezes my hand. "They have a football stadium there. Not like the Mercedes-Benz Stadium or anything, but it's pretty good. The Buccaneers."

"The Bucs. Wait. Why are we discussing football?"

"Because I'm trying to get you to relax. You have family in Florida?"

Goodness, it's so warm in here. Bordering on sweltering. I press my free hand to my forehead. "A cousin and an aunt."

"Interesting. You didn't go live there after your parents died?"

I scrunch my face up. My aunt is a single mom who runs a bar and didn't have the time or money to take us in. "Um . . ."

"Sorry. I ask too many questions. Anyway, the travel will involve the Georgia coast. Savannah, to be specific, and Tybee Island. I'll be your personal tour guide." He shifts so that we're both sitting with our backs to the wall. His arm is still around my shoulders.

I've read that responses to pleasure and terror originate in the same part of the brain. Which might be why I'm having such a difficult time discerning my emotions when Alex's voice rumbles through me. I'd unpack my inappropriate feelings—like why I enjoy having my boss's arms around me—later.

Once I get out of this elevator. If I get out of this elevator. How many stories up are we? Can we survive a plunge to the basement?

"What will I do in Savannah?"

"The assignment involves discretion. Can you keep a secret?"

There's a hint of conspiratorial amusement in his voice, and something about his words makes me uneasy. Probably he's making fun of me. Or wants to hire me for something stupid, like dressing up as a clown for his niece's birthday.

"Of course. NDA, remember."

"I was going to discuss this with you over dinner. You're sure you don't want to wait? I could take you to Aria. Tonight, if you're free."

Aria's one of the nicest restaurants in all of Atlanta. Or so I've read. "I'll have to check my social calendar."

"Or we could go wherever you'd like."

This is so weird. I shift a half inch away from him. He squeezes my hand again. Good lord, the tingles. I'm not supposed to feel tingles before I'm about to die in an elevator.

"Will you have dinner with me tonight?"

"If we live." Now I'm sweating everywhere.

"Oh, Evie. We're going to live. Is that a yes to dinner?"

"That depends."

He chuckles. "On what?"

"What's your proposal?" *Proposition* has a slightly dirty tone to it.

"This isn't the most optimal setting. I'd rather do it over a bottle of champagne and a steak."

At the word *steak*, my stomach growls audibly. I'd had a cup of coffee for breakfast and was hoping my emergency instant oatmeal cup is still in my desk drawer. It's been stolen on two occasions.

"No time like the present." I'm trying to remain chipper and not openly terrified. I shift my legs and I can feel the fabric of his trouser brush against my bare thigh.

"All business. I appreciate that. Here's the situation: my entire family will be in Savannah for a long weekend. A reunion. You've met my grandmother, and can see she's rather hardheaded."

"I have a feeling that trait runs in your family."

He laughs, a genuine, rich sound. Another hand squeeze. I squeeze right back but only detect the slick, slippery perspiration on my palm. He's likely disgusted by me.

"And you met Beau."

"Yeah." I draw out the word, like I tasted something foul.

"What did you think of him?"

"Would it be inappropriate to say I'm on Team Alex?" I reply.

He laughs, hard. "I like that answer. I want to prove to Gram that I've settled down and that I'm more capable than him—"

"You are. I can already tell." The mood subtly shifts, as if we're on the same team against his snarky cousin. I like this; it's a pleasant diversion. Still, it's starting to be oppressively hot in this elevator. It seems like we've been in here for a lifetime.

"Thank you. This is where you come in. I'd like for you to accompany me there, and to a handful of other events. I appreciate your tenacity and your wit, and think that you and I will work well together as a team."

My stomach feels like a washing machine on the spin cycle. "Perhaps my brain's not working because I'm scared out of my mind, but I'm not following."

"Let me tell you an entertaining story. Hopefully, it will take your mind off our present situation. Remember my grandmother talking about my sister, Savannah, and her husband, Dante? The Italian guy?"

"Mmm-hmm." I also recall staring at photos online of Alex at their wedding, because the lavish affair had been featured in some big European newspaper that I stumbled across while snooping into Alex's past.

"Do you know how they met?"

"A car race? Something to do with tires?" I have a vague idea that her husband is some sort of former auto racer in Europe. I shiver. It's impossible to even watch the NASCAR segment on the local news because it's too unnerving.

"Yes, and no. Yes, they met while Dante was driving for an American team and Savvy was a pit crew member. But the way they started dating was unusual. She told me this in confidence, and I'm telling you privately, as well. And I will sue the daylights out of you if you sell the story to a tabloid."

"Threats. Thanks for ratcheting up the tension, dude." I try to swallow, but my mouth is seemingly devoid of liquid.

"This is the part you can't tell anyone about." His voice has dipped a half octave and it's gravelly and low.

"Who am I going to tell? For the third time: nondisclosure, remember?" A trickle of sweat creeps down the back of my neck and I grimace in the dark.

"Right. Savvy and Dante pretended to be together before they actually were together."

I stammer a few half-formed words and end with, "Really?"

"Amazing, isn't it?"

"I'm still not quite sure what you want from me. All this stress has erased my critical thinking skills."

Another squeeze of my hand. Another electric shock to my system.

"Evie, I'd like you to pretend to be my fiancé."

CHAPTER NINE

ALEX

She doesn't respond.

There, in the dark elevator, all I can hear is the sharp inhale of her breath. All I can smell is her. Maybe it's her shampoo, or it's her perfume. She smells like flowers, or candy. Candied flowers. Something absolutely delicious, a scent that makes me think of sex. Well, to be fair, I seem to harbor incredibly inappropriate thoughts every time I'm around Evie Cooper.

Shit, she's not responding to my proposal.

"Evie?" I ask.

At that moment, the lights in the elevator blaze on, making me wince. Evie gasps and jumps to her feet.

It's then that I notice she has a broken heel. Poor thing, she's having a bitch of day. As I rise to standing, the elevator smoothly glides upward. Like nothing ever happened. I straighten the lapels on my coat and step a few inches away from Evie.

She's staring straight ahead. I can't tell if she's pissed at me or scared the elevator is going to plunge down the shaft. Or both.

The elevator goes down and when the doors slide open, we're on the ground floor. A cluster of concerned-looking employees are standing there, along with two paramedics with a stretcher. Evie shoots out of the elevator, and I follow.

"Evie, are you okay? What happened?" Everyone questions her at once. The paramedics ask her if she wants to lie on the stretcher.

"Maybe you should," I encourage.

"I'm fine. Fine! Feeling great." Her voice is an octave higher than it normally is.

She turns her head to me and her eyes flash a warning. As if to say, *Don't cause a scene, dude.*

"Please inform me of your decision regarding my proposal, Ms. Cooper." I keep my voice neutral. The lingering and curious employees have no business knowing about *this* particular proposal of mine.

Evie nods curtly. For someone who's afraid of so many things—fast cars, elevators—she has a side that's made of ice. I watch her walk toward the hall leading to the stairs, shooing the paramedics away.

I spend a couple of minutes chatting with a few employees about the incident, then take the building's second elevator up to my office on the fifty-fifth floor. The one that malfunctioned on us is being checked by maintenance. When I'm finally on my floor, my PA Nadine—my usual PA, not a temp—rushes to me with a worried look.

"Alex. My God. Are you okay? We heard the elevator trapped you and an intern."

"Welcome back from vacation." I wave her off. "I'm fine. Did you reschedule my nine thirty? I sent you an email about it earlier."

As Nadine follows into my office, going over the rescheduled nine thirty and the various meetings and obligations of the day, I loosen my tie. It's already later than I thought and every minute to come is jam-packed with pressure. Not to mention the meeting with Beau on Monday. The little slime puppy will crawl out of his two-bit fitness equipment store to present his quarterly report alongside the other managing directors of Jenkins. Really looking forward to that.

I stand behind my desk, still listening to Nadine. She's ten years older than I am, smart as a whip, and doesn't take my shit. She also has a love of leopard print, and I notice that she's wearing a pink-and-black ensemble today, as if a wild feline fell into a vat of Pepto-Bismol.

"I have a question."

Nadine looks at me over her glasses. She's like a tough-ass aunt. "Shoot."

"If a man was trying to impress you, what kind of flower would you want to receive?"

Nadine inhales. "Why don't you send the usual pink rose bouquet?"

"No. This is someone special. I want it to be different."

She arches an eyebrow. "What's her favorite color?"

I scratch my chin. "Dunno."

"Where does she shop?"

I shrug.

"What kind of perfume does she wear?"

"It's sort of like, ah, candy?"

Nadine shoots me a blank stare. Hell, I know nothing about Evie. If she decides to go along with my plan, I'll have to find out some salient details about her life. Otherwise my family will see right through my charade.

My family is notorious for prying. When my sister brought Dante home that first holiday they were together, you'd've thought he was under investigation by the FBI. By the end of Christmas Eve dinner, the poor guy was sweating rivers from the pressure—and he'd been the fastest man at Monaco three years running.

"Roses. Red. A dozen. But wait, is there a difference between red and pink?"

Nadine blows out a breath so her cheeks puff out. "Yes. Pink is more casual. Red is more serious."

I gnaw on the inside of my cheek. "Let's go with red."

"Will do. When do you want them sent, and where? What should the card say? I assume this isn't your typical 'thanks for last night' message."

This is Evie's final day here. I need to seize the moment. "As soon as possible. Location is the fourth floor. No, third."

A look of confusion crosses her face. "Third? Are you sure?" She points at the floor. "Marketing?"

"That's right." I sit in my chair and grab a pen. On a sheet of monogrammed stationery, I scrawl Evie's name and a short message.

"Here's what it should say. Word for word. And the recipient's name."

Nadine stands up and takes the paper from me. "'Evie Cooper.

It would be my pleasure to take you to dinner to discuss my proposal.'" Nadine glances at me. "Kind of wordy, but whatever. Done."

◊
EVIE

"These are breathtaking! And they're a special delivery for . . . where is the damn card, anyway?"

Josephine roots around in the massive bouquet of red roses that arrived. It's perched at the front of our open-air, cubicle-dotted office, on the desk of Darla, the Corp Comm's head assistant. Darla joins Josephine in gushing about the flowers.

I glance up, give them a lopsided grin, then snap my focus back to my computer screen. It's not like they're for me—they're never for me—and I still have to pack up my desk. I've finished the online application for the Georgia Aquarium. The fact that I meet all the qualifications for the entry-level public relations job boosts my mood a little.

I still haven't gotten over the mortification of melting down in front of Alex while in the elevator—or being forced by HR and Josephine to be checked out by paramedics afterward. They'd declared me physically A-OK, but suggested I seek counseling for an "untreated panic disorder."

I'll get right on that, I'd wanted to yell, *with all that free mental health care available in the United States*. Instead, I'd nodded and escaped to the bathroom where I gulped in lungfuls of much-needed cool air.

Now, hours later, my heart rate's come down, but I'm still painfully embarrassed as I work on an exit interview for Jenkins interns. It's at least ten pages long, and every question brings me right back to the horror show that happened in the elevator this morning.

Q6. How do you feel about management at Jenkins?

My fingers hover over the keyboard, unsure of what to type. How do I answer that after this morning? Part of me wants to call Sabrina and tell her everything that's happened today, but she's in school and can't use her cell until the afternoon. Josephine's been so worried that she stopped at my desk twice and stared at me, her brown eyes filled with concern.

"I'm claustrophobic, so being in the elevator was a bit traumatizing," I'd replied truthfully. Obviously, I didn't tell her about Alex's proposition. She's been something of a mentor to me these past six months. We've eaten lunch together several times, and even gotten drinks after work once. I could see our relationship developing into a friendship if I'd gotten a full-time job here.

But as of now, we're not on such friendly terms that I'd tell her about *this*. Probably because I was a little ashamed that he'd even asked me at all.

"Quite a way to end an internship. I don't think any intern's ever had a last day that was so exciting. And we haven't even gotten to the cake yet! That will be at three, by the way."

I'd been looking forward to the cake. I hadn't had anything decadent in a couple of months, since no one had left Corp Comm recently and I didn't exactly have the time or money to splurge on dessert. Hopefully I could relax and enjoy it.

Now that the Horrific Elevator Incident is firmly behind me—
that's what I've been calling it in my mind—I've decided that I'd
misheard Alex while we were trapped together. There was no way
he'd asked me to pose as his fiancé. That had to have been a hallu-
cination due to stress. A figment of my imagination. Some weird
Freudian projection due to trauma tangled with claustrophobia.
The mind plays tricks, you know.

Clicking over to Google, I type in the words *stress hallucinations*. Sure enough, twelve million results pop up. Stress can make
people particularly vulnerable to hallucinations.

"There you go," I mutter to myself, scanning a medical journal
article about anxiety causing verbal hallucinations. I nod sagely
at the screen.

There's no other logical explanation. I either hallucinated
Alex's proposal or interpreted one of his questions as a weird
proposition. That's all. Probably I replied and said something
extremely embarrassing, but oh well. It's my final day here, and
I'll never see him again.

"Evie. Evie. EVIE!" Josephine shrieks, jolting me out of my
psychological research.

"Yeah?" I peek up over my computer like a meerkat.

"These roses. They're for you." She waves the card in the air.

"No, they're not." I turn back to the screen.

"They are, and I think I know who they're from. Come here!"
She's chortling and speaking in a singsong tone.

A bad feeling washes over me. Now the entire office is staring
at me as I rise and walk on rubbery legs to the front of the room.
Dear God, no . . .

I snatch the card from Josephine's outstretched hand.

Evie—

Apologies for my company's faulty elevator. Can we continue our discussion over dinner? I promise it will be at a restaurant on ground level. Call me.

—Alex

My free hand flies to my chest, as if I'm trying to trap all the swirling confusion inside. When I glance up, I'm greeted by the mirthful eyes of Josephine and Darla.

"Looks like the big boss wants to *personally* make amends," Josephine says with a saucy grin.

"Sure," I respond, dragging the word out as if it has ten syllables. "Thanks, I guess."

She thrusts the flowers into my arms and I'm even more mortified than before.

"Or maybe he wants to discuss a *new position* with you?" Josephine's dark eyebrows shoot up to her hairline. "He's super handsome. And single, you know. Notoriously single. You could do a whole lot worse."

What must they think went on in the elevator? Oh crap, who cares at this point? I'm leaving and won't be getting a job here anyway. All I can hope for is a good recommendation, perhaps from Alex himself.

I scurry back to my desk and set the flowers down. They seem to engulf every other thing in the room, as if I'm sitting inside the bouquet. Did he have to be so extravagant? A ten-dollar gift card to Starbucks would have been enough. My hand jerks the mouse around and the screen flickers to life.

Q6. How do you feel about management at Jenkins?

I bury my face in my hands, not knowing whether to laugh or cry.

CRASH

0

ALEX

As the day drags on, I'm beginning to wonder if I'll need to rethink this plan with Evie to get Gram on my side. The florist delivered the flowers around noon, and here it is, four o'clock. She hasn't acknowledged the roses or my question. Or my existence.

Not that this is the only thing I've thought of this afternoon. I've also been busy preparing for Monday's confab with the company's managing directors.

My phone buzzes and I snatch it up. It's Nadine.

"Alex, Evie Cooper is on the line. Shall I put her through?"

"Please."

I swivel my chair around to face Atlanta's skyline. The idea of her, downstairs, with a serious, stern expression, makes me grin.

"Hello, Mr. Jenkins." Evie's voice is clear and firm.

"Hello. You can call me Alex, you know. Have you recovered from the elevator incident?"

"I'm planning to take the stairs when I leave. And I found some decent glue for my shoes in maintenance. Does that answer your question?"

I chuckle. "You didn't call to talk about that, though."

"No. I did not."

There's an awkward silence.

"Thank you for the roses. They're beautiful. My coworkers know it's you who sent them."

"Is that a problem?"

"I guess not, since it's my last day. I'd like to bring them home to show my sister tonight, but I'm not sure I can do that."

Note to self: send more flowers to her house. Wait.

"Why? Jealous boyfriend?" My stomach drops. Idiot. Should've asked that in the beginning. A boyfriend would muck up the fiancé plan. Sometimes my arrogance gets in the way.

Note to self: temper arrogance around Evie.

"I don't have a boyfriend, jealous or otherwise. I don't know how I'll get the flowers home on the train."

"No problem. I'll work out the flower transport. And dinner?"

"That, too. Dinner, I mean."

"Yes?"

"When were you thinking? What night?"

I scan my brain. It's Friday. The weekend's packed. I have that big meeting on Monday, more meetings on Tuesday. Wednesday is a day trip to Tampa. Thursday is a business meeting. Tonight? I'm supposed to have dinner with Travis. Planning the details of his bachelor party. Dammit. Tomorrow? No, Travis can wait.

"Tonight." The sooner the better.

I'm starting to become familiar with the sound of Evie's sharp inhale. Every time she does it, my muscles tense with anticipation. It's rather satisfying that I affect her so much.

"Tonight is fine." Her voice sounds glummer than expected.

I'll have to text Travis to reschedule. He's not going to want anything raucous for his bachelor party, anyway. He's already told me: no Vegas, no heavy drinking, no strippers.

"I'll make reservations. What time is good? Seven?"

"Make it seven thirty. I have a few errands to take care of first."

"Fair enough. I'll come to your floor and pick you up."

"No," she says sharply. "I mean, no, thank you. Some of my coworkers could be here. I might need them for a reference, and I don't want them to think I'm sleeping with you to get ahead."

Most women would want to show off that they're leaving with the boss, that their careers were on an upward trajectory. "Okay. Lobby, then?"

"Outside. By the main doors. See you then." And she hangs up.

She hangs up, on *me*. As if she can't spare a second to say goodbye. I lick my lips. I love a challenge.

CHAPTER TEN

ALEX

"See anything you like on the menu?"

It's nearly four hours later, and we're at my favorite downtown restaurant, Southern Oak. My first instinct was to take her to a quiet, impressive place, like Aria. But all of my usual haunts in that vein seemed a touch too romantic. As gorgeous as Evie is, I don't want her to get the wrong idea. So, we're at a place that's busy, boisterous, and modern. It has high ceilings, an open kitchen, and blond wood everywhere. Sleek and hip.

It's also within walking distance to the office. I didn't want to risk jangling her nerves by getting into my car. It was kind of nice to stroll alongside her in the warm early evening air. She hadn't talked much on the way, and yet the silence was easy. Comfortable.

It took a Herculean effort for me not to flirt. Not to touch the small of her back when we walked side by side. Not to get lost in those blue eyes.

"I like . . . everything," she says, snapping the menu shut. "I'll start with the shrimp and okra."

"Good choice. For dinner?"

"Definitely the country chop. I haven't had pork chops in forever."

"A woman after my own heart."

She stares at me, and thankfully I'm saved from any further flirtation when the waiter comes. She orders sweet tea and her appetizer. I order a bourbon and a charcuterie plate.

Once we get our drinks, I take a good-size sip. "I love me some Pappy's."

She stares at my glass of liquor.

"You ever had this?"

"I've never had bourbon."

It's so charming how she tucks her hair behind her ears. How she opens her mouth and pauses before she speaks. How her eyes light up when she's taking in new things.

I hold up the glass. "It's call Pappy Van Winkle. Among the most expensive bourbons in the world. Aged twenty-three years. Tastes like caramel and cream."

Exactly what I imagine she would taste like. My mouth waters, and not for liquor. I slide the glass toward her. "Here. Try this."

She lifts the bourbon, sniffs, raises her eyebrows. Takes a sip. A big one.

Her eyes bug out as she swallows. "You like that?"

I reach for my drink. "Every last drop."

"I don't get the vanilla or cream part. Maybe a hint of spice.

But burning spice. As if someone tossed a lit cinnamon stick down my throat."

I chuckle. She really is adorably honest. "About my proposal. I thought we could discuss it before the food gets here."

She straightens her spine and puts her hands in her lap. "Yes. About that. Do you mind going over it again? I'm afraid I wasn't at my personal best today in the elevator."

"Of course, of course. I want you to pretend to be my fiancé. It's really important that I prove to my grandmother and my entire family that I'm stable. Willing to settle down. Capable of running the company."

I go into greater detail about Beau's managerial short-comings—I probably go on too long about this, but there's simply so much wrong with him—and then rehash my sister and the beginnings of her relationship with Dante. Evie sits, sipping her tea and staring at me. Her face is an expressionless mask.

"You've heard my pitch, what are your thoughts?" I grin at her. It's impossible not to smile in her presence. She's gorgeous. Her cheeks are rosy and plump, like an apple. Her ass is shaped like a peach. I groan inwardly at the food metaphors. I'm obviously a cheeseball.

She daintily dabs at her lips with her napkin, then sets it back in her lap. "I realize you're a very wealthy man. I don't know much about wealthy people. Or you. But I'm thinking that your family, and friends, and probably most people at work, say yes to you. They go along with what you want."

I stare at her. There's no telling what's going to come out of her mouth yet. She almost looks . . . sad.

"Alex, I think underneath all of your arrogance, you're proba-bly a good man." Her voice softens, like she's speaking to someone in distress.

"Probably?" I croak.

She reaches across the table and touches her fingertips to my hand. "I saw the way you treated the security guard one day."

"What?" Now I'm confused.

"Do you recall being in the lobby on a Saturday, about two months ago?"

"Why was an intern at work on a Saturday?" he interrupts.

"Because I'd offered on a Friday to collect quantitative data for a marketing campaign and figured I'd get a head start it."

"Impressive."

"Anyway. You were wearing sweatpants and a T-shirt. You stopped to chat with the guard. I promise I wasn't trying to snoop, but I overheard the guard say that his truck had been damaged in those bad storms we had. A tree fell on it."

"Oh, yeah, I remember. Lewis. Good guy. Has worked for Jenkins for years."

"You offered to buy him a truck. I thought that was so sweet." She pats my hand.

"So, you noticed me back then." I sit a little straighter.

"That's what you're taking away from my story?"

I shrug and sip my whiskey. "I like helping people. I've been privileged my entire life, so that means I have a responsibility to help others, however I can. Contrary to what you might have heard about me, I'm not a bad guy. Heart of gold, right here." I pat my chest.

"Right! I could tell from that conversation with Lewis that you have a lot of compassion in your heart. Plus, your stance on the environment, from what I heard during the meeting with your grandmother."

"I do think climate change is the biggest challenge of the

coming century." I mean, it's true, I do think this, but if talking about it helps me get in with Evie, I'm going full-on Al Gore over here. "What are your thoughts on solar?"

She runs a hand over the smooth white tablecloth, between her tea glass and my whiskey. "Alex, I feel it's my duty to encourage you to seek help. I've heard there are some really effective treatment centers in the Southeast."

"What?" I squint at her.

"I'm sure your friends and family don't feel they can be candid because you're so charismatic and powerful."

"You think I'm charismatic . . . what?"

She lowers her voice. "Addiction is a very real thing, Alex."

I shake my head. "What are you talking about?"

She stops touching me and presses her hand to her chest. "To propose something so strange. Make me your fake fiancé? My goodness. That's the kind of question someone on drugs asks. Or someone under the heavy influence of alcohol." She eyes my bourbon. "It's nothing to be ashamed of. I'm sure a man in your position feels pressure from all sides. And since I'm no longer an employee, I can be brutally honest with you without consequence."

I take a long sip of bourbon. Then I study the lines and contours of her face. Her high cheekbones. Her long lashes. Her plump lips.

Then I laugh. For a solid thirty seconds. The couple at the table next to us glance over, but I don't care.

"Evie, I'm not a drug addict. I've never even smoked pot. And I'm not an alcoholic. This is the first drink I've had in days."

She frowns. "It's often difficult to admit. I had a friend in college—"

I hold up a hand. "I made my proposal in all seriousness, and while I was stone-cold sober. I first thought of it the night you were in my office, and I've been thinking about it now for two weeks. I want you to help me get this position, so I can bury my cousin Beau once and for all."

"Goodness." Raising her eyebrows, she picks up her sweet tea and wraps her lips around the straw. I swallow at the sight. She stops drinking, and suddenly the restaurant seems too boisterous under the circumstances. "You're truly serious? You want me to pose as your fiancé for your family? For some weird power play, revenge thing?"

"Yes. Attend the reunion and a few other events. Be seen around town. I need to appear stable and responsible for my grandmother. There will be a formal contract and generous compensation."

She's quiet for a beat, then bites her bottom lip. I shift in my seat. This isn't going as I planned.

"I think you're a little unbalanced," she says gently.

"Really? Did you meet my grandmother? I'm absolutely unbalanced. Wait till you meet the rest of my family." The expression of pure astonishment on her face is worth the discomfort. "Now I have another question for you. If you thought I was a drug addict, or an alcoholic, or off my rocker, why did you agree to have dinner with me?"

She looks at the table, her eyelashes brushing her cheekbones. She shudders in a breath. What's with the sudden somber face?

Her voice is so low that I almost can't hear her over the din of the busy restaurant. She's not looking at me. "For the past week, I haven't eaten anything other than oatmeal, boxed mac and cheese, and the occasional item off the dollar menu at Taco Bell. I haven't had a proper meal in forever, and I'm starving."

My jaw drops. I don't know what makes my gut tense more: what she told me, or the fact that she's lifted her eyes and is staring at me, defiant and hard. Most women would probably shed a tear under these circumstances. Evie is sitting as still as granite, her gaze challenging me to say something. To react. I can't form words. This beautiful woman, my former intern, is going hungry? It's unfathomable.

Then, the waiter comes over and sets the shrimp-and-okra appetizer in front of her. She looks at the dish and her face lights up. Here's Evie, looking like a kid on Christmas Eve because of a ten-dollar appetizer.

And here's me, with a heart that's cracked right in two.

CHAPTER ELEVEN

EVIE

I didn't plan on telling Alex that I hadn't eaten a good meal in days. But something about his self-assured swagger, the way he carries himself so arrogantly, got under my skin. He says he's all about helping people less fortunate, but don't all rich people say that?

And his offer. Pretending to be his fiancé? Ridiculous. He could've asked anyone to do this, and probably lots of women would even pose as his fiancé for free.

While he's staring at me with those intense midnight blue eyes, I'm turning my attention to my shrimp and okra. Mom used to make this every few weeks, and it had been my favorite growing up. She'd proudly tell her friends that her girls loved the classic spicy southern stew. She'd make it with tomatoes and okra from our backyard—when we had a backyard, when we were a family living in a nice Atlanta suburb—and her secret ingredient was ginger.

My mouth watering, I grab my spoon and tuck into the gumbo. Then I cast a quick glance at Alex. He's staring through those long sooty lashes, gaping as if I'd shocked him with fifty thousand volts of electricity. Good. It's about time he finds out how the other half of the world lives.

I scoop up a chunk of tomato, okra, and broth, and slide it into my mouth. Closing my eyes, I allow the prickly heat of the cayenne pepper and the earthy texture of the okra to coat my tongue. It's enough to make me want to moan out loud—it's that freaking good. So similar to Mom's stew that it nearly makes me weep.

Smell and taste are two senses that grief can't numb.

I open my eyes and smile beatifically at Alex, who's loosening his red tie and swallowing hard. He's also scowling. Probably disgusted at the way I eat.

"I'm glad you're getting so much pleasure out of that stew." He grabs a piece of cheese on a cutting board between his thumb and forefinger, and shoves it into his mouth.

I slide another spoonful between my lips, then another. The comforting food is like an embrace of my soul. I'm sure I'm eating like I was released from prison, so I set the spoon down and try show a little class by dabbing at the corners of my mouth with my napkin.

"My mother used to make the best shrimp and okra," I say in a soft voice. "I haven't had it since she died."

By the aggressive way he's chewing that chunk of cheese, I suspect that my admission of poverty and rotten luck probably is harshing his buzz. Probably he thought I'd be ecstatic and bubbly about his offer.

Instead, it's highlighting all the things I lack. Money. Power. A future. Still, I don't care what he thinks. He's the one asking me to do the most absurd thing ever. And I'm the one seriously considering his offer. Not that I want to. I *have* to.

I don't want to appear too eager, though. And he needs to know I'm doing this because I'm desperate. Not because he's handsome or rich or annoyingly charming. Even though he is those things. I'm doing this for my sister. So she can have a chance in this hard world. And maybe it will give me the possibility of digging out from under all this student loan debt.

Although . . . how much will he really offer? I'll bet he'll low-ball me.

"I'm sure you didn't ask me here to talk about my life." I wave my spoon in the air. "Now let's go over your proposal."

"Right." He clears his throat, "I know it's unorthodox, but it might work. I'd like to pay you to come to Savannah with me for a long weekend. We'll pretend to be a lovey-dovey couple. We'll probably have to attend a couple of other events, too. Oh, and my best friend's getting married in about six weeks. You'll need to go to that, as well. Possibly other events. People need to believe we're engaged. I'm guessing this'll take about three months, total. So, the entire summer. Let's say into September, to be safe. Gram sometimes takes her time in making a decision, but her ninetieth birthday is in October, so I'm sure she'll want to do something about the company before then."

"She looks amazing for almost being ninety." I scoop the last chunk of shrimp onto my spoon and then savor the final bite. It's only a little cup, which is too bad. I could eat an entire pot.

"Gram's incredible."

"Why me, though? I'm sure you know lots of women who are better suited for this. Women who were in sororities, in society, debutantes, whatever. I'm not that, in case you had any doubts."

Might as well acknowledge that we're from two different social classes. Well, he's in a social class. I'm a nobody. God, I don't know where all this anger is coming from. Maybe it's because everyone around us looks so happy, so shiny, so wealthy. And I'm here in my old dress, carrying a purse I'd bought three years ago at Walmart, forced into considering the unthinkable.

I pick up my glass, wrapping my lips around the straw so I can vacuum up the rest of this delicious sweet tea. He's distracted, looking over my shoulder, probably seeing who he knows here. No, he's flagging down the waiter, who hustles over to the table.

"Yes, sir?" the waiter asks.

"Another tea for the lady. And, Evie, would you like another cup of the shrimp and okra?"

Oh, now he's treating me with kid gloves. Great. I shake my head and the waiter rushes away.

"Why don't I ask another woman? Well, let's see. Some of the single women I know want to marry me. I wouldn't want to get their hopes up. Others think I'm a confirmed bachelor and would never be able to play this straight. And most people wouldn't know how to be discreet."

He continues. I'm sipping as he talks, but his self-important tone is too much. I burst out laughing. Which means I choke on my tea. A drop of liquid dribbles down my chin. I reach for my napkin and press it to my face. His attention snaps back to me, and I'm sure he's wondering whether he's going to have to perform CPR.

"You have got to be kidding, Alex." I wheeze and laughter and cough, patting my chest. "You really do think that highly of yourself, don't you? You assume every woman wants to trap you into marriage. Wants to be your wife. That's hilarious."

"I'm glad you think I'm funny." He cocks an eyebrow and takes a sip of his ridiculously expensive bourbon. Damn him for looking so rakish. I'm sure it's true that most women would like to be his wife because of his looks and wealth. But I'd rather wear a wool coat on a summer day in Atlanta than admit that to him.

"Don't worry, dude. If I take you up on your offer, I won't get my hopes up that you'll fall in love with me," I declare sarcastically.

"Thanks, I guess." He chuckles, and the sound makes the corners of my mouth turn up. He's annoyingly cute and genuine when he laughs. "And that's exactly why I'm asking you to do this. You're not a yes man. Er, woman. I like that."

"I'm sure you can guess I'm desperate for money, so it was a good guess that I'd say yes to anything." I roll my eyes. "But hey, don't get your hopes up. This is a business deal. No funny stuff, 'kay?"

"Absolutely not." He clears his throat, and an uncomfortable silence hangs between us. The restaurant suddenly seems way too loud, with clanging utensils and people laughing at top volume.

"Like you say, it's business, so let's get down to brass tacks. How much would you like? I thought you should make the first offer and then we can discuss. I'd like to see how well you negotiate."

"What is this? *Shark Tank?*"

Under normal circumstances, I'd never agree to something like this. It's only a few steps away from prostitution, in my opinion. But under normal circumstances, my parents would be alive, they'd be paying for Sabrina's camp and college, and I'd have a full-time job. And a life.

I'd been thinking about this all day. "Twenty thousand dollars." That will cover Sabrina's science camp, three months' rent, a solid six weeks of groceries, and more than a few months of my student loans. This money plus three weekly shifts at the restaurant will allow me to take my time looking for a good job. Maybe I need to be more assertive. "I won't take less than that."

I raise my voice a little and am impressed with how firm I'm being. No way would I have been this brave five years ago.

If Alex was staring at me before, he's now gaping. I'm about to tell him to close his mouth or he'll start catching flies, when he chuckles. It's a deep, warm sound, and I'd love to hear more of it. He should laugh more often.

"Evie." His Adam's apple bobs as he swallows hard. His gaze takes a slow journey from my eyes to my mouth. And lower. The air between us suddenly crackles with unexpected tension, and I can't hear the din of the restaurant because of the blood whooshing in my ears.

"I can afford more than twenty grand, Evie." His voice is so soft that I can barely hear his words. "Way more. I think you need to aim a little higher. You're giving me your time. Your entire summer. You're giving me you."

At that, my entire body flushes with heat. Like I do when I'm nervous, I grab a strand of my hair and twist it around my finger.

He's right, and it's deeply unsettling. I'm giving my time, my life, my attention, in exchange for money. The implications of that are huge, and I'm not sure I'm willing to acknowledge them. The waiter comes at that moment, toting our main courses. Although the pork smells incredible, I'm suddenly not hungry.

"Okay, so do we have a deal? Shake?"

We're in Alex's car, parked in front of my house. The magnitude of our arrangement is sinking in, and I'm feeling a hot poker of shame jab at my stomach. He undoes his seat belt and turns to me with his hand extended.

"I have another question," I say.

"Hit me." He withdraws his hand.

"I've been applying for jobs over the last month. There's one in particular that I'd really like to accept if it's offered to me. What happens in that scenario?"

He inhales and tilts his head, as if he's contemplating a major business deal. "I think that would be okay. In fact, it would look even better. Make us appear more responsible, and you wouldn't come off like a gold digger."

I contort my face into a grimace. "People will think that?"

"People will think all sorts of things." He shrugs. "You're going to need to learn to ignore a lot."

My mouth moves before my brain has decided that this is all acceptable. "Okay. We have a deal. I'm all in."

I'm the one to extend my hand and he accepts. Tingles. All the tingles, up and down my body. His clasp is firm and when he eases his grip, I wriggle my hand out of his.

"A hundred grand. You sign the new nondisclosure form and I'll deposit a quarter of your compensation in your bank account on Monday. We need to do this legitimately, so I want you to send me an invoice. You're going to say it's for consulting fees."

I snort aloud. "And you're going to submit that to accounting?"

"No. I'm going to pay it out of my personal account. I'm a lot of things, but I'm not sticking the company with my expenses. I'm loyal to a fault. I don't screw over the people or companies I love."

His voice sounded a touch fierce, as if I'd hit a nerve. "Fine," I reply.

"You'll get the rest in weekly intervals over the next three months."

A hundred thousand dollars wasn't my idea. He'd insisted on that amount. It took all of the main course, dessert, and a coffee with Bailey's Irish Cream for him to convince me it was a fair amount. (It was my first time drinking Bailey's and I have to admit, it was quite yummy.)

A hundred grand is enough to pay for camp and Sabrina's first year at college. And to make a massive dent in my student loans. And pay rent, and eat three meals a day, and if I can manage to get a job, then I'll really be set . . . I stare down at my new black flats, the ones I'd bought at the discount store at lunch. When I agreed to have dinner with Alex, I worried that the heels wouldn't last. The flats had been twelve dollars, and the expense gnawed at me. The broken high heels were in my bag, and I'd hoped to repair them with glue this weekend.

But now? I drag a shaky breath into my lungs. From the morning's near-death experience in the elevator, to being offered more money than I'd ever dreamed of at dinner, it's almost impossible to process how my luck has changed so drastically in the span of one day. Maybe I could go to the mall and buy new shoes—but I'll have to wait until the money's in the account.

I shift in my seat to face Alex. In the yellow light of the streetlamp, his face is all sharp, beautiful angles. So much power that it steals the breath from my lungs. A hundred grand is probably a week's worth of earnings for him.

"One more thing. I'd prefer that no one at the office knows about us. About this." My tone is steely.

"They might hear that we're engaged, Evie."

Another stab of shame. Hopefully I'll never see the people at that office again.

He slowly traces the edge of the Tesla's touchscreen on the dashboard, a motion that's so sensual it's almost obscene. I can't focus on that, or worry about what the people at the office will think. I need to do what needs to be done: pose as his fiancé.

"We should probably get together a few times before the reunion. That way we can get to know the basics."

"Make it plausible," I murmur, tearing my eyes away from his thumb. "A fake date. When do you want to do that?"

He grips the knob with his entire hand, probably annoyed that I'm taking up this much of his time. "I have a big meeting Monday, a work trip on Wednesday, I'll be back in the late afternoon. What are you doing this weekend? Sunday? Is that enough time for you to look at a contract? I'll write it up and send it over tomorrow. Then we could meet for coffee somewhere."

"Community garden." I point into the darkness, down the street. "Sunday's my day to pull weeds and do some maintenance. You can join me, if you want."

Yeah, right. Like he'll do that.

"Sounds perfect. What time?"

Why does he keep staring at my mouth? I squirm in my seat, sweating, wanting this night to be over. My tummy is full from all the food. I'd eaten all of my pork chops, and then he insisted I try his fried chicken. Which was delicious. And he'd ordered two desserts. A chocolate lava cake and a thing I'd never had. Crème brûlée. It was amazing.

And that Irish cream coffee. I feel like I'm going to burst.

"You. Want. To. Garden?" My brows knit together. Does he even own a pair of pants that cost less than two hundred dollars? Getting down and dirty in the red Georgia earth to pull weeds seems highly improbable.

He smirks. "Sure. I know a thing or two about plants."

"You do?" I screw up my face, and he laughs.

"Hell yeah. My aunt had a garden in Savannah, and I picked beans as a kid. Loved the pumpkins. I'll garden with you. It'll give me a chance to get to know you. In your element. You got any tomatoes?"

His wide grin sends prickles of electricity through me. *Whoa, Evie. Control yourself.* This isn't real. He doesn't give a crap about you, your tomatoes, or your *element*. This is a business deal.

"Okay. I'll be there at ten." I try to sound chipper as I slip my fingers through the door handle.

"Ten is perfect. Gives me time for a run beforehand. But Evie? One more question."

Why does he sound so gentle now? I swallow. The car is too small. He smells too spicy and soapy. This is way too awkward.

"Yeah?" I bite my lip.

"I was thinking. I have a condo downtown. Well, several. We use them for visiting executives and people we hire who need temporary housing while they're getting settled in the city."

"Okay." I drag out the last syllable.

"Would you like to stay in one of the condos? They're all in an excellent, safe building with a concierge. Within walking distance of everything. I know you don't have a car. I could arrange it so that you and your sister could live rent-free for a while."

Why is he being so nice to me? No one has ever been this kind. All this, to put on a show for his grandmother? Something's not adding up. "Sabrina's leaving in a couple of weeks for science camp. Her graduation is next week."

"You could live the condo alone after she goes to camp. It would be much easier to look for a job downtown, wouldn't it?"

I look out the window at the little wooden house that I rent for eight hundred a month, with its beige paint peeling on the left side, near my bedroom window. It seemed cute and cozy when I rented it after the bank repossessed my parents' home; now it looks like a dump.

This is all too much, too fast. "Let me think about it."

He licks his lips, and for a hot second, I fantasize about what he'd do if I leaned over to kiss him. I imagine how soft his mouth would be, how he'd slide his hand to the back of my neck and pull me closer.

"Okay, Evie. You think about it."

I tell him thanks, climb out of the car, and get into the house in record time. The sound of the front door slamming echoes through our sparsely decorated living room. I slide the chain lock, flip the dead bolt, and even turn the lock on the knob, something I never do. It's as if I want a barricade between me and the memory of what happened tonight.

"He drove you home again?" Sabrina's shriek is a sharp contrast to Alex's velvety tone. "Are you keeping a secret from me? Why must you deny me the juicy details? Tell me everything! Pleeeeaaasseee?"

Without looking at her, I stalk into my room, slam the door, and crumple onto my bed, my heart banging against my rib cage the entire time. Somehow, I can still smell Alex's spicy cologne in my nose. I grab a pillow and hug it tight to my chest. If I'm to survive the summer, I need to remember one thing.

This isn't real.

CHAPTER TWELVE

ALEX

Gardening. On a warm Sunday morning in Georgia, no less. I almost laugh out loud as I lock my car door and dash across the street to the block-wide city garden where I'm supposed to meet Evie. I could be golfing or riding my motorcycle. Or preparing for tomorrow's management team meeting.

Dear God. I slow my pace so I can savor the stunning sight before me. There's nowhere I'd rather be than here, now.

Evie's already here, next to a raised bed of tomato plants. On her hands and knees. I have the sweetest view of her ass. In olive-colored shorts. Short, olive-colored shorts. And a thin white tank top. She's also wearing pink gardening gloves. Come to think of it, I can't remember when I'd seen a woman so alluring.

Okay, maybe this gardening thing won't be so bad. It should concern me, I suppose, that I'm so attracted to her. But there's something about her that I'm drawn to, a detail I can't quite discern. It goes beyond the physical, and ever since our dinner two nights ago, I've thought about her nonstop. I can't seem to forget the details she told me. How she's worked hard since her parents died, how she's struggled to keep her teenage sister in line while getting a college degree for herself.

It made me feel a bit embarrassed by my own life, which has been smooth and fairly uneventful. Evie has more grit and determination than I'll ever have. And I admire the hell out of her for that.

Although seeing her in a doggy-style pose is wiping my brain of anything but carnal thoughts. I've got to get my dirty mind under control when I'm around her.

I walk to her and crouch down. "Hey, garden girl."

She leans back on her heels and wipes her face with her wrist, leaving a smear of reddish-brown dirt on her cheek. "Hi, Alex."

Her dark hair is in two short loose pigtails, a sweet contrast to her pink cheeks. She must have been wearing makeup the other day, because I see a sprinkling of freckles on her nose.

The freckles slay me.

My gaze lingers on her face and I'm tempted to brush the dirt off her skin. "How's your weekend been? What did you do yesterday?"

She shrugs, then drops back to her hands and knees, leaning over to pull a weed. I stifle a groan when I take in the backs of her thighs, which are deliciously smooth. I scratch my head, wondering how I'm going to make it through the summer with her. She's tempting precisely *because* she's off-limits. That's it.

"Not bad. I spent the day cleaning and then I had a shift at Chili's."

I scoot closer to her midsection so I'm not staring at her ass. "Wait. What? You have another job? You didn't mention that. How do you get there if you don't have a car?"

She yanks a weed out of the ground and tosses it in a pile. "Yeah, I'm a hostess a few nights a week. It's about a mile away, so I can walk."

The greater Atlanta region has a lot to offer, and I'll love it until my dying breath. It is not, however, pedestrian-friendly. A scowl spreads on my face. "When's your last day?"

"What do you mean, last day? At Chili's?"

"If you're going to come live downtown in Atlanta, you're going to trek out here to work as a hostess?"

She narrows her eyes. "Should I quit? I haven't given it much thought. I'm still getting used to all this." She waves her glove-covered hand at me and a clump of dirt bounces off my knee.

While she leans over to collect some scattered gardening tools into a bucket, my stomach tightens as I think about her in a restaurant late at night. Drunk guys harassing her. Walking home alone. "You feel safe doing that? Walking at night in this area?"

When she looks at me over her shoulder, my heart stutters. "Yeah, why not? You going to help me with these weeds?"

I clear my throat and bend over, dropping my palms into the dirt next to her. Maybe she'll quit once I give her the money.

Our bodies are now about six inches apart, and I can smell her sugary scent, mixed with sweat. "Where do you want me?"

She tilts her face in my direction, her sparkling eyes meeting my gaze unblinkingly.

"Where do I want you? Hmm." Her lips plump into a pout.

Oh Christ, is she flirting with me? I'm close enough that I could lean over and kiss her. I cock an eyebrow.

"I want you over there, on the other side of this bed." She waves a few feet away. *Weeds. Focus on the weeds, asshole.* I rise to standing and position myself where she was pointing. As I'm about to tug something green out of the ground, she tells me to wait.

"You sure you know a weed from a plant? Show me what you're about to pull." She sits up and peers over a foot-high tomato plant.

"I told you, I'm a plant expert. See?" I yank a weed and hold it up.

"Good job. Not so sure that you're a plant expert, but you'll do for today." Then she giggles, and I swear to Christ, the temperature rises ten degrees. Sweat forms on my forehead.

Perhaps I need to rethink this whole deal. Give her fifty grand and bow out gracefully. Say adios. Write her a glowing recommendation and ask around if anyone has a job open for an excellent young employee in their marketing department.

Because I foresee several problems being around Evie for any prolonged period of time. I grip a weed where it's coming out of the earth and tug. This one's a strong-rooted bastard.

One. I want her.

Two. Under no circumstances can I sleep with her.

Two and a half. Okay, I could abandon my rules and sleep with her, but things would get complicated, fast.

Three. I don't do relationships or complications well. Or at all. And something tells me that if I were to sleep with Evie, she'd get attached, despite what she claimed. I can't have that on my conscience.

Four. I admire her too much to hurt her.

"What did you do yesterday?" Evie's voice is relaxed and happy. She's on her heels now, and I notice another smear of dirt, on her chin. An image of us in the shower comes to mind, and I grunt.

"Here, sometimes those weeds are tough to get out." She passes a little shovel to me through a break in the vines.

"I took my dirt bike out on a trail up near Dahlonega. Ripped through the woods. Then went out for beers with the guys after."

"That doesn't sound safe."

"It's totally safe. I wear a helmet and protective gear. It's probably safer than being on the roads here in Atlanta."

"You have a point there." She winces, and I realize what I've said. God, I'm an idiot. Her parents died in a car crash on the interstate. She'd told me all about it over dinner.

"Sorry," I say softly.

She shakes her head. "No, you're probably right. I'm sure it is safer being in the woods than on the road with all the crazy drivers."

We go back to the dirt and work in silence for a few minutes. The air is thick with humidity, and smells like tomato plants—spicy and tangy, a unique scent that reminds me of the country. Except we're not in a rural area. I can hear the traffic from the six-lane highway just a few blocks away.

"Why do you like to go fast? Is it the adrenaline rush?" She's not looking at me. We're only a couple of feet from each other, separated by tomato vines.

"Yeah. That. That edge. It's addictive. It's difficult to explain, but it's a rare chance to feel truly alive."

"Then you must miss being a pro motorcycle rider."

"I do." My voice is rough, as it is whenever I talk about that part of my life. A past life, is what it is. "But I got injured and had to grow up sometime."

She laughs. "It doesn't seem like you've grown up at all."

"Why would you say that?" She apparently has the same view that my grandmother—hell, my whole family and the entire world—does.

"You seem to live this magical life with your man toys and parties and expensive dinners. I mean, you do work hard at your company and all. But you have it pretty easy, in my opinion."

"Yeah. I do, I guess. Hey, who owns this property, anyway?" I search around, wanting to change the subject because I'm uncomfortable. I detect a hint of judgment in Evie's voice. My eyes land on a scraggly rosemary bush.

"It's a nonprofit. They buy vacant lots and organize community gardens around the city. This one was quite a fight because the group bought a property that a developer was eyeing. We didn't want a store here, and the neighbors rallied."

"How'd you get involved?"

She gestures with her hand toward a row of wooden houses. "My friend Ida is on the board. She lives across the street and asked me to help out. She can't garden as much as she used to, because she's eighty. Then I offered to do the monthly newsletter for the group. We're up to twenty thousand subscribers now."

She has a tinge of pride in her voice, and something inside me softens. "That's really cool. They're lucky to have you."

Evie sighs. "I don't know how much longer I'll be able to do it, though. They're facing a funding crisis because the state didn't renew their grant. They might have to shut down. I worry that the nonprofit's going to fold and have to sell the land."

She moves closer to me, using a little rake to smooth the dirt. She's a tiny little thing, a fact that's apparent when she's next to me.

I pick up a pile of weeds and sit up, turning to throw them into a nearby garbage bag. "How much do they need?"

"Their grant was for fifty thousand dollars. It's not a big operation, plus they spent a lot in buying this property." She brushes her elbow against my arm and a surge of desire runs through my veins. She jerks her arm away and rubs her elbow, as if she'd slammed into me. "Sorry."

The two of us launch into small talk about the weather, and she sprays a row of tomatoes with a hose. More neighbors come out to work their own plots in the garden, and as I pull weeds, I wonder whether I should pull some strings to donate to the nonprofit that owns this land.

It would be easy enough to do; Jenkins has many corporate giving projects all over Georgia. But if I swooped in and helped save Evie's cause, would she interpret it as trying to buy her, even more than I already am?

Something tells me she would.

*

Over the next couple of hours, we work in comfortable silence. Funny how my mind's been wiped clean of those annoying business details that constantly haunt my thoughts. Evie's easy to be around, more than most people. It's also adorable how she hums softly while she's working. She has me haul a couple of bags of mulch to one side, then spread the contents over one bed.

"I'm pleasantly surprised by you." She's standing up, tying a garbage bag closed.

"You doubted my gardening skills."

It's beginning to sink in that she doubts many things about me. I'm going to have to work hard to get her to trust me. If we're going to pretend to be engaged, it's important that she believes in me.

"I did. But you've redeemed yourself. I think we're done here. You probably have stuff to do. Work or whatever."

It's true, I do have work. There's always work. I stand up, brushing loose dirt off my sweatpants, thinking of tomorrow's meeting and sitting across a conference room table and staring at Beau's smarmy face. "Hey, could you give me the name and website of the nonprofit? I'd like to check it out online."

She rattles the info off, and I make a mental note as we walk to the street.

"You want a ride home?"

She shakes her head. "No, I'm around the corner. A block away. Oh, I almost forgot. I signed the contract. I'll email and send you a hard copy in the mail. I printed it out and everything."

"You live a block away—why don't we go get it? Probably safer that way, so it won't fall into the wrong hands, and all." Why am I angling for more time with her? I should go home, shower, look over some reports, call my buddy Travis and see if he'll meet me at our favorite bar.

She chews on her cheek. "My sister's home."

"Perfect, I'd like to meet her. Isn't she graduating soon?"

"Tomorrow, four thirty in the afternoon, the Woodward High football field."

"You sound as though you're counting the minutes."

She snorts a little laugh. "That's because I am."

"Well, I'm intrigued after everything you said about Sabrina. She sounds like quite a character."

She looks me up and down. "I don't know about this. About you meeting her."

"Our relationship is going to be a lot more authentic if I know real things about you," I point out.

"True. But what are we going to tell her? I don't want to lie to her and say we're . . ." She waves her hand in a circle. "You know."

"Engaged?"

"That." She winces, as if she bit into a lemon. Obviously there's not a mutual attraction here. It's almost as if she's repelled by me.

"We'll tell her I'm hiring you for a special assignment over the summer. Or that we're friends."

"There's truth in at least one of those, I guess." She doesn't look convinced. "Fine. Let's go."

She takes off down the sidewalk, and I jog to catch up while thinking of the possibility that she doesn't consider me a friend. As we're about to cross the street, she beams at an older woman sitting on a porch.

"Hi, Ida," she calls out, stopping at the small white-picket fence around the property. Like Evie's house, it's a tiny wood-frame home with a tin roof. It must be older than the woman sitting on the porch.

"Hello, my dear! I was at the garden earlier and it looks so wonderful." The woman rises and walks down the porch steps, moving stiffly. She's got bright-blue eyes that sparkle, and they light up as she gets closer to Evie.

"I did a lot more work today. Well, we both did." Evie gestures toward me.

"Who's this handsome young man?"

"My friend Alex. We worked together downtown." Evie's southern accent is a touch more pronounced, and something about it makes my heart molten and gooey. "Alex, this is Ida, the lady I was telling you about."

So, she does think of me as a friend . . .

"Nice to meet you, ma'am." I extend my hand and Ida shakes it while scrutinizing me from head to toe. "Evie put me to work."

Evie chuckles. God, I love the sound of her laugh, and how she presses her shoulder into my arm. Her words convey one message, but her body language is sure speaking something entirely different.

"Good for you. It's nice to see you young people do something other than play with your phones. Alex, it's wonderful to meet you." Ida winks. "Nice sweatpants, too."

"I'll be over later," Evie calls out.

I chuckle as we walk away. "She's cut from the same cloth as Gram, I can tell."

"I think you're right about that. Ida's tough. She was a nurse during the Vietnam War. The stories she tells are wild."

Evie points out the homes of other neighbors as we walk. She's apparently a social butterfly because she knows details about everyone who lives within a three-block radius.

"Is that why you didn't immediately take me up on my offer to live in the downtown condo? Because you know everyone?" It's a relief that she knows her neighbors. At least she can call on them for help if needed.

"Dude, you only asked me two days ago. I need more time to think. But yeah. It's part of the reason." We're at her house, and she stops on the sidewalk. "And because I'll be taking enough from you. I don't want to depend on you for everything. It doesn't seem right. It feels like I'm a kept woman or something."

I open my mouth to reply, but she leans in.

"Brace yourself. My sister's a handful."

A *handful* could describe any and all members of my family, so I've got this, no problem. When we walk inside, I take two steps and I'm in an immaculately clean living room. The furniture is older and cozy, and everything's well kept. Books on shelves, arranged by color. No clutter. The only nod to the fact that two young women live here is a poster of a Korean boy band is tacked up on one wall. She'd mentioned her sister loves K-pop, a detail I'd filed away for later use. There's even a rack for shoes near the door.

My admiration for Evie grows. She's got her shit together.

She goes to a desk in the corner and riffles through a stack of papers. My eyes sweep down her body, from her little waist, to her curvy ass, to those legs. I force myself to look away, and my gaze lands on one of the few decorations in the place, a silver-framed photo on the wall. I take a step forward to get a better look. There are four people in the picture, which looks like it was taken years ago in front of Cinderella Castle at Disney World. Two adults and two little girls, all smiles.

A pang of sadness stabs at my heart. Goddammit. Life is a true bitch sometimes. At that moment, a door opens.

"Hey, Evie," a girlish voice comes from the hallway.

This must be the infamous Sabrina. She's standing in the hallway, wearing a blue robe printed with white cartoon sheep. She has a towel around her head and glasses on her face. This girl looks like Evie, only younger and not as stressed out. And nowhere near as gorgeous.

"Oh my GAAAAHD. Evieeeee. I didn't expect company. I woke up a half hour ago. Why didn't you text me?"

She sounds nothing like her sister. Her voice is high-pitched, while Evie's voice is throaty and like an aural orgasm.

"Hi, I'm Alex Jenkins." I step forward, my hand outstretched.

She looks me up and down, batting her lashes behind thick black glasses. "Why hello. I'm Sabrina. Evie's sister."

"I've heard a lot about you," I say.

"Same," she squeaks, pumping my hand.

Interesting. Evie didn't mention that she'd told her sister about me. Wonder what she said. In the background, Evie exhales a long sigh. I let go of Sabrina's sweaty hand.

"What are your intentions with my sister, Mr. Jenkins?" Sabrina asks, squinting one eye.

"Please. Call me Alex."

"I will, *Alex*."

Evie appears next to me, holding a piece of paper. "Ignore her. Sabrina, stop."

I take the paper. "Your sister is doing a special assignment for me this summer. She's a trusted colleague, ex-employee, and soon-to-be consultant. I'm quite indebted to her."

I look to Evie and notice her slanted mouth and downcast eyes. I try to catch her gaze, but she won't look at me. Did I say something wrong?

"Thanks for visiting the garden today, Alex." She wraps her small hand around my biceps and gently turns me around. "Here is the paperwork you asked for. I'll see you next week."

"Yes, I'll call you. We need to meet to go over our project. We still have a lot to discuss." I wink at her, and she stares, stone-faced. What the hell?

I turn my head and look at Sabrina, who's beaming. "Nice meeting you."

Evie steers me to the door, opens it, and eases me through. "Talk soon. Bye!" She shuts the door and I hear the snick of three locks.

Weird. Why do I get the feeling that she's rushing me out of her house? And why am I so disappointed?

CHAPTER THIRTEEN

EVIE

The smell of earth and Alex's spicy, masculine cologne hangs in the air of our living room after he leaves. I can tell Sabrina's ready to grill me about him and I don't feel like talking. Pretending to check my phone, I wander into my bedroom and shut the door.

The day with him was reasonably fun—at least until he called me a consultant. That stung, as painfully as if I'd walked into a beehive. I figured he'd at least use the word "friend," like I did with him when we ran into Ida. I can't ever forget that I'm not his friend, his equal, or his real fiancé. I'm another cog in his corporate machine.

It sucks that I feel nervous around him. Annoyed that he makes my stomach flutter and parts of my body ache. Loathing how I resent his wealth and arrogance. The last thing I want is to fall for him, because he obviously thinks of me as nothing more than a paid helper. An asset. Someone whose only purpose is to assist him in getting what he wants.

And what he wants isn't me. There's a weird, full feeling in my chest, and from years of experience, I know what it is.

Disappointment.

Still, he knew how to pull a weed instead of a plant, didn't mind getting dirty, and showed a generous side. And I liked that he was interested in the community garden program. Maybe he'll throw some of his vast wealth at the organization.

Maybe this summer I can convince him to donate to all sorts of good causes. He might not ever appreciate me as anything more than an ex-employee, but he can help in other ways. If he's going to use me, I'll use him right back. For noble causes. Things that will help the world. God knows he's got enough money to spare if he's willing to pay me six figures to pretend to be his fiancé.

I'm making a mental list of charities and brushing my hair when the door bursts open.

"Hey, what is this? I need some privacy. Get out." I point at Sabrina, then the door, with the brush.

With a squeak, she flings herself on my bed. So much for privacy. "Well. Alex is a snack."

"A what? Don't put your shoes on my bedspread." A snack? Where does she get these sayings?

"A snack. Delicious and hot." She's lying on her stomach, kicking her feet on her butt and smacking her lips.

Can't argue there. But this isn't a conversation I want to have with my seventeen-year-old sister, so I shrug. "I suppose some women find him handsome."

She snorts in response.

I resume brushing my hair. "You all packed for camp?"

She buries her face in a pink throw pillow and squeals like a tween who's at her first boy band concert. Come to think of it, I think she used to make noises like this when she watched her favorite BTS videos. I'm glad she's so excited about going away. She might be overly exuberant at times, but when it comes to science, she's brilliant.

"I take that as a yes. Good job."

Maybe she's maturing after all. I set the brush on a bureau and lean into my wall mirror, inspecting the pores on my nose. Are they too big? Am I going to have to wear a lot of makeup when I go to Alex's family reunion? Hell. What am I going to wear? I'll have to go shopping, and the thought that fills me with dread.

"No. Not yet. Did you notice what Alex was wearing?"

I sigh and sit on the edge of the bed. My sister is pink-cheeked and giggling. "A T-shirt? Sneakers? The unmistakable scent of male privilege?"

"No, dummy. Sweatpants. Gray sweatpants." She takes her phone out of her hoodie front pocket.

"That's usually what people wear to garden." God, she's so weird sometimes. But wait. I scrunch up my face, recalling how Ida had complimented him on his sweatpants. They looked pretty normal to me. Maybe the most normal thing I've ever seen him wear. "So what?"

I mean, he did look fine in those sweatpants, but I have yet to see Alex look bad in anything. Or nothing at all. The image of him shirtless that night in his office flits into my mind. It's awful how I can't stop thinking about his muscles.

My sister's staring into her phone. "Haven't you ever searched the hashtag 'gray sweatpants' on Insta?"

"What are you talking about? You're such a goof. No, I haven't. Why would I? I only use Instagram for work."

She sits up, swinging her legs over the edge of the bed so our thighs are touching.

"Look." She shoves the phone two inches from my face.

I flinch and grab the phone from her. "Is that . . . oh my God, Sabrina!" I shriek.

There, on her phone, are photos of muscular men in gray sweatpants. With erections. Obvious, insistent erections under the sweatpants. Shirtless guys only in gray sweatpants and large boners. Dancing guys in sweatpants and hard-ons. Dudes crossing the street in sweatpants. Posing in front of bathroom mirrors in their sweatpants. Getting coffee. Lying on beds, working out, walking dogs.

All. With. Erections.

"You are such a pervert." I hand her the phone, then bust out laughing, thinking about Ida. "Where do you find this crap, anyway?"

"I've been following the gray sweatpants challenge for a while now." She pokes me in the ribs and I yelp. "Try to get a photo of Alex in sweatpants. With a hard-on."

I bury my face in my hands. The very idea of him like that makes me uncomfortably warm.

"Gahhhhh," I cry. "Shut up. It's not like that with us. He's a-a . . . colleague." My stomach plummets once again.

She shoves the side of her body into mine and I tumble onto the bed.

"Whatever. I saw how he looked at you. He has lust in his heart.

CRASH

Make sure to send me a sweatpants photo when I'm at camp."

My heart pounds against my chest. She stands up and I hurl a pillow in her direction.

When she shuts the door, I roll over and sigh. My sister is a lot of things. Boy crazy. Oblivious. Intensely focused on a career in research science. She's also a far better judge of the opposite sex than I am. And if she says Alex was looking at me, it's almost certainly true. Maybe he does think of me as something more than an employee. I know it's stupid to even entertain the thought, though, given our deal.

But it's nice to fantasize a little.

I press my palm to my forehead, then my cheeks. My face is fever-hot, either from gardening in the sun or the X-rated fantasies going through my mind. There's no way I'd admit this to anyone. For once I agree with my little sister. I'd like to see Alex wearing nothing but gray sweatpants and an erection, too.

As I'm about to walk out of the bedroom to shower, the door flies open again, and Sabrina is there.

"What?" I ask.

"I almost forgot, since I was so distracted by the sweatpants."

Oh God, what now? "Is there a problem?"

She leans against the doorframe and crosses her arm. Her earlier salacious expression is gone. "You don't have to do this, you know."

"Do what?"

"Be his fiancé."

I gasp. "What? How did you know about this?"

"Did you think I wasn't going to snoop in your paperwork on the desk?"

I sink down onto the edge of the bed and bury my face in my

hands while groaning. "Sabrina, why did you read that file? It's none of your business."

"You've been acting weird for days. And last night I watched you sitting there, carefully printing everything out. And remember when you messed up at the printer and refused to let me help, then tore a couple of sheets into little pieces?"

I groan again. "I thought you were watching YouTube videos on your phone and not paying attention."

"I can multitask, bitch."

I stare at her, hard. "You can never utter a word about this. Not to anyone at camp, not to anyone, ever. After today, we won't be discussing this at all."

"Seriously, Evie. Please don't do this for me. We'll get by." Her voice is uncharacteristically kind, and this isn't the reaction I would have expected from her.

"I'm doing this for you and for me," I say slowly.

"You're sure you're okay with doing it?"

I nod.

"That's all that matters to me: that you're comfortable. I don't want you to feel obligated. What happens if you get that job you want, the one at the aquarium?"

"I'm impressed that you were paying attention the other day at breakfast when I mentioned the job." I don't tell her that I've felt obligated to do so many things since our parents died, and this is the latest example. "It's attending a few events with him and his family. Not a big deal. We've agreed that if I get a job in the next few months that I'll take it."

She tilts her head. "No sex?"

"No sex, you pervert."

"A little sex?"

"No. No sex."

She sighs.

"Is that a swoony sigh, or a relieved one?"

She taps her index finger against her chin. "It's a real conundrum. On one hand, you're basically a paid companion. I mean, no judgment there. I get it. We need the money. If you're okay with it, I'm okay with it. Take that cash from the multimillionaire. Don't apologize, don't feel ashamed. On the other hand, you're going to hang out with a rich and eligible bachelor who's super sexy. I'm not sure what to think."

With a sigh, I stand up. "You and me both."

CHAPTER FOURTEEN

ALEX

Nadine and I march down the hall to the management team meeting.

"Did you get a chance to look over the agenda for today?" she asks. "That lawsuit in Germany's a little concerning, no?"

"Those climate activists also sued Volkswagen and Daimler. I don't quite understand how they can sue a tire company for exacerbating climate change, and I hope the European team explains that today."

I yank open the door and let Nadine walk in first. We're among the first in here, except for the head of HR, and Dad, of course. Dad's always early, always prepared. Since he's the CEO, he sits at the end of a long conference table, his bald head gleaming under the recessed overhead lights.

"Son," he booms out, beckoning me with his hand. He pats the table, and I take the empty seat next to him, while Nadine sits nearby, against the wall. The HR director is across from me, and she and Dad are talking about "team upskilling," a term that sets my teeth on edge. Why not say "training"? Even after eight years at Jenkins, I still loathe the corporate jargon.

I scroll through the emails on the phone, then tap in a search phrase on Google:

Woodward Graduation Ceremony

It's later today, starting at four thirty. I frown at my phone. That doesn't give me much time; these meetings usually last all day, sometimes into the evening. But the agenda is pretty light, so if there's a benevolent meeting goddess somewhere, this will wrap up in plenty of time.

The idea of surprising Evie at her sister's graduation has been on my mind since I left their house yesterday. Evie still seems skeptical of me, and I want to ease any fears she might have. It's important that she trusts me before we embark on this entire charade, and something tells me that she needs convincing that I'm on her side.

Maybe going to her sister's graduation with a gift would help. I google *graduation gifts for teen girls* and scroll through several options. Evie's sister doesn't seem like the inspirational-quote-mug type. Maybe I'll leave it up to Nadine.

I'm about to ask her to buy Sabrina's gift when a stream of people walk into the room. The executive VP for the European division. The CIO. Marketing VP. And . . . Beau.

"Hey, hey, hey, all you cool cats and kittens," he says. Everyone lets out a tepid laugh. Everyone but me, that is. I catch Dad's eye and he gives me a subtle yet sharp look, one that says, *Don't be a dick.*

So I give a little one-finger wave to Beau, who's sitting almost directly opposite me, next to the HR director.

"What's up, DJ?" He knows that I've only ever been called by my middle name, but persists in his ham-handed joke, trying to tie me and Dad to the NASCAR father-son racing team. It's some subtle class jab that always falls flat because that's Beau's level of humor.

"Beaumont Jenkins the third. How the hell are you?" I ask.

"Never been better. Trying to pack in all the child-free things before the bundle of joy comes. You know how it is."

I nod once.

"Rose is due in five months. Time flies, doesn't it?"

"Sure does."

There was a time when this conversation would've been impossible. A time when I couldn't even be in the same room as Beau without wanting to throat-punch him. But eight years and the gift of hindsight have brought me to a place where I can be gracious. For better or worse, he is family, and I've come to accept that.

It doesn't mean I have to *like* the sniveling little weasel, though. In fact, he looks disturbingly like a weasel today, more so than when I saw him last. Maybe it's his new haircut, the close-clipped sides and the longer mop up top. It accentuates his sharp nose and the beady, bland hazel eyes.

Thank fuck he mostly works out of the sporting goods headquarters in the suburbs. I'd never have survived this long if I'd had to look at his jerk face every day for years. And if he takes charge of this company, well, my days are numbered. I've stopped asking myself what Rose sees in him because if I live ten lifetimes, I'll never understand.

"All right, everyone, let's get this meeting off the ground. I'm going to jigger the meeting agenda a bit and front-load with the strategic items." Dad's voice booms through the conference room.

I snap into action, opening my leather notebook and taking the cap off my Montblanc pen.

In truth, I was far happier as a semipro racer, enjoyed being on the track and in the garage much more than a corporate boardroom. But I'm also a realist. I wasn't a top rider, and would never be; I was too tall, too muscular. In so many ways, I'm much more suited to this life.

Dad brings up a huge print ad campaign, and the group quickly gets bogged down in discussing the plan. An hour passes, and Beau raises issues about the campaign's look and feel. I try not to register any emotion while I watch him speak, but still. What the hell? He runs the sporting goods stores. Why is he bloviating about ads?

"Son? Any thoughts?" Dad shifts to look at me.

"I have full confidence in the marketing team. That's their expertise, and it's why we pay them."

Dad chuckles. "I like how you're always willing to delegate."

What the hell? I hope that wasn't a jab. Sometimes it's difficult to tell with Dad. That's one thing I loved about being a motorcycle racer: I always knew where I stood. On the podium, off the podium, first place, last place. Everything was clear. Here in corporate America, each word, every concept, needs to be scrutinized, unpacked. Memos are picked apart for meaning, and utterances from Dad are often taken as gospel—when really, he likes to speak off the cuff.

Next up is a briefing about factory automation in the tire-manufacturing plants and that leads into lunchtime. Caterers swoop in with trays of sandwiches, bags of chips, and giant cookies.

"It's a working lunch, so take ten," Dad declares, which means we're all supposed to piss, (hopefully) wash our hands, and then grab a tuna fish wrap to wolf down while listening to more reports. It's exactly what we all do, and the minutes tick by as the sound of crunching chips practically drowns out the European VP, who has somehow brought the discussion back to the dreaded "team upskilling."

Discussion bleeds into a two-hour, all-out bitch-fest about the Atlanta IT department. Everyone loathes IT. I glance at my watch. This entire day has slipped by without a single productive moment. If we can wrap this up in the next half hour, I'll have a chance at making the graduation ceremony.

Dad jumps in, holding up his large weathered hands. "Your concerns over IT are noted. I think we're going in circles. I have one more item on the agenda. I wanted to bring you up to speed on my new planning process."

This was Dad's signal that the meeting was about to wrap up. Everyone seems sufficiently beaten down and/or exhausted, and no one counters with any other issues or complaints. I exhale softly when the meeting breaks up.

"Alex, give me a call later so we can debrief. No rush." Dad claps me on my shoulder on his way out.

"I've got an off-site meeting. Won't be available until much later."

"It's fine. I'll be up late. Or tomorrow."

I'm about to follow him out when I'm ambushed by Beau, who has somehow slithered from his side of the table to mine. The other managing directors shoot us glances and scurry out, until it's only the pair of us left.

"I was hoping to chat with you before the reunion."

I nod once. "Oh yeah?"

"I have ideas, dude. Big ideas. Ideas that will take this company into the next stratosphere. This was a shit show today. They always are. Did you see how everyone walked out of here, cynical and sour?"

I did notice, but I wasn't going to agree with Beau. "I thought it went okay."

Truth is, Dad isn't great at running meetings, and both Beau and I know it. Dad allows people to drone on too long, and then certain managers steer the discussion, which means we end up off track more often than not. Wasting time. Never making decisions. It'll be different when I'm in charge. I close the cover of my leather notepad, hopefully signaling that this conversation is over.

"We could grab coffee and toss a few thoughts on the table. I figured it's better if we're on the same page," Beau says.

"Same page about what?"

"The future."

"I've got a thing tonight and I still need to get on the road." I insist, "Traffic, you know."

"Alex. I'm willing to discuss and cut a deal with you."

I snort and shake my head. Persistent little fuck. "A deal? About what?"

"If I'm made CEO, I'll agree to two permanent board seats. One for your dad and someone else in your family. Also stock options and veto power. But I can also carve out something for you. Something lucrative. Let's get our ducks in a row now."

I'm not into hunting, but right now I want to shoot Beau's ducks in midair. "Save it, Beau. It's not the time. Gram hasn't made any decisions, and I don't think she will anytime soon."

"We'll see." He smirks. "This would give you plenty of room for movement within the company. I'm planning on making these suggestions to Gram when we're all there for the reunion, by the way."

A snort comes out of my nose. "Pure class. Talking shop at a family reunion. But what else could I expect from you? You're the master of propriety, aren't you?"

He studies me, a half smirk on his face. "Dude. I won. I won Rose, and I'm going to win the CEO job."

"We'll see, Beau." *Dick*.

I walk out of the room without a goodbye, but more determined than ever to show my family that I'm capable of the CEO position. Beau must be defeated, at all costs.

CHAPTER FIFTEEN

ALEX

It's a damned good thing I arrived early to this graduation cer-emony, because the place is huge and packed. A quick scan of the bleachers reveals crowds of people, all dressed in their sum-mer best. Sure, I'd attended my share of graduation ceremonies back in the day, but they were always at small private schools. The events were ticketed affairs, sometimes held in theaters or community centers. The commencement of the fifty-fourth class of Woodward High School is more like a Pro Bowl game. There must be thousands of people here.

My initial plan was to show up, wander around, spot Evie, and sit with her while her sister walked across the stage. Now that I'm here, though, I realize there's no way I'm going to casually bump into her.

I pull out my phone as I stand at the end zone, then swipe to Evie's number. It's close to five in the afternoon and the summer sun is beating down, making me sweat. From across the football field, a high school band strikes up a tune that I don't recognize.

I happened to be in the neighborhood of your sister's graduation ceremony and thought I'd stop by. This place is jammed! Where are you? I'd like to say hi.

Three dots appear on my screen, then disappear. Then flash again.

You're here at commencement?

At the end zone, near the goalpost, all the way across from the stage at the other end of the field. Where r u?

I'll come find you.

For the next ten minutes, I answer a few emails, catch up with friends on Facebook. I'm about to call Dad to debrief about the meeting when I spot a woman in a pink-and-black polka-dot dress gliding toward me on the grass.

It's Evie, looking stunning. She's in the same black shoes she wore to dinner, and as she comes closer, I notice her outfit is in two layers, with a see-through pale-pink polka-dot fabric over a pink satiny slip-like dress underneath. Her legs are bare, and her hair is shiny and bouncy, like a shampoo commercial. The overall look is elegant yet a little edgy. My sister would call it *vintage*.

Whatever it is, I like it.

I grin, but she doesn't. She stops about a foot in front of me. "You were in the neighborhood. Late afternoon on a Monday. Wearing a button-down shirt and suit pants. And a tie, like you'd wear to the office. Sure."

"I thought you'd want company. Where are you going to sit?"

"You could've texted to ask if you could join me."

"I assumed you'd probably say no."

"You assumed right," she grumbles.

There's a screech of feedback from the sound system, and Evie claps her hands over her ears. "Ladies and gentlemen, we will begin the commencement ceremony in five minutes. Please take your seats."

Evie slides her hands away from her ears and stares at me accusingly. "What if you'd needed a ticket? Let's find a place to sit together, I guess."

She stalks off and I jog to catch up with her. "I looked online about tickets, but it said they weren't required. If there had been a problem, I'd have sorted it out."

A snort erupts from her mouth. We go up a few steps to the bleachers, seeking a place in the shade.

"Over there," I point, slipping around her to lead the way.

We settle onto the hard metal bench. "How's Sabrina doing today? She excited?"

Evie thumbs through the program and doesn't meet my gaze. I'm starting to feel unwanted, which is a new experience.

"I guess. She left early to get ready at a friend's house. I think she's swept up in the excitement of it all, and that she's got a lot to look forward to."

"And you? How are you doing today?"

Evie looks up. "I'm okay. Why do you ask?"

"I kind of figured this might be a tough day for you, with your parents being gone and all. I wanted to show up to support you."

"Thanks, I guess. You really didn't have to. I'm sure you have plenty better things to do."

I lift a shoulder. "This helps me get to know you better. We'll have something to talk about with my family."

"We still haven't had a real talk about what's going to happen in Savannah."

"I thought we could hang out this week and I'll explain everything. Ah, check it out." I scoot closer to her and point to the stage, a little zing of desire shooting through my body at her nearness. "I think it's ready to start."

We lapse into silence and listen to the superintendent, the principal, the valedictorian, and a couple of others. I stop listening after the first speaker and zone out, thinking about various things I need to finish before Evie and I head to Savannah in a couple of weeks.

The announcer says that the diplomas will now be handed out, and I try not to laugh when Evie mutters, "Finally."

We can barely see the graduates walking across the stage in their maroon caps and gowns, but the order is alphabetical. Holy crap, this is going to take all freaking night. I stifle a yawn and immediately feel like a shithead.

Families and friends erupt with cheers when their graduates strut across stage to accept their diploma, and I notice Evie sitting straighter as the C group is called.

"Sabrina Cooper, National Honor Society," the announcer calls.

It's hard not to chuckle when I see Sabrina walk up to the stage, holding her fists in the air. Judging from the whoops and hollers from her classmates, it's apparent she's quite popular.

I slide a glance to Evie, expecting her to applaud, jump, cheer, or yell for her sister. Instead, she sits, ramrod-straight, her gaze boring a hole at the front of the field. She doesn't move.

When a single tear rolls down her cheek, I turn toward the

stage and clap loudly, pretending not to notice Evie's expression. I feel like an interloper.

Unsure of what to do, it hits me that Evie might want photos of this moment, and she's far too emotional to take them with a steady hand. I whip out my cell and snap several pictures of Sabrina receiving her diploma from the principal, and then doing a little triumphant pirouette onstage.

Evie pats at her wet cheek with her hand, shudders in a breath, then shoots me a bashful expression. "Sorry. I was thinking of Mom and Dad," she whispers.

I slide an arm around her and pull her in with a squeeze. Suddenly my back-and-forth with Beau earlier today seems insignificant—stupid, even.

"Thanks for being here," she says.

"Babe? That's what friends are for."

EVIE

"I can't believe you sat through all that. And hey, thanks for getting those photos, that was really sweet."

Alex and I are on our feet, ready to shuffle out of the bleachers. Like me, the rest of the crowd is sweaty and sun-weary.

"It wasn't that bad," he says cheerfully.

"Not that bad? It was three hours long."

He nudges my arm, indicating that I should take the opportunity to slip into the group of people walking single file down toward the football field. I do, and he follows, his hand on the small of my back.

Once we're on the field, I pull out my phone. "I told Sabrina I'd text her immediately after and we'd meet up."

Alex, who doesn't look as though he's sweat a drop, surveys the scene calmly. "Tell her to meet us at the forty-yard line."

"Like she'll know what that is."

"By the photo arch with the balloons." He points to an area where entire families are taking photos, next to a big banner that says CONGRATULATIONS VIKINGS!

Alex takes a few steps away to inspect the balloons and I exhale. His sudden appearance today didn't just take me by surprise; it nearly gave me a coronary.

I message Sabrina my location, and within two minutes she bounds over, talking nonstop.

"I can't believe I found you this quick. Did you see me walk across the stage? I thought I was going to have a wedgie and have to pick my underwear out of my butt. I don't even know why I wore underwear since I have on a dress and a gown. This thing is sweltering. Did you see that I gave the principal a high five? I need to show you all the photos I got while sitting there at the ceremony. Good lord, it's hot. Are we still going out for—" Her stream of consciousness ceases when she spots Alex coming toward us.

"Holy guacamole, Evie. You're not going to believe this but . . ."

A grinning Alex greets her. "Congratulations. You looked great up there. Your sister was really proud of you."

My sister looks to me, then to him, then back to me. "Did you two sit together?"

I nod.

"You didn't tell me he was coming with you."

"It was a surprise to me, too."

Alex lifts a shoulder. "I happened to be in the neighborhood."

Sabrina snorts. "Yeah, right. So, are we still getting food?"

"Definitely." I glance at Alex. "We were planning on going out to celebrate. I was thinking we could take an Uber to Chili's, I'm sure they'll give us a discount. They have those salads you like."

Sabrina's face falls.

"Or, uh, where else would you like to go?" Even though Alex's first payment is showing as "pending" in my bank account, I haven't been able to think of it as real. Haven't wanted to go hog wild. I'll be able to wire money to Sabrina's camp, but haven't thought of buying anything else. Probably because I'm afraid. Of what, I'm not sure.

"Anywhere you want," Alex says. "I know this great steakhouse—"

"Slutty Vegan," Sabrina squeals.

Confusion crosses Alex's face. "What?"

"Sabrina's eating only plants now. Slutty Vegan is a plant burger place, but it's kind of far," I chime in.

"It's not just any vegan place. It's the hottest vegan restaurant in the country," she says.

"Let's do it," Alex says.

"It's kind of a haul, Sabrina. Surely Alex has better things to do than sit in Atlanta traffic on a Monday night."

She gazes at him with a pleading look.

"I don't have anything better to do. C'mon. I'm parked over here. Slutty Vegan it is."

He turns to stride off and Sabrina and I scurry to keep up with him. She keeps elbowing me and trying to get my attention because I'm sure she's going to say something embarrassing or inappropriate.

At Alex's car, I let Sabrina sit in front so I can have a panic attack in peace. I grip the door handle as we drive away.

"You okay back there?" Alex stares into the rearview mirror and our eyes meet. There's a definitely look of concern, if the little wrinkle in between his eyebrows is any indication. Or maybe it's pity. I can't tell.

"I'm great," I chirp.

"Evie doesn't like cars," Sabrina says from the front as she fiddles with the stereo. "That's because of my parents' car crash. She has a lot of triggers when it comes to cars. I don't. Isn't that funny how people are different?"

I shut my eyes as Sabrina babbles on. She's such a good kid, but sometimes I wish she had an internal filter. I snap, "I'm sure Alex doesn't want to hear about our family tragedy and my anxiety issues."

"Fine, fine. I won't talk about the bad stuff. Not today. Oh, let me tell you what happened during the commencement ceremony. Lola Snyder, you know, the one I'm always talking about, she has the purple hair . . ."

Sabrina regales us with a detailed story about poor Lola, who apparently was still drunk from a party the night before, and barely missed puking on Sabrina. She finishes right as we arrive to the parking lot of the restaurant.

"Thank you for that uplifting tale," I say, then mouth *sorry* to Alex.

Alex is laughing his butt off.

Slutty Vegan, as it turns out, is not just any burger joint: it's a wildly popular vegan burger joint, if the line out the door is any indication. As we wait to get in, Sabrina gives us the rundown. She's still wearing her commencement gown.

"It's owned by a kick-ass woman, and there are multiple locations around the city. The owner's thinking about doing a national franchise."

She then grills Alex about his stance on factory farming. To my surprise, he doesn't respond with a snarky answer. He's thoughtful, and speaks to Sabrina like she's an equal, not a kid who graduated from high school a half hour ago.

Even though I'm a carnivore, I have to admit that it smells incredible once we get inside. I order a plant-based "chicken" sandwich, Alex gets two vegan hot dogs, and Sabrina decides on something called a Fussy Hussy, which involves caramelized onions and a Hawaiian bun. We also get french fries and fried pickles, and Alex adds in several other sides, desserts, and drinks.

"This is starting to look like a celebration," Alex says.

At the table, I stare at all the food, my mouth watering at the sight of the sweet potato pie. I haven't eaten this big of a meal with Sabrina since our last Thanksgiving that Mom and Dad were alive, which makes me feel bittersweet. We'd skipped homemade holiday meals since they died, relying on microwave dinners in front of the TV.

We dive into the plates and eat mostly in silence that's punctuated with *mmm*s and *ooh*s, and small, satisfied groans.

"I'm shocked at how tasty it is," I say between mouthfuls.

"You should trust my judgment more." Sabrina stuffs fries into her face.

Alex, too, seems relaxed and pleased, much more than I would expect. It's weird how he seems to be an entirely different person than when I first met him in his office. Like a regular guy, not a corporate executive. This makes me wary, though, because I'm not sure of his motivation.

That someone like him would want to spend all this time with me—with us—doesn't add up. And he even picks up the check.

Still, I'm grateful, and when we're done, we drive back home. Alex stops the car in front of our walkway. I'm in the back, fretting about whether to invite him in. The place is a disaster because Sabrina couldn't figure out what to wear for commencement, and her rejected outfits are strewn everywhere.

Okay, a few of my own are, too.

"Thanks again for dinner, Alex. I'm gonna head inside and give you two some time alone," she says. "To talk business."

She says the word *business* in a funny voice, then shoots out of the car and skips up the walkway, her maroon commencement robe fluttering in the breeze.

I ease out of the car at the same time Alex climbs out. We walk slowly to the broken sidewalk in front of my house.

I look up, into his dark-blue eyes. "Hey, you were incredible today. I can't thank you enough for bringing us to dinner. She's wanted to go to that place for months now, but it's so far away and we couldn't afford it. This was really special."

Gah. I feel like a loser even saying those words. Why can't I keep my mouth shut? Maybe I'm like Sabrina, too. All talk, no filter.

"It was truly my pleasure, Evie. I know I barged into your life tonight, but I did want to be there for you. You're the one who got your sister to this moment, it's a big milestone. You deserve to celebrate, too."

My brain seizes up at the compliment. No one in the past two years has acknowledged my effort in raising my sister. Most people want to ignore it, since our circumstances are rooted in tragedy, and no one wants to discuss that.

"Thanks," I say, shyly. "I don't want to take up too much of your evening, but if you'd like to come inside . . ."

"I'd love to, but I have to get going. I'm supposed to hop on the phone with my dad about some business stuff, and I need to make sure my assistant made reservations for a bachelor party. We're going deep-sea fishing in the Bahamas."

"Oh. Oh! Of course." I pause. "Uh, who's getting married?"

Alex's dimples make my icy heart thaw a few degrees. "Travis. He's my best friend. Really great guy, funny as hell. You'll meet him soon, I'm sure. He's getting married later this summer at the Buckhead Country Club. We'll be attending the wedding."

I nod slowly. The concept of *we* is going to take some getting used to.

"In fact, we should probably get together to chat about our schedule and go over some other details. I can make dinner at my place so we won't have any distractions."

"That works." I can hear the blood rushing in my ears. Alex and I alone, with no distractions? The thought of that makes me perspire, and I pat my forehead with my fingers.

"Great. And keep thinking about my offer of the condo. I think you'd really love living downtown." He steps toward me and presses his lips to my cheek. "Thanks for letting me tag along today."

My face feels like it's been held against the surface of the sun, and I stand there, mute. He's grinning as he walks back to his car, and all I can do is stand on the sidewalk and wave goodbye, marveling that it had been the most perfect day I'd had in a long, long time.

CHAPTER SIXTEEN

ALEX

"Did you want a larger carat, Mr. Jenkins? Would you like to see a two? Or a three?"

I run my hand through my hair. Tiffany's is the most intimidating place I've been in a while, and believe me, I don't intimidate easily. All this sparkle and bling is blinding. Trying to pick out an engagement ring for Evie is taking longer than I expected.

Just thinking those words is surreal. I could simply buy her a lab-created stone, I guess. A fake stone to go with a fake engagement. But all my relatives and friends will stare at the ring, and I want Evie to be confident in the face of that scrutiny. So, nothing but the best. She deserves it, after all she's been through. And, really, what's fifteen grand? She can keep the ring and sell it, for all I care.

That thought leaves me unsettled, for some reason. It's like all this glitter and shine is short-circuiting my brain.

"No, one carat is fine." Probably most women would want more than a carat, but I'm trying to be practical. And I don't get the impression that Evie would be comfortable with a larger rock. "What happens if it doesn't fit? I guess we can get it sized after I give it to her, right?"

I have no idea how this engagement stuff works. When I popped the question to Rose all those years ago when I was twenty-one, I'd given her a ring that had been in my family for three generations. She returned it, possibly one of the only decent things she did in the final days of our relationship. I'd stashed it in the back of one of Mom's jewelry boxes when no one was looking, and I assume it's still there.

The clerk, a guy about my age, nods patiently. "That's one way to do it. Many men often come in to select a ring *with* their fiancé."

Well, we aren't most couples, buddy. I pluck the ring out of its velvet nest and turn it slowly, its angles and edges catching light and throwing off shards of white illumination, like sparkling ice.

"I'll take this one."

It will look amazing on Evie's slender finger. The one-carat, square-cut platinum ring is elegant, beautiful, and sleek, like my fake bride. Who has haunted my thoughts for days now, a detail I'm trying to push into the back of my mind.

CHAPTER SEVENTEEN

EVIE

Two nights after my sister's graduation, a hundred thoughts race through my brain as Alex opens the door to his condo and ushers me inside. It looks like something out of an expensive catalogue, from the floor-to-ceiling windows overlooking Atlanta's skyline to the rustic, exposed wooden beams in the combined kitchen and living room.

I assumed it would be a sterile, cold space, all black and white, punctuated with perfect coffee-table books and statement sculptures. But it's surprisingly homey for a place so big. Maybe the wood floors add to the warmth, or the simple tan sofa with the fuzzy blue throw over the back gives it a casual touch.

Or perhaps it's the cat.

"That's Fuzz Aldrin," Alex says as I stand in the middle of the space, setting my purse on the eat-in kitchen counter.

Fuzz is the largest, fluffiest feline I've ever seen in my life. He's orange, and has to be at least twenty pounds. Maybe twenty-five. His size and his bright-green eyes are glorious.

A chuckle slips from my mouth. "Aww, Fuzz!"

The cat gives me a withering look and saunters off. "He's magnificent. I've always loved cats, but Sabrina is allergic, so we never had one."

Alex chuckles and stands behind the counter, chopping tomatoes. "He's part Maine coon. I did a fundraiser for the local Humane Society and took a tour of the shelter one day about six months ago. When I saw him in a cage, practically taking up the entire crate, I knew I had to spring him loose. He takes his time getting to know new people, though."

"A wise animal," I murmur, wandering the room so I can check out Alex's taste in art. He has several large framed photos on the walls, mostly of nature landscapes like the Everglades and Yosemite. There are also pictures of groups of people, and by the looks of it, they're probably his family.

"Do you have any other siblings?" I call out, while staring at a photo of at least two dozen people mugging for the camera. They're all near the ocean, and it looks like something you'd see in a society magazine.

"Nope, just Savannah." He's in the kitchen cooking something that smells delicious.

On top of what Alex had already told me, I'd read more about Savannah in several magazines, since I'd been furiously Googling Alex and his family in recent days. "Who are all these people?"

He walks over and stands close to me. So close that I can feel the heat of his body. I stare at his finger, which is pointing to a woman in the picture. It's essential to focus on anything but his gorgeous face. For some reason I thought I'd get used to Alex's looks. I haven't. He—and obviously his family—are blessed with superior DNA. They're never going to buy that he fell in love with me. It's not that I'm hideous or anything, but I don't have that sparkle that this crowd does. Tragedy and poverty will do that to a girl, I guess.

"This is my mom. And here's my dad. And my sister, Savannah."

"She's got great hair. Wow. It's naturally that red?"

"Yeah. Takes after my dad. He had red hair before he went bald."

He goes through the rest of the people in the picture. Cousins, uncles, aunts. More cousins. "You'll meet all these people in a few weeks."

When he's explaining the family dynamics between the second cousins, I start to laugh.

"Am I expected to remember the names of all these people? I'm not used to a family this big. I only have a couple of cousins in Florida."

Alex looks at me with those deep-sapphire eyes, and he has an air of casual amusement about him. "Don't worry about it. Remember my dad, my mom, and my sister. And Gram, of course."

"How could I forget her? Oh, and hey, where's Beau, the diabolical cousin you want to vanquish? I notice he's not in any of these photos."

A muscle in his jaw ticks. "No, he's not."

"So, Dale Jenkins, Kathleen Jenkins, Savannah Jenkins-Annunziata," I recite. "Her husband's Dante, from Italy, and their daughter is Gabriella. You adore Gabriella."

"Excellent memory." Alex's eyes turn soft, and warmth floods my body. He obviously doesn't know how that one little encouraging phrase has affected me, because he's calling me down the hall to see the rest of the condo, seemingly oblivious to my flushed face and flustered tone.

"These are the uninteresting rooms. The guest rooms, the master bedroom. But here's a space I think you'll like. It's my favorite room in the condo."

With a dramatic flourish, he opens a door and I gasp. "A library. Wow!"

Only rich people have libraries like this, with bookshelves twice as tall as me. There's a cozy-looking, older green sofa facing a gas fireplace, and I imagine myself curled up with a book.

"This is definitely the best room. What are these?" I peer into a glass case and recognize a few authors on the books, which are displayed cover out, as if we were in a store.

"Vintage science fiction paperbacks. These three here were signed by Isaac Asimov. And here are some Ray Bradbury titles. Have you ever read sci-fi?"

I shake my head, but I'm impressed, nonetheless. "I didn't take you for a reader, much less a science fiction kind of guy."

"There's a lot you don't know about me. A lot no one knows about me."

He gives me a saucy wink and a grin, and for a second, I'm caught up in the excitement. Of him. I'm starting to like the idea of us being a team against the salty cousin Beau.

0

"Okay, let's go over this again. You like reading, gardening, and watching *Animal Planet*. What else?"

"Umm . . . " I inhale deep, then slowly let out the breath. "I really loved those meatballs you made for dinner. They were perfect with the sauce and spaghetti."

"That's good insider information. Likes Italian food." He pretends to jot a note down on his hand. "Seriously, though. Let's go deeper. What do you desire out of life? What's your five-year plan?"

I lean back into the sofa, stumped at the random deep question. All through dinner we'd briefed each other on our likes and dislikes, and now we're in the library on the cozy sofa. It's a little too hot for the gas fireplace since it's June, but the warm ambient lighting and the Lana Del Rey on the stereo are contributing to the overall heat in the room.

Well, that and the wine. And the flirting. Maybe I'm projecting blind hope here, but it sure seems like Alex has been flirting with me all night. And touching me. Fingers brushing against mine, his hand on the small of my back in the kitchen, a squeeze of my shoulder.

I crave all of it. Probably too much.

"My five-year plan? Hmm." I take a sip of my wine in an attempt to stall. It's the kind of question I always stumble on during job interviews. This is good practice in case I'm called for an interview with the aquarium. I'd applied on my last day at Jenkins and had checked my email approximately every half hour since, even ducking into the bathroom at Alex's to see if they'd gotten back to me. They hadn't, of course.

"Yeah, you know, beyond caring for your sister and making rent. What would you do if you could? If money was no object?"

"That's a tough question, because for the past couple of years, money's been the only object," I say dryly.

"You were dealt a bad hand, that's for sure. But money's not an issue now, is it?"

For the first time since I arrived at his house, I'm acutely aware of the strange situation I've agreed to. That he's created this *Pretty Woman*-esque setup for me. I scrunch up my face, unable to think of anything. "Survival mode is a bitch," I joke.

"What did you want to be when you were a kid? Let's start there."

"Oh, that's easy. I wanted to do something with oceans and sea mammals."

He tilts his head. "Like a . . . dolphin trainer?"

I playfully swat his arm. "No, silly, like an oceanographer. I wasn't great at science, so when I went to college, back when Mom and Dad were alive, I decided to major in business marketing. I'd hoped to get an internship at an aquarium, but . . ."

"But what?"

"Well, my first internship was in Florida at a small marine aquarium. I lived with my cousins. That was amazing. Then Mom and Dad died and I had to line up work and paying internships. A lot of places don't pay their interns, or pay terribly."

Alex winces. "Like Jenkins?"

"Honestly, Jenkins pays pretty well as internships go."

He nods slowly. "So, your dream is to work at an aquarium?"

"I applied for a marketing position at the Georgia Aquarium recently, so I'm waiting to hear back. If that doesn't come through, I'll look into a nonprofit that does something with animals or the environment."

"That seems feasible, the aquarium job. An attainable goal, no?"

I lift a shoulder and take another sip. "Everything seems attainable when you have money. When you don't, it's a struggle to get through the day. But yeah, now that you've offered me this"—I wave my free hand between us—"I can concentrate on my original goals."

We sip in silence and I hope I didn't kill the vibe. It's difficult for me to ignore the obvious class differences between us.

"So, you like nature. How about hiking?"

I'm relieved he's returned to more superficial topics. "I love to hike. When my parents were alive, we'd all go exploring in the north Georgia woods and sometimes on the Appalachian Trail in North Carolina."

Alex leans in. "I love hiking. Maybe some weekend we could go together. I know some great spots with waterfalls. We could swim, bring some food. Or, if you're up for it, we could go camping."

Is he asking me on a camping date? Or is this part of our fake relationship? I'm so confused. The image of us kissing near a waterfall and snuggling in a sleeping bag comes to mind. "Yeah, maybe," I mumble.

"Let's see. What else do I need to remember?" He holds up his index finger and I wonder if my soliloquy about poverty even registered with him. "You broke your arm at seven climbing a tree in your neighborhood. You won a writing competition in ninth grade. And you wanted to be an oceanographer, but decided on public relations and marketing instead. Your favorite is roast pork, you have a deep dislike of flavored coffee, and you're obsessed with calendars because you're incredibly organized."

I laugh. "Planners. Not calendars. Planners."

He snaps his fingers. "Right. You like planner accessories.

Stickers. Folders. Stationery. I need to find out where to buy those things for you."

There's a weird pause as we look at each other. Does he realize how familiar he's being? As if I'm his real girlfriend? I imagine him buying me expensive pens. Little waves of happiness flow through me every time he flirts, every time he makes a promise. I'm starting to think I'm in trouble here.

He bites his full bottom lip and I swoon a little. Nope. This isn't good.

"Okay. What do I like to do?" he asks, grinning.

I can't help but coyly bite my bottom lip, and lean back against the plush sofa cushion. His library is well-decorated in dark-brown and cream tones, but also cozy. This might be the most comfortable sofa I've ever sat on, in fact. It's like a cloud. Or a hug. A hug from Alex.

"Ride motorcycles. Ride dirt bikes. Buy cars. Drink expensive and gross Scotch. Read vintage science fiction paperbacks."

"What else?" He's studying my face in that intent way, like he did that first night we talked in his office. Like I'm the only person alive. Between the wine and him, it's dizzying.

"You can make a mean meatball. Seriously, they were amazing. Your best friend's name is Travis. You were born and raised in Savannah and started motorcycle racing at twelve." I rattle off Alex's high school, college, and graduate school information. I turn my head in time to see the cat peek into the room, give us a withering look, then strut toward us. "And you were engaged once."

Alex ignores the last statement, and leans into me and says in a low voice, "Pretend like you don't see him."

"Okay," I whisper.

The cat jumps onto the sofa, in between us. He circles a few times, then plops down his girth. I slowly work my fingers into his silky fur. "Good kitty," I say quietly. "Alex, I should know more about Rose in case your family asks. Sometimes people like to do that, you know. You were engaged to her—and now we're pretending we're engaged. It's bound to come up."

It's not like I have experience with this, of course. But I've read about it in plenty of books.

He lets out a soft sigh. "It was a long time ago. We were young."

Something about his halting voice tells me that there's an epic story here, and I'm insanely curious to know who captured Alex's heart. Okay, curious and a little jealous.

"How old were you? And what happened?"

He takes a long sip of his wine that turns into a guzzle, then leans forward and sets the empty glass on the coffee table. He sits back and his hands clench into fists, then flex wide. The cat jumps down and sprints out of the room.

"We met in high school. Stayed together through college. Probably should've listened to my inner voice that told me we were too young, but I cared for her. And thought I was doing the right thing. Doing what everyone expected of me. We got engaged right after graduation. On the weekend we were supposed to be married, I canceled everything."

"Canceled. Everything? As in the wedding? Why?"

A bitter chuckle erupts from his lips. "Do you want the official story? Or the truth?"

"Both, I guess."

"Officially, I called it off because I wasn't ready to settle down. I wanted to sow my wild oats. Date every debutante in the city. Become Atlanta's most eligible bachelor and all that shit.

Unofficially, and only one other person knows about this, here's what really happened. Two nights before the ceremony, I walked in on her screwing another guy. As in, doing the naked horizontal tango in my family's pool house."

My face freezes in shock. "Oh. Oh! Oh, wow. I don't even know what to say to that. My God. I'm sorry, Alex. That's terrible."

"Oh, it gets better. Or worse, I guess."

"Yikes," I whisper, wishing I hadn't prodded him to tell me about this.

"The guy she was screwing in the pool house? It was my cousin Beau. She married him a year and a half later. She's now pregnant with his child and they live a perfect life in Buckhead."

"Beau? The guy from the other night?" I stare at him, horrified.

He points a finger in my direction. "Exactly."

His words hang in the air. They make my stomach churn with indignation. I'd assumed that his entire life was blessed by money, good looks, fortune. All this time I didn't realize he'd gone through something so humiliating. You never know the pain people go through, I guess.

"I'm beginning to understand the big picture here. You don't want Beau to become CEO because you obviously, rightfully, justifiably, loathe him."

"Bingo."

"You want to prove to your family that you're stable, not a womanizer, and can handle the responsibility of running a company. Because your family, especially your grandmother, thinks you're the biggest playboy since Hugh Hefner."

"There ya go." His voice is grim.

"Are you?" He squints at me. "Are you really even a womanizer? Or is that all an act?"

He drags a breath into his lungs. "No comment."

"Come on," I tease.

"Mostly an act."

I trace the rim of my wineglass, wishing Sabrina was here to unpack all of this with me. His revelations have changed the way I view him—yeah, I still think he's a privileged rich guy, but he definitely has more texture and depth than I anticipated. It doesn't take away from the fact that he's a man-whore, though.

And no one deserves being cheated on with a family member, especially not two nights before his wedding.

I reach out and rest my palm on his forearm. He's wearing a black T-shirt, and his skin is warm. His eyes meet mine. "I'm over Rose. We were a terrible match; I can understand that now. I don't like to talk about any of it. I want Beau out of the picture when it comes to running the company. He's an incompetent little prick and I don't want to have to report to him."

"Obviously." I rub his muscular arm in little back-and-forth motions. "I'm sorry. What an awful thing to happen when you were so young."

He shrugs. "I'm over Rose. But, see, I miscalculated."

"In what way?"

"When I broke off the wedding, I told my family and everyone that I was doing so because I wasn't ready to commit. From that day on, everyone thought I wanted to screw my way around the city."

"You grew into your reputation."

"No. I let everyone go on thinking I was a fuckboy. I should've shut it down, but my reputation preceded me, and I stopped caring." He shifts in his seat, and I take that as my cue to pull my hand away. The look on his face is so hard, so intense, that I want to hug him tight. But he doesn't need a hug now. He needs help.

"But you're not."

"At the beginning, I had a couple of one-night stands. They didn't feel right. So, since then I've gone out on a lot of dates. Am spotted by all the right people with beautiful women on my arm. But I always go home alone." He scratches his neck, looking incredibly uncomfortable. "Christ, I don't know why I'm telling you all this."

I set the glass down on a nearby end table, now resolute in my mission. "Well. I'm Team Alex, and we're going to put on a good show for your family. Because I am outraged on your behalf. I'm glad you told me all of this. It makes my job much easier. We're going to convince your grandmother and the world that you are the best man for the job."

"I knew there was a reason I liked you, Evie Cooper." He holds out his hand to shake. "I'm glad we have a deal."

I clasp his hand in mine and we grin conspiratorially. This will be amusing in an odd, perverse way, and for some reason, knowing Alex's backstory takes some of the pressure off.

It doesn't, however, remove the sparks flying back and forth between our hands. I slowly release my grip and fold my arms over my chest.

"You know, I probably should be going," I say slowly. "I can still catch the late train."

"I don't think so." His voice is a growl.

"What?"

"You're not taking the train home. That won't happen on my watch. I'll drive you."

For some reason, I don't argue with him. "Okay. I'd like that."

0

We make meaningless small talk all the way to my house, as if we hadn't discussed for hours how to deceive his family. When he pulls up in front of my walkway, I thank him with a smile and pop open the door.

He opens his, too, and by the time I'm on the sidewalk, he's next to me. Tingles go through me when he gently clasps my elbow as we walk up the three cracked concrete stairs to the porch.

"Your sister's not home?" he asks when we're at my door. "I don't see any lights on."

I dig in my purse for my keys. My hands are shaking, because this seems a little too much like a date. He's too close. Smells too incredible. The situation is suddenly way too emotionally complicated for me.

"She's at friend's house for a sleepover. Her last before she goes to camp in a few days." I find my keys and look up. Alex is scowling, his dark brow heavy.

"You're home alone?"

"Yeah. It's no big deal." I shrug. "It's nice having some privacy."

I swear, his scowl has deepened and he looks almost angry. "Evie, would you please consider my offer of the condo downtown? It's only a couple of blocks from me, so you'd be closer. If you needed anything or had an emergency. And if you need to get out of your lease early, I'll pay whatever it takes."

I freeze. The way he said my name, hoarse and desperate, slays me. My insides liquefy, leaving my skin a shell. After a second, I slide the key into the lock and cast my eyes about the neighborhood. Anywhere but at him. It would be nice to leave here, and life would be easier downtown. I guess I could return on the weekends to garden and visit Ida, and to work my shifts at Chili's.

"I'm still thinking about it," I say in a soft voice.

Something about his worried look makes me so sad that on impulse, I lean up and kiss his cheek. It's a brief kiss, a brush of my lips on his smooth skin. I'm surprised to hear his sharp inhale.

"Night," I whisper.

He swallows. "Night."

I rush inside and twist all three locks. My heart's hammering as I lean against the wall and close my eyes. My index finger goes to my mouth, tracing my bottom lip. I can still feel the skin of his cheek against my lips.

My fake relationship with Alex got real complicated, real fast.

CHAPTER EIGHTEEN

EVIE

The more I think about it the next day, and the day after, the more I come to like Alex's idea of living downtown.

Of course I don't want to rely on him any more than I need, but I know that between my sister's camp and her college tuition, plus my student loans, that hundred grand will go fast. He's already deposited a quarter of it in my bank account, and already I've transferred thousands of dollars to Sabrina's school, to my student loans, to the overdue electric bill. Cash is going out as fast as it came in, leaving me with a familiar panicked feeling.

I'm sitting on my sofa Thursday morning, drinking coffee, looking at job listings online and doing my monthly budget, when I finally settle on a decision. If I don't have to pay rent for a few months, I'll be able to have an even bigger cushion. I could save money, then rent my own place, and if I do get that job with the aquarium, I'll be able to walk to work.

It's not like I'm depriving Alex of much-needed cash. Or rental income, even. He won't go hungry if I stay in that condo for free. The company owns those units and uses them for employees and executives, he'd said.

Moving downtown will mean quitting Chili's, though, unless I want to schlep out here on the train for a few shifts a week. I'm about to text my manager my two-week notice, but I hesitate. Something tells me I should hang on to the job at least until I get another one. Don't want a gap in my resumé and all that.

I study the map of the area around the condo building. It's a prime location, walkable to everything. As I'm staring at it for the tenth time, I work up my courage, swallow what's left of my pride, and pad into my sister's room.

She's sitting in the middle of the floor, surrounded by mountains of stuff. Today she's packing for camp and her room looks like a clothing boutique and a cosmetics store exploded. I approach an open suitcase on the bed. It's empty except for one thing.

"You're bringing a feather boa to science camp?" I pick up the feathery pink accessory.

"I'm bringing a lot more than that. I can't decide. I'm trying to do a capsule wardrobe and I can't decide if I should go with smart emo goth or smart Harajuku Girl. The boa goes with either."

I shove a pile of shirts out of the way and sink onto her bed, rubbing my forehead. "I have no idea what you said. Listen, I'm going to be moving out of this place, so I'll be packing up everything that you don't take. Let me know if you want me to trash anything."

"What? Where are you going?"

"Alex—"

She screeches. "Are you moving in with him already?"

"What? No! Calm down. Alex's company has a few vacant apartments downtown. He's offered to let me stay there while I look for a job and while we . . ." I flop back onto a stack of sweatshirts.

"While you pretend to luuurve each other?" She dissolves into giggles.

I ponder whether I should tell her about Alex's saga with Rose, then decide against it, even though Sabrina would love nothing more than to possess such juicy knowledge. It doesn't seem fair to tell her though, because it's his private tragedy. His business.

"It makes way more sense for me to live there while I look for jobs. It will also mean we can save money on monthly rent for a while."

"He's letting you live for free?" She grabs a black beret from one of the piles and places it on her head, tilting it to the left and staring at herself in the full-length mirror on the wall.

"No. Yes. I don't know." *Crap, I should offer to pay him something.*

"Hmm."

"Is that a disapproving hmm, or a hmm of acknowledgment?" I sit up.

"I'm not sure. I can't really disapprove because this setup will benefit us financially and I think we shouldn't feel guilty about taking money from millionaires. But he seems like a cool guy, so I guess I'm worried you're going to fall for him. It would be hard not to—he's so hot. Hey, do you think I need to bring a scarf and mittens to camp?"

I stand up with a groan. "It's summer, Sabrina. Even in Massachusetts, I think that might be overkill."

As she grumbles a response, I walk out of the room and back to the sofa, where my phone awaits. It's time to tell Alex of my decision. I swipe to his number and dial.

"Yes?" His voice is so abrupt and stern that I nearly drop the phone.

"Hi. It's Evie."

There's a pause, and my stomach sinks. Oh, this was a terrible idea. I hear honking and cars in the background.

"Evie. Evieeee," Alex's voice is a velvet growl, and when he draws out my name my stomach tightens, but not from nerves. "Hi. How are you? Sorry, didn't mean to be short when I answered. I'm in Miami on business for the day."

"Oh. Sorry to bother you. I can call later, or if you want, call me some other time."

Once again, our different life circumstances are painfully evident. He's hundreds of miles away for a meeting, probably wearing one of those suits that make him look incredibly gorgeous and powerful. I'm in my living room, in a faded yellow T-shirt and pajama pants decorated with smiling cartoon coffee cups.

"No. I'm never too busy for you. Everything okay?"

My entire body flashes with heat at his words. "Yeah. I'm really good. Thank you for the flowers and the gift card." After our dinner "date," he'd sent the bouquet and the card for a well-known clothing store. Obviously a hint that I need to upgrade my wardrobe. "I was thinking. About your offer for the condo. I hate asking you about this."

Maybe I shouldn't do this. I could hang up now. Pretend we have a bad connection.

"You can ask me anything. I know we're in a rather unusual arrangement, but I want you to consider me a friend. Someone who can help you. Okay?"

Why is he so damned nice now? He's nothing like that arrogant guy I met in the office. It's like he cares about me. What's that about? I wipe one sweaty palm on my pajama pants.

"I would like to stay in that condo for a few months, until I get back on my feet with a job. If the offer's still open, of course. And I'll pay you what I normally spend in rent. Eight hundred a month. How's that?"

"Consider it done, but no, I don't need payment."

"Please?" I gnaw on my thumbnail.

"We'll discuss it later. I'll send my assistant Nadine an email now, and get the ball rolling. You want the penthouse? I think we have one of those. Fortieth floor."

"I don't think that's a good fit."

"Wh . . . Oh, right. The elevators. We also have a second-floor unit in the same building, I believe. It's smaller, though. But you're going to love the building. Concierge, gym, pool, there's even a spa on the ground fl—"

There's no need to hear any more. "Perfect. I don't need a big place or bells and whistles."

"Okay. Cool. We'll get movers to help you with your things. The place is furnished, so bring only what you want."

I glance around my living room at the few pieces of furniture that used to be in my childhood home, the stuff my mom and dad had picked out, the things I hadn't sold for cash. Do I want to part with these things? They bring back so many memories, many of them sad. Maybe it's time to let them go. The rest is secondhand stuff I'd picked off curbs and in charity stores.

"Thank you. You've been really kind with all this."

"Listen, babe, I have to get into a meeting. I'll send that email. Also, make sure you're ready to go out Friday night. I have something special planned, 'kay?"

I drag air into my lungs. Babe? We're at the "babe" level of friendship? I mean, I guess we are. We're getting engaged, right? We're a team, conspiring against his family. Working against Beau. Still, I'm so shocked that all I can muster is grunting out an *okay* and a *goodbye*.

He probably wants to go over more details so our story's straight for his family. That's it. Still, for a fake boyfriend, he sure is attentive. Maybe we are friends.

It's not like I've had many guy friends as an adult. In high school, sure. But friends of both genders have been scarce in the past few years because I've been drowning in work and responsibility. My few high school friends moved away for school and haven't returned. The couple of women I met in college faded away after I became too busy with work and caring for Sabrina. Sure, there are people I'm friendly with at Chili's, and at my internship.

Alex is merely a buddy, like a step up from my coworkers at Chili's. Of course I wouldn't recognize this because I'm a friendless loser.

That's why he called me babe. It's a friend thing.

An hour later, I get a call from his assistant, who doesn't seem to remember me from the office. Or if she does, she's discreet enough not to mention it. Then one from a moving company. And like a rocket, the week takes off, into a flurry of gathering Sabrina's stuff into only two suitcases, then dropping her at the airport on Thursday.

I'm a mess as we say goodbye in the packed terminal. She's bouncing off the walls, excited for her new adventure.

"Please be careful. Don't get into trouble, okay?" I whisper into her ear as I squeeze her tight.

"Don't worry, I won't. And don't you get into trouble, either." She breaks apart from me, wags her finger in my face, and leers. "Use condoms. And send photos of Alex in gray sweatpants."

"You are so gross."

"You love me, though."

"I do." A thick lump of tears forms in my throat, and I will myself not to cry in front of her. "You need to get through security so you don't miss your flight."

I watch her walk into the security line, keeping an eye on her until she goes through the metal detector and disappears from view. It feels like part of my heart has been ripped out.

Outside at the airport's curb, I inhale exhaust and swipe to the Uber app. I want to go home, but I should check out the new condo. With a shuddering sigh, I type in the address that Alex gave me. I've already memorized it.

The moving guys are coming in a few days to pack up my few possessions and bring them to the new place. It seems like a lot, to say goodbye to my sister and to the little house all in one week.

An hour in hellacious traffic later, I walk into a gleaming, restored building.

The historic lobby is impressive—there are actual brass doors on the elevators—and the concierge offers to walk me up the multiple flights of stairs to the gym and the rooftop lounge. I don't tell the concierge that I hate elevators. Instead, I pass it off as wanting to get settled in the condo first. He seems to appreciate that.

Then, he led me to the door of my new place. Thankfully, it's on the second floor.

"Oh my God," I whisper over and over, as I walk around the furnished condo. My legs feel heavy, as if they're suddenly filled with stone. This is too wonderful.

By Alex's standards, it's probably a dump. But to me, it's the most sophisticated city apartment, even nicer than his. There's a golden granite countertop, an eat-in kitchen bar, and vintage windows that overlook one of downtown's pretty, tree-lined streets. The sofa's a golden brown, too, and is every bit as comfy as the couch at Alex's house. Everything smells new and clean, like fresh linen, and there are no hints of mold or traces of termite damage on any of the wooden windowsills.

There's only one bedroom, and it's somewhat spartan and white—a perfect palette for me to decorate. Perhaps I can take a little of the cash he's already given me and buy a pretty duvet and some throw pillows. I've had enough of sleeping with my parents' old bedding.

I flop onto the sofa. When Sabrina comes home between camp and college, she'll have to sleep here, or in the big bed with me. But that's fine. It's not like she'll be home for long.

I LOVE IT, I text Alex. *THANK YOU*

I almost text a heart, but refrain. That would be way too much, set up far too many expectations.

I'm glad. Knew you would. Remember: I'm picking you up tomorrow at eight.

Oh crap. I'd almost forgotten in the frenzy of moving. I have so much left to do, and to celebrate, I order an entire pizza for myself, and get it delivered to the condo. It feels like room service, it's so decadent, and I sit by the window and check my emails. I'd neglected reading them all day because of the move.

My heart skips a beat when I see the words "Georgia Aquarium Human Resources."

We are pleased to inform you that we would like to set up a preliminary interview for the content development team specialist position . . .

I shout a loud yes, and my voice echoes through the condo. While the sun goes down, I finish my pizza, adoring my life for the first time in forever.

CHAPTER NINETEEN

EVIE

"You look nice tonight," Alex says in an even voice.

We're in his car, and I'd hoped for a compliment better than *nice*. I'd gone to the boutique that he'd given me the gift card for— it was a downtown shop that I'd walked past on my lunch break during my internship but never could afford.

Tonight I have on a pretty pale-pink shift dress and gold sandals. The dress is a little short, around six inches above my knee. The sales lady said it looked "amazing," and even though I was skeptical of that particular adjective, I bought it because it made me feel good. Put together. Adult.

Plus, it has pockets.

It's the most expensive thing I've ever worn, and I'm worried I'm going to spill something on it.

Honestly, I'm a little ashamed. Apparently Alex can throw his money around and impress me. I'll have to analyze these emotions later, because he's slowing the car and I suddenly recognize where we are. I've been here more times than I could count, and would spend every weekend here if I could. Again, those stupid money and time things have always been my excuses.

"The Georgia Aquarium? What's here? It's not open at this hour." I glance at the building. Funny, I assumed the next time I'd come here would be for the job interview . . .

Alex beams wickedly. "It is for us."

He pulls into the empty parking lot.

"What? Why? Alex, why are you doing this? It's not like we're really . . ." My voice dies in my throat.

He kills the ignition and looks at me. "I know we're not really." He waves his hands around. "But I wanted to surprise you tonight. So you could be genuine around my family when talking about our time together. I want you to have an experience that will take your breath away, and you can tell everyone how amazing this night was."

Of course. It's all business. Forced enthusiasm. Great. I nod, and my stomach sinks a little. I try to refocus on the task at hand: making sure his family believes our story.

My eyes go to his crisp navy blue suit jacket and white shirt. He's not wearing a tie, and combined with the stubble on his cheek, it makes him look older, more dangerous. A corporate wolf. A sexy corporate wolf. I inhale. God, he smells good. Is it soap? Cologne?

He leans in. "Anyway, I enjoy your company." He flicks my nose gently with his index finger, and I laugh.

As it turns out, Alex rented the entire place for the evening. Which is mind-boggling when I think about it. The only other people here are the security guards and a waiter who hands us champagne when we walk in.

Awestruck doesn't even come close to what I'm feeling. Normally this place is crawling with thousands of visitors every day. Tonight, it's us and thousands of sea creatures, which is pretty much my dream date.

"Can you believe I might be working here?" I murmur to Alex, breathless with anticipation as I take a sip from my glass.

"It would be pretty damn cool," he admits.

Now, the Georgia Aquarium is famous for two things. It's one of the largest in the world, and they have beluga whales.

I adore beluga whales. It's something about their goofy expressions, their melon-like heads, their almost cartoonish smiles.

So I'm almost giddy and feeling like a kid as we grow closer to their exhibit. Basically, I'm trying to impress a classy, gorgeous guy while managing my excitement, and doing a fairly crappy job. Oh, well. This is too much fun to really care what he thinks.

Alex leads the way and starts at the tropical fish exhibit.

"I haven't been here in years. Not since before Mom and Dad died. We used to have an annual pass. You didn't have to do this," I keep repeating reverently every twenty feet.

He chuckles. It's interesting. Tonight he seems to be in a different mood. More relaxed? Happier?

Then, he puts his hand on the small of my back and it makes me so nervous that I start babbling about how I'd read that the aquarium was going to bring eighteen wild belugas from Russia, but the government denied the permits. I talk on and on about the whales, about the aquarium's field research, about the animals' blubber layers, and how the belugas manage in captivity. He glances at me, probably because I've suddenly become the world's foremost whale expert.

I use the word *blowhole* multiple times.

It's like I'm a marine biologist readying a months-long transoceanic expedition. He shoots me a confused look.

I groan. "Oh, God. I'm sorry. You don't want to hear this. It's not like you care about whales."

"I do. It's interesting. You're quite knowledgeable." I'm sure he's saying that because he has impeccable manners, but inside he's thinking, *Holy crap, did I have to choose someone so dorky? What if she talks about blowholes with my family?* "Why do you like belugas so much?"

I shrug. The waiter materializes seemingly out of thin air with more champagne. I take a giant gulp and try to rein in my nerves. "They're fascinating. And cute. I read about one that mimicked human speech."

Alex pauses, his champagne glass in midair. Maybe that impressed him. "Really?"

"Happened at a research facility in San Francisco."

"See, I'm learning new things with you, and about you."

I'm glad the light in here is blue so he can't see me blush. "I really hope I get the job here."

"It would be perfect for you and your, uh, vast whale knowledge."

Okay, so I did go overboard on the beluga details. I down the champagne in a few hasty gulps, and thankfully Alex has taken my glass and put it on a tray resting on a nearby bench. I step over to the window, thankful for the fresh silence.

I'm transfixed by the schools of fish. My shoulders relax downward, and I realize they'd been up near my ears. Which must have been attractive. My mind's spinning from standing in this incredible place with the thought that I might have a shred of a chance at a career here. Plus, being alone with Alex in this hushed, dark aquarium is a bit dizzying.

At first I thought it would be awkward for the two of us to stand in silence, but like when we were gardening together, it feels perfectly normal. Too normal. Too wonderful.

When he's not looking at me or touching me, I'm calm.

That kind of thinking needs to stop, now. It's not productive or healthy. I can't keep on dreaming that he's acting like a boyfriend or that I have a chance with him. This is a business transaction, and if I don't guard my emotions, I'll be devastated when this ends.

But this is so perfect, a little voice whispers. *He wouldn't do all this if he didn't like you.*

I shove the thoughts out of my head. Why can't I enjoy this amazing moment?

We're bathed in an otherworldly blue light, and the hush is almost reverent and mystical.

See? It's already perfection, even if we're only friends. We peer into the tank together, shoulder to shoulder, mesmerized.

I'm glad he's not talking nonstop. I'm glad I'm not talking nonstop.

"Let's go this way. We can come back here later and drink more champagne. I think we also have chocolate-covered strawberries for later," he murmurs, again putting his hand on my back.

Chocolate-covered strawberries? Who am I kidding? I don't care if this, us, is all a lie. Maybe the champagne has gone to my head, but I don't think anything will ever compare to tonight.

"Are we going to the belugas?"

"Not yet. We'll get there. I promise we'll spend a lot of time there. Come this way."

CHAPTER TWENTY

ALEX

Why am I so nervous?

Is it because she looks amazing and leggy and polished tonight in that little pink dress? Everything about her tonight is distracting, more than usual. I can't even concentrate on the sharks or the seals or whatever the hell's swimming around because she's so crazy hot.

Seriously, the Loch Ness Monster could float by in that tank and I wouldn't have noticed.

I love her legs.

She's so adorable, talking about the whales. I don't really follow that whole thing about belugas talking, though. I'm too busy thinking about what I'm about to do, and whether I should kiss her.

I shouldn't kiss her. This arrangement between us should be all business, and we should be focused on one thing: persuading my family that I should be the one to take over the CEO job.

But my mind isn't on any of that tonight. I'm sweating my ass off in a tunnel that's making me feel like I'm at the bottom of the ocean. There's a curved, transparent roof, and it's hot as hell in here, either because they don't air-condition this particular part of the aquarium, or because I'm anxious.

Maybe we need to go to the arctic exhibit with penguins, where I won't sweat buckets. No, that won't work. Penguins stink.

Every time she leans into me, a charge runs through my body. It's electricity mixed with desire and an added dash of something I can't quite identify.

Tenderness. Is that it?

I love the way she smells.

Do all men feel like this when they pop the question? Like they're about to have a heart attack?

Wipe that sweat off your upper lip, dude. And stop fucking shaking.

What am I thinking? I'm going insane, obviously. This isn't even real. This is only to surprise her so she has a genuine reaction. She'll be able to authentically tell my family about the moment I proposed. They'll grill her about the moment I asked her to marry me. Maybe I went a little overboard in planning this surprise. Made it a little too real.

Sweet Christ, why *does* this feel so authentic?

◊

EVIE

He steers me through a door, and even though I've seen all of this before, I make a muffled squeal of excitement. We're in a tunnel, with a see-through acrylic window curving overhead. Fish swim above us, all around us, really, and it's as if we're nestled deep in the ocean.

Everything's serene and perfect and absolutely stunning. I stop to gaze upward, probably looking like one of the fish because my eyes are bulging and my mouth is open. But I can't help it. It's too impressive, being here alone, without thousands of annoying people.

Like a dream come true.

There's a shark, and a school of silver fish and . . .

"Evie," Alex says softly, and I tear my eyes away. He's standing in front of me, smiling.

"Yeah?" My voice is a whisper. It doesn't seem right to talk at full volume.

He clears his throat, and that's when I notice that he's frowning a little.

"You okay?" I ask.

"Yes, I'm good." He shrugs one shoulder twice, almost like he has a tic.

Why is he acting so weird all of a sudden? Maybe he has a muscle cramp. He did mention something earlier about working out.

"What did you want to ask me?"

"I wanted to see if you're enjoying yourself."

I take a step toward him and study him in the blue light that's bouncing off the angles of his face. He looks a little stern. Or maybe it's the shadows of the aquarium lights. We're only about six inches apart and I notice his pulse at the base of his throat. It's quite strong, pulsing insistently. He's also sweating. I wonder why, because it's pleasantly cool in here.

Oh. Maybe enclosed spaces make him anxious. I understand claustrophobia, and hope I can ease his mind.

"I'm having the best time. Thank you for this. It's a once-in-a-lifetime experience."

"Want to go see the belugas?"

"You know I do."

Again, he puts his hand on my back as we walk. Our footsteps echo in the big empty rooms, and we pass by several smaller tanks of other sea creatures. There are signs explaining what's in each tank, but we don't bother to stop to read.

The viewing area for the whales is dark, illuminated only by the blue of underwater lights. I see a ghostly form swimming in the clear water. I'm so excited that I let out a little yelp and grab Alex's arm with both hands, dragging him toward the window.

He laughs and follows.

There, in the tank, are three beautiful white whales. They swim past gracefully and I'm transfixed. How can something so strange, so perfect, even exist?

"They look like they're smiling, see?" I say softly. "Aren't they amazing?"

I turn to Alex, and notice that he's not looking at the whales. He's staring at me with the most intense eyes I've ever seen.

"Evie, I have something to ask you."

When he gets on one knee at my feet, I press my fingers to my mouth. Not that I'm in danger of saying anything, because

I've been rendered mute. Blood whooshes in my ears, and on the other side of the window, the white whales pause, as if they're on board with whatever Alex is about to do. There's a small box in his hands. He's fumbling with the box. He opens the box.

Oh no. He's not. He didn't. This isn't what I think it is. Why? Why? *Why?*

"That's a diamond ring," I whisper weakly, flattening my sweaty right palm on the cool acrylic window so I won't lose my balance.

My heart and my stomach and every other organ do somersaults. He looks up with big, hopeful eyes. Oh, God, that *expression*. It almost looks *genuine*.

The lone chance that I won't fall for Alex Jenkins glides away silently like the smiling whales in the tank.

"Evie, will you marry me?"

CHAPTER TWENTY-ONE

EVIE

"Am I supposed to say yes?"

Still holding the open box as if it's a sacrificial offering, Alex seems stunned by my question. I'm sure he's planned everything in excruciating detail up to this very moment. Because that's the kind of thorough, organized, plan-ahead man he is.

And now my confused expression and strained voice has shattered the natural order of his carefully constructed fake proposal.

What should I say? Does it matter? Why does my stomach feel like it's folding in on itself?

That's when I notice how much he's shaking as he takes the ring out of its velvet cocoon. He fumbles so much the box drops to the floor. He ignores it and holds the ring up for me to see. It sparkles in the blue light, and I stop breathing for a second.

"Well, technically, yeah. You're supposed to say yes." His expression isn't one of control. It's more feverish and wild.

"Well, technically, the answer is yes." I hate to respond sarcastically during such an important moment, but I can't help it. My emotions are all over the place.

There are smiling beluga whales staring at us.

And my right hand is so sweaty and gross that it's suctioned to the window at this point.

I extend my left hand toward Alex, my fingers splayed and stiff. Still trembling, Alex goes to slide the diamond onto my third finger.

"Relax," he says, jiggling my hand.

It's a fact that no one ever relaxes when told to relax. I finally allow my fingers to go slack and he slips the ring on easily.

Don't read too much into that. It's not a symbol. It's not a sign.

I twist it around with my thumb and bring it closer to my face so I can get a better glimpse in the semidarkness. It really is a gorgeous ring—a simple cut, probably platinum, large enough but not too ostentatious. Exactly the one I'd choose. If I had money. If I were getting married for real. Why does it have to look so pretty and sparkly on my hand?

"How did you do that?"

Alex straightens to standing, and that confident expression, the self-assured mask, is firmly back in place. "Do what?"

"Choose the ring that exactly fits my finger." I gaze into his eyes and wonder if my heart will ever stop pounding against my chest.

"Luck," he says in that honeyed voice. "Or maybe I pay attention to you. D'you like it?"

Before I get a chance to answer, his hand reaches to me. Toward my face. At first I assume I'm drooling and he's going to wipe my chin or I've got a blob of makeup on my shoulder and it's been annoying him all night.

But then he tucks a strand of hair behind my ear. Slowly. Tucks. My. Hair. I swallow hard. I think there was a slight ear caress in there somewhere. Tingles shower down my body, and I shiver, as if I'm cold.

I'm not cold. I'm on freaking fire.

"It's beautiful. Truly," I murmur. "Is it real?"

I immediately feel ungrateful and petty for asking.

Alex pauses to swallow. "Of course. It's from Tiffany's. And you can keep it. When we, ah, are done."

Oof. It's like a punch in the throat. *When we're done.*

This is what happens when a guy has limitless money and arrogance. He can make anything work, to hell with everyone else. What's several thousand dollars if it means his grandmother will give him full control of a company? What's a woman's heart, for that matter?

"No, I wouldn't do that." I frown. "I'll give it back."

"Well, why would I want to reuse—" He abruptly stops short.

Why would he want to give the woman he eventually falls in love with a used ring?

"We'll talk about it later." His voice is brusque.

"You really did surprise me. It seemed kinda real there for a second or two." I should be more grateful, I suppose. But I'm still unsettled.

He studies my face for a beat. "It did, didn't it?"

If it was quiet in the aquarium before, it's like the eternal, existential silence of the universe in here now. I peel my hand from the window and I detect a faint *squoosh* noise as my sweaty palm unsticks from the clear acrylic. He bites his lip.

"Strawberries," I blurt. "You said something about strawberries."

"Right! Yes, strawberries!" He claps his hands together. "They should be in the other room, the one near the big windows and the main tank with the sharks."

I glance over at the whales. One ghostly white beluga is suspended in the water, floating near the window. It's eyeballing us and smiling in a puzzled way, as if it isn't quite sure what's unfolded.

That makes two of us.

◊

ALEX

If this were a normal date, I'd hand-feed Evie the chocolate-covered strawberries. I'd kiss that cute-as-a-button nose. I'd lick that little smudge of chocolate off her bottom lip and then slide my tongue into her mouth.

But this isn't a normal date. I asked her to marry me, for Christ's sake. I'm still unwinding from the most harrowing ten minutes of my life. Going down on one knee was scarier than any motorcycle crash on the track in my days as a semipro racer. And it was nothing like my stiff and formal proposal to Rose, which was done one Christmas in front of both of our families.

Tonight with Evie has a sweetness to it, something I can't quite explain.

Ours isn't even a normal relationship. It's . . . I don't know. My hand goes into my hair and tugs. I'm not doing any of the things I normally would with a woman. Even though I want to.

The things I want from Evie, my thoughts and the fantasies, all eclipse what I've felt with other women. That's sending up a big red flag in my brain. Several red flags. A parade of red flags.

I want to slide my hand under that pink dress. I want to find out what color underwear she's wearing. I want to believe she's not wearing underwear at all.

She glances at me as she picks up a third strawberry and puts it between her beautiful, lush lips. I let out a low groan.

Why does everything about her have to be a turn-on? Her sugary scent. The curve of her waist, and how she keeps slipping her hands into the pockets of that dress. Those gold sandal straps around her delicate ankles.

Her eyes slide to me. For someone who lives such a simple, humble life, she sure has the cool and haughty look down. She doesn't deploy it much, but I have to confess, when she does, it brings out the caveman in me. Like I must work hard to impress her.

She's a challenge, all right.

"You want some water?" she asks, all innocent, while pointing at a glass pitcher on a table arranged with the fruit and champagne.

I shake my head and guzzle the rest of my bubbly. An image of doing even filthier things with her comes to mind. Would she like it if I bound her hands with a silk tie? If I spanked her? If I played with her . . .

She drops a napkin and before I can bend to reach it, she leans forward, giving me an eyeful of her long legs. I cough as she straightens.

"You're coughing a lot tonight. And your voice is a little hoarse. Do you think you're getting sick?"

"Nah." I growl, clearing my throat. "I think there's something in the air here."

Something that's making me want to drag her to me and kiss her senseless.

◊

EVIE

I'm not sure how I make it through the next hour and a half. I stuff my face with the delicious chocolate-covered strawberries and down another glass of champagne. As I'm munching and drinking and gazing from the ring to Alex, something occurs to me.

What's going to happen when we're around his family? Will we have to act all lovey-dovey? Part of me wonders if he'll kiss me in front of his family. I take a sip of champagne and shoot Alex a flirtatious little grin.

"What are you smiling about?" he asks. I shrug coyly, and he chuckles in response.

How, exactly, am I expected to make it through the summer without swooning every time he laughs? Maybe this is too much of a risk. *No, Evie. Don't start obsessing now.*

Another part of me is terrified of getting any closer than I already have.

We put the champagne down and stroll to another room that features a different view of the massive aquarium. I spend several long minutes pretending to read the posters about the life cycle of a grouper while he's several feet away, looking intently at a horseshoe crab.

"You okay?"

"Fine. Well, no. Not fine. I mean, I'm okay but I'm not fine." I walk in his direction, acutely aware of his presence the closer I get. "This is a little weird."

"What? The horseshoe crabs?" He jerks his thumb to the aquarium. "Yeah, they're mating over here and it's pretty wild. Check it out. Who knew that two things that look so weird could actually have sex."

"No," I say sharply. "I'm not talking about the screwing horseshoe crabs."

At first his eyes go round, then he laughs. "You're cute when you talk dirty."

I take two steps toward him. "Shut up. You know what I mean. This. Us. It's weird."

He runs a hand through his hair and sighs. "It is. I agree."

"I'm worried it'll be strange in front of your family."

"Oh, that."

I tilt my head. What did he think I was talking about? "I'm worried that I'll mess up somehow. The reunion's in a couple of weeks and we have a lot to go over."

"I'm in New York all next week, so this is it."

Must be nice to jet off so frequently. My plans for the coming days include searching for other jobs in case the aquarium position doesn't come through, and working two shifts at Chili's.

"And I'm sure you'll do great with my parents. Act natural. My entire family will be their crazy selves and won't even notice us. We'll do great."

"I have questions. On top of my guilt about lying."

"Stop feeling guilty. Leave that to me. What do you want to know?"

"Well, we're there four nights, right?"

He nods.

"What are the sleeping arrangements, anyway?" My eyes narrow.

For a nanosecond, his eyebrow quirks up and I suspect he's about to flash that arrogant smile, but then he sobers. "You'll have your own room. My parents' house is huge, and I'm sure they won't want to scandalize my grandmother by letting us sleep together."

I doubt that Mrs. Jenkins is scandalized by anything. "Crisis averted," I mutter. "One more question." I can't hold it in anymore.

"Ask away."

"Are we going to act like, you know, an engaged couple?"

He frowns. "Uh, yeah. That's sort of the whole point."

"Engaged couples touch each other. Hold hands. Kiss." I fold my arms over my chest.

"I was thinking about that."

"Don't sound so excited." I shift my weight from side to side and he laughs.

"We'll probably have to hold hands. I'll put my arm around your chair or shoulder or other body part."

I glance to my right, where the two crabs are, indeed, going at it. The idea of us holding hands makes my face blaze with heat. I can't even imagine how I'd react if he kissed me. I'd probably spontaneously combust. Better not to think about that. I squeeze my eyes shut. "And kissing? No kissing, right?"

"Hmm. I dunno. I think it might be odd if we never kissed. My family's pretty affectionate and if I wasn't that way with you, it would be a red flag." By the sound of his voice, he's somehow moved closer to me. My eyelids snap open, and he's only a foot away now. Stealthy, like a panther.

I try to play it off like it's no big deal, and so I shrug. "We don't want any red flags. I understand if you have to kiss my cheek or something. But could you give me a heads-up? A warning?"

"A warning?" He snort-laughs softly.

"Yeah. Like say a code word or something before you're about to touch me? Give me a few seconds to prepare myself?"

"A code word? Morse code? Pig Latin? Code red? Can you handle a kiss the cheek? A peck on the mouth? Or do you find me repulsive, Evie?"

I take in his dark hair, his full lips, the angled jaw. The broad shoulders and the big hands and the straight Roman nose. No. I do not find him repulsive one bit. Which is precisely the problem.

"That's not the point. I don't want to be caught off guard and act shocked in front of your family." I refold my arms tighter, aware that my nipples are feeling oddly sensitive against my bra.

"Okay, I won't catch you off guard. What's our code word?"

I shrug.

"Hm." He taps his finger on his lips and I have to glance away because he looks so adorable. "You choose."

"I don't know. You're the one running this show. You choose."

"Okay." His eyes glance around. "Crabs?"

I bust out laughing. "Crabs? We're going to insert the word *crabs* in casual conversation with your family? There's no way that will end well."

He presses his lips together, trying not to laugh.

I do laugh. It's impossible not to. "You're kind of a dork, you know that?"

That's when he gives me the sweetest, sexiest smile. Complete with twinkling eyes and dimple. "You're getting to know a side of me that most people don't know exists."

"Aren't I lucky?" I murmur.

"I'm ignoring that. Okay, so how about *whale*? Beluga whale?"

I quirk my mouth to one side. "Still a little strange. But I guess that would be okay. The word *whale*? It's more generic."

"Whale it is." He chuckles low. "Let's practice. C'mere. Let's pretend we're talking to one of my aunts."

"Which one? Don't you have, like, fifty of them?"

He faces the crab tank and points to the floor next to him. I'm not sure I want to practice, but I'll humor him. So I take a few steps and stand at attention at his side, my arms still clamped tight to my chest.

"Why, yes, Aunt Mary, we did go to the Georgia Aquarium, it's where I popped the question," he says, gesturing at a school of fish floating by the window, as if he's talking to a person.

"You deserve an Oscar for this performance." I giggle. He really does have a silly side, for all of his corporate rich-guy bluster.

"We did see the beluga whales, in fact. Evie here loves whales." He slips an arm around my waist, turns his head, and beams at me. "Don't you, Evie?"

"I do," I respond in a clear, fake voice, trying to block out his delicious smell. And the force field of his beautiful body. Sweat pricks at my neck. On instinct I drop my arms and gesture wildly with my hands. "I'm oddly obsessed with them, in fact."

I'm such a goof.

My laughter dies on my lips when I glance up at Alex. I expect him to let me go, but no, he's looking at me like he's starving. He licks his lips. I stop breathing.

In one swift motion, he draws me a little closer, cups my jaw in his big hand, and presses his mouth to my cheek. Frighteningly close to my lips.

"Like that," he murmurs against my skin, his breath feather-light, his nose grazing my cheekbone. His mouth lingers, and my entire body lights up. "A little kiss. Not too bad, is it?"

"No. Not bad, exactly." My brain is exploding like an electric transformer that's been hit by lightning. I cannot think straight with him so close.

"How about this?" He turns my chin gently with his fingers, so my mouth is next to his. Then his lips are on mine, soft yet commanding, while his hand cradles my face. *Whoa.* This guy really knows how to kiss. He's all soft lips, gentle tongue, slow and sensual while exploring in an unhurried, yet intense, way.

He's so good at it that it wouldn't shock me one bit if he said he kisses for a living. *Dang.*

All of my other kisses suddenly seem like they came from human Hoovers, guys who wanted to suck my entire face into their mouth.

I return Alex's kiss, hesitant at first. For a second I get swept away and nibble on his bottom lip, then break away, horrified. What if I'm a human Hoover? I probably seem needy and touch-starved. *Gah.*

"And that? How was that?" He's positively triumphant.

"It was. Uh. Okay." I swallow and step away.

He looks at me with big eyes and a horrified open mouth, like a startled Muppet. "Okay?"

"It was nice, I guess." Way more than nice. It was freaking phenomenal. So awesome that I don't know what to say.

"Tough crowd here." He smirks, but his eyes seem a little vulnerable and I wonder if I've hurt his feelings.

To break the tension in the air, I swat him on the arm and force myself to snap out of this dreamworld I've slipped into. "Come on, dude, it was great. You're an awesome kisser. We've got this. We can kiss in front of your family, no sweat. Pfft. By the end we'll be randomly making out in your parents' house."

He busts out laughing. "You said it, I didn't."

After a few awkward seconds, he breaks the silence. "Want to go look at the belugas again?"

"Absolutely." I power walk back toward the whale tank.

We don't kiss again. Not while we double back through the aquarium and gawk at the all the fish a second time, and not when he drops me off at the condo. For the rest of the night, until I lay my head on my pillow, I feel my lips tingle from that kiss. And I wonder how I'm going to make it through the summer without pinning him down and demanding to be kissed again.

CHAPTER TWENTY-TWO

EVIE

The next day, still feeling a little dizzy from Alex and his sinfully hot kiss, I board the train to my old neighborhood and try not to think too much about what happened at the aquarium. Surely Alex isn't thinking of me as much as I've thought of him this morning.

What does he do on Saturday mornings, anyway? Does he sit in his fabulously decorated living room in that condo of his, drinking coffee in gray sweatpants and a black hoodie, his dark hair tousled? The idea makes my entire body feel warm.

Or does he go out to brunch with his family? He seems to be quite fond of Savannah, his kid sister. Maybe they hang out together when she's in town. Probably he plays golf with his father. He said something about that last night.

As we approach the stop for my old neighborhood, I'm still thinking of the kiss and how it complicated everything. He claimed that he'd only had a couple of one-night stands since he broke up with Rose. Was that true? I mentally chew on this, realizing I have no reason to doubt him.

Last night, after we kissed at the aquarium, he was a total gentleman driving home. He held my hand, drove up to my condo building—where I proceeded to thank him about fifty times for helping me find the place—then walked to the building's door with me.

I'd hoped for another long kiss, but instead, he'd walked me to the elevator, then smacked his palm against his forehead.

"Sorry, I remember your thing about elevators," he'd said.

"It's okay. I'll take the stairs."

A lot of people would've teased me, or said goodbye in the lobby, since the condo's on the second floor. Not Alex. He followed me up the stairs, then outside my door, planted a chaste peck on my cheek.

He didn't even try to worm his way into my apartment, which surprised me a little.

Alex certainly seems like a gentleman.

I ponder this as I exit the train station. A fat drop of rain splats on my forehead and my immediate instinct is to sigh in frustration.

But wait! I can afford an Uber to take me the half mile to Chili's. Duh. There's a bank account with my name on it, containing more than two figures in the balance. This realization lifts my mood, and I decide not to think about Alex while I climb into the hired car. It seems almost decadent to only go such a short distance in the rain.

Along the short drive, I take in everything along the road that I normally walk: the massive chain stores and vast parking lots, the fast food garbage that clings to the curbs, the chaos of suburban sprawl. It looks even more dismal now that it's pouring, and I'm glad I didn't walk.

Part of me feels like I'm the luckiest woman in the world, now that I'm living in a gorgeous downtown condo, with enough money so I don't have to worry about necessities. It would be easy to live in this new world and never look back. But another part feels a bit ashamed, like I didn't work hard enough to earn these blessings—or that everything I'm enjoying right now will be pulled out from under me at a moment's notice.

And that includes Alex Jenkins.

Good lord. Don't think about him in that context. Think about how you're going to survive this restaurant shift, and how you're going to eat some of Ida's homemade cookies later.

I know a lot of people in my position would've quit Chili's on the spot and never returned once Alex made his offer, but not me. I can't leave anyone in the lurch, even a faceless corporation.

The other reason I trekked here from downtown was to see Ida so we can talk about the future of the community garden. I plan on doing that after my five-hour shift, since I'm working the lunch rush today.

The first person I see when I walk to my hostess station at Chili's is Gabe. Great. I'd hoped to avoid his accusing, surly stare. He's lingering at the front desk for reasons I can't fathom. And frankly, I don't care. I ignore him as I grab an erasable marker for the laminated table map.

"Excuse me, I need to get ready for my shift." I slide the map closer.

He shoots a smirk at me. "I'd like to say I'm going to miss your sunny disposition, but I won't."

I narrow my eyes. "What do you mean? Where are you going?"

"This is my last day on the job. Don't miss me too much."

"Good for you, I guess." My tone is flat. I won't miss Gabe, or this job—if I ever work up the courage to quit. That's for sure.

The shift is mercifully quick, and Gabe doesn't give me any grief, even when I give him three tables of two in a row. At three thirty, the end of the shift, I watch as he yanks off his apron and tosses it onto an empty table. He stomps past me and yanks the door open.

His vibe is too weird and angry for me to say any parting words, and I'm glad that my shift is over, as well.

"Yikes," I say to the hostess who's replacing me for the rest of the afternoon, a woman named Maria.

We stand at the hostess desk and watch out the glass front door as Gabe climbs into the passenger seat of a white truck. It roars away.

"He's pissed off because his car broke down," Maria says.

"What?" I'm half distracted and didn't quite follow where she was going with her statement.

"Gabe. He didn't want to quit, but felt he had to. His car died and he doesn't have the money to replace it. His stepdad has been bringing him to work and picking him up, but apparently the stepdad and his mom are getting a divorce, and he won't have a ride. Says he's too far from public transportation."

I gnaw at the inside of my cheek. "That sucks."

The manager approaches and the next ten minutes is a flurry of gossip about Gabe, who apparently also broke up with his girlfriend recently. He's had such a bad run of luck that I feel terrible about being snarky to him.

"Not everyone can be lucky in love like you," Maria points out.

"What do you mean?" I squeak.

"How's she lucky?" the manager asks, a question that I, too, was pondering.

Maria practically doubles over with laughter. "Are you blind? Or do you not see that rock on her finger?"

My eyes zoom to my hand and my breath hitches in my throat. Why am I still wearing the engagement ring?

The manager, a woman in her forties, grabs my hand and whistles. "Whoo-ee. That's some ring. Who's the lucky guy, and does he have an older brother? Or a dad?"

Laughter bubbles through my two coworkers.

"H-he's someone I've been seeing for a while," I stammer, while racking my brain in an effort to figure out if I've ever told anyone here that I was single. Fortunately, I'm a pretty private person and haven't discussed my love life with anyone here.

"Well, congratulations! You'll have to bring him around so we can meet him." The corners of Maria's eyes crinkle. "When's the big day?"

"We haven't set one. Yet. A while. A long while," I reply.

After a round of congratulatory hugs, I slink out the door, feeling conflicted. The fact that I've been working a restaurant shift that would net me a fraction of what this diamond ring cost leaves me feeling . . . gross. Icky. Like I'm selling out the working class or something.

It's stopped raining, but the gray sky remains, giving all this suburban sprawl a tired, dull patina. For a second, I stand outside the restaurant and stare at the ring until I finally slip it off, into my purse. Then I walk away.

For some reason, I can't get my mind off Gabe. I assumed that, because of his decent looks and his ability to earn lots of tips, his life was pretty easy, far more comfortable than my own. Now that I know otherwise, I feel terrible. Maybe I should've been kinder to him.

Instead of taking an Uber to Ida's house, I walk the mile to my old neighborhood. With every step, I'm starting to seriously doubt the choice I've made with Alex.

Or maybe it's Alex and his entire lifestyle that I'm uncomfortable with. He's too rich, too cavalier with money, and way too different than me. No matter what I wear or where I live, I'll never be like him.

CHAPTER TWENTY-THREE

ALEX

Evie seems to be in a good mood today.

How do I know? She's not gripping the door handle as we drive the three hours to Savannah. Of course, we're stuck in hellacious Atlanta traffic and we're crawling at the speed of snails. If there's one thing I truly dislike in this world—other than my cousin Beau—it's traffic.

"Do you own two cars? Why are we not in your . . ." She waves her hand at the dashboard. "Taurus? Toyota?"

"Tesla?"

"Yeah."

"I thought I'd rent this big SUV so you'd feel safer on the drive over. It's a Ford Expedition. Feels pretty solid, right?" SUVs aren't normally my thing, but I have to admit, it is comfortable.

"You didn't have to do that. But thanks. I do feel a little safer in this. But please don't take any turns fast. I've heard these roll over easy."

"No fast turns. Got it."

We've been in the car for a half hour, and I'm taking it slow when it's not bumper-to-bumper, and driving like a grandma (someone else's grandmother, not Eleanor). It's Thursday morning, and we're headed to my parents' house to kick off the four-day Jenkins family extravaganza.

To say I'm nervous would be an understatement. It feels like my entire future is riding on the next four days.

"How was your week? Did you do anything fun? How was New York?" Evie asks. She sounds genuinely interested, and not like she's trying to make small talk.

Other than think about our kiss last weekend at the aquarium? I want to say this, but don't.

It's true; I've been thinking about Evie nonstop. Aw, hell, I'll admit it. I've got a wicked crush on the girl. It's going to be quite easy to pretend I'm head over heels in front of my family.

"The tire-recycling initiative went through, although I had a hell of a time convincing the CFO that it made financial sense." I take one hand off the wheel and gesture, then put it back when I see Evie make a move for the door handle. "Other than that, lots of meetings. No time for fun or sightseeing. We've been in discussions about taking the company public."

Her face lights up. "That's exciting."

"It is. It was my grandfather's dream, and I think Gram is eager to see it happen in her lifetime. And you? Did you do anything exciting this week? How's the condo?"

"Love the condo. It's perfect. Lots of room for . . . stuff."

"Yeah, have your friends over, or whatever." *Oh, crap.* The last thing I want is for her to bring dates there. Wait. What am I thinking? She's single. She can date anyone she wants. But not publicly, per our contract.

She lets out a laugh. "Yeah, I'll be sure to have a party with all my vast numbers of friends."

"Oh, come on. You must have tons of friends. You're charming."

She snorts and looks out the window. We're finally moving a little.

"I used to have a lot of friends in high school. And my first couple of years in college."

"But?"

"But when my parents died, I fell off the map, socially. I was so upset, then so busy, that I let all my friendships fall apart. It was totally my fault."

"There's still time to change that. You're twenty-two, not eighty."

"This is true. I did have a good week, though. Worked a shift at the restaurant, then applied for a bunch of jobs. Oh! The aquarium scheduled me for an interview. I thought they'd do it sooner, but apparently it takes a while to get through the process."

"Excellent. Let me know if you need a reference. And I happen to know a couple of people on the board of the Georgia Aquarium, and I can put a word in for you. I should've thought of that earlier. Jeez, would you look at this traffic? I can't believe how bad it is." We roll to another stop and I glance over at Evie.

She's staring straight ahead, a faint furrow in her brow.

"What?" I ask.

"You've been so nice, but no. I would not like you to speak with anyone at the aquarium on my behalf." She purses her pink lips.

"Why?" My gaze ping-pongs from Evie to the sea of brake lights ahead of us.

"Thank you for offering to put in a good word for me. I'll think about it, okay? I have the preliminary interview on Tuesday. It's a phone call. I need to get through this weekend with your family first. Then the interview. I might not make it past that."

"If you want to do a practice interview, I'm your man. And I can call my aquarium buddy anytime. He owes me a favor."

"Hey, where's Fuzz Aldrin this weekend?"

"Way to change the subject, babe. My assistant's son takes care of him when I'm away."

"That's a relief. I was worried you were one of those guys who left a bowl of food and shut the door."

"Nope. Only the best for Fuzz. Getting back to the topic at hand, pretend I'm a hiring manager at the aquarium and tell me why you want a job. Go."

"So bossy," she grumbles. "Fine."

She clears her throat and launches into interview mode. Her voice is clear and her words smart, and something about her voice makes me happy. The traffic lets up and I accelerate while I listen to Evie talk about her passion for sea life.

That's when it hits me that this is the best time I've had while driving to Savannah, ever.

0

"Where have you been hiding her? Look how stunning she is!"

We're about two feet into my parents' place—my childhood home—and already, Mom is glued to Evie. No amount of preparation would have been adequate for this, and even though I'd tried to warn her on the drive here, Evie looks wide-eyed for a brief second.

Serves me right for encouraging her to listen to tunes, sing along, and laugh while we drove here. Okay, I'd encouraged all of that because I loved seeing her happy and carefree. Something I suspect is a rarity. Still, I'd tried to warn her one last time. Tried to tell her that Mom's intense, Dad's a bit scattered, and Gram, well . . .

"Mom, let Evie go, please. You don't need to take her prisoner yet. Yes, I know, she's beautiful."

Mom breaks away from her deep embrace, and I notice Evie's eyes drift to the now-closed door. If she doesn't flee in the next half hour, it'll be a miracle.

"Oh, Alex. Stop. I'm so thankful that you've finally brought someone appropriate and lovely and obviously smart home to meet the family." Mom clutches Evie's arm and looks her up and down, then whispers. "It's been forever since he's brought anyone home to meet the family."

"I see," Evie says. She's now sporting a saucy little grin.

This warrants a groan as I kiss Mom on the cheek. "Let's not go there," I say gruffly.

Mom ignores me. "I adore that dress, Evie. Lilly Pulitzer?"

Evie smiles knowingly and nods. There we go. She's in character now. Whew. I knew she was a great choice for this. She's unflappable. Cool. Pride swells in my chest. I set our bags down in the front hall, only to turn around to see Mom patting and squeezing Evie's hips.

Jesus, take the wheel.

"Perfect childbearing hips," Mom declares. "When are you two going to give me babies?"

There are a lot of reasons why I don't often come home to Savannah, and why I never bring home the few people I've casually dated since the Rose fiasco. What Mom said is exhibit A. I clear my throat and slip my arm around Evie and tug her toward me, trying not to meet Mom's eyes. If I do, she might be encouraged to say more stupid shit.

"You know, Mrs. Jenkins, that's a great question."

Evie's voice is like orange blossom honey, thickly southern and perfectly syrupy. And sensual as hell, but I'm trying to ignore that. My eyes snap to her face and she's beaming. I didn't expect Evie to do anything more than let out a sparkling laugh. What's she planning to say next? Fear stabs at my stomach.

Evie presses her left hand to my chest and rubs in a soft circular motion. Her engagement ring is practically blinding, it's so sparkly. Her hand runs down my chest, to my stomach, then back up. She's going to make me hard if this continues. "Alex and I haven't decided whether we want two or three children, but I know I'd love to have a boy and a girl someday."

"Oh my God!" Mom shrieks, and lunges for Evie's hand. "That diamond! Dale Alexander Jenkins, you did not tell us that you popped the question! Evie, tell me everything. Oh, my word!"

The sound of her voice shocks the thoughts out of my brain, so much that I don't even stop Evie when she slips her arm into Mom's. They walk off, chattering like old friends.

I am so screwed.

CHAPTER TWENTY-FOUR

EVIE

I didn't set out to annoy Alex, but that's obviously what I'm doing. I felt his scowl from the moment his mother hugged me, and especially when I chatted her up. He's probably rethinking this whole idea. As he should. I'm going to have a serious talk with him, because his mother is a gem.

Practically the moment we walked in, Mrs. Jenkins complimented me, fawned over my dress, then whisked me away for a tour of the house. Maybe she's putting on a polite show, but if she likes me even half as much as she seems to, she'll be devastated when Alex and I eventually "break up."

Whatever. I'm here and agreed to play this ridiculous role. I have only myself to blame, and I can't wallow in insecurity. I need to stay razor-sharp for this crew.

It's so difficult, though, because everything is stunningly beautiful. The house is a four-storey, pale-yellow, nineteenth-century Queen Anne Victorian mansion in downtown Savannah. To say it has southern charm would be an understatement. It's like *Midnight in the Garden of Good and Evil* come to life.

On the outside, it looks like a wedding cake, with decorative plasterwork, ornamental ironwork, and white moldings evocative of sugary, piped icing. The inside is a showroom of antiques and history. Of culture and class and everything I don't possess.

Alex grew up here? If I wasn't wary of his wealth before, I am definitely suspicious now. All I can do is gawk at all the pretty things. It's almost absurd that I'm even allowed inside. I'm even a little shocked that no one is directing me toward the maid's quarters.

"This used to be the servants' kitchen way back," Mrs. Jenkins says. *Yep. Here we go.* "I use it when it's just me and Alex's father. When we're entertaining, like this weekend, I'll use the big kitchen."

Inside, the place is decorated in soft colors and expensive-looking fabrics. There are views of oak trees draped in Spanish moss from seemingly every window. Stained-glass windows and ornate chandeliers grace almost every room.

Third, it even has a name in Savannah, one that's known by people all over the city, according to Alex's mom. After the family.

The Jenkins House. Unreal.

"It looks like something out of a magazine," I whisper as Mrs. Jenkins takes me through the formal dining room, where place settings for dinner are already on the table. Not only did Alex not fill me in that he grew up in a mansion, he also didn't tell me that I should have learned how to eat at a formally set table like I'm in an episode of *Downton Abbey*. Guess I'll hole up in the bathroom in a little while and Google it on my phone.

"It was in *Southern Living* back in 2014," Mrs. Jenkins says casually.

Of course it was.

Drapes that seem to whisper in the breeze. A courtyard. A terrace. A porch, where mint-green comfy chairs look like the perfect place to relax with a glass of ice-cold sweet tea. Alex's eventual wife—who will undoubtedly be as graceful as the curve on the wooden handrail of the staircase and as beautiful as the fresh flowers in every room—will fit in seamlessly here.

Even in my expensive little designer dress, I feel like the human version of a 7-Eleven store. Tacky, trashy, and pedestrian.

"You know what would be lovely"—Mrs. Jenkins gestures to the cream-colored wood lattice detail hanging over the end of the porch—"is if you hang your wedding dress there, suspended from that overhang. My daughter did that for her wedding, and the photographer took the most beautiful picture."

That comment hits me hard, makes me feel even worse. If only my wedding dress were hanging there for some expensive photographer to capture in an artsy shot. I imagine golden light filtering through yards of pure white lace and tulle. Maybe a graceful ribbon at the waist, floating in the genteel breeze. A princess neckline and a bodice laced with Swarovski crystals.

It's enough to make me sigh out loud.

"Have you and your mom picked out a dress yet, dear?"

My knees go rubbery at the question, so I reach out to grasp a wooden rail. The mention of my mother, and the knowledge that we'll never pick out a wedding dress, hits me like a kick to the stomach. I shake my head.

Then, Alex emerges onto the porch, right in time to save me from answering. He looks from his mom, to me, then back to his mom.

"We were discussing whether Evie and her mother have started dress-shopping," Mrs. Jenkins says. "I recommend Joan Pillow in Buckhead for designer gowns. They even carry Oscar de la Renta."

Alex pales. He slips his arm around me and hugs me tight to his body. "Mom, didn't Dad say anything? I told him about this yesterday and asked him to mention it to you. Evie's parents have passed. Together. In an accident."

Mrs. Jenkins looks taken aback. She's obviously embarrassed, because her face has turned the color of the scarlet cushions in the library.

"I had no idea." She squeezes my arm and I swear I see tears pooling in her big brown eyes.

"It's okay." I wave my hand. "Really."

"I am so sorry. I feel awful. Alex, you should know better than to trust your father with important information." She gently pats my cheek. "Alex's father has a terrible memory for personal details, dear, and he never mentioned it to me. Listen, you and I will go dress-shopping together. If you'll let me, I'll fill in for your mom and do her proud, 'kay? Now I'm going to get us some tea. You two stay right here."

I didn't realize how much I missed my mom until this very moment. That Mrs. Jenkins is so kind and gracious, offering to take me shopping, reminds me of everything I lack. Namely, parents. A real family. Roots. It's hard not to feel this way when hundreds of years of Alex's family history is literally surrounding us.

I try to wiggle out of his grasp so I can take a deep, sloppy breath, but he holds me in place. Then he puts both arms around me, and for the first time, I'm engulfed in him. In his scent. In his heat. In what feels like . . . affection. He strokes my hair softly. I press my face into his solid chest and sniffle. It probably sounds more like a honk, but he rolls with it and hugs me closer.

His big hands run down and around my back, and the tingles bloom on my skin. I've tried not to think about the tingles since that night he kissed me at the aquarium. But I have a feeling that this trip will be an express train to Tingle City.

"I'm sorry about my mom," he whispers.

And then he does the one thing that sends fractures through my heart: he cups my face, gently tilts my head up, and then presses his lips to my forehead.

◊

The next several hours are something I don't expect.

Fun.

Despite all of Alex's warnings and cautions, his family is pretty cool to be around. They all have a wickedly dry sense of humor. They're all warm. Everyone's welcoming. My initial worry was that they'd be snobby or arrogant because they're rich—kind of like how Alex came off initially. But no. They've accepted me into the family with kind words and a deep curiosity about my life. Alex keeps telling them not to barrage me with questions, but I don't mind.

It makes me all the more melancholic, of course. If I were to marry into any family, I'd choose this one. His mother, scattered and silly. His dad, clearly sharp about business, but a little befuddled about things like computers and social media. His sister, Savannah, who is gorgeous and runs her own Formula World team. And is a mother to the most beautiful daughter, Gabriella.

That little girl adores Alex. They've been playing while I've been chatting with Savannah on the terrace. It's so beautiful up here, with a fragrant jasmine vine wrapping around the posts. We're standing at the railing, overlooking a tree-lined park with a fountain.

She's telling me what she and her husband do in Europe. As she talks, I think about what Alex told me: how Savannah and Dante pretended to date when they both worked for a racing team.

"Ahh, so that's why Dante and Alex get on so well. They both love speed. You're all a family of daredevils." I'd seen Alex talking intently with the handsome older Italian man.

Savannah rolls her eyes. "Wait until there's a race on TV. Then you'll see all of us go crazy. We all root for different teams. It gets intense."

I imagine the four of us—well, five, including Gabriella—hanging out on Sunday, watching a race on TV. We'd eat nicely arranged snacks on an elegant platter, and laugh a lot. The idea of that level of domestic bliss is something I'd never wished for. And now I want it so bad that my chest hurts. Damn Alex for giving a glimpse of what happy families have, and what I never will.

"My brother's similar to my husband," Savannah says, and I widen my eyes.

"How so?"

She shrugs. "They're both a little arrogant. Okay, a lot arrogant."
I snort and nod.

"But they've got a gooey core, and we're their weakness. Alex is like a cinnamon roll. Spicy on the outside, sweet on the inside. Don't take his shit. He'll respect you more if you don't," she says. "Although you don't seem like the type who will put up with his stupidity."

"I'll keep that in mind."

"We all knew that when Alex fell in love, he'd be totally devoted. He's clearly crazy about you. I've never seen him this way with anyone. Ever. It's so like Alex to propose without telling any of his family first."

Really? How is that possible? I turn this over in my mind. "Yes, well, we're really happy together."

"And there's Mommy!" Alex's voice is loud and comes from the vicinity of the doorway. Gabriella is in his arms, wearing what appears to be a pink princess outfit and the most adorable pair of red Converse high-top sneakers.

"We had a wardrobe change," he says, while handing the girl to Savannah. "We played princess."

"I see. Nice sneaks, kiddo," Savannah says.

"Were you the prince or the frog?" I lightly jab Alex in the side with my elbow, and he laughs.

"What are you two talking about?" He looks from his sister to me.

"I was telling her all your deep, dark secrets. And was about to ask her how you proposed. I still haven't heard that story."

A mischievous look spreads over Alex's face. "I was waiting to tell everyone at dinner. But"—he slides an arm around my shoulders—"maybe Evie wants to tell you now."

My arm snakes around his midsection. "Oh! Yes. He surprised me by taking me to the Georgia Aquarium. He'd rented the whole thing, so it was only us. It was truly magical. He got on one knee. It was super romantic."

No lies detected here.

Savannah seems pleased by this. "Where in the aquarium? I love that place."

"Yeah, Evie, tell her *where* I popped the question." Alex's hand is on the back of my neck now, his fingers buried in my hair. Forget about tingles—this is like being electrocuted. And then I realize: he's forcing me to say the word *whale*. And since he's already touching me, what's he going to do next?

"He proposed in front of the beluga tank. I think all the whales watched him get down on one knee. It was incredible. Like something out of a movie."

None of that's a lie, either.

Alex kisses my temple, then takes my chin in his fingers and tilts my face to his. "Only the best for you."

And with that, he puts his mouth on mine and kisses me. Not a peck. Not a small smooch. A kiss. A long, lingering, totally-inappropriate-around-family-members kind of kiss. A kiss that relaxes my jaw and my lips and pretty much every muscle in my body. It's harder and more possessive than the kiss at the aquarium, and steals the breath from my lungs.

"They're kissing," Gabriella whispers.

"My God, in front of my daughter, Alex?" Savannah snorts, and I break away, embarrassed. My entire body feels like someone's thrown kerosene on my skin and lit a match.

"See you two at dinner. If you even make it to dinner," she adds, then wanders off, cackling.

Alex is still holding my face and staring at me. Why does he look so serious?

"What . . . why . . ." My voice dies on my lips.

"Because I want to, that's why. And because you said the word *whale*. We had a deal."

He leans in for another kiss, only this time, he parts my lips with his tongue. I wrap my arms around him, savoring his mouth. His taste, which is minty. His smell, soapy and spicy. His hands slide from my face down to the sides of my body, and he presses me into the terrace railing. Every part of me is throbbing, even parts of me that haven't ever throbbed before.

We're making out, hard and dirty. It's dusk, and the crickets are singing. Every cell in my body is humming, boiling, *alive*. I'm nipping at his bottom lip; he's sucking on my tongue. I'm tugging on his hair; he's making little groaning noises.

It's like he's desperate for me. And I'm more than desperate for him—it wouldn't take much for me to tear off this dress and press my fever-hot body to his. It's wildly inappropriate, what we're doing here on his parents' terrace, with his family milling about inside.

But I don't care. I can't help but give in to how good this feels.

"I've wanted this since the moment I laid eyes on you." Then he growls and cups my ass. Actually makes a low noise like a feral animal.

"You did? That's . . . interesting." I breathe, then go in for another kiss.

There's absolutely no denying that I'm thinking along the same lines. Because I'm inhaling his mouth like I need it to breathe.

Yeah, I'm going to take a risk with him tonight, this weekend, and see where it goes. Live the fantasy of being his princess in this picture-perfect home. I'll probably regret it, but I'm sick of being afraid of anything and everything.

I've never felt this way about anyone, never been kissed like this, never been so physically crazy for someone like Alex. I'm going to seize this moment of joy with both hands. Even though it's the most out of character thing I've ever done.

"Fuck, you taste so good," he whispers, his eyelashes brushing my cheek.

"So do you," I whisper back.

His mother's voice and the word *dinner* wafts up the stairs. Probably a good thing, because who knows how far we'd take this. We break away, staring at each other and panting.

"Wow. That happened," I murmur.

"We're not finished," he growls, and grabs my hand, pulling me toward the door. "Nowhere near finished."

CHAPTER TWENTY-FIVE

ALEX

I'm so distracted I can barely chew.

The kiss with Evie left me starving. For her. I'd had to go into the bathroom and wash my face with cold water and think about the driest of business reports to make my raging hard-on subside. Maybe this is a result of not hooking up with anyone recently, or perhaps I'm just that attracted to Evie. I'm not sure.

Now that we're sitting around my family's dinner table, making small talk about the weather and auto racing and neighborhood gossip, I can't help but slide my hand under the tablecloth and caress her thigh. Her smooth, toned, bare thigh. My mind goes to that kiss, and whether she's wearing panties and . . .

No. I can't think about that at dinner. Christ. I'm a thirty-year-old man, not a teenager.

"So, what time is everyone getting here tomorrow?" I ask between bites, hoping to get my mind out of the gutter. I look around the table. Only immediate family is here tonight, which means Mom, Dad, Savannah, Dante, and Evie. Gabriella's eating in the kitchen with her nanny.

Mom launches into a detailed rundown of aunts and uncles. "Uncle Stan and Aunt Dolores will be here early tomorrow, and will join us for breakfast, along with their kids. And Beau and Rose are expected to show up this year, by the way."

Mom stares at me with a pointed expression. Everyone except Evie studies me.

"And why wouldn't they?" I ask, then shovel another potato into my mouth.

"Well, I'm sure you've noticed, but they've skipped the last several years." Mom says, pursing her lips.

Yeah, probably because I got silently drunk one year and glared at them both from my spot on the sofa. I'd been aware that I made them uncomfortable, but didn't care. It wasn't even that I wanted to get back with Rose; it was the sheer hubris of their smarmy faces that made me surly.

"Well, good for them."

Sometimes I wonder what would've happened had I not launched this entire charade, if I'd told everyone that I caught Rose and Beau screwing. As it stands, I took the fall and have remained the bad guy, the wild child, the one who cut poor Rose loose.

Dad clears his throat. "Please be on your best behavior this year, Alex. You made your choice, Beau and Rose made theirs."

"Of course," I say, genuinely. "Although we all know why Beau's showing his face this year."

"Why is that?" Dante pipes up. He's a bit clueless about our family dynamics, probably because his family has their own dysfunction, if the way his mom and dad screamed at each other during their wedding rehearsal dinner was any indication.

"Sweetie," Savannah says, in a warning voice.

"What? What am I missing?" Dante looks around the table.

"It's because Beau wants the same position Alex does in the company." Savannah elbows her husband.

"Oh, well that won't happen, will it?" Dante asks, ignoring Savvy.

"Who knows? My mother's liable to do anything. She keeps saying she's going to make an announcement on the CEO job at the next shareholder meeting, but she's said that before the last three meetings. We're pretty certain I'll take her position when she steps down. Who else moves up, that's anyone's guess." Dad throws up his hands. "Let's not talk business at the dinner table. Dante, tell us all about that new winery you invested in. We really loved that Pinot noir you sent us. You know, Alex, that might be a great honeymoon for the two of you. Italy. Vineyard."

"Absolutely romantic," Mom sighs.

I turn to Evie.

"Italian vineyard." She raises an eyebrow.

We nod at each other. "We'll definitely discuss it, Dad."

Under the tablecloth, Evie grabs my hand and squeezes, then shoots me a sexy little smile.

Why does she have to fit in so well with my family? They love her. Why does she have to look amazing in that little blue-and-white dress?

What is up with me? When my mom made that stupid verbal blunder on the porch, I saw the pain in Evie's eyes. I felt the sadness radiating off her, and wanted to erase her discomfort. It's why I hugged her—that gesture had nothing to do with sex. It made me feel fiercely protective. I want to shield her from any more awfulness.

Which made me wonder whether I'm falling for her.

But that's ridiculous, right? This is all for show. Even so, the intensity of my physical attraction to her is almost frightening.

Dante drones on about Italian wine varietals, and Dad is acting like he's the most interesting man in the world. As I'm chewing on a mouthful of Mom's excellent potato salad, I try to calculate what time I can safely sneak into Evie's bedroom tonight. One in the morning? Too late? Which room did Mom give her? Did I bring condoms with me? I haven't been with anyone in so long, I can't remember if I have any. Maybe she has some; she's always so prepared, so organized and well put together.

I shove another forkful of potatoes into my mouth. I need to sleep with Evie. That's it. It's pent-up sexual desire. Nothing more than that. Once we screw, I'll be able to approach this whole weekend much more rationally. Deal with her more like I'm a friend with benefits, and not a lovesick boy. Get her out of my system, then attack the situation at hand: convincing Gram to retire.

Evie traces the back of my hand with her index finger and my entire body prickles with awareness. It's all I can do not to sweep away the plates and the food, haul her ass onto the table, and do her right here.

0

EVIE

"My dear, you look sleepy." Alex's mom pats my hand. We're all in the living room, and I'm squashed between her and Alex on a tiny antique sofa that was probably intended for elves. Alex's fingers are threaded in mine. He's chatting with his dad and Dante, and Savannah is sprawled on a divan.

"Why don't I take you up to your room? I know we're a lot to deal with, plus you traveled today. You need your beauty rest. Tomorrow will be even more intense, with Alex's grandmother arriving, and all the aunts and uncles and cousins," Mrs. Jenkins says.

Alex lets go of my hand. Ugh, he's probably done with me for the night. Who could blame him since I've been an awkward, sweaty mess for hours. The entire room is done in cream and gold, and one of the Jenkins family ancestors—one of the few Union Civil War heroes in the city, according to Alex's dad— stares down at us from a stern painting on the wall.

"Is it really midnight?" I say to Mrs. Jenkins.

She chuckles and rises. I don't know why Alex and his grandmother say she's flighty. I think she's absolutely lovely.

"It's late. Please, come with me, Evie. I'll show you where your room is. We've already put your things in there."

I stand up. My head's a little dizzy from the champagne and all of Alex's kisses and hidden caresses throughout the evening. I'm way overstimulated. My body is like a stretched rubber band— strung tight, ready to snap. How Alex can do that with kissing and touching, I'm not sure.

After saying good night to the others in the room, I follow Mrs. Jenkins out. To my surprise, Alex tags along. What's he doing? Probably wants to say good night. He is a gentleman. Or debrief on how this first day went. Critique my performance. That would be like him.

We climb up the grand wooden staircase, walk down a hall, and enter a room at the end.

"This used to be Alex's bedroom as a boy, but we've had it redone," says his mom.

If I was sleepy before, I'm wide awake now. It's the most romantic room I've ever been in. The walls are painted a faint blue, the valances on the windows are a shade darker, and the bed . . . God, the bed. It's probably a hundred years old, but perfectly restored. It's a wooden four-poster, with a half canopy over the headboard and pillows. The duvet and pillows are white and fluffy. I can't wait to nestle between the sheets.

My eyes take in the fireplace on one wall, and the beautiful, soft paintings of flowers that are tastefully hung around the room.

"I liked it better before with my motorcycle-racing posters," Alex snorts.

I run my fingers over the footboard of the bed. The posts are intricately carved into pineapples.

"Evie, go peek in the bathroom, it should have everything you need." Mrs. Jenkins gestures.

I didn't think I could be more impressed, but I am. The bone-white stand-alone bathtub is a curved, sensual shape, like a slipper. It looks like it could fit two people easily, and I block out the image of Alex and me soaking in hot, bubbly water. Kissing. Naked.

My face flares, and I catch a glimpse in the oversized,

gilt-framed mirror. I'm flushed, and my hair looks wild. Probably because Alex has been playing with it all night. My eyes are wide and manic. I heave in a breath and realize I'm mentally saturated from hours of nonstop conversation.

Sleep's what I need. Time alone to collect myself. That's all.

I step out to see Alex kissing his mother on the cheek. He murmurs a good-night.

She holds out her arms and I give her a quick hug. His family sure is handsy, but I don't mind. My own parents had been affectionate, too.

"Thank you, Mrs. Jenkins. You've been so nice to open your home like this to me."

"You're welcome, Evie. I think you're delightful. And I know that Alex's grandmother will probably be scandalized, but I decided to put you in here together. There's no need to be old-fashioned. She'll get over it."

Alex snickers, and I'm not sure if I'm supposed to laugh. So instead, I nod slowly, letting the weight of her words sink in. We're sleeping in here? *Together?*

Mrs. Jenkins pats her son on the cheek. "You're getting married, for God's sakes. We're all adults here, and we know what adults want to do at night."

Alex stands there, not protesting, not chiming in. All he does is stare at me in that lazy, sexy way. Mrs. Jenkins just gave us the green light to have sex in her house. My stomach constricts, either from nerves or desire. Or both. I glance at the bed.

"Sleep well, you two." Mrs. Jenkins gives us a little wave and pads out.

I'm still rooted to the carpet. Alex looks like a hunter who's caught the most elusive of prey.

But what about the vow I'd made to myself earlier? To live the fantasy? To say yes to new experiences? To enjoy myself for once and stop being so responsible?

A grin spreads on my face. I might be a virgin, but not for much longer. In fact, I can't think of a more romantic, perfect place to lose my virginity. I'm twenty-two, in a gorgeous bedroom, and the hottest man I've ever seen is a few feet away. Looking like he wants to devour me.

"Alex?"

He's leaning against the closed door and quirks an eyebrow.

"Come here," I murmur.

He saunters over and stands in front of me, his hands jammed in the front pockets of his jeans. He's so close that I can feel the heat of his body. I take one step closer, so my breasts brush his chest. That sharp inhale of his breath is so satisfying. It means I'm doing something right. That I might have a chance of making that careful control of his shatter.

"What?" he asks in a rough, desperate tone.

I stare into his eyes, which are the color of twilight before nightfall. I don't think my heart has ever beat this hard.

"Kiss me. Please?" I whisper.

And he does.

CHAPTER TWENTY-SIX

EVIE

His kiss is soft and slow. A faint brush of his lips, enough to make everything inside me coil tight. It takes me by surprise because he'd looked so intense before our mouths met. Almost scary, his intensity.

But his kiss is featherlight. Careful. Focused. He cups my face in his hands, and his touch is also heartbreakingly gentle. It's as if he thinks I'm breakable. As if he wants to savor me, delight in every last drop. Warmth spreads from my lips into my entire body with every movement of his mouth. My hands are flat on his broad chest, but I can't bring myself to touch him more than that.

It's as if I'm discovering that he's flesh and blood. Plus, I'm too stunned by the sublime kiss and the fact that this is happening.

He nips at my lower lip. I do the same to him. We go back and forth like this for a while, exchanging little bites of each other's mouths with only the slightest of contact, only a breath separating us. Finally, our lips barely touch. He smiles. I smile back, and shudder-inhale, opening my eyes to look at him. It's a sublime moment.

"Do you know what you do to me, Evie?"

I shake my head. Could my heart beat any faster?

One of his hands goes to mine, which is still on his chest. With the same maddening slow pace as the kiss, he guides my hand down his chest and over his stomach. He's so solid. I didn't think humans could be this firm. He moves my hand past his belt and presses it firmly against his zipper. I gasp when I feel his erection straining against his jeans.

"That's what you do to me."

"Ohh." My voice comes out as a breathy sound. I'm shaking. Not out of fear, but from mild confusion. I turn him on that much? Me? How?

He draws my face closer and kisses me again, this time with a bit more urgency. Oh, God. Yes. This. This is what I want. But I'm not entirely sure what to do with my hand on his erection. Does he want me to unzip his pants? Or keep pressing my hand there? He seems to sense my indecision because he moves my hand up and down his hard length. Good lord. Is he big? He feels big. Are all men that size? So many questions, all of them leading to one fact: I'm way out of my element here.

Apparently I'm touching him the right way, and with the perfect pressure, because he lets out this little growl-groan, the same as he did earlier when we kissed. Only now, the sound is lower in pitch. More wild. It makes my heartbeat spike again, and I wonder if I'm going to screw this up because I'm so inexperienced.

Our tongues slide against each other, and I press a little harder with the heel of my hand. I slide my hand down, and he stops kissing, and sucks in a breath.

"Oh, fuck," he whispers.

Well, I guess he likes *that*. I lean in to taste his mouth again, and I bite his bottom lip a little harder while sliding my hand up his erection, then down. I'm trying to match how slow he'd been when kissing me but it's difficult because he's breathing heavy. So I'm rubbing a little faster.

He grabs my wrist, holding it place. "No. You could almost make me come like this."

And with that he stops kissing, stops touching, and picks me up in his arms. He carries me across the room to the big bed and gently lays me down. I expect him to pounce on me, but instead, he stands at the side, running both hands through his hair. Staring at me. Still breathing hard like he's run several blocks.

I prop myself up on my elbows and realize my dress is halfway up my thighs. My hair's probably a mess, my face is probably flushed, and I'm sure I look disheveled. Does it matter? I'm going to lose my virginity to this gorgeous man. Who was once my boss. Whose entire family thinks I'm marrying.

Life is complicated, isn't it?

A wave of panic goes through me. Alex is used to perfect-looking women. Experienced women. Older women. The bedside lamp isn't that bright, and casts a perfect, soft glow. Every lamp in this house seems to be designed to make people look their best. Still. I'm not sure I want him to see my pale body and my awkward limbs. Not to mention my breasts and my . . . I turn over and flick it off.

"What are you doing?" Alex is on top of me now, pressing me back against the pillow, caging me with his arms and legs.

"Don't you want to turn off the light?" I trace his sharp jawline.

He shakes his head while staring into my eyes. For some reason, the gesture and expression are the most erotic exchange I've ever had with a man. Heat pools in my belly, and I'm suddenly hyperaware of how wet I am between my legs.

While still gazing at me with those dark-blue eyes, he leans on one forearm, and with his other hand rests his palm on my throat, almost as if he could choke me. His touch is light and I start breathing from the top of my lungs as he drags his hand down the hot skin of my neck and over my right breast. He skims there, and I want more. I arch into his hand, but he moves down my body, caressing the dip of my waist and the swell of my hip. He shifts to his left and his hand's on my thigh, caressing the bare skin.

Feeling dizzy and feverish, I let out another breathy *ohhh*. He squeezes the top of my leg, his fingers digging into my skin. It's a little scary and exciting all at once. Especially since I can sense the power in his hands. And it's driving me wild.

The spot between my legs, the one that's drenched, is aching. Positively throbbing for him to touch me. But my legs are closed and I'm not sure what exactly he wants, so I lie there, panting and wanting and hoping he'll do something soon.

His hand moves higher, under my skirt. With a small sweep, his palm is between my legs. Instinctively, I part my legs a little, enough so he can slide his fingers there. He presses against me, the wet fabric of my panties the only thing stopping him from touching me for real. I'm practically hyperventilating now.

"Oh, Evie," he murmurs, almost to himself. This is something

I've never experienced—not because I didn't want it to happen, but because life kind of cut me down at the knees right when I was ready to date—and a little cry escapes my lips.

"Please?" My voice comes out as a plea.

He opens his eyes and refocuses on me.

"Please what?"

I shake my head. I'm not even sure what I'm pleading for. My eyes squeeze shut, unable to handle his handsome face so close to mine. "Please kiss me, please touch me, please do whatever you want with me."

He moves his hand back to my thigh, and his head dips so that his forehead presses into the hollow of my neck.

"The one thing I want to do with you, I can't." He kisses my neck.

Maybe I should wrap my arms around him. But he's so solid, so in charge, that my earlier confidence has gone out the window. "Why?"

Alex lets out a little laugh and raises his head. "Evie, I want to make love to you. But I'm an idiot and didn't bring condoms. It's been so damn long for me, that I don't have condoms. Do you have any?"

I shake my head, partially in disbelief that he's admitting that it's been a while since he had sex. "Of course not," I say with a lopsided grin. "I'm a virgin. I've never bought condoms in my life."

And for the first time since I've known him, Alex Jenkins looks truly caught off guard.

CHAPTER TWENTY-SEVEN

ALEX

Evie's *what?*

"Oh. *Oh.*" *Jesus, man, don't make her feel bad about it. There's nothing to be ashamed about.* I allow my body to stretch out next to hers, so I'm lying on my side. "Cool, cool. Totally fine."

She shifts to face me. Her brow is lightly furrowed, and I hope she's not offended by how I reacted to her news.

"I decided that you should be my first. That is, if you want to be." When she leans in to kiss me with those beautiful lips, I want to groan.

Once she starts biting my bottom lip, I'm lost. Done. It's impossible to stop kissing her. I shift so I'm half on top of her. Her being a virgin shouldn't bother me. She's old enough to decide what she wants to do with her body. That's none of my business. But I've never been in this position before. I know lots of guys who are into that sort of thing. I'm not one of them.

Or am I? I don't know what the hell I am right now.

And what was up with me telling her I wanted to make love to her? I never use that phrase. During my rare one-night stands, I'd use the word *fuck*, and women seemed to like it. I'd always thought *making love* was a cheesy thing to say. Until tonight, I guess. It slipped out. Now I'm glad I said that instead of something raunchy.

Maybe I should feel a sense of obligation about being her first. Then again, I could be merely a convenient and trustworthy stand-in, better than the college boys who probably hit on her nonstop.

Most guys would take her, wouldn't bother with a condom. But I'd never do that. She has all of my respect, and while I was ready to ravage her all weekend, I realize I need to proceed even slower. Maybe. If she wants.

Because we're back to making out, as intense as before. My dick's like iron, my mind's a whirlwind of questions, and all I want is for us to get naked.

Maybe not having condoms tonight is a good thing. It will force us to go slow.

She slips her hands under my T-shirt and the sensation of her fingers on my skin makes me inhale a sharp breath. How the fuck can I go slow when I love everything she's doing to me? I break away from her kiss to study her face.

"God, you're beautiful," I blurt. I lean in for another kiss and our teeth clash.

"Ack," she yelps.

"Sorry," I mutter.

She goes to kiss me, but we awkwardly mash our noses together. We both laugh, then grow silent as we stare into each other's eyes. She probably thinks I'm a total goof, a guy who has no game. The most eligible bachelor in Atlanta is a clumsy kisser who didn't come prepared with condoms . . .

Finally, she breaks her silence. "Do you not want to be with me because I'm inexperienced? Do you have an existential problem being my first?"

Evie's directness, and her honesty, can be disarming at times. Especially in that sexy-as-fuck voice. I lick my lips, biding my time. I'm not sure how to respond. Part of me wants to be responsible. Tell her no, being a girl's first lover comes with way too many expectations. I should tell her that kissing's fine, cuddling all night is peachy, but I'm not the guy who should deflower her. I'll leave that to someone who is less of an asshole, who is more her age, who wants a commitment.

But the next guy might not know what a precious jewel she is. Jesus, that thought slays me. She deserves the best of everything. I am the best for her, right? Right?

Another part of me is wildly, inappropriately, turned on by the idea that I could be the first man to touch her. That line of thinking is all kinds of wrong, and even I recognize that. But that part of me is so strong, so loud in my brain that it's roaring like the crowd at the Georgia Dome during a Falcons game. It's as if all my senses are blinded by a lust and tender desire I've never experienced with anyone.

I dip my head to kiss her neck, bathing in her sugary scent. She's too innocent, too beautiful, too complicated. And yet, I can only think of two words, and they crowd out all the others in my mind.

Claim her.

Okay, and a third.

Now.

But I can't. Not yet, anyway. Sometime this weekend, definitely.

I bite her soft skin, slightly harder than I intended. She gasps, and I kiss the spot, hoping to soothe it. Her little mewl sends a fresh surge of need through my body, and I trail my mouth up to her ear.

"Evie, baby?"

"Yes?" She wraps her arms around me for the first time and it feels so damned perfect.

"I'm going to be your first. I promise. If you'll let me. It's totally up to you."

0

EVIE

We lie there for a long time, kissing. I'm relieved that he doesn't have condoms, because it gives me time to get used to all of this. Him. His body. The way he moves.

I've never been in such close physical proximity to a man. It's heady. His hard body. The way he takes control of the rhythm of our kisses, then backs off and lets me lead. The way his hands skim my body and leave trails of heat and light in their wake.

After a while, he sits up, on his knees and reaches for me. I sit too. For the first time tonight, I notice how wrinkled my dress has become.

My lips feel almost bruised from all the kissing—my entire

body aches like every nerve ending is exposed. He cups my face in his big hands. Why does he look so serious?

"I want to make sure that you want all of this." He smooths back my hair.

"All of what? I thought you said we couldn't tonight because you don't have a condom."

"All of this, everything else we're going to do. I want you to know that you can say no. At any time. I want to respect your boundaries. If you say no, that's okay."

Ignoring him, I walk on my knees a couple inches closer and grasp the bottom of his T-shirt and lift it. "Can I take this off?"

"Yeah."

I swallow hard, while my eyes take in his muscles. "I want this. Whatever this is. Whatever we do."

"It's a big step, though."

"Alex, I'm twenty-two."

He winces.

"What?" I tilt my head, curious.

"I'm thirty."

I shrug. "So? My parents were ten years apart."

God, I love to run my hands over his skin. It's so smooth.

"I guess, but I don't want you to regret this."

"Why would I regret this? I've missed out on so much of life, taking care of my sister and working. It's not like I planned to be a virgin at this age—it just kind of happened. This is me having some fun, joining the human race, being a normal twentysomething for a change."

"This is different for me, too," he says.

I tilt my head, tearing my gaze away from the ridges and valleys of his chest muscles. "How so?"

"It's, ah, been a while for me. Remember? I'm not a fuckboy, I just play one on TV."

A soft chuckle slips from my mouth. "That's okay."

"Can I take off your dress?" he whispers in my ear.

Thought you'd never ask. "Absolutely."

He lets out a groan as he lifts the dress over my head. I'm wearing a new bra and panty set I'd bought when I went shopping the other day. It's not like I went and bought all sorts of sexy lingerie—this is a pretty basic matching lace set in light blue—but the way Alex is staring at me you'd think I have on something out of the Victoria's Secret fashion show.

The way he's staring at me sends a fresh flood of wetness between my legs. I'm aching for him to touch me. He looks both carnal and afraid.

"Evie. You're fucking perfect." His eyes linger on my chest. Long enough to make my nipples stiffen. I can't wait to find out what he'll do when I'm totally naked. With a devious grin, I slowly lower the bra strap on my right shoulder. Then I do the same with my left. My hands go around my back to the hook. I don't let the bra fall off me; at first I clutch it to my chest.

And slowly, so slowly, I let the fabric and my hands slide away.

He looks stunned, and I move toward him until my nipples brush his chest. At the moment our bare bodies touch, it's like there's an explosion.

While I cling to him, he pins me to the bed, kissing me hard. I reach for his belt buckle, fumble with it, and then he takes over, stripping to his black boxer briefs. Then we're back to kissing, only this time, my legs are spread, and he's grinding his hips into me.

"I love how strong you are," I whisper.

"I'm so fucking weak around you, though." His mouth finds my nipple and I gasp. Oh, wow. His tongue, flicking like that. His mouth, sucking. His other hand, rolling the other nipple between his thumb and forefinger. It's as if there's an invisible thread between my nipples and my clitoris, and everything is pulsing insistently, so much that I'm almost shivering.

"Can I take these off?" He tugs at the elastic of my panties.

"Yes. Please do."

When he sits up and fixes that intense stare on me, I feel helpless. And wet. And out of control. When I think he's going to take his time removing my underwear, he pauses.

"Lift your butt up."

Obediently, I do. And he whisks my lacy panties down my legs and off, tossing them onto the floor.

I am naked. For the first time. With a man.

Who I'm falling for.

He swears softly under his breath, his eyes taking me in. I have a feeling I know what he wants. Or maybe it's me who wants this.

Hesitantly, I open my legs. Alex swallows. I'll be honest. It feels a little weird, being spread out on a bed with a gorgeous man. While a nearby lamp casts soft light on my skin, making it look the color of milk.

"You are so, so pretty. I want to . . ." His voice dies on his lips.

"To what?"

"Touch you?"

I nod, and with one index finger, he traces the seam of my sex. It makes me gasp.

"You're already so wet," he says, his voice rough.

I don't know how to respond so I moan and wiggle my hips from side to side a few inches. Then he does it again, traces the seam. And the lips. And then—oh God—he goes in a little deeper. Between my folds.

"Oh, God, that. Alex. That."

He stretches out next to me, his hand still between my legs. "That's where you want me to touch you?"

His fingers are now exploring more, probably coated in my wetness. "Yeah," I grind out.

"Mmm. I'll bet it feels good right—" he kisses my cheek and I feel like I'm almost electrocuted when his finger makes contact with my clit "—here. Is that a good spot?"

He's circling and rubbing and I've never felt this physically needy. This sexual. This amazing.

"Oh. Oh! That's the spot. Yes. Right. There. To the left."

He hums low in my ear. "You're a virgin and you know where you want to be touched."

I hum. "Being a virgin doesn't mean I haven't had an orgasm."

"That is so fucking hot. Want to tell me more?"

I shake my head, not wanting to talk and ruin this perfect moment. He's exploring and stroking and I'm practically going out of my mind. I think he is, too, because of the way he's breathing hard.

I gather the duvet in one fist, and grab a hold of Alex's bare thigh with the other. He's too muscular, of course, to truly grasp, so I settle for digging my nails into his flesh. I've gone from wet to swollen to ready to explode.

And then I do.

CHAPTER TWENTY-EIGHT

EVIE

It's eight in the morning on Friday, our first full day in Savannah, and I'm still in bed, half naked. It was the first time I've slept in bed all night with a guy, and it was surprisingly wonderful. When we weren't kissing, we cuddled.

I stretch, feeling decadent and wanting to eke out a bit more time here. Immediately I feel guilty about this. Alex showered and dressed without waking me, and now he's nuzzling my neck.

"Staying in bed all day is a better option than anything else," he murmurs. "But I guess we have to brave the crowd downstairs. I'll stay here while you get ready."

"No, don't wait for me." I pinch his butt. "I'll meet you downstairs for breakfast after I shower and get ready. Don't let me hold you up."

Alex is wearing a black hoodie and gray sweatpants. I giggle, thinking about my sister. About how loud she would screech if I told her about last night.

He leans in and kisses my nose. "What are you laughing about?"

I consider telling him about the sweatpants challenge. Maybe later. "Nothing, you look cute is all. I'll see you downstairs."

He brushes one quick kiss on my lips, growls, then kisses me harder. Every time he puts his lips to mine, warm tingles flow through my body.

"Okay. I might take a few minutes now to go to the drugstore to buy some necessities. Oh, and hey, I meant to tell you . . ."

"Tell me what?" We kiss again.

"If you happen to talk with Beau or Rose today, keep it light, okay?" He strokes my hair.

"About what? Us? Or what happened with you and Rose, or Rose and Beau? I'm confused."

"They might try to pump you about me. What I'm planning if Gram appoints me as CEO. They might try to get you to divulge my plans for my takeover. Or try to get at me through you."

"I don't know your takeover plans. So they'll be out of luck if I'm part of their fact-finding mission. Can't get blood from a stone and all that."

"I know. Don't let them get under your skin. They're . . ." His eyes dart around as he eases himself off me, and the bed. "They're a bit ruthless."

A grin spreads on my face. "Something to look forward to. Don't worry. I've dealt with worse."

"Okay. I want you to be prepared for all possibilities today."

"Consider me the princess of possibilities. I'm all yours."

His lips part, and he pauses while his gaze scans my face. "Yes. You are."

He bounds out of the room like an eager Labrador retriever fetching a particularly juicy bird while on a hunt.

The tingles stay with me as I shower, and while I put on one of my new dresses. This one is a little black-and-white number, with a floral print and a tie at the waist. As I slip my feet into black sandals, my stomach flutters with nerves about going downstairs and facing his family. Hopefully I'll sort of blend in. And my still-flushed face and shining eyes don't scream: *Hey, fam, we've been getting it on all night, sort of, and we'll definitely have sex later.*

Maybe everyone will be finished with breakfast, and I can have a cup of coffee and a piece of toast in peace. This family looks like they'll have the really excellent bread, and probably a selection of jams.

On the way downstairs, I pause in the hall to look at some family photographs. Unlike the historic ancestor paintings downstairs, these are all of Alex and his family. More normal, if yachts and auto races and motorcycles are normal. I pause to look at one picture that looks like a wedding. Or prom? Oh, *cotillion.* That's what it says in embossed gold script at the bottom of the photo. Of course.

All the girls have perfect straight hair and beautiful long dresses. The boys in back are in tuxedoes. I locate Alex at the far right of the frame. He was handsome even then. I doubt if he even had a teenage awkward phase.

The girl next to him is adorable. Blonde, wearing a pretty white dress and clutching pink flowers. I wonder if that's Rose. How could anyone do what she did, screw Alex's cousin a few nights before their wedding? It's too revolting to think about.

The house is so big that I almost get lost on my way to the kitchen—Alex said his mother would have breakfast waiting for us—and I'm stunned to see several people around the formal dining room table.

"Good morning," his mother trills, waving me in. Everyone at the table, around ten people, turns their eyes to me.

I give a little wave. "Morning. When Alex said there would be breakfast, I didn't think it would be a sit-down like this."

His mother pats the empty seat next to her. "We're catching up over coffee."

With the gold-rimmed china, it looks like more than a casual coffee, but whatever. As Mrs. Jenkins piles my plate with bacon, croissants and fruit, she introduces me to everyone around the table. Aunts, uncles, cousins. People from Charleston. People from Jacksonville. I immediately forget everyone's name. By the time I spear a strawberry, I'm in a light sweat. These adults are all between twenty and fifty years older. They all look exceedingly well-dressed. Where is Alex?

"Alex said he'd be right back, dear." Mrs. Jenkins can obviously read my mind. "He said he had to run a couple of errands."

I nod and smile weakly, hoping she doesn't guess what he's going to buy. I'll keep myself busy by eating until he gets back. Hopefully if my mouth is full, I won't have to make casual conversation. Mrs. Jenkins stands up, saying she'll get more champagne for the mimosas. This is a family that likes to drink, that's for sure.

One of his aunts, a lady with white hair, leans in. "Dear, where did you say you were from? You look so familiar."

I'm certain I don't know this woman, but I smile patiently. "I grew up in the suburbs, but I live in Atlanta now."

The woman beams. "That's where I know you from." She turns

to the man next to her. I think it's her husband. I spear a juicy piece of pineapple and shove it in my mouth.

"Sam, she was in cotillion."

Sam nods thoughtfully and pops a slice of bacon between his thin lips. How is Alex related to these people?

The woman mentions a year. "You were in cotillion that season, weren't you? I knew several of the girls in that chapter because of my daughter-in-law. You might know her. Rose Jenkins? Well, that's her married name. It was Rose Richardson."

"I'm sorry, how are you related to Alex? I'm trying to get his family tree straight. He has so many relatives." My tone is soft, deferential.

"Alex's father and my husband are brothers. I'm Beau's mother."

"Oh. Oh!" *So this is the woman that gave birth to the smarmy Beau. Interesting.*

She says her name—Bunny, short for Barbara—and I spear another piece of fruit. Cotillion is a staple of people like these. A formal ball where "debutantes" are presented to society. A throwback to another era. It's for the rich and snooty, in my opinion, and there was never a thought in my parents' minds that I'd be a debutante. My mom once mentioned it, but only in the context of how sexist it was. Of course Sabrina also wasn't a debutante. The very idea makes me want to roll on the floor in hysterics.

"Like I was asking, Evie, what year were you in cotillion?"

"No, I'm sorry. You must be mistaking me with someone else. I wasn't in cotillion." Again, the eyes of the table turn to me, and I grow uneasy.

"You weren't?" The woman frowns. "I could have sworn there was an Evie in that class."

I glance around, and everyone is looking at me with curious

expressions. Is it that unusual that I wasn't a debutante? I know it's a popular thing in parts of the South, but I met plenty of girls in college who weren't.

"No," I say firmly, thinking of my mother. And I'm proud of it, I want to add, but don't.

I tear a corner off the croissant and put it in my mouth. Bunny purses her lips. This is Alex's aunt? I'm disliking this branch of the family more and more.

Mr. Jenkins, who's seated at the head of the table, chuckles. Obviously he sees the absurdity in this.

"I think she's the first non-debutante Alex has ever dated. Guess he went through the entire social register." Mr. Jenkins guffaws, and the entire table laughs.

Oh. My. God. Did he say that out loud? I look around nervously, and no one will look me in the eye. He sounded so convincing that I'm now doubting Alex's assertion that his play-boy persona was all an act.

The croissant mingles with the lump of discomfort in my throat, and I gulp water to wash everything down. How long do I have to sit here after that little humiliation? Ten minutes? Five? Thirty seconds? I feel like hurling coffee at everyone and smashing this expensive china against the wall. One thing was made clear to me, whether Alex's family meant to do it or not: I'm an outsider here.

Alex isn't. He's as firmly rooted in this upper-crust life as any of these people at this table. And he can tell me a million times that I'm beautiful, that I'm smart, that I'm hardworking. He can give me a thousand passionate kisses. He can tell me, like he did last night, that I'm so different than the other women he's slept with, and how he adores that.

But he will never, ever choose me to live in this world as his real girlfriend.

The next ten minutes are excruciating. Everyone at the table is silent, the clacking of silverware against plates the only noise.

"Lovely day," someone says in a pleasantly fake tone.

Everyone enthusiastically begins talking about the weather and how it will be perfect for croquet in the garden later, and I'm left to marinate in my humiliation. Of course these people would subtly make fun of me—I'm a zero in their minds. It takes all I have not to start bawling. The bitter coffee helps a little.

Mrs. Jenkins returns with an open bottle of champagne, and pours me a glass, topping it off with orange juice.

"Here you go, darling," she says.

I beam at her, grateful she wasn't in the room when her husband made the crack about Alex and the debutantes—and when everyone laughed.

"It's such a beautiful day out, I think I'm going to drink this on the porch and wait for Alex. I also have to make a phone call." Mustering all my courage, I stand up, and push my chair in. I don't even have my phone with me, nor do I have anyone to call.

"I'll tell him you're out there, dear," Mrs. Jenkins says.

I thank her and hold my head high as I grab my mimosa and walk out. Screw these people. Well, not Mrs. Jenkins. She's nice. Everyone else is awful. No manners. Money can't buy class, my mom used to say. I'd doubted her when she said it all those years ago, but she was proven right.

The porch is a welcome respite. I sink into the comfy cushion of the wicker love seat and take a sip of my mimosa. Ugh. It mixes with the gallon of coffee in my stomach, and I feel like I'm digesting rocks. And I haven't even met the infamous Rose.

Can't wait for that.

Last night was perfect. Something out of a dream. Or a romance novel. We kissed for what, eight hours? It probably wasn't that long, but it felt like it. He was so gentle. Yet dominant. And patient. Probably a lot of guys would have tried to have sex without protection. But he didn't. Alex said he wanted us to get to know each other's bodies, to feel comfortable with each other.

And the way he whispered in my ear when he touched me? I'm unsteady and turned on as I replay the night in my mind.

Will you come for me again, Evie? Please? I love watching you.

Even though I'm sitting here swooning, I should be rethinking everything after that scene at breakfast. I have no place here, or with him.

My sigh is drowned out by the sound of happily chirping birds. At least someone's in a good mood.

"Hey, beautiful."

I look up, and Alex is coming through the doorway. A charge of adrenaline goes through me, like it always does when I see him. He looks unusually alive, a flush of color on his sharp cheekbones. Good lord, he's handsome. More so today, I think. Maybe it's because of what we did last night, or because he'll never be mine for real. Grinning, he plops down next to me.

"How is my fiancé?" he whispers, taking the mimosa out of my hand and finishing it. He sets the glass on a table, then leans in, his hand on my neck, pulling me toward him.

"Kiss me," he murmurs.

Denying him is impossible.

As his lips touch mine, I consider whether I should tell him about what went down at breakfast. What would I say? *Your dad was snarky and everyone laughed at me because I'm not a debutante from a rich family like your other girlfriends?*

God, why does he have to be such a good kisser? His tongue slides into my mouth.

Alex breaks from our kiss and sucks in a breath while putting his forehead to mine. "I went to the store and purchased the things we need. They're in our room," he whispers. "I'm tempted to take you upstairs right now."

If only we could do that and forget about everyone else. "Don't we have to make an appearance for your family? Aren't there games? Someone at breakfast mentioned croquet."

Even uttering that phrase aloud seems foreign on my tongue. I wasn't even aware people still played croquet.

He sighs and sits back, running a hand through his hair. "Yeah, I guess. Did you meet everyone at breakfast? I grabbed a bagel and left. C'mon, let's go do our duty." He stands up and holds out his hand. I allow him to pull me up, and he tugs me in for a hug. "Why do you feel so damned good, Evie Cooper?"

Hearing him say my full name makes me melt into his body. And then his words echo in my ear.

Do our duty.

I can't forget the real reason I'm here. I'm hired help. And now, hired help with benefits. The thought sends a hot poker of pain through my stomach. He's probably fooling around with me because I'm convenient. It's not like this will continue when we get back to Atlanta. If I tell him what happened at breakfast, he'll wonder why I care. I won't see these people again. He might even laugh, like his family did.

And he'll probably assume that I'm falling in love with him, and that might be a correct assumption. It was the one thing I told him I wouldn't do, and here I am, wondering if what we have could be real.

CHAPTER TWENTY-NINE

ALEX

Most of the morning is spent chatting with my family, making sure Evie meets all my aunts and uncles and cousins streaming in, and making sure Gram doesn't monopolize all of Evie's time.

Gram loves her. Mom loves her. The three of them spend a solid hour looking through my baby photos in the library. I make myself scarce for that trip down memory lane and retreat into the family room with Dante to watch a MotoGP race on TV.

Our family reunion weekends have been going on for decades: one of the many Jenkins traditions handed down through the generations, like shrimp and grits on Christmas Eve and an intense love of the Georgia Bulldogs. They are always chaotic affairs, with people showing up at all hours, mixing cocktails, eating the massive catered spread ordered by Mom and displayed in the lavishly decorated garden. The actual reunion isn't until tomorrow, and it will be held at the Gibbes Museum. While the days before and after the event are often raucous, boozy affairs, the reunion itself is a bit more formal.

At first I worried how Evie would handle it, but now that I'm sitting on the porch and relaxing with a beer, I realize my fears were unfounded. She's circulating in the backyard, talking with relative after relative. Turns out that Evie's much more social than I imagined.

But then, since all peaceful and calm events in the Jenkins family must come to an end, Rose and Beau walk in. A brief hush falls over the seven people sitting near me, as if they're anticipating something dramatic.

When I stand up and call Beau's name, I hear everyone around me inhale.

"Hey, bro," he calls out while walking over. Assorted family members let out audible exhales when they notice we're both smiling. It's been like this for years, whenever family sees the three of us in the same room. But on my part, there's no drama left in this theater.

Rose waves, then stops to chat with an uncle. See, we're civilized. At least these days. It's a far cry from that first year they were together, when I'd considered punching his smarmy face right on this very porch.

Beau and I shake hands like we're at the office. I spot Evie glancing at me from the appetizer table on the lawn. She's standing near a cousin who is gesturing wildly, and I motion for her to join me.

Beau hitches up his pants. "Good to see you. We'd hoped to

come sooner, but she gets tired easily, you know. Did we miss anything?" Beau asks.

"Other than Mom's homemade strawberry jam this morning and a killer game of cornhole, I don't think so."

He sucks his teeth and looks around. "Where's Gram? She say anything important? Like when she's going to announce her decision?"

"Don't know, and nope." I take a swig of my beer and watch as Evie comes our way.

"She's gotta have a plan. That's what the board wants."

Evie stands next to me and kisses my cheek. I slip my arm around her and make a clicking sound with my tongue. "Dude, I'm not talking business this weekend. Beau, this is my fiancé, Evie Cooper. Beau, I think you met Evie in my office the other week."

Beau's eyes widen and take in Evie, who looks stunning in a summer dress. I immediately want to punch him for staring at her, but instead I paste on a smile.

"Nice to see you again, Beau," Evie says sweetly.

"Likewise, ma'am." Beau's pouring on his southern charm, and I have to fight not to roll my eyes. I rub the small of Evie's back and can't help but notice that my hand seems to fit perfectly there. "I didn't realize you two—"

At that moment, Rose saunters up. Her eyes zoom in on the ring. "Who is this gorgeous girl, Alex?"

"This gorgeous *woman*," I emphasize, "is my fiancé. Evie, this is Rose, Beau's wife."

"I've heard so much about you," Evie says. There's an imperceptible edge to her voice, and honestly, I'm kind of digging it.

"I'm sure you have. Are you having fun at your first Jenkins family weekend? This is your first, isn't it? I don't recall seeing you around. But that's quite a rock on your finger. Congratulations." Rose's default smirk has made an appearance.

Yikes, the barbs are out. I can tell by Rose's tone.

"Thank you. That's so sweet. It is my first reunion with the family, and I'm having such a blast. Alex's family is wonderful. Especially his grandmother, whom I've met before. She's the real deal, don't you think?" Evie's eyes glitter, and I swear she's subtly needling Rose for sport. "I think she and Alex have so much in common, personality-wise."

"Yes, she sure is something else." Rose smiles tightly and rubs the swell of her stomach.

"When are you due? Congratulations!" Evie says, sounding a touch more genuine.

Rose says something that I don't hear, because I've turned to Beau. "Seriously, man, I wouldn't approach Gram this weekend. It's tacky to talk about succession plans here."

Beau lifts the corner of his smarmy mouth. It's hilarious how he and Rose have started to look alike. "That's the difference between me and you, Alex. I'm a doer. A visionary. I choose to seize the moment, while you're content with tradition."

"I wish you'd choose to get me a ginger ale, Beaumont," Rose says, making a pouty face. There was a time when I'd jump to do her bidding when she made a face like that. Now I can see it for what it is: manipulation, laziness, a way to control.

"Of course, sweetheart. Let's go over to the bartender and I'll hook you up. Evie, Alex, see you around."

"Toodle-oo," Rose says, and they strut off. I can't help but notice that Gram's at the bar, which is set up under a canopy.

"Mercenary little snake," I mutter.

Evie and I walk off the porch in the opposite direction.

"So that was Rose," she says in a clipped tone.

"Yep. What did you think?"

Evie gives a small shrug. "She's pretty."

"I guess."

"You guess? You're not attracted to her anymore? I'm asking not out of jealousy, but curiosity." She tilts her head to the right and stares at me like she looked at those belugas the other week.

"No. It's weird. I feel nothing for her. We were way too young to make that kind of commitment. It's so obvious now, and even though everything happened like it did, I don't regret the outcome. I can't imagine being married to her."

Odd, but I've never said that out loud to anyone other than Travis. I wrap my arm around Evie's waist and kiss her temple. "I see Dante's at the grill. He makes a real mean hamburger. You want to eat one with me?"

"Sure do, babe." The sun hits her eyes and my entire body is bathed in warmth.

To the people at the party, my happiness must have appeared genuine as we walked across the lawn. Because it was.

◊

EVIE

Alex and I are sitting in the library, listening to one of his uncles tell a story about some politician. It's kind of funny how Alex's family constantly discusses status, power, and wealth, whereas my family—well, what was my family, plus a few relatives in Florida—discussed normal stuff. You know, football, the weather, food, whether dogs or cats make better pets. Light stuff. Conversation that doesn't go nuclear within five minutes.

Not the Jenkins clan. They go full-on, in whatever they discuss, and things get more heated with the addition of alcohol. I'd initially thought them genteel and polite, but there's already been one shouting match between two cousins who backed two different candidates for governor.

During a lull in the conversation, I lean into Alex and breathe in his delicious smell. "I'm going to the bathroom and to freshen up my drink. Want another?" I point at his beer.

He kisses my temple. "Sure, babe. I'd like that."

I slip out of the room and into the bathroom, where I spend a solid five minutes sitting on the edge of the gleaming claw-foot tub, breathing deep. This day has been super stressful, but I feel like I've done well. I've even made Alex's parents laugh a few times, and talked to his sister for a long while about women in racing. That was interesting.

Somehow I expected to be more on guard when it came to Rose and Beau, but honestly? They're easy to ignore. Rose seems to be like one of those people in college who was like a butterfly, flitting from sorority to football game to the hottest parties in campus. That kind of woman wasn't in my circle—no judgment—so I didn't pay any mind to Rose. She was like her name, pretty, decorative, but I'm sure thorny if I crossed her. Best to stay out of her way.

After washing up and putting on a new layer of lip gloss, I make my way into the kitchen, expecting to see the hired help. Instead, I'm greeted by none other than Rose and Alex's mom.

They look incredibly chummy, laughing and drinking sodas

like old friends. Which seems odd to me, but I guess it's one more quirk of the Jenkins family.

"Hey, there," I say in a warm voice.

"Oh, Evie! We were talking about you," Mrs. Jenkins says, waving her wineglass. Rose snickers. I paste on the expression I use while working at Chili's, but I'm not getting the best feeling about this.

"I came in to grab Alex a beer. And I'm looking for a water."

Mrs. Jenkins crosses the spacious kitchen and pulls open a fridge. While she's grabbing a beer, Rose stares at me with a smirk.

"So obedient. Just how he likes them," she murmurs.

I keep my face in place, but my breathing turns shallow like it always does when I'm nervous. Why would she say such a thing? Alex has never struck me as someone who wants an obedient woman around.

"Here you go, dear." Mrs. Jenkins hands me a beer and a bottle of water. "I was saying how gorgeous you are. How happy I am that Alex finally found someone he cares about. After that whole situation with Rose, well, he broke a lot of hearts that day, including Rose's and especially mine. But Rose here has moved on and found herself a wonderful husband."

I think Rose found her wonderful husband in the pool house, I wanted to say. Lord. I knew Alex had saved his family—and Rose—from the humiliation of a scandal, but holy smokes. This level of drama on the part of his mother seemed excessive. "Hmm," I say noncommittally.

"Well, I'm glad Alex is settling down," his mother says.

Rose looks like she's holding in the funniest joke. "I am too."

Mrs. Jenkins chimes in. "We wondered where you two really met. Was it online? Or through, ah, an agency?"

I frown. "We met at the office. I recently finished my internship in the marketing department."

"Sure you did," Rose whispers, raising her eyebrows as she takes a drink.

My internal gauge for uncomfortable situations tips into the red zone. I need to get out of here. "Thanks! See you out there."

Mrs. Jenkins rubs my back. "I'll join you in the library soon."

Rose doesn't say another word. Doesn't even bother to say goodbye. Maybe it's because she's trying to play some weird mind game, to or show me that she's connected to this family in ways I'll never be. Or perhaps to her, I'm that insignificant. And what was that about Alex and I meeting through an agency? It dawns on me that they might think I'm an escort, which is so ridiculous it's hilarious.

Whatever it is, I don't care. I've faced far worse than her, or than the barbs directed my way today. That knowledge is like a little flame inside me, warming me so I can hold my head high and walk out of this kitchen with a smile even though my heart is heavy with shame.

CHAPTER THIRTY

ALEX

Every time I catch Evie's eye from across the room, or when I walk up to her and plant a kiss on her temple, a thought goes through my mind:

Why can't this be real?

I mean, maybe not the engagement. She's too young for that, and I'm not sure if I'm ready for that level of commitment. But I'm comfortable with her. Happy in her presence. We're beyond physically compatible. Sure, she's a virgin, and is still hesitant about some things. But so deliciously eager to learn. I can't think about it too hard while around my family because it's distracting.

Last night was the most erotic night I've spent in . . . I don't know how long. I'm not that experienced with women, but being with Evie was incredible.

Plus, I can be myself around Evie, say stupid shit, make her laugh. I can be my geeky self with her.

Yeah, maybe we should continue this. Try it out. Would that be weird, me giving her money while we date? I mull this over throughout the day as my relatives drone on about horse farms or their second homes on the coast or whatever. Unlike with other people, I don't feel the need to talk about that crap. My career and my past as a motorcycle racer seem inconsequential to Evie.

She seems a little uncomfortable with wealth, and occasionally I notice her looking around, taking in the details of my parents' lavish, historic mansion, or the gaudy gold-and-diamond neck-laces on my elderly aunts. I've yet to ask her what she thinks of all this, and frankly, I'm a little scared to hear her assessment. My family can be a bit snobby when it comes right down to it, and I've never noticed it as much as this weekend, since I'm trying to experience things through Evie's eyes.

Take right now, for example. It's been a long day of socializ-ing and we're in the garden courtyard, having a nightcap with my cousins and Gram. Rose and Beau are still here somewhere. When they first got together, I would've been drunk and sullen by this point in the night.

Tonight, I barely remember that Rose and Beau are even here. They've mostly steered clear of me. Beau has flitted around Gram like a moth all day. Surprised he's not out here now, in fact.

I keep trying to wrap things up so Evie and I can get upstairs. My need for her has been on a low boil all day and now that we're under the light of the moon, her skin looks so fucking beautiful that I can't wait to get her naked. It's going to be difficult to make love to her gently because I feel like a Neanderthal of need.

I can tell Evie's exhausted—who wouldn't be, after listening to my family all day—but she's being attentive as all hell while listening to Gram's story about when she met my grandfather. We're sitting next to each other on a rattan love seat, while Gram is holding court in a comfy matching chair in front of a fire pit.

I've heard this one a million times before. Gram's talking about how she was a from a good southern family and a debutante, and how my grandfather was from a more unusual southern family—a poorer one, with ties to Union soldiers in the Civil War. To hear Gram tell it, their love story was like something out of *West Side Story* or *Romeo and Juliet* or some shit. How her family didn't want her to marry into the Jenkins family, who were like the black sheep of Savannah.

"And you know what I said?" Gram asks triumphantly, taking a dramatic sip of her bourbon.

Beau slithers up and takes a seat next to Gram. Of course. *There he is.* "What?" he asks, pretending to be interested.

Evie's wide-eyed, and I can tell she's enthralled. I can practically recite what Gram's going to say next, and squeeze Evie's hand.

"I told my father to go to hell, I was going to marry for love and not money. And look where we are now. My husband made it all on his own. Well, and I helped. A lot." She sweeps a gnarled hand around the courtyard.

"Of course you did. I wish I had your kind of courage," Evie murmurs.

Gram pauses. "Young lady, I detect more courage in your little finger than all of these people have in their entire bodies."

Evie's obviously taken aback that Gram would say such a thing out loud. Beau and my other cousins titter and roll their eyes. Gram's well-known for getting a bit tipsy at these things and making wacky declarations. Still, I'm glad she adores Evie, and I know her words are genuine—and true.

"Well." I lean forward. "It's going to be a long day tomorrow. Gram, isn't it time we get some rest?"

"Oh, hell, Alex. Say the word. You want to take your girl upstairs. I know your mother put you two in the same room to spite me. Well, I don't care. I'm not a prude. Or if you all want to drink bourbon and smoke your marijuana, I'll make myself scarce." She flicks her hand at the door and I crack up.

"Gram, we won't smoke pot unless you agree to do it with us."

Gram giggles and swats the air in my direction. "Oh, you."

There's a beautiful smile on Evie's face. I stand up and stretch, letting out an audible yawn. So much for Gram being old-fashioned.

"I probably should head to bed," Gram sighs dramatically. "Youth is wasted on the young."

Beau stands. "Er, Rose and I need to be getting to the bed-and-breakfast. I'm going to find her now. Last I saw her she was in the kitchen with your mom, Alex. See y'all tomorrow."

He wanders into the house while I rub Evie's shoulder.

Evie stands and goes to Gram. "I've had a wonderful time talking with you today. I'm glad we've gotten to know each other."

Gram sets down her drink and offers her hand. Evie clasps it gently, then leans down to give Gram a kiss on the cheek. To my surprise, Gram kisses her back.

Gram is not the kissing-strangers type of lady. She wags her weathered index finger in Evie's direction. "You're the best thing that's happened to my grandson. Don't let anyone try to tell you otherwise. Good night, dear."

CRASH

◊

EVIE

Alex shuts the bedroom door softly. For some reason, being alone with him seems awkward. My feet are glued to the floor. I look around as if I've never been here. There's a paper bag on the nightstand that wasn't here this morning, and I know what's inside.

"Hey." He rubs his hands up and down my bare arms, and I shiver. "You seem nervous. Don't be. We don't have to do it tonight if you aren't ready."

The thing is, I am ready. It's probably a terrible idea because I know my heart will be shattered eventually, but I want him. I'm anxious because of the impending heartache, and because of the stress of the day, of having to smile and nod with a few dozen of his relatives.

My virginity is an afterthought.

My eyes sweep down his face and body, every angle and muscle. His deep-blue eyes and his sensual mouth. His broad shoulders barely contained in a white linen shirt. His near-black hair, and the matching dark brows. I'd waited to lose my virginity because I'd been busy with death and life, not because I was holding out for someone perfect.

But somehow, I'd found him. Even though this perfect man is only mine for the weekend. I gently take his face in my hands and kiss him. With a possessive sweep of his arm around my waist, he drags me toward him, kissing me harder. We walk to the bed, still kissing, and when we're at the edge of the mattress, his mouth hovers over mine.

"I'll be gentle. I promise. If it hurts, tell me."

I begin to unbutton his shirt. "That's . . . quite kind. Considering you're more experienced and all."

He stills and captures my hand that's on a button. *Uh-oh.* I think I've said something wrong because he's frowning.

"Evie. I'm not that experienced. And whatever I've done in the past doesn't matter now. Doesn't have any impact on what's going on in this room, between the two of us. And I'd never want to hurt you physically. In any way."

I shrug. "I'm sure you're used to women who—"

"Stop it." His voice is a little too rough. "Don't ever compare yourself to anyone."

He pauses.

"I want to share this with you. Enjoy every kiss and every thrust and every second with you. I haven't felt like this since . . ." His voice fades.

"Since?" I whisper, as I finish unbuttoning his shirt. His bare chest is too tempting, and I run my hands over his muscles.

"Since never," he says, pushing me back onto the bed.

Since never? What's that supposed to mean?

My thoughts are wiped from my brain because I'm surrounded by his smell, his touch, his bites on my flesh. He kisses me so deep that I forget whose air I'm breathing, or why I even need air. It doesn't take long for both to us to get naked—I don't even mind that the light is on, and I don't try to hide the fact that I'm staring at his huge erection—and Alex parts my thighs with his hands.

"Don't you want the condom first?" I ask, confused.

"No. I want to lick you until you come first. I want you wetter than the ocean and nice and relaxed. *Then* I'm going to be inside you."

"You're so dirty and I love it." He's between my legs, licking and touching, and I gasp at the sensation.

"You're so wet and I love it."

All the day's doubts vanish into the humid night air.

Everything seems to happen quickly, too quickly to process. We're in a frenzy of absolute need, and he's bringing me so close to release with his mouth and fingers. Over and over, until I'm on the brink.

And he keeps me on the edge by toying with me, by changing his rhythm, by looking up at me with those eyes and saying dirty, filthy things. I can barely see straight, and can't hold out any longer. My orgasm comes fast and hard, and I cry out a little louder than I intended while pulling on his hair.

"Sorry, I don't want your whole family to hear," I whisper, totally embarrassed. I try to roll onto my side, but he flips me onto my back again.

"I don't care," he growls, moving up my body, sucking my nipples on the way to my mouth. "I love it when you're loud. I couldn't care less who hears."

"I love what you do to me. How greedy you are with my body. But maybe your family doesn't need to know."

"Baby, if you think I'm greedy now . . ." He chuckles. "Just wait."

He sits up on his heels and leans over, grabbing for the bag on the nightstand. It takes him a few seconds to open the box and the foil packet, and I watch, fascinated, as he holds himself while he rolls on the condom.

"You like that," he murmurs. "You like watching me."

I grin bashfully. "Maybe."

He leans down to kiss me. "I'm going to be on top, okay?"

I nod. It would be awkward for me to take charge for my first time. But perhaps later . . .

"Open your legs wide. Wrap them around my hips." His voice is gentle, far softer than when he was talking dirty while licking me.

When I spread for him, I feel a jolt of nerves. *This is really happening.* His arms are close to my body, and he's staring intently into my eyes. I reach up and trace his lips. He kisses my finger.

"You know you might not orgasm with penetration, right?"

I nod.

"And you know that if you don't, I'll make sure you do afterward?"

I nod again. We'd talked about this last night.

"Are you ready?"

"Yes, Alex."

"I like to hear you say my name."

I feel his tip between my legs. A slow push of his hips. A hot, quick pain makes me suck in a breath and squeeze my eyes shut.

"Alex," I breathe.

"You okay?"

"Yes."

He's not moving anymore, and despite the fullness, I get the feeling he's not all the way in. I open my eyes to find Alex breathing hard.

"I'm okay, really," I whisper.

We stare at each other, and it's both hot and awkward. I giggle, and he laughs a little while rubbing his nose against mine. Then things turn serious.

He gives a little nod and moves his hips into me. "There," he says. "How does that feel? I'm all the way inside."

"Ohhh. Whoa. Alex." I grip his arms. It's like nothing I've ever experienced. Intense. Intimate. Like we're joined together. Cliché, I know. And the fact that he's talking about it in a low voice is making me even wetter than I was before.

He slides out slowly and groans. "Evie, you feel incredible."

"I do?"

He slides in and smiles wickedly. "Oh, yes. You don't even know."

There's another spear of pain, this one duller, and I force my muscles to relax. How can something feel painful and amazing at the same time?

He's slowly thrusting in and out, and I'm glad I'm so wet. Otherwise this would be unpleasant. It's a different sensation than when he was bringing me to orgasm with his fingers or tongue. Not worse, not better, different. More carnal and raw. I probably won't orgasm like this, not yet, not my first time. But that's okay, because this is incredible in a whole other way.

His mouth is next to my ear, his body heavy atop mine, his breath coming in thick gasps.

"Evie," he rasps. "I'm going to come. You're so fucking tight and you feel so good."

He whispers my name again and the sound is so desperate. Like he's coming undone because of me. I wrap my arms around his back, digging my nails into his skin. Maybe I'm too rough because he props himself on his hands so he's looking down at me while he slides in and out of me, faster now.

Oh my God. I am having sex. With a gorgeous man. Who looks savage with his unruly dark hair and wild, half-lidded eyes. There's a slight snarl on his lips, like he's going to lose control any second. I shut my eyes because it's too much. Too intense.

"Look at me," he whispers.

TAMARA LUSH

I do. A second later, I watch his eyes roll back in his head, his full lips part. With a strong thrust into my core that makes me whimper, he moans, unable to hold on any longer. His arm muscles strain; his ab muscles tense. Now I'm glad the light's on, because he's incredible to watch. Erotic, sure. But also vulnerable. Which inspires something protective in me.

I feel him pulse inside of me, and I don't think I've ever seen anything so captivatingly masculine. Still panting, he dips his head to kiss me. I feel the sweat and heat radiating from his body.

"Was that okay?" he murmurs against my lips.

If by okay, he means, *Did that make you fall fully and uncontrollably in love with me*, then yes.

"It was more than okay." I smile and kiss him again.

◊

Over the next few hours, we do it twice more. I don't orgasm either time, but he makes up for it with his fingers and tongue. I'm officially addicted to the way he touches me.

By his third orgasm—and my fifth, I think—I'm an exhausted, quivering mass of flesh. We're both sticky and sweaty. Somehow most of the bedding's ended up on the floor, and we haul it back onto the bed.

"Sleep. I need sleep." I laugh, giddy from being overtired and sex-sated.

He reaches to turn out the lamp. "You and me both, babe."

A cozy silence fills the room, and I'm almost asleep when he says, "You did so well today with my family. With Rose and Beau. I'm in awe. You showed no fear."

"Mmm," I exhale, snuggling into his side. The last thing I want to think about after this amazing night is Rose and Beau. Especially the way she was so dismissive in the kitchen. But it's easy to forget about all that, now that I'm in Alex's arms.

"It's so funny, I wondered if you'd be able to handle my family. A couple of times I wasn't so sure, since you're afraid of other things. Like elevators. And cars. I guess that's your past, though, and it's totally understandable. Aww, hell. I'm babbling. Sorry. I'll let you sleep."

"I am afraid because of the past. It's true. And you know, you are too." My voice is gravelly. Somewhere there's an important message in this conversation, but my brain and body are too tired to process everything. "You've been afraid, too. Not telling your family about Rose and Beau, taking the fall for that whole situation. You did it to protect your family's reputation while ruining your own."

Now it was his turn to hum a *mmm-hmm* sound. "You're pretty smart, Evie Cooper."

He gently uses his fingers under my chin to tilt my head up. I let out a little coo. "I love how you kiss me," I murmur.

"I thought about kissing you a long time before I actually did." He's trailing his fingers up and down my bare back.

"That first kiss. It was deep. Mmm." I'm so drowsy now, especially since the room is dark.

"So deep that it was like our souls were making love even before our clothes were off."

I giggle. "I'm not sure that makes sense, but I love that."

"I'm not sure we make sense, but I love it."

Did he say that, or did I dream it? I drift off, my mind a jumble of thoughts and emotions that dissipate like fog over the beach.

◊

I'm jarred out of a heavy sleep by a pounding on the door.

"Alex? Alex?" It's a masculine voice. *Mr. Jenkins?* I struggle to open my eyes as Alex's dad says a few more words that are muffled by my sleepy brain and the door. Alex is next to me, snoring. We're still tangled together, naked, covered only by a white sheet.

I shake Alex's shoulder. "It's your dad. He's knocking. It's sounds urgent."

"Hunh?" He jerks his head and opens his eyes, lifting his head. "Dad? Is that you? What's up?"

"Alex, you'd better get out here. It's Gram. We found her . . . well, come out here and we'll tell you."

CHAPTER THIRTY-ONE

EVIE

As the casket is lowered into the earth, Alex draws me a little closer. I feel him trembling, and I lean into him slightly, wanting to reassure him with my presence.

He turns his head toward my ear. "She adored you," he murmurs.

I smile weakly. "She loved you," I respond.

He inhales a giant breath and glances at the Spanish moss–covered oaks, the beautifully tragic marble headstones in the shapes of angels, the cheery purple azaleas that line the walkways of Bonaventure Cemetery. It's the best-known burial ground in Savannah, and the most beautiful, especially this morning, when it's not yet too humid and the sun filters through the trees. Gram is buried next to her husband, at the foot of an imposing and intricately carved marble arch. Even in death, she's dramatic.

Alex's eyes are flitting everywhere but the grave, and I know exactly how he's feeling. Vulnerable and anxious. Like the world has tilted off its axis and will never right itself.

It's been an absolutely awful week. Ever since Gram—even I call her Gram in my mind now, which is odd, since I never knew my own grandparents, and barely knew Alex's grandmother—was found dead, it's been a whirlwind of grief and the gruesome tedium of death. Arrangements, wakes, food for the wakes, the scheduling of plans and airport pickups, hugs and sympathetic glances. Alex has taken care of most of the preparations, and I have to say, he's been a rock for his parents and sister.

The reunion was canceled, and instead of returning to Atlanta as planned on Monday morning, we've stayed here. I even did my phone interview for the aquarium—I'd considered canceling, but Alex encouraged me, and set me up in the quiet library for the half-hour call. It went well, I thought.

Being around grieving people has brought up my own traumatic memories of my parents, but oddly, I've surprised myself and summoned an inner strength. I'd even like to think I've helped Alex and his family by listening to their stories, and holding their hands when they've been sad.

Doctors said Gram died in her sleep of a heart attack.

For the first time since we've arrived in Savannah, I realize what Alex means about his family being a little eccentric. Their grieving is more like a party. Instead of somber reflection, everyone's drinking and hanging out, much like they were for the reunion. I haven't raised my observations with Alex because he's the only one who seems shaken. Well, his sister, too. She's been visibly upset, but has made herself scarce, choosing to spend much of the past week in a nearby beach rental with her husband and daughter.

Alex hasn't cried, though, and that worries me.

"As we hold Mrs. Jenkins in our hearts and memories from this day forward, we commit ourselves to carrying her with us always. We honor her memory by the following promises," the pastor says in a loud, clear voice. "To be gentle and kind. With a caring heart and honest interaction. With a soft voice and an even softer heart."

Someone in the crowd snorts softly, and a few others titter and comment how nothing about Gram was soft. Good lord. I glance around, but I appear to be the only one who thinks it's odd that people would act like this at a funeral. Rich people, to boot. Then again, Gram was pretty unconventional herself, and from the little I know about her, I'm not sure gentle or soft were adjectives she'd have chosen for herself.

"I ask all who wish, to now come forward and take this soil in your hand and bless Eleanor Dorothy's final resting place here beside her husband. If you have any final words for her, please feel free to share them from your heart and soul. I only ask you to be mindful of the heat and comfort of the others here with us."

Alex and his sister exchange uneasy glances, and they watch as their red-eyed father scoops dirt into his hand and tosses it on the casket. He's followed by Savannah, and then she nods at Alex.

"Come," he murmurs, and propels me toward the grave.

I take a deep breath. This isn't difficult because of Alex's pain. It's forcing me to remember when Sabrina and I buried our parents. But for Alex, I'm holding those emotions inside. The last thing he needs is me weeping at every turn. Although when I return to Atlanta, I'm planning on sitting in the bathtub and crying for a solid hour.

We take a few steps to the mound of dirt and Alex scoops a big handful. Looking mournful, he turns his palm slowly and watches the dirt fall. I follow suit, but much quicker, and then we move back from the open grave. I feel like a fraud. Everyone here believes I'm practically part of the family. It was fine and fun for a family reunion. For a funeral, it seems downright immoral.

My stomach tightens uncomfortably. I'm in a new black dress, and I'm wearing shapewear underneath that's making me feel and look like an angry, trussed ham.

It's all incredibly awkward. I'm a virtual stranger to Alex, and yet, because his entire family thinks we're engaged, it's not like I can waltz back to Atlanta. *See you! Bye! Good luck with everything and thanks for the cash!*

No. A real fiancé would stay. Would want to stay.

And so I've stayed.

Mostly I've remained quiet, listening to Alex and his family tell stories about Gram. I've come to think of myself as Alex's security blanket. He seems to need me near at all times, and won't stop holding my hand. I'm glad I'm here for him because he seems so lonely, so set apart from his family. While the rest of them are boisterous, he's turned strangely silent.

Maybe he's considering what Gram's death means for the business. I'm trying not to think about what that means for us. I'm no longer needed, of course. But that's incidental right now, because he's grieving. I can't bombard him with questions—not yet.

In the back of the limo, he wraps his arms around me and buries his face in my hair.

I hold him until we arrive at his parents' house. He sits up and sighs.

"We have to get through the wake today." His voice is gravelly from all the talking—he gave the eulogy for his grandmother at the church earlier.

"You're doing so good," I murmur, placing my hand on his cheek.

"I couldn't have done any of this without you. You and Travis. I'm glad he's here. Sorry you had to meet my best friend under these circumstances." Travis arrived two days ago, and is staying at the Jenkins family home in a room down the hall from us. He's a gem of a human who looks like a cross between a country singer and a football quarterback. He's also someone who truly cares for Alex. I could tell by the long embrace he'd given Alex when he first arrived.

"C'mon. Let's get inside, babe."

He's been saying little endearments like that all week, and I don't know what to think. Maybe because I'm also tired from all the residual grief in the air. I tell Alex that I'm going upstairs to change shoes, and he nods, wandering off to join his dad in the living room.

I haul myself upstairs and quickly change shoes. Something about Alex's tone makes me not want to leave his side. As I'm coming out the door to our room, I almost run smack into . . . Rose?

"Oh! Hey!" I can't hide my surprise. Of course, I'd seen her at the funeral and interment, but we hadn't had any significant exchanges, only a few murmured "I'm sorrys" and "Wasn't Gram an amazing woman" in the receiving line.

"I know exactly what you're up to," Rose says while leaning against the white wainscotting on the wall.

My eyes dart around. "Yeah, I was changing my shoes. Sometimes heels really pinch your toes, you know?"

"Don't be dense with me. You can't fool me, with all of your fake tears and kind condolences. Alex is paying you. The only question I have is whether you're a professional escort or whether this is some private arrangement between the two of you."

"Wh-what?" I manage to stammer.

"Don't deny it. I can tell you're not his type. So can his mother and the entire family," Rose simpers, rubbing her belly.

"This is ridiculous." I clear my throat. "And anyway, what do you care? You rejected him and screwed his cousin two nights before your wedding. What kind of a woman would do that?"

A flash of anger appears in her eyes, then she's back to her amused expression. "Is that what he told you? And you believed it? Silly girl."

She lets out a soft snort, like a haughty pony, and shakes her head while walking off. Me? I can't move. I'm tempted to go back inside the room and stay there. But I can't seem to make myself do that, either, so I slump against the door and shut my eyes, willing my heart to stop thrashing in my chest. How had she guessed?

A door in the hall opens and I peel my eyes open to see Travis, Alex's best friend, barreling out. His broad frame seems to take up the entire space.

"That little witch," he hisses.

"Huh?" My hand finds the doorknob to the room. I'm definitely ready to retreat. Maybe feign PMS and hide under the covers for a while.

"Rose. I heard your entire conversation. She claimed Alex was lying about what she did before their wedding. She's the liar. She's a snake. Alex came to me an hour after he walked in on them. He was devastated. Trust me. She's not telling the truth."

I open my mouth, but words don't come out.

"Look, I know his family's a lot to handle. But he likes you. Really likes you. He told me that, and he doesn't ever get involved with women. Don't forget that, okay? Stay strong, not only for him, but for you. You've got to be mentally tough to run with this crowd." Travis, who is big and looks like something out of central casting for apple pie, hot dogs, and pickup trucks, furrows his tawny brows in concern.

"Thanks," I mutter. "I-I'll keep that in mind."

◊
ALEX

Our family's lawyer downs a long sip of his Coca-Cola.

"This is how Miss Eleanor wanted me to tell you. It's spelled out in her will, which she updated the Thursday before she passed. She wanted me to inform the four of you of her intentions prior to the reading of the will."

It's been a long and difficult day, and now it's almost eleven. Evie's upstairs because my parents didn't want her or my sister's husband to be part of this conversation. It's the longest I've been away from Evie all week, and I feel her absence acutely. I've relied on her this week probably more than I should, but she's been so damned wonderful and sweet.

"Couldn't we have waited to discuss this?" I'm furious that my parents and the lawyer want to talk about the company's future with my sister and me right now, of all times. "Gram was buried this morning, for God's sake."

"You're going back to Atlanta tomorrow, and we're going to

need to convene the board. The will won't be read until next week. She wanted you to be CEO, Alex, and for your dad to be chairperson." The lawyer, whom I've known since I was a child, is at least as old as my dad, if the gray hair against his dark skin is any indication.

"Is it crucial we do this now?" my sister says. She's also annoyed with this.

It's as if we're carrying on with business as usual.

"You should be happy about this, son," Dad says.

"I . . ." My voice trails off and I'm suddenly lost in thought.

"Alex?" Mom asks.

I shake my head. "Sorry. I'm wiped out. Happy? That I was Gram's choice all along? Yeah, I guess I'm happy about that. I'd rather have her alive."

"We all would," Dad sighs. "I'll convene a board meeting tomorrow morning, and we'll make the announcement. This will only help when we go public."

"She wanted you to be in charge all along, Alex," my sister chimes in.

"She did," the lawyer says. "She told me herself on Thursday when she came to sign the papers. Said you'd really grown into the position, and that you had changed a lot over the years. Also mentioned that fiancé of yours. Mrs. Jenkins said you have a future with her."

Mom and Dad have triumphant looks on their faces, and something about that makes me uncomfortable. I want space to grieve, not talk business. But the fact that Gram could see the potential in Evie, well, that makes a lump lodge in my throat. Gram knew Evie was good for me even before I did.

"I have a trip to Malaysia scheduled later in the week." Putting on a suit, flying around the globe, talking business—the thought of those things leaves me cold. What I really want is to go home to Atlanta with Evie and lie in bed in my condo and watch movies. Something to take my mind off the past several days.

"This will all be pretty routine," Dad says. "Beau doesn't have a leg to stand on now."

"Feels like a hollow victory." I reach out and squeeze Dad's shoulder, and he folds me into a hug. "I'm headed upstairs."

After I say good night to my family, I find Evie in bed, reading. She's using one of those little book lights, so the room is dark except for the focused beam of illumination.

"Hey," she says softly, shutting her book. The little light remains on.

Jesus, she looks so pretty right now, it makes my heart ache. Her dark hair is brushing her collarbone and I want my mouth there.

I crawl onto the bed and take the book from her, snapping off the light.

"How are you doing?" she murmurs. "How did the talk with the lawyer go?"

Kneeling at her side, I stroke her hair.

"The position. It's mine. The lawyer said Gram had that in her will all along." My words come out slow, the tone hollow.

Evie lets out a little gasp. "The CEO job?"

I nod, feeling raw and stunned.

"Oh, sweetie," she whispers.

"It doesn't feel right to be happy about this." I choke back tears.

"It's okay to feel whatever you want to feel."

What should I say? That being appointed CEO doesn't seem to matter as much now? That something about death and cemeteries makes me realize how fragile life is? That it makes me understand what I've been missing all these years?

I pull her down on the bed with me and kiss her hard. We haven't had sex since that first night, for obvious reasons. Tonight feels different. She's been by my side all week, patient and loving. Selfless, even though I know this must have been difficult for her because of her parents. Because she came here to pretend, and things got terribly real.

"Evie," I whisper.

She cups my face in her hands, and a pleasurable shiver goes through me. "Alex?"

"I need you. Now."

All week, my heart's been clenched like a fist in the center of my chest. As I slowly slide Evie's shirt over her head and kiss her soft skin, as I close my lips around her nipple, the fist unclenches. When I trail my tongue down her stomach and peel off her panties, my shoulders relax. As I taste her, as she tugs at my hair, I feel the heaviness lifting from my chest.

I want to lose myself in her, and that's exactly what I intend to do for the rest of the night.

CHAPTER THIRTY-TWO

EVIE

I won't tell Alex this, but I'm glad we're leaving for Atlanta today. It feels like we've been away for years. Grabbing my purse, I take a glance around this beautiful room for the last time. I'll always remember this bed, the way the morning light filters through the curtains, the paintings of flowers.

Alex is downstairs, loading our luggage into the SUV, and I'm supposed to meet him in the kitchen to say goodbye to his parents and sister; it's back to reality. I'm hoping I can explain my feelings to him soon. I won't tell him I love him, of course. That'd be too intense.

It's probably a good idea to wait a week or two—to let him take his first business trip after Gram's death and to get settled back into real life. I remember when my parents died, those two weeks after the funeral were the most difficult. It was like sleepwalking through life, and I'd been unable to make any decisions. I can't imagine Alex having to do business in the state he's in.

I make my way down the steps, past Alex's baby pictures on the wall, past the prom photos and the ones of him standing proudly at the side of his motorcycle.

On the first floor, I round the corner into the small family room and bound into the foyer. Alex and his parents are there. To my dismay, so are Beau and Rose. They look like they stepped out of the pages of *Southern Living*. I didn't realize that anyone under eighty actually wore seersucker, but here we are. Beau is in a blue seersucker suit and Rose is wearing a pink seersucker dress and a wide-brimmed straw hat.

"Good morning, everyone," I burble. "Rose, I love your hat."

"Thank you. We're going antiquing today. That's where we spend a lot of money on old treasures. You probably have never done that." She sneers and I look around, horrified, hoping someone will step in.

"Rose, please," Alex says, his voice strained.

Well, this family goodbye isn't going as planned.

Mrs. Jenkins looks me over, and it's clear that I've interrupted something.

"Alex, come clean. Evie's not really your fiancé. Puh-lease."

"Mother." Alex's deep voice rumbles through my body.

What. The. Hell.

I freeze. Flatten my body against the wall. All eyes turn to me. I gape at them, mortified that they're talking about me.

"Oh, let's get this out in the open." Mrs. Jenkins waves her hand. "I had a long discussion with Rose, and I know my son paid you to make him look more stable. That's despicable."

"Son, did you really do that?" Mr. Jenkins holds a coffee cup in midair, looking about as perturbed as he would if his golf game were canceled.

"Rose, how do you know this?" Alex's voice is tinged with anger.

Beau guffaws. "It came from me. I heard everything, DJ. Your entire conversation in the elevator was recorded."

"What?" Alex sounds incredulous.

Oh, shit.

"The elevator. When it malfunctioned the other week. Everything was recorded for safety reasons. There's a speaker and a microphone there, and a video camera. You didn't know? I asked security for a copy of the recording, and they gladly gave it to me. I figured I'd get a good laugh out of it, maybe hear you panic like a little bitch, but I got so much more."

"You asshole." I clap my hand over my mouth, but can't muster any guilty feelings. Oh, well. My moments with this family are numbered. I guess I can say whatever I want.

Everyone ignores me.

"I know you did that for the benefit of Gram, Alex. You'd never marry a waif like that," Mrs. Jenkins says.

I stop breathing when I hear Alex groan. Mrs. Jenkins doesn't like me. Probably never liked me. They're discussing me as if I don't exist when I'm standing feet from them.

"And what if I did?" Alex's nostrils flare.

What? What if he did what? What does he mean by *that*?

"I'm standing right here, you know." My tone is sharp.

"This doesn't concern you, my dear," his mother says in a dismissive tone.

"Excuse me?" I say sharply.

"You're going to have to let her down gently, Alex. This girl adores you."

Stick up for me, dammit. I squeeze my eyes shut, not wanting to hear Alex's response. But needing to, so I can face the horrible reality of our relationship.

Alex's loud, impatient sigh echoes through the kitchen. "You seemed to like Evie. You and Gram showed her my baby photos, for Christ's sake. I don't understand you at all. You're being duplicitous, and you know how I hate that."

"She's a wonderful girl, Alex. And yes, Gram did like her. She told me so, she told everyone. But you know Gram and her weird taste. Evie's not for you. She's not one of us."

The emphasis on *us* is now branded on my soul. I am an Other. Because I wasn't a debutante. Because I'm not from a wealthy society family. Because of a thousand imperceptible reasons, none of which I can change. My throat thickens.

"Why don't you let me live my life, Mother, and stay the hell out of my business? Out of *our* business!" Alex's voice has turned cross and haughty, like it does when he's talking about work on the phone.

"You know I was hoping to set you up with Bree, the girl from the tennis club. She's so lovely, and her parents are well-connected. No offense, Evie. This is something I thought of before he, ah, met you. I want him to stop sleeping around and settle down with someone appropriate."

I let out a snort as all my warm feelings toward Alex's mom evaporate.

I cannot believe this is all happening *right in front of me.* My stomach folds, origami-style, into a tight package. Of course.

Lovely Bree. She's probably working at a meaningful job, or maybe volunteering, since she's got family money and no student loans. I can imagine what she looks like. Tall. Willowy. Honey-colored hair. I look down at my feet. My toenail polish, once perfectly shiny and pink as a spring tulip, is chipped on one toe. Bree never has chipped toenail polish.

Alex does appear furious, to his credit. "I don't have time for this. We're going back to Atlanta. I've got a ton of things to do, and I can't stand here and subject someone I care about to this abuse. Evie, let's go."

As he takes my arm and propels me to the front door, I wriggle out of his grip.

"Hold on a minute." I turn and face his parents, Beau, and Rose. I'm so angry my vision seems sharper, brighter. I am done with these people. "Since we're spilling secrets, here's one. Alex called off the wedding with Rose because he caught Rose and Beau screwing two nights before the ceremony, in the pool house." I point dramatically in the direction of the backyard.

Everyone gasps, an oddly thrilling sound. Good. I shocked all these jerks. His mother grips the side of the counter.

"You liar," she cries.

"Ask Travis. He knows the truth. He's known all along."

Alex is staring at me with wide eyes. Beau is as pale as the mayonnaise in the fruit salad in the bowl next to him. Mr. Jenkins clears his throat a few times. Rose shoots me a sour look.

"You're so low-class," she mutters.

I shoot her a simpering look. "And Alex? He took the blame. He said the breakup was because he wanted to play the field, that he wasn't ready to get married. That wasn't true at all. He's never played the field. Hell, the other night, he didn't even have condoms with him because he hadn't had sex in so long. He did all of this so your precious little family wouldn't be scandalized. So, take your secrets and shove them up your tight, society asses."

I'm acutely aware that this will end my relationship with Alex, but it's so satisfying to stun these terrible people into submission. It also feels damn good to let go and tell people what I really think. Freeing. Authentic. Maybe I should try this more often.

I whirl and stomp out the door, not caring if Alex is following or not.

CHAPTER THIRTY-THREE

ALEX

We're a half hour outside of Savannah before I finally break the tense silence in the SUV. I still can't believe she said that stuff about the condoms. *Damn.*

"I'm sorry about my parents." I reach for Evie's hand, bring it to my mouth, and kiss the backs of her slender fingers.

"It's no big deal." She lifts a shoulder into a shrug. "I'm sorry about spilling your secrets. But I couldn't control my anger. They were being so awful to you, and to me. I exploded."

"Like a goddamned volcano. It was pretty incredible to watch. It rocked." I'm still shocked, to be honest. "Mom was awful. She can be like that sometimes, but at the end of the day, she's still my mother. And Jesus, Beau. I can't believe he went to the trouble of getting a recording from the elevator. I didn't know any of that was being captured. I'm sorry."

I release a long sigh and the terrible silence overtakes us for a few long moments. "I'd like to talk with you about, ah, this. Us."

She pulls her hand from my lips and wraps her arm around her midsection. "Maybe not right now, if that's okay. I'm beat. And my stomach kind of hurts. That was a lot back there."

Poor thing—she wasn't prepared for any of this. And I can't get over how fierce she was. Somehow, I'm not even angry that she revealed all of that to my family. None of it seems as important as it once did. I know one thing, though: Gram would've loved Evie's outburst.

"Understood. It was a lot to take in over the last ten days. Thank you. Thank you for being there for me. Thank you for standing up for me."

She glances at me with skittish eyes, then stares straight ahead, unblinking. "You're welcome. One question, though."

"Yeah?"

"Why didn't you tell your parents what happened with Beau and Rose? Why did you let that secret fester? Why did you allow people to think of you as a man-whore all these years?"

I snort. "I don't know. At first I was ashamed. Like I'd done something wrong to drive Rose away from me. It seemed easier to take the blame. And then it kind of snowballed. At first it was hilarious, me, a motorcycle and sci-fi geek who worked all the time, being a playboy. I rolled with it. It was stupid. I should've told them."

"I can't imagine keeping those kinds of secrets from one's family."

"Evie, not everyone has simple relationships."

"True." Her voice sounds sad, and exhausted.

I glance over at her. "Why don't you try to sleep? I promise I'll drive like a normal person."

She nods and rests her head against the passenger window, shutting her eyes. I sneak looks at her face every so often, pride swelling in me. I'm even more enamored of her today.

◊

Evie wakes up two hours later when we arrive in downtown Atlanta. She's still silent as I park and as we hike up the flights of stairs to her condo. I don't even mind that we're not taking the elevator because I'm feeling out of shape after all those days of eating and drinking.

When we get to her door, she turns to me.

"Thanks." Her expression is tight. "You don't have to come in. I know you're busy and all, and you probably want to get home. And I need a bit of space."

"Oh. Uh, yeah." I'm a little startled by her flat tone. She's exhausted, though, and it's beginning to be clear the toll my family took on her.

I rake my hand through my hair, the mountain of work at the office edging out all other thoughts. "I've got a lot going on over the next few days. I don't know if I'll be able to see you because I'll probably be in my office from about, well, now, until the time I leave. Might have to sleep there. I'm really behind. But I'll text you. Or call."

"Totally understandable." She bites her lip.

"Hey. Evie. Baby." I cup her face in my hands. "I'm sorry you had to go through all that, with my family. But thank you. You were impeccable. Amazing. Fierce. Truly."

"Well, that's why you hired me."

"I'm glad I did more than hire you." I go in for a kiss. Her lips are supple and warm. Willing. I inhale sharply. Jesus, she's so tempting. Maybe I should stay for a little while. No, there's too much to prepare for tomorrow's board meeting. "I need to go. As much as I want to do other things with you."

I pull back to gaze at her, my hands still on her face, thumbs stroking her cheekbones. I can't tell if her eyes are unusually shiny or if it's the fluorescent lighting in this hallway. This is awkward. It's a moment I didn't anticipate when we were sharing a bed in Savannah. Normally I'm smooth around women, but right now, I don't know what to say. Every word I could utter to her would scare the shit out of her, I think. I'll tell her everything I'm feeling when we're rested and not rushed.

"I'll text you, okay? And call."

She wriggles out of my hands, then nods and scratches her neck. "'Kay. Hope you get all of your work done."

I lean in for another quick kiss. Oh, I have an idea to lift her mood. "Bye. Get some rest. I'll have my assistant to set up a spa day for you, okay? You deserve some pampering."

"We'll see. I need to focus on the in-person job interview at the aquarium. It's tomorrow."

"You're going to kick ass. I know it. But you can make time for a spa afterward. It's on me. Please?"

Brushing my lips on her forehead, I try to ignore her shuddering breath. Part of me wants to insist that I stay with her, that I bring work back to her place. But she's an adult, and she's sending me all the signals that she wants me to leave. I need to respect that and not bulldoze my way into her life. She probably needs some alone time.

"Bye, Alex." She waggles her fingers at me and slides her key into the door.

"Spa day," I call out. "Make sure you go, babe. Good luck on that interview."

As I walk out and run down the stairs—Christ, it feels good to stretch my legs—I wonder if she could come to Malaysia with me. *Hmm.* But I'll be in meetings. The negotiations there are tense, and days are long. She'll want to sightsee . . . no, maybe another time. I'd rather our first trip out of the country not be tied to business.

So, I'll buy her one of those sarongs I've seen in shops over there. She'll love that. I drive away, imagining Evie's beautiful body wrapped in silky fabric.

Yeah, I've got it bad for this girl.

EVIE

I've only slept a few hours since Alex dropped me off yesterday, but I'm as wide awake as if I'd drank a gallon of espresso. Maybe because I did drink close to a gallon of espresso early this morning from that fancy coffeemaker in the condo.

I'm wearing one of my old dresses, the black sheath I'd had on when I first met Alex. It matches my mood.

Dark and determined.

I take an Uber to the aquarium and give myself a pep talk

along the way. Alex probably won't be part of my life, but my dream job could be. I need to pour all of my energy into this, and then I'll tackle the tough stuff later in the afternoon.

The interview, with a kind lady in her fifties, goes well. Better than well. Somehow I manage to turn on a sparkling expression and an excited vibe, and I can tell the interviewer is impressed with my resumé, my honors diploma, and my answers. Toward the end of the hour, I pull out the big guns—my knowledge of beluga whales—and the interviewer lights up, saying she adores them as well.

A kindred spirit.

"I am so impressed with you, Evie. You should expect to hear from us soon. Thank you for coming. I'll walk you to the exit."

I beam as we both rise to our feet. "You don't know how much it would mean for me to work here."

We stroll along the corridor, with her explaining about the newly renovated offices and where my desk would be if I were hired. Excitement surges through me. This is really happening.

We pause at the employee exit and I thank her again.

"It was lovely meeting you," the HR director says. "And please tell Alex Jenkins hello the next time you see him. He's been such an invaluable donor to the aquarium."

My face falls. At no point did I mention him during the interview, and I'd gone out of my way to talk about my internships prior to Jenkins. "Yes. I'll definitely do that."

We shake hands and she lets me out of the building. As I wait for the Uber to take me back to downtown Atlanta, anger rises in my chest.

Did Alex pull strings to get me this interview? There's only one way to find out, and I was already planning to stop by Alex's office today to tell him what's on my mind.

I know this is for the best. I have a scrap of dignity left, and I must gather it and end this situation before I'm any more damaged. All night I'd turned the pros and cons over in my mind, and now his interfering with my job prospects is the final straw.

I could continue like I hadn't told off his family. As if I didn't know what they thought of me. Eke out more time with him, bask in his affection. Have blind hope that he'd learn to care for me, that we weren't so different, that we came from the same social class.

The probability of any of that is about the same as me becoming governor of Georgia.

Even if he did care about me, would I want to deal with Mrs. Jenkins? She'd sabotage our relationship in a hot second.

The more likely scenario is this: his texts and calls will become more and more scarce; he'll throw some money my way, and figure he did a good deed by recommending me for the aquarium job; I'll see him in some local scene magazine with a beautiful woman on his arm; and then, I'll fade into obscurity. When he's older, he'll joke with his friends at the country club about how he once paid a destitute woman to pose as his fiancé.

Or, worse, he'll continue to screw me, which is probably why he was so nice when he dropped me off. He wants to leave the door open to call me at two in the morning when he's half drunk. What was that crass phrase Sabrina used one time when gushing about some celebrity?

Side piece. Or was it *side chick*?

I cringe as I climb out of the Uber in front of the Jenkins building, repeating the phrases over and over in my mind. Side piece. Side chick. Either way, it's an awful fate.

Alex should be finished with his board meeting by now.

Yesterday in the car, he said he didn't expect it to last long once his grandmother's wishes were announced.

It's easy to slip past security since I never returned my company badge. I was prepared to chat up the security guard I know and like, but there's a new guy today, so I sail on past.

I think about taking the stairs up to his office on the fifty-fifth floor. The last thing I want is to run into any of my former coworkers and endure their questions and pointed stares. I'm sure the news of our "engagement" is all over this building—and I'm certain that like Mrs. Jenkins, not one person believes it's real.

But no, I don't feel like slogging up fifty-five flights of stairs. That's ridiculous. I defiantly punch the button for the elevator and keep my eyes shut the entire way up. Thankfully, I don't see anyone I know, and I step out on the top floor.

Gathering all of my courage, I march up to his assistant, Nadine.

"Hi. I'm here to see Alex."

She greets me, the corners of her mouth curving upward. "Evie Cooper, correct?"

I nod.

She picks up the phone on her desk and punches a button. "Alex, Ms. Cooper is here to see you. Yes, Evie Cooper. Will do." Nadine nods. "You may go in. You're in luck, since the board meeting ended fifteen minutes ago."

"Thank you." I keep my voice clear and even and stride toward his office.

My heartbeat is so loud that I almost can't hear the snick of the door closing behind me. Alex is standing at the window, hands on hips, back to me. He turns, and my breath catches in my throat. With the skyline and the bright-blue Georgia sky in the background, he's like an advertisement for the Chamber of Commerce.

Power, wealth, control: they can be yours here in Atlanta . . .

Why does he have to look more delicious today than any other? He's wearing a perfectly tailored navy suit, and it makes his eyes appear all the more magnetic. The dark stubble tells me that he probably didn't get much sleep either—for different reasons, of course.

"Hey," he says in a warm voice, crossing the room. "This is a nice surprise."

He bends down to kiss me, and I turn my head away before his mouth makes contact. If I feel his lips on mine, I'll lose my courage. That aftershave he wears is seductive enough, and I feel like my plan is already faltering.

"How was the board meeting?" My words come out slow and thick, like I have peanut butter in my mouth.

"Well. Beau didn't put up a fight. Thought he would, but he knew he didn't have a leg to stand on."

"Good."

He reaches for me, attempts to draw me in for an embrace.

Hug him. Put your arms around him. Beg for his affection.

No.

"Alex." I step away so I can put a chair between us. "We need to talk. You said that yesterday, and I agree."

Like a languid, predatory panther, he rounds the desk and sits in his chair, gesturing to the seat on the other side of the desk. "What's going on? Are you okay?"

It feels like my heart is going to leap up my throat and out of my mouth. *Tell him. Don't waste his time or yours.*

I sit on the chair's edge. "I can't do this any longer."

"Do what?" His voice is low.

Oh, God, why does this have to be so hard? I don't want to utter these words out loud, but I have to, for my own sake. I need to save myself from heartbreak.

I love him and he'll never love me in return. He's genetically incapable of loving someone like me. From the slightly confused expression, I almost feel bad about telling him—after all, his grandmother did die.

"This. Us. I thought you should know before you left. I . . ." My voice falters when I see the slight frown on his face. "I think it's best if we don't see each other anymore. You're getting what you wanted out of your family now that Gram, ah, your grandmother, is gone. You said so yourself. And so you have no need for me anymore. I've fulfilled my duties. I'd like to end our arrangement. I think it's best."

It's clear that he's angry by the way the tops of his cheekbones have reddened. And how his jaw ticks from clenching his teeth. He's angry. Of course he is, because I've wounded his pride. Men like him greedily guard their pride.

"Excuse me? I don't think I understand, Evie." His voice is so icy and frightening that I fight the urge to run out. "Your duties?"

I shift in my seat. "You hired me to do a job. Like a contractor."

"This is true. And we signed a contract. In good faith."

His glare sends a wave of fear through my body. Could he somehow force me to continue this charade? No, that's ridiculous. Oh, dear. This isn't going well. I'll try a different tack.

"Listen, Alex," I say in a softer voice. "You've helped me so much. I can't thank you enough for that. And I had a wonderful time in Savannah with you."

I stop to drag in a breath. That sounded weird. *I had a*

wonderful time in Savannah the weekend your grandma died! And that last conversation with your family, when I told them to shove their secrets up their asses? I'd love to do that again!

But he knows exactly what I mean. His lips form a harsh line, something I've never seen.

"Okay, well, an interesting time in Savannah. We shared something special, I'll admit that," I continue. "And I realize that it was a one-time-only kind of thing. Something that would never work in the real world, for so many reasons. And I don't want you to have to go through the motions of being with me out of pity or obligation."

He squints. "Pity?"

"I didn't expect things to be the same now that we're back in Atlanta. Of course we wouldn't continue . . ." I wave my hand in a circular motion.

"Fucking?" Oh crap, he's sneering. And he sounds so harsh.

"Yeah. That. So our deal is over, and I release you from any obligations."

He picks up a pen and twirls it in his fingers, then tosses it on the desk. His eyebrows lift and he makes a little face, as if to say, *Okay, whatever, I don't have time for this drama.*

"I think it's best if I go on my way, move out of the condo, and get on with my life. Alone."

His eyes narrow, and he leans back in his chair, his hands clasped behind his head. A classic man-in-charge pose. Unsettlingly, he says nothing. Why is he acting like this? I thought he'd take this more in stride.

Oh. Right. The money. People like him are always thinking of the bottom line. I'd offer to return the cash, but I'd spent most of that first twenty-five grand on my student loans, Sabrina's camp, and on her first semester at school. I figure I have enough to move, and that's about it.

"Naturally, you don't need to pay me the rest of the sum we agreed upon. And"—I fumble with the clasp on my purse—"I wanted to give you this."

I dig around in a purse pocket until I find the little black velvet bag that contains the diamond ring.

"Here." I set it gently on the desk and stand up. I can't be in this office any longer, enduring his sharp, irate stare. Truthfully, this is going far worse than I'd expected. I'm about thirty seconds from sobbing.

He leans in, resting his elbows on the desk and threading his fingers together. "It was a mistake, wasn't it? I should have—" He squeezes his hands together so tight that the skin of his knuckles turns white.

Of course he thinks we were a mistake.

"You see?" I interrupt, trying to muster his cold tone while inside, I'm a muddy puddle of despair. "You said it yourself. It was a mistake. I totally agree. And that's why I'm here to end it. Thank you again for all your help, and I hope your business trip to Malaysia goes well. I should probably also thank you for the aquarium interview."

"What?" Alex scrunches up his face.

"You called the HR manager, or someone, at the aquarium. Pulled strings for me. Even though I asked you not to." I try to summon the anger I felt when I was leaving the aquarium, but I'm incapable because I'm too sad.

I scurry toward the door, and when my hand is on the knob, Alex's sharp voice slices through my soul. "Evie."

Oh God, what if he says he really cares for me? Would I

apologize and throw myself into his arms, then beg for forgiveness?

I turn my body in his direction. His handsome face is expressionless. Of course he's not going to tell me he cares. That's absurd.

"I didn't call the aquarium."

"The HR director told me to tell you hello. Of course you did."

"I didn't. Honest. They might have seen the news coverage of Gram's funeral. I think you were in a couple of the photos."

I inhale deep. "Whatever. I have to go."

"Wait, Evie. Do you regret our time together?"

How do I answer that? There are a million things I could say.

No, I don't regret anything because I loved every second we spent together and will hold those moments in my heart and soul for the rest of my life.

Or how about: *I regret falling in love with you and being captivated by your charm.*

My mouth feels sticky and dry. A lump of tears has formed in my throat, and I'm really going to bawl my eyes out if I say one more word to him.

Instead of answering, I shake my head and walk out the door, trying to harness what's left of my dignity so his assistant and every other person in this building doesn't see me cry. I even take the elevator down to the lobby because I figure death would be preferable to what I'm feeling now.

I make it out of the building and run across the street to a park, where I sink onto a bench and double over, sobbing.

CHAPTER THIRTY-FOUR

ALEX

My breath comes in short, shallow gulps as I rub a hand over my chest. For some reason, I can't look out the window at the downtown skyline because I feel too light-headed and dizzy. That entire conversation fucking blindsided me like an unexpected tornado. Between Gram dying and Evie saying goodbye, it's like a one-two punch in the face.

Did that happen with Evie? Or was it a figment of my exhausted imagination? I'd stayed here last night, grabbed a nap on the sofa, and showered in the morning. I wondered why she hadn't returned my text that said, *Good morning, beautiful.*

Now I know.

I reach for the little velvet bag and shake the ring into my palm. It doesn't sparkle today. Maybe it never did. I replay the entire conversation I had with Evie, trying to figure out what the hell I did wrong. Her words left me speechless, they were so unexpected.

"It was a mistake, wasn't it? I should have—"

If she hadn't interrupted, I'd have said this: *It was a mistake, wasn't it? I should have told you how much I cared about you before I made love to you.*

I thought it was so obvious. We'd stayed up talking for hours. We laughed until tears leaked out of our eyes. We kissed until our lips felt raw. I held her hand the day of Gram's funeral because that was the only thing that made me feel whole. Why doesn't she understand that?

Wait. What if she never had the same feelings for me as I did for her? Could I have misread the entire situation? Perhaps she was with me for the money. Maybe the time we spent in Savannah was something she endured out of a sense of duty. Like a job.

Holy shit.

Evie Cooper broke my heart.

CHAPTER THIRTY-FIVE

EVIE

Fortunately, I don't have much to pack.

It had only taken a couple of days to remove everything from boxes when I arrived at the condo, which was a couple of weeks ago. It shouldn't take long to put everything back in boxes.

Except now, I have to stop to cry. And sleep. It's incredible how much I miss Alex's presence in my life.

I've been doing a lot of sleeping since that morning in Alex's office, but even that hasn't been a respite from my sadness because I dream of him.

I need to speed up the packing because he's returning to Atlanta in a couple of days, and I want to be out of here by then. Maybe I'll stop thinking about him when I'm away from this place.

So today I've started in on the books. Sighing, I pause at the built-in bookcase on one wall. I love this bookcase. All of my books are nestled like little babies. I take a few down and am organizing them neatly into a box when I hear the phone ring. I dash across the living room, where I'd left it on the coffee table.

Stupidly, every time my phone rings or buzzes with a text, I hope it's Alex. I get a call from my alma mater about donating, and I politely tell them to call back. There's the obligatory robocall about car insurance. But the aquarium did call with a job offer—at least that's one thing going in my favor.

The HR director doesn't mention Alex, thank God, and says she will send over the offer package in an email. I start in two weeks, and that's the only thing keeping me going now, the little light at the end of a pitch-black tunnel.

I can do this. I can do this.

The phone rings again. It's not Alex.

I glance at the screen. *Sabrina.* I'd only told her scant few details about what was going on in my life, and had tried to claim that this condo was a temporary situation until I could get a job downtown. Alex was only helping me out, I'd said.

She's been too busy at camp to pay attention to my drama, and that's worked to my benefit. She hasn't asked too many questions, and I hope today's not the day she starts.

"Hey." I wedge the phone between my ear and shoulder, shuffling into the bedroom. My muscles are exhausted lately. I guess that's what heartbreak does. "How's camp?"

"Why didn't you tell me?"

"Tell you what?" I flop onto the bed.

"That Alex's grandmother died. You were there at the funeral with his relatives. What the hell, Evie? Why would you hide this from me?"

Crap. She's going to ask questions. "How did you find out?"

"I was scrolling through the *Journal-Constitution* to see if our graduating class photo was in the paper on Sunday. They always run them a few weeks after the ceremony, pages and pages of the city's high schools. I wanted to see ours because I'd made a funny face with my tongue for the photo."

I roll my eyes. "Great. I'm sure that must have looked classy."

"It looked awesome. But while I was scrolling I saw the story about his granny's death. And a photo of the funeral. With you standing next to Alex."

"I'm no longer an employee and we're no longer fake-engaged. Hey, can we have this conversation later? I have to pack up. I'm moving out of this condo. And look, I got a job at the aquarium."

"Whoa, congratulations!" Sabrina's screech makes me hold the phone away from my ear. I stab a button so I can listen on speakerphone. "Tell me about the job."

I spend the next five minutes on the details, reading to her from the email I'd received.

"So what the hell?"

"What the hell what?" I respond crossly. Something about Sabrina can turn me into a twelve-year-old, I swear.

"Why do you sound so depressed when you got your literal dream job? Evie, I'm worried about you."

I groan.

"Genevieve Cooper." She's using my full name, like Mom used to when she was angry with me as a girl.

"Fine. I'll tell you everything."

I burrow under the covers and for the next fifteen minutes, tell my sister everything. And I mean everything. I almost don't stop to breathe, I'm explaining so fast, and for once, she's silent.

"Sabrina? You still there?" Maybe I'd lost the connection while I was ranting.

"You told a bunch of rich people to shove their secrets up their asses?"

"Yep."

Sabrina laughs hysterically for a full minute. "I'm crying. Oh my God. Evie. I love you so much."

"I couldn't help it. They were all so awful. Well, except for Alex. He wasn't awful. His sister was also nice."

Her laughter dies down. "You had sex with that man." Her tone is reverent.

"I told you that my heart is forever broken and that's your takeaway?" I mash my face into a pillow for a few seconds.

"Was it good?" Her voice is a whisper.

I chuckle for the first time in days. "I am not dignifying that question with an answer, you little pervert."

"So that's a yes."

"Anyway. I'm moving out and never talking to Alex again. I'm going to an Airbnb for a month while I look for a new place."

"Are you an idiot?"

"What? I can't stay here."

"Why didn't you tell him how you feel?"

I let out a strangled grunt. "Didn't you hear what I told you? I don't have a chance with him. This was merely a business arrangement. Now that he's in the CEO job, he doesn't need me."

"God, Evie. He had lost his grandmother. You remember when Mom and Dad died. He probably doesn't know what to say, or when."

"Yeah." My voice is weak. She's got a point, I suppose.

"You probably broke his heart at the worst time of his life. Way to go."

A pang of guilt shoots through me. "Aren't you supposed to be in my corner?"

"I am. I want you to be happy. And it sounds like he made you happy. Jesus, Evie. Live a little. Stop acting like you're elderly. Who gives a shit if you get your heart broken or go into debt or whatever. That means you've lived life."

"Spoken like a seventeen-year-old."

"Crap, I gotta go. I'm late for class. Let's talk more tonight."

"Wait. How's camp?"

"Good. I've been doing a lot of research on cholera. Working on improving the statistical significance of genome-wide association study by applying machine-learning to the problem of identifying cholera-linked genes."

I have no idea what she said. *Cholera*? She is so weird. She's like Marie Curie. A foulmouthed, horny, teenage Marie Curie. Better if I don't ask for details. "Okay, that all sounds fun and important. Call me later. Love you."

"Love you too, even though you're obtuse."

"Throwing around the big words. Nice."

"Byeeee."

I roll over and scroll through my phone until I get to my photos. Alex made me take a selfie with him that first day at his parents' house.

In the photo, he's hugging me close and pressing his lips to the side of my head. I'm laughing. We were in his parents' courtyard, and the dusky sky was the color of his eyes.

Could Sabrina be right? What if I did break his heart?

CRASH

0

ALEX

I'm jolted awake by the ringing of my cell phone. Squinting, I snatch it off the nightstand. Nadine.

"Jesus Christ, what now?" I growl. "It's not that contract from Japan, is it? This is the first night I've been able to get any sleep."

"Sorry, Alex. I figured you'd still be up."

Well, yeah, I usually would. But I'd had three bourbons tonight from the hotel minibar and I'd fallen into the bed, hoping for a coma-like sleep. Either because of jet lag or grief or anger, I've slept like shit on this trip. Which isn't usual for me. It's probably because I've been thinking of Gram, who never got the chance to retire.

And thinking about Evie, and how I miss sleeping next to her.

"What's going on?" I roll onto my back.

"You got an urgent personal call that I thought you should know about."

I sit up, and my mind begins to churn. Savannah? Mom? Dad? They all have my number. Or . . . no. It wouldn't be Evie. She has my number. Unless something happened to her.

"Yes? Who called?"

"It was a woman, well, a girl. Her name's Sabrina Cooper."

Something's happened to Evie. An icy trickle of fear runs down my spine, the same feeling I had when I'd first heard Rose was missing all those years ago. "What did she want?"

"She didn't say. She was very, ah, animated. Insisted on speaking with you. She's also emailed several times. I wouldn't give out your private information, of course. But I told her I would pass along the message."

"I see."

"She's called five times this morning already. Started in at eight thirty, the minute I arrived."

As angry as I've been with Evie these past few days, I won't be able to handle it if something happened to her. I flick on the light and grab the pen and notepad lying nearby.

"Give me her number."

Nadine does, and we hang up. For a couple minutes, I stare at what I've written. Ever since Evie marched into my office and told me she didn't want to see me again, my anger has boiled and simmered, then turned to sadness and despair. I started my trip thinking she was ungrateful. That morphed into believing she was the best gold digger who ever lived. By day two, I'd softened and wondered if she broke it off because I scared her somehow or did something wrong. That's where I'm at now, but it doesn't make me any less angry. I treated her like a queen, a thousand times better than any other women.

I miss her. And I hate that I miss her. Feeling vulnerable isn't something I'm used to. Dammit.

Now that she's probably in trouble—or worse—I need to decide if I should set aside my emotions and help her. I let out a sigh. Fine. I'll call. I'd feel terrible if I didn't and she was physically hurt in some way. But if she's asking for money via her sister, so help me God.

"Fuck me," I curse while I dial Sabrina.

"Hellooooo!" Her high-pitched voice slices through my brain. I'd forgotten how girlish she sounds compared to Evie.

"Hello. I understand you've been harassing my assistant."

"Is this Alex Jenkins?"

"That's me," I say, irritated. "Let's get this over with. And please stop calling my office."

"Well, that's the only way I could think to get your attention, my dude."

I mouth the words in the dark. *My dude?*

"I know you're a big-shot CEO and all, so I tried sending you, like, ten emails but I didn't get a response. Plus, I didn't know you were halfway around the globe." She doesn't sound particularly upset, which makes me think that Evie's okay.

"Okay. You have exactly two minutes of my time. It's eleven at night here in Kuala Lumpur, and I'm an adult with a job, which means I need to sleep."

"Good lord. You and Evie really are alike. Total fun-stealers."

"I'm not much fun when I'm woken in the middle of the night. What's going on, anyway?"

"Okay, okay, I'll get to the point. I don't know if you're aware, but my sister is pretty stubborn."

"I've gathered that."

"You need to know that she's in love with you. Full stop. I talked to her yesterday, and she's devastated. She's moving out of the condo. I figured she has too much pride to call you, so I'm taking matters into my own hands."

I stop breathing for a second.

"Alex? You there?"

"Yeah."

"She thinks you don't care. She's convinced you're going to break her heart. Or that your family is going to convince you not to date her. Your mother should be proud to have Evie walk through her front door and give her the time of day. My sister's the best person. She's a badass. Oh, and your ex-girlfriend Rose sounds insufferable. I'm glad you broke up with her."

I pinch the bridge of my nose.

"Evie thinks you'll eventually side with your family. Something about class differences. Said you mentioned a mistake, I don't know, she was ranting and raving. I told her that was stupid, that you were upset about your grandmother. Maybe I'm wrong. Maybe you are a jerk—"

"I'm not. Honest. I'm not." My breaths are coming in shallow gulps.

"Okay, good. Because you've gotten my sister to take risks. No one's ever done that."

"Risks?" What's she talking about?

"Yeah. Moving out of that little shack we lived in, going to Savannah with you, heck, even agreeing to your stupid idea of being your fake fiancé. Those are all things she'd never have done a year ago. You know, she would have done all that even if you hadn't given her money. If she felt that someone she liked needed help, she'd give her heart. Evie's sweet, sweeter than most people. And wound tight."

There's a pause. "Probably like you," Sabrina mutters.

She's in love with me? I can hear my heart beating in my ears. It's all coming together now. Evie took a risk—on me.

"Thank you for telling me this."

"Dude, you need to give her another chance. And if she's right and you don't care, you need to let her down easy, okay? Don't be a dick. Got it?"

"Uh, got it."

"Cool. No dickish behavior. Oh. And did you pull strings to get her the aquarium job? I think that's kind of cool, if you did. But Evie doesn't see it that way."

"I didn't. She asked me not to, and I respected her wishes."

Another pause. "Okay, I'll believe you, for now. I've got my eye on you, though. Be good to my sister. Bye." Sabrina hangs up, and I scrub my hand over my face. What the hell was that? What am I going to do now? How can I fix this? How can I make her understand that we're so completely perfect together?

Don't be a dick. I laugh out loud.

I just got lectured by a teenager, but I don't care. Evie Cooper loves me. And I love Evie Cooper.

0

EVIE

"Ah, yeah. Take that box, and"—I point at a large fern that I'd brought from my old house—"that."

The building's concierge was kind enough to ask his two sons to help me move with their truck, and they're here, stacking boxes onto a dolly and trying to figure out how many trips they'll need to take.

There's a sharp knock at the door. "That might be Dad," one of the guys says.

"Oh, go ahead and open it." I grab a few more books from the shelf. I'm not as finished as I'd hoped to be.

A sudden, uncomfortable silence floats in the room. I turn.

Alex is in the doorway, looking big and mean.

I gasp and lose my grip on the books. They fall to my feet and one hits my big toe. I don't feel the pain because I'm so shocked to see him here. His presence is so large it's as if he's crowding out everything inside this living room.

He steps into the room like he owns the place. *Well, okay, he does own the place.* "What are you doing here?" I blurt.

"Evie and I need a moment in private. Take the rest of the day off, guys," he says, staring at me all the while with those dark-blue eyes.

"But—" I respond.

The two men scramble out the door, and I'm about ready to tell them to stay when Alex shuts the door.

His long legs eat up the distance between us. I'm trying to interpret the expression on his face when he's suddenly right in front of me. Before I can ask any more questions, he cups my face in his hands and kisses me. Hard enough to make me lose my breath and make my legs feel like limp noodles.

He breaks away, his hands still on my face, his thumbs grazing my cheekbones.

"I love you."

My breath catches in my throat. He . . . *what*? I can't do anything but stare at him. If I try to move, I'll collapse. His hair is unusually disheveled. And his stubble is longer than I've ever seen it. And he loves me?

"I know it's so soon and we haven't been together long, but Gram dying seemed to bring us closer together. It seems like we've been with each other forever, and I want it to stay that way. I'm sorry about what my mother said. She can be like that. I'm used to ignoring it, but you're not, and that's understandable. When she said that you weren't one of us, I wanted to argue, but I didn't have the energy. I wanted us to get home. I'll talk to her, though. And I hope you know I don't care about you spilling my secrets to my family. It's better this way."

"How did you—"

"Sabrina. She called. Asked me to give you another chance. Told me not to be a dick."

I wince.

"And I'm sorry about something else. I apologize for offering you money to be my fiancé. It was totally inappropriate and arrogant. You deserved better. You deserve better. Hey. Evie, baby, don't cry."

He brushes fat tears off my cheeks with his fingers. I shake my head. "Your mom is right. I'm not one of you. I don't come from money. I'm not like you, and that's the truth. You're clueless about this kind of stuff, because you've always had privilege."

He gulps in a breath. "You're right. But do you think I care that you're not from money or my social circle?"

I shrug and snort-sniffle.

"I don't care. Not one bit. Here's what I care about. You. I love you. You're brilliant and you're kind. You make me laugh. I love to hear you laugh. You didn't want to kill me after three hours in the car together. You handled my family at their worst moment with grace. You stood by my side at my grandmother's grave and held my hand. You stood up for me, and for yourself. Those are the things I care about."

I lean into him, unable to hold myself upright. *He thinks all those things about me?*

Alex wraps his arms around my body, stroking my hair. "And you know what else you are? Brave. Strong. Your parents died, and you didn't give up. I admire that. You continued to go to school, and you raised your sister to be a successful person. She's kind of strange, though."

I gurgle a little laugh into his white button-down shirt.

"Your sister doesn't think you took risks before me. But I disagree. You took a lot of them. They're risks people are too afraid to take, or are incapable of taking. You took on the damned world by yourself, Evie, and that's why I love you."

Breaking free from his embrace, I look at him through my tear-dappled lashes. "But don't you want to be with someone gorgeous and experienced? Someone who looks perfect all the time. Who will have wild sex every night?"

"You are perfect for me, all the time. I don't care you were a virgin. I think we're sexually compatible, don't you? We had pretty wild sex. And I'd like to have a lot more."

"God, me too," I mumble. I nod and rub my nose. He pulls me close again.

"You are so beautiful, Evie. I had to stop myself from staring at you while you slept because it felt too creepy. And when you told me you didn't want to see me, I was devastated. This past week has been hell."

"You were? I'm sorry." Shame washes over me. I was so, so *wrong*.

"But now I understand why. And there's no need to apologize."

I'm sobbing now. He picks me up in his arms and carries me to the bedroom. When he sets me on the bed, he stands to undo his tie. I gaze up at him, feeling so lucky that he's here. The tie makes a *swoosh* noise as it goes through his collar, and he allows it to drop to the floor.

I extend my arms toward him, and he lowers himself on top of me. My hands go to his hair, my mouth to his ear. His spicy scent surrounds me, and I sigh contentedly against his skin.

This is real. This is us.

"Alex?" I whisper in his ear. "I love you."

EPILOGUE

EVIE

I peer over the side of the boat, eyeing the gray-blue water that's only a few feet from our inflatable vessel.

"Don't worry, the water's only five Celsius," the captain reminds us, his Canadian-accented voice turning jovial.

"What's that again in Fahrenheit?" I look to Alex, worrying my bottom lip between my teeth.

"About forty-one degrees." He's grinning from ear to ear.

This is right up his alley: an adventure. He'd organized this as part of our honeymoon trip across Canada. We'd been planning this trip for months, but I didn't know about this particular excursion until the night of our wedding.

We're both in two-piece wet suits that are fourteen millimeters thick, and so tight I can barely breathe. Booties, a hood that covers my neck and chin, and gloves round out the ensemble. I look a little like a rubber tire.

A snorkel covers my eyes and my pulse races. It's almost as though I'm trapped in this suit, this mask, this place. I practice my deep breathing to calm down; I'd learned this through meditation classes to help me get over my fears.

In the two years I've been with Alex, I've gone out of my comfort zone and taken so many risks. Like going on a sailboat with him and his friends on the Gulf of Mexico. Like riding behind him at slow speed on his motorcycle (it was on a track, so we were the only vehicle). Like learning to drive a car. Right before the wedding, I even drove to pick up Savannah and Travis's wife, Kayla. The three of us went to the bridal store together for my final fitting.

And maybe the biggest risk: standing up to his mother and proving to her and the rest of his family that I'm not inferior. I'd learned that a closed-mouth half smile, a sharp stare, and a well-placed *bless your heart* can quell even the most snarky of comments.

And now that we're married, Mrs. Jenkins has to accept me, because she's hoping for more grandchildren. We're going to wait a long while for that, though.

This, our first adventure as a married couple, might be more exciting than anything that's come before now.

"You ready?" Alex shouts. He's also wrapped in a tight wet suit, and he doesn't look like a tire. He looks more like Aquaman.

I nod and push the snorkel into my mouth as we'd been instructed during the hour-long class back ashore.

Alex sits on the side of the inflatable boat, then slides gracefully into the water. He bobs for a moment, then reaches toward me and nods.

I swallow. Will I freeze to death? We're on the Churchill River estuary in Manitoba. The subarctic. I'm a southern girl, and even though it's summer, it's still the coldest weather I've ever experienced.

And what about polar bears? We saw them during a tour yesterday. They were far enough away that I wasn't scared, but today . . . yikes. I know they swim in these waters. Still. The tour companies wouldn't bring people out here if polar bears routinely ate people, would they?

Hesitantly, I ease my butt onto the side of the boat. Then I swing my flipper-covered feet into the water. I expect it to be cold, but it's not. I don't feel a thing.

Taking a deep breath, I slip into the water. Alex grabs my hand. As we planned, he's going to hold me until I'm comfortable. His body goes horizontal, and his face is in the water.

My heart is banging against my chest. I have no choice but to mimic his pose since he can't float like that and hold on to me. I surge forward, my face in the water. The cold shocks what little skin is exposed, and it's like a jolt of electricity.

Alex gently swims, tugging me. I kick my feet gently and swim beside him. Well, *swimming* isn't the best word. Gliding as he tugs me along is better.

The water is a murky, icy green, and there's nothing in sight. He stops, and we float on the surface of the water. I concentrate on taking deep breaths through the snorkel and am amazed at how easy it is to breathe through it. Duh. It's a snorkel. It's not like we're deep-sea diving with Jacques Cousteau here.

And then I hear it. A whistle. It's almost like a bird. Alex squeezes my hand. There's another whistle, this one longer. Then, a cacophony of chirps and songs.

Alex tugs me closer and points.

There, in front of us, is a beluga whale. I can't really scream, but I let out a little cry into my snorkel. And then there's another. And a third. And a *baby*.

I'm almost crying into my snorkel because the sight of the ghost-white creatures in the water is so beautiful. They seem to be singing and dancing, for us.

I let go of Alex's hand, because I'm no longer afraid.

◊

Later that night, after eating the best burgers we've ever had in a little hole-in-the-wall pub, we're in our lodge. I'm still on an adrenaline high from the whales, and have finished taking a hot shower.

When I walk into the bedroom wearing a fuzzy white robe—no silky numbers for me; it's too cold—Alex has already built a fire.

"You did good, reserving a hotel with a fireplace in the bedroom," I purr. "So romantic."

He dips his head to kiss me, and within seconds, we're devouring each other.

"Mrs. Cooper-Jenkins, I have a request," he murmurs in my ear.

"Tell me, sir," I tease.

"I'm sure you noticed that our headboard here in this romantic honeymoon suite is made of iron rails."

My fingers work into his hair. "I did notice that, in fact."

"And what were you thinking of when you noticed it?"

My hands go to the tie on my bathrobe, and I undo it, allowing the terry cloth to pool at my feet. "It sure is warm in here."

I'm wearing a silky white bra and panties with gold lace accents. It's the skimpiest, sexiest set I own, and Sabrina had bought it for me. She'd also bought me several other gifts, ranging from dirty to *OMG is that even legal in Georgia?*

Alex sucks in a breath. Turning him on has become my favorite pastime.

I press my breasts into Alex's chest, the bare skin of my back feeling the warmth of the fire. "So, about the bed."

My hand goes to his jeans, pressing against his already huge erection that's straining against his zipper.

He lets out a small growl.

"I was wondering if you brought the silk ties."

"I did."

I stroke him through his jeans for a few seconds, teasing him. Then I giggle and stop touching him.

With an exaggerated sway in my hips, I prance over to the bed and climb on top, sitting on my knees. My hair's gotten long, almost touching my breasts, and tonight, it's soft and straight, the way he loves it.

Alex goes to the closet where our suitcases are, and emerges with the black silk ties we both love so much.

He moves onto the bed and kisses me, then snakes his hands to my back and undoes my bra.

"Lie back."

I do as I'm told. My nipples are hard. Legs together. I spread my arms in a Y-position, and by the time he loops the silk around the second wrist and ties it to the bed, he's breathing hard.

I'm a little disappointed when he stands up. I love when he kisses me while I'm restrained. Since that first summer we had sex, I've explored so much with him. I've come to realize that I love being submissive in bed—but nowhere else.

Alex takes his time unbuttoning his heavy plaid shirt and his jeans. When he's in his black boxer briefs, I squirm and mewl, hoping he'll ease that rock-hard body on top of me. I'm wet from the way he's looking at me. Wet from anticipating how he'll lick, stroke, tease, and thrust.

"You're so perfect, you know that? I think I want to fuck all night long."

Talking dirty doesn't shock me anymore. Quite the opposite. I let out a throaty laugh. "I know that's what I want."

Finally, I get my wish. He's caging me with his arms and he kisses me softly. "Are you wet?"

"Why don't you find out yourself?"

He chuckles wickedly, then runs a hand over my breasts, pinching the nipples. Tingles race over my skin as he strokes my stomach. His middle finger slides between my tight-together legs, and I press my hips into his touch. "Yes, please," I say.

"Your panties are soaked," he whispers in my ear. Of course they are. It's already been the best day of my life, and it's only getting better. "Please what?"

"I already want to come."

"You do? So soon? You've gotten greedy, Evie. And I love it."

He sits up and hooks his thumbs into the sides of my underwear, and teases me by stripping them off slowly.

"Spread your legs for me."

I bite my lip and wriggle against my restraints. First, I allow my legs to part only a few inches, because I want him to beg.

"Wider. I want to see you."

My skin feels like it's on fire when I open them all the way. He tells me that I'm a *good girl*, and then says something super dirty. Something that sends a fresh rush of wetness to the place he loves.

Alex glances at my face with a harsh, needy look, then lowers himself between my legs. His warm breath hits my inner thigh. Abruptly, he sits up and shakes his head.

"That's for later. I think you need this instead."

He slides his boxers off and his erection springs free. And that's when he positions himself between my legs and guides his hard cock inside. It slides in easily, and I cry out, my hands now gripping the silk ties.

He feels so incredible, maybe better tonight than he ever has. It could be the adventure of the day, or the fire, or the fact that we're married, and he's mine. He thrusts into me, slow and deep, the shadows and flames of the fire flickering off his beautiful, angular face.

"I love you, Evie."

I tell him I love him, and can't wait to keep telling him—and showing him—how much, for the rest of our lives.

ACKNOWLEDGMENTS

Fiction doesn't exist in a vacuum. I have many people to thank for this book, but none more than Deanna McFadden, the editor who has gently and expertly encouraged me to be a better writer. Her suggestions, her support, and her willingness just to listen have been a saving grace many a time.

This book was easy to write, and difficult to edit. Readers might not know this, but an earlier, shorter version was first published on Wattpad. When I initially wrote the story, I never dreamed it would end up in print. Deanna helped me take a fun story and turn it into something meaningful, and I'll always be appreciative.

Thank you to all of my Wattpad readers for your support of this and all of my work. You will never know how much your comments and encouragement mean to me.

Also a tremendous thanks to my husband, who has been there every step of the way for my fiction career.

And lastly, I wanted to acknowledge the one I dedicated the book to: my heart dog, Dino. He passed during the editing of this book, and I will miss him until my final breath.

ABOUT THE AUTHOR

Tamara Lush is a Romance Writers of America Rita award finalist, an Amtrak writing fellow, and a *USA TODAY* bestselling author. She's a former reporter who writes steamy and heartfelt romance set in tropical locations. You can find her on a Florida beach with her husband, a kombucha, and her Shih Tzu.

Turn the page for a preview of Book 1 in

The **PRETENDERS** Series

DRIVE

by **TAMARA LUSH**

Available now,
wherever books are sold.

CHAPTER ONE

DANTE

"I will not allow a girl to change my tires. Absolutely not."

Jack, my chief engineer and oldest friend, shot me an acerbic look that indicated he wasn't in the mood for my attitude. We were the only two at a twelve-seat conference table, where team principals normally met to discuss engines, tires, and race strategy.

My Italian accent turned thick with derision. "What the hell, man? I'm not going to dignify your laughter with a response. This is serious. This is world-class auto racing, not some reality TVshow."

Jack, an intense and sardonic Australian, finally sobered and turned his gaze out a window. My eyes rested on the vibrant green grass flanking the smooth asphalt of the Maranello test track. In the distance, the turret of a Renaissance-era palazzo peeked over a cluster of trees. I could practically smell the eucalyptus and lavender mixed with the burning rubber of tires. It was the scent of home. Of motorsports in Italy.

"Look here, mate. I know you don't want a woman on the team. But it's boss's orders. Might as well get used to it. She's part of us now. That's what I'm hearing, at least. And apparently she's quite competent."

Boss's orders. A woman in the pit crew was a responsibility I didn't need. A distraction I didn't want.

"There's never been a female tire changer in the history of Formula World. She'll ruin the team. And where the hell is Bronson? He called this meeting and now he's ten minutes late. You know how I feel about being late. Or coming in second."

Jack plucked a small model of our team's Formula World car off the conference room table and turned it around in his hands. He set the little white car back down and ran it back and forth on its toy wheels, avoiding my stare.

"Just because your sister—"

"This has nothing to do with Gabriella," I growled.

Jack pushed the little car across the table toward me. "It has everything to do with her. I've known you since before she . . . before the accident. And you didn't use to be so against women on the teams."

Slapping my hand on to the rolling car, I halted its journey. Jack was my savior on the track, my wingman. We'd worked together my entire dozen-year career. He was one of the few people on earth who treated me like a regular guy and not a racing super-star. But he knew how—and when—to poke at my tender spots.

"Gabriella shouldn't have tried to be a mechanic. She should have gone to school to be an engineer and gotten involved in the behind-the-scenes of racing. Or taken a job in the corporate offices of a motorsports team . . ."

"We've had this conversation a thousand times. But hey, we can have it again, I don't mind. I was on the track the day it happened six years ago." Without the car to fiddle with, he drummed his fingers on the table, unable to be still. "She didn't die because she was a woman. She died because of a faulty design in the fuel-rig. She happened to be the unlucky soul who was draining the rig after your practice lap."

The familiar feeling of sadness churned in my gut at the memory of my older sister, and the flash of terror I'd felt when I'd staggered out of my car, screaming her name. Every time I walked into the pit, the smell of gas reminded me of that day. Reaching into my pocket, I touched the silver medallion she'd given me for luck the year I started racing, back when I was twelve and into go-karts. "And you never listen. Or agree with me. She didn't have the upper-body strength to wrangle the hoses on the fuel rig. Which is my point. Women don't have the capability or stamina to be part of this."

Good God. How difficult was it for people to understand?

"Also, a woman will be distracting. Can you imagine how the guys will react to her? It won't matter what she looks like, someone will want to . . . you know." I waved my hand dismissively.

"Screw her?" Jack offered.

What a disaster. It was difficult enough to stomach that Brock Bronson, the team's owner, barely knew an open-wheel car from a junker in a demolition derby. He was a Silicon Valley billionaire with a fascination for speed. But he'd offered me such an astronomical amount of money to sign with Team Eagle—had assembled such an incredible car, drawn such lucrative sponsors—that it was impossible to say no.

Eagle was new and risk taking, my agent had said. *Sign the contract*, my agent had said. Six world championships in, I had been looking for the ultimate challenge. To win a seventh in my final season with a rookie team would be the biggest conquest of all, and it would bring both visibility to a new team and plenty of retirement sponsorships my way.

Good karma and a ton of cash, my agent had said.

"All I want is to win and stay drama-free. Can you imagine the headlines if she screws up?" I said.

"Really? Will she distract us? How will we even know she's a woman? She'll be done up in coveralls and helmet during races, like the rest of us. Surely you can control yourself. And look, Rolf is gay, and he's on the pit crew. We don't worry about him being distracted by other blokes." Jack reached across the table to grab the little car.

Hell. His logic was solid. "This isn't about controlling *my* libido. Like I would be interested in a tire changer when I've got models and actresses and that singer . . ."

What was the name of the pop singer I'd hooked up with last season in Malaysia? I couldn't recall. Women were among the many perks of being a driver, and I hadn't ever felt the need to settle down with only one.

"A lone girl around a group of men will always be a distraction to someone. And it's our championship and my safety on the line." I threw my hands in the air. "And what does she know about tires and cars? She won't have the hand-eye coordination needed to change a wheel in seconds. *Porca miseria*.

"Oh, we're trotting out the nonsensical Italian swear words, are we?" Jack asked, annoying me even more. "She's starting at Monaco. And testing with us soon here on the track. In a day or two."

"We'll see about that. She can't waltz in now and begin a week before the season," I snapped. "I'll meet with Bronson and try to knock some sense into that stupid American. He thinks he knows everything because he made more money than God with his computer chips, but he knows nothing about cars, tires, or racing. He's a—"

"Who's a stupid American?"

It was Brock Bronson. In all of his friendly, casual glory. Regarding him with a surly smile, I decidedly ignored what he'd overheard. Other drivers would have quaked in fear had they insulted their team owner. But Bronson needed me, so I smiled. Fuck him.

"*Buongiorno*, Signor Bronson. We were just discussing the team's new hire."

Bronson took a seat across from me at the conference table. To my ears, his thick American accent sounded like syllables scraped against a cheesegrater.

That's one of the reasons I wanted to sit down with you two. I knew it would get some of you boys in a snit. But first, I wanted to update you on our other situation, in private."

Jack and I straightened our spines in tandem. This was far more interesting than any woman.

"The Praxi steam is still considering going to the FIA World Motor Sport Council about Max and his engineer," Bronson said. If the Fédération Internationale del'Automobile got involved, it could lead to terrible press and even worse morale for an organization as new as Eagle.

Jack stared at me as if to say, *I knew coming to this team was a terrible decision.* We'd had a bit of a quarrel over whether to sign the contract when we'd found out that Max Becker, a hot shot young German who'd been in the sport only a year, would be the other, junior driver.

"So they're serious? They think Max and his engineer stole the technical information on the chassis last season?"

Jack sat back in his chair and folded his arms. There was no love lost between him and Max's crew. We'd competed against them last season on opposing teams, and never trusted them. Now we were on the same side, but apparently Max's past slippery nature was catching up to him. And we could be collateral damage.

Bronson held up his hands. "Look. Max assures me that his guys are clean. No one stole anything last year, he said."

"Was he or was he not in possession of the Praxis chassis information?" I asked.

"I'm still looking into that. He claims no."

The way Bronson evaded my question was concerning. "I didn't sign onto a rookie team and bring my trusted crew with me to be embroiled in drama. I wouldn't have signed at all had I known you were bringing on that kid."

"Max is no rookie. He's been driving for three years and isthe future of the sport. People are saying he's the next . . . you," Bronson said.

Max was only twenty-four, and as hungry as I once was. A fact I didn't like to be reminded of at my age. "Still. I don't enjoy the scandal."

"There's no scandal. No drama. Don't worry, dude. We've got this. I know the press is sniffing around, but I'm confident everything will turn out fine. I'll make sure of it."

Figures. Bronson was the kind of guy who thought money could fix everything. Admittedly, it usually could in Formula World, but I liked to think that talent always rose to the top.

"When will we find out whether Praxis is taking the case to the FIA?"

"A few weeks. A month, maybe."

We'd be in Montreal by then, perhaps Belgium. "Fine." I sighed. "Let's try to put it behind us, especially before the first race in Monaco. And what's this about the girl? Please tell me it isn't true."

"Oh, right. Savannah." Bronson chuckled. "You'll meet her soon. She's doing onboarding with HR as we speak. I spoke with Max earlier, and he said he doesn't have an issue with her."

He spoke with that kid before me? "Then assign her to his pit crew."

Bronson tilted his head. "Nah, I think that would be a little too obvious. As if we were purposefully trying to distract the public from the chassis info situation."

"Max would definitely try to sleep with her," I muttered.

My German teammate was as legendary on the party circuit as he was on the track. The two of us made quite the tabloid fodder, actually. Two months ago during a promotional event in Chile, he'd had a threesome with two flight attendants after the exhibition race that somehow got leaked to the press, and I'd gotten a speeding ticket the day after.

On a Vespa. With a soap opera actress riding behind me. Later, back at the hotel, she'd ridden *me*. Then proceeded to divulge everything about our night together to a gossip site.

The media never ceased in their attempt to stir the pot, whether it was with the drivers' on-track problems or their off-track escapades. "Terrible Twos," the tabloids had recently dubbed me and Max. We were the biggest celebrities in motorsports and could pretty much do anything we damn well pleased.

And now, with Max's crew and the accusations of possible

stolen technical information, Eagle was in the press every day. Hell, every hour on the blogs, which I tried not to read.

"With all due respect, I need to tell you there's a million reasons why it would be disastrous to have a girl on the pit crew. What if she becomes involved with someone?"

"Not a chance in hell. She comes highly recommended by some of the top IndyCar executives. She interned there. And at NASCAR too. Pretend she's a guy. She's one of three hundred people on the entire Eagle payroll. Ignore her. Your only job is to win."

Bronson reached across the table and clasped my muscled forearms with his smooth, chubby hands. "With the car we've put together and your skills, you've got a serious shot at a seventh championship. Then you can retire in glory, bro."

Nothing was more irritating than that man calling me bro. A man with his wealth should be more formal, less crass. But the American was right: if I won a seventh championship, I'd be remembered as one of the greats of motorsports, alongside Hamilton, Schumacher, and Andretti.

"Have you told the guys?"

"I'm making it clear to everyone, including Max, that they're not to harass Savannah. I'm telling you the same thing, and that's why I wanted to sit down with both of you today. I want you to welcome her and turn on that Italian charm of yours when you meet her in the coming days. I think it looks good to have a woman on the team. I'm not going to lie: it'll help our image, given Max and his alleged 'espionage' controversy."

"Espionage. I'll strangle him myself if it's true." I swore under my breath.

"And Savvy will practice with us next week."

"Savvy? What kind of a girl name is that? It sounds like the moniker of an exotic dancer."

"She's not a girl, she's twenty-four. She's a woman, and you should respect her as such. And Savvy is short for Savannah. As in Georgia, USA. Which is where her father, Dale Jenkins, the owner of Jenkins International—one of the largest parts distributors in North America—makes his home and his corporate headquarters. I'm surprised you don't know her, he's such a high-profile man in the industry and all."

Hearing the name of Jenkins International sent a frisson of awareness through my body. Of course I'd heard of her father and his company. The brand was known the world over.

"Why does *she* want to be on the team?"

Bronson guffawed. "It might have something to do with the fact that her father is now one of our sponsors. She asked her daddy if she could work with us, and I couldn't say no. He and I met at a party in the States—he's a stand-up guy. It was too good a PR opportunity to pass up. But you can always ask her yourself. Maybe she's got her own reasons."

I leaned forward, gesturing by turning my hand upward, pressing my thumb against my four fingers, and flicking for emphasis. "Let me get this straight. Our new tire changer is the daughter of the man who owns one of America's largest auto parts companies? The outfit that sponsors NASCAR teams?"

"What are the chances of that?" Jack and I stared at each other.

Bronson stood up. "Sounds like you two will have a lot to talk about."

So much for a drama-free season.

CHAPTER TWO

SAVANNAH

Showtime. Well, not exactly. It was only practice. But every practice needed to be perfect, at least for me. This was the final run at the test track before the season opener in Monte Carlo, and my heart practically raced in time with the RPMs coming from the gleaming white car.

I pulled on a white helmet and adjusted the strap under my chin until my head was safe and snug inside. Snapping the visor into place, I knelt between two men, one of whom was holding a tire. I picked up the pneumatic wheel gun, and it was heavy and comfortable in my hands.

Finally. It felt amazing to be in the pits, the roar of the engine echoing in my head. I'd spent the last three weeks here at the Eagle headquarters, mostly doing boring onboarding with Human Resources during week one. Life had gotten more exciting in week two, when I'd shadowed crew members from the team's other car. After all this, I was assigned to Dante Annunziata's crew and had recently learned the fascinating—and highly confidential—technical aspects of his vehicle from the engineers.

Fun fact: The steering wheel for the car on the track cost close to a hundred grand. It was made of carbon fiber and silicone and controlled up to forty functions for the vehicle.

And now, it was time for me to control my own destiny.

Everyone was clad in identical white, fire-retardant jumpsuits, with heavy black gloves and boots. Not to mention the white helmets, which made us look like aliens. Even the most ardent of racing fans wouldn't be able to tell I was a different gender—the other tire changers were also trim, small, and nimble. Sure, maybe I was a bit shorter than the rest, but I didn't feel like I stood out.

Giorgio, the tire carrier next to me, gave a thumbs-up, and I responded in kind. He flipped up his visor.

"*Che calor,*" he yelled, and I recognized his words as Italian, something about the heat, because I'd been studying the language for the last month in preparation for my first practice with the team. I wanted so much to be accepted by them, and each time anyone talked to me, I tried to be superpleasant. So far, everyone had been respectful and kind, and I was grateful.

It didn't feel hot outside to me, not after a lifetime spent in the steamy south of Georgia. This heat had nothing on my hometown, where palm trees, moss, and people visibly withered in the summer months. I grinned wide inside my helmet.

Girl, you've got this.

I'd signed with Eagle to show everyone a woman could break

barriers in racing's most glamorous sport. I'd also wanted to prove something closer to home.

My mother assumed I'd choose something genteel, a branch of the motorsports profession with a whiff of glitz, like public relations. She'd gone along with the engineering diploma from the University of Georgia and the internships with NASCAR and IndyCar. But my traveling the world with a race team for the better part of a year had been a bridge too far.

"You're going where, to do what?" Mom had asked a month ago, during our weekly bottomless mimosa brunch at a place not far from home. Her incredulous tone had caused many of the well-heeled Southern women at nearby tables to turn in our direction. "But what about that assistant public relations job with the racing team in Atlanta? Or something with our family's company? You'd be close to me and Dad, and you'd be able to find a nice Southern boy to settle down with."

Then came the inevitable guilt-trip. "How could you leave *me*?" she'd wailed.

The emotional manipulation had become too much to bear, and for the first time, I stood up for myself. "I don't want nice, I don't want a Southern boy, and I don't want Atlanta," I shot back. "I want international travel and fast cars and Formula World."

She'd fixed her hard blue stare on me and doubled down on her toxic tactics. "You'll never succeed in that world, Savvy. That's a rich man's game, and you have no business sticking your nose into places it doesn't belong. Don't even bother. You'll fail."

That conversation, and no small measure of satisfaction, raced through my head as I stood there, waiting for the car to pit. I was here in Italy. I was succeeding. *Thriving*.

Crouching into position again between the two men, I sent a

silent thank-you to my unconventional father, who had always encouraged me to follow my dreams. It was Daddy who had introduced me to the world of motorsports, and who had been the only one to know my secret dream: to help run our family's company, alongside my brother, and sponsor my own racing outfit—an all-female team in one of the top circuits, proving that women could be successful athletes and equals in motorsports. First, though, I needed *experience*.

"Get in place!" yelled a voice.

With a high-pitched roar, the powerful machine whizzed into the pit. The guy standing at the hood—the lollipop man—held up a sign to signal to the driver to keep his brakes on during the pit stop.

I moved fluidly, pressing the gun into the middle of the tire, unlocking the single lug nut at the center of the wheel. I eased back. The man to my right slipped the tire off, and the man to my left slid a new tire on in one seamless motion. I moved forward and quickly locked the lug nut with a fierce blast of the wheel gun.

Zip. Whoosh. Zip.

It was an intricate dance, albeit one that happened in a few blinks of an eye. The twenty-one strong pit crew that hovered around the car stepped back with uniformity. The lollipop man at the front raised his sign and the car sped off. With that engine, it would eventually reach its peak of fifteen thousand revolutions per minute—up to two hundred and twenty miles per hour.

Faster than a hot knife through butter, I thought.

I thought something else too: *You're a beautiful girl, Savvy, which means you have to work harder and smarter than everyone else to be taken seriously.* That's what Daddy always said, and I'd reminded myself of his words a thousand times during my first weeks with Eagle. It was a mantra I repeated every time I was asked to do something new.

Work harder.

Work smarter.

Don't show any fear.

The team practiced the pit stops four more times, each one more efficient and faster than the last. The pit crew manager took off his helmet. "Three point one seconds on the last stop. Nice work. Let's take a break and recap the day."

One of the tire carriers who'd stood nearby during the pit stop clapped me on the shoulder as we all walked into the pit garage. After a few moments, a hand firmly eased me aside. From the specially tailored uniform, the uniquely decorated helmet, and the swagger, I knew it was Dante Annunziata, our driver. I'd seen him earlier when he'd climbed into his car for the test laps.

Pulling off my helmet, I watched as the team parted for him, a king given the privilege of entering the air-conditioned garage first. Drivers, even the most decent of guys in any semi-pro contest, usually displayed a hint of entitlement and brashness off the track, and an exacting, calculating iciness behind the wheel. He was no different, from what I could tell.

I followed everyone inside. Although the team was American owned, the headquarters were in Italy because the owner loved it here, I'd heard. The Team Eagle operation was like nothing I'd ever seen in other circuits back home. The place was a vast motorsports complex that had been recently built with an eye for detail. Everything from the polished concrete floors to the mahogany conference room tables to the tools with their surgery-theater-level gleam screamed money.

Owner Brock Bronson had spared no expense for the building

or the cars. This was how I'd explain the place to my dad next time I called: cleaner than a bar of soap, with the added bonus of a catered pasta bar for lunch. Hopefully Daddy would be able to visit during a race at some point later in the season. Making him proud was important to me.

As I started to pull a chair out from the sleek mahogany table, Giorgio tugged on my sleeve and wagged his finger.

"We sit back here during these briefings," he whispered in a heavy Italian accent.

I winced, wishing I hadn't drawn attention to myself. "Sorry," I whispered. He was my dad's age, a guy with salt-and-pepper hair and a handlebar moustache. He motioned for me to sit next to him, front and center in a row of folding chairs.

The team's engineers and computer technicians took their places at the conference table.

I set my helmet at my feet on the gleaming terrazzo floor, mimicking the other guys, and undid my ponytail. Goodness, that cool air felt amazing on my scalp. I combed my hair back with my fingers, letting it fall loose over my coverall-clad shoulders.

My gaze alighted on a man at the head of the table. For a second, everything around me—the two dozen pit crew members, the assistants serving coffee, the strong blast of the air conditioner—fell away, because I was spellbound by a pair of dark, molten eyes.

Dante Annunziata.

My first thought was that it was too bad he wore the foulest, angriest glare I'd ever seen. With his longish raven-black hair tumbling over his forehead and his matching dark brows, it was a waste of a handsome face to look so nasty. My second thought was one of sheer curiosity. Why were his full lips curled into a sneer as if a foul odor permeated the room? Our pit stops had been flawless, and he'd driven as fast as the wind around the track. He should be thrilled that we'd worked so well as a new team, especially since the season opener in Monaco was just days away.

What was he staring at? I glanced to the men on either side of me, then quickly over my shoulder at the two other rows of chairs, which were filled with pit crew members and team staff. I looked again at Dante. He hadn't stopped staring in my direction. And his flashing dark eyes were still unblinking and furious.

Well, that was rude. Surely he wasn't raised by wolves?

As if he'd heard me calling him names inside my head, Dante turned to Jack, the chief engineer, who sat next to him. The two men huddled for a minute until the team's owner ambled in. He was lanky, and wore dung-colored cowboy boots, jeans, a black T-shirt, and thick, black-rimmed hipster glasses. He took up a lot of space when he moved his long arms and legs.

He was followed by Tanya, the team's head of public relations. She was also from the US—Boston, I think, if her clipped accent was any indication. I'd only met her once, and thought she was pleasant in a slightly frosty way. But since we were among the only women employed by the team and both from the United States, I hoped to get to know her better. Being surrounded by all these dudes—and missing my best friend, Kayla, back home—made me crave female friendship.

Bronson passed by Dante and Jack, squeezing both men's shoulders before taking the empty seat next to Jack. "Take it away, Jack. It's your show," he said.

Jack climbed to his feet. "You all looked incredible out there. Bravo, team." He pumped his fist. "Now, let's go over what we could've done better, and talk about the weather conditions for our first race."

I concentrated on his post-practice wrap-up, trying to put Dante's blazing stare out of my mind. Something about him left me with a squirmy feeling.

"We'll likely be starting the Monaco race on soft tires, since they've done so well in practice this week," Jack said, then launched into a long explanation about the weather in France.

I studied Dante. He was a world champion in the sport. A legend. Which meant I needed to be deferential and extrarespectful.

He furrowed his brow. His full lips plumped into a faint pout. He ran a thumb across his jawline, which was sharp as a knife.

I'd bet a hundred bucks that he practiced that brooding, intense look in the mirror just to perfect his sex appeal. The thought almost made me laugh, but I had to admit an uncomfortable truth: he had more sex appeal than his car had RPMs.

It was not something I often thought when looking at a man. Actually, I'd never had a visceral reaction to a guy like this. Not during either of my internships, not in college, not ever.

Guys rarely affected me one way or the other, much to the dismay of both my mother and Kayla. Oh, sure, I thought some were cute, or even handsome. I liked men. I'd kissed a few. But Dante, and his searing, brooding expression, was a different story entirely, stirring in me something both unnerving and unfamiliar. Dangerous, even. I was usually so unaffected by men.

But *this* man was different.

His forehead was high and his nose aquiline, a classic Italian look. He often posed for edgy modeling shoots for various Italian clothing designers, and I'd seen lots of photos of him online.

But in person, he was way different. Rawer somehow, and more arresting. All charisma and attitude. His lips were plush and sensual, which made his sharp jaw seem all the more masculine. He was clean-shaven and I pondered how the olive-gold skin of his face would feel under my fingertips.

Egad. I made a mental note to text my best friend back home about this troublesome thought. She'd probably laugh at me and tell me I was jetlagged or dehydrated.

"And I'd like to again introduce our newest team member, Savannah Jenkins. Some of you met her during this morning's meeting or have had the chance to say hi over the past couple of weeks. Our team's grown so much, though, and we've hired so many new people that I wanted to do another round of introductions, since I know some of the staff and techs haven't yet been acquainted. In case she doesn't stand out, Savvy's the one in the front row of chairs with the long red hair. Savannah, stand up, please."

Oh dear.

I hurriedly smiled and stood, all while being acutely aware of Dante's smoldering eyes. He'd caught me staring, and I watched as his own gaze skimmed down my coverall-clad body. *Just great.*

"Thank you," I said, drawing out the words in my most syrupy Southern accent. I'd been trying to temper that around all these international people, but when I was flustered or put on the spot, my roots bloomed in my voice with a vengeance.

"I'm thrilled to be here in Formula World with all y'all, simply honored to be in your presence," I said. "It's a world away from Atlanta, where I'm from, but I know we're going to win the championship for Eagle. Get 'er done. Shake and bake, and all that. At least that's what we say back home. And Mr. Annunziata,

I must say that was some of the finest driving I've ever seen on a track. You are incredible."

A ripple of laughter and applause went through the room. Except from Dante. He winced. Didn't nod, didn't smile, didn't acknowledge my compliment in any way.

Jack smiled warmly. "We are equally as thrilled to have you. In case you didn't know, Savvy—that's what she likes to be called—has an engineering degree and has interned with a top NASCAR team. She and Eagle are also part of history, because she's the first female tire changer in Formula World. She's a great asset to Eagle, and I hope you'll join me in making her feel welcome."

Bronson stood. "I'd also like to give Savannah a big hello. I know you all got my memo about her, but consider this a formal welcome. Having a woman on the team puts us at the forefront of motorsports. We should all be proud of that. And look at her. She's something, isn't she?"

When everyone again turned to stare at me, I froze. In an instant, my face felt like I'd pressed it into a bowl of jalapeno peppers, and I knew it was turning red. "Thanks, y'all," I replied.

The team applauded, and I sank back into the chair. The guy next to me patted my shoulder. I let out the breath I was holding and pasted on my best pageant smile. Even gave a little wave.

My eyes went from Bronson to Jack to Dante. He wasn't clapping. Instead, he was scribbling on a piece of paper in front of him. Looking like he couldn't be bothered.

What a *jerk*.